Tempered Illusions

Whitney Hill

BENU
MEDIA

TEMPERED ILLUSIONS

Benu Media

6409 Fayetteville Rd

Ste 120 #155

Durham, NC 27713

(984) 244-0250

benumedia.com

ISBN (ebook): 978-1-7376311-8-7

ISBN (pbook): 978-1-7376311-9-4

Library of Congress Control Number: 2022919006

Cover Designer: Pintado (99Designs)

Editor: Jeni Chappelle (Jeni Chappelle Editorial)

Content Warnings

This book contains strong physical violence and gore, on-page death, swearing, slurs (not toward any real racial or ethnic group/identity), alcohol use, knife violence, threat of sexual violence, mention of past abuse by a guardian, deadnaming, kidnapping, state-sanctioned violence, blood-drinking, and consensual on-page sex scenes.

For those who have fought to build new lives for themselves in the ashes of the old.

Chapter 1

The darkness weighing on my aura and the chill biting down my spine wasn't just from being underdressed in the forest on a February night as the moon waned. It was a power signature, a strong one.

A psychological play as well, I suspected.

I slipped through the trees, staying low and placing my feet carefully, as I'd been shown, shields tight. It reminded me of another night in these same woods, one I almost hadn't survived but had because the man hunting me now had pulled me out of the lake he'd thrown me in with a concrete block tied around my ankles.

I shivered, remembering it, then pushed the memory aside.

Focus. I needed focus.

Troy Solari was even deadlier than Troy Monteague had been two and some years ago, and I couldn't afford to lose this hunt. Mostly because it was my final exam for the first course new Darkwatch agents were put through, and I had to prove to the rest of the East Coast elves that I was not to be fucked with.

The energy in the woods shifted.

With our bond locked down tight and me shielding like hell to keep my own power signature from giving my position away, I had to rely on all my other senses to both navigate through the forest and evade Troy. He might be my fiancé and my king, but when it came to training me, he was as brutally unforgiving as he'd be with any other recruit. My life depended on it, and there was nothing he held more valuable.

I'd gotten the flag from the locked box hidden in the bole of a lightning-struck oak. That'd been the first test—whether my senses, amplified by the massive boost in my power during the Wild Hunt, had reached elf-level and whether I could evade the physical and Aetheric traps that'd littered the path to the tree and surrounded the box itself.

Now I had to escape the woods with my prize.

Nothing moved. Even the wind had stilled, like it wanted nothing to do with this. If I eased up on my shields, I could find Troy and everyone else hiding among the trees by reading the wind's movement. I could read air currents as a passive power, but Troy had figured out my range months ago and usually managed to stay out of it until he was ready to strike. Then he was all terrifying speed, devastatingly strong Aether, and sharp teeth.

Goddess, I loved the man.

Shaking off the thought, I took another silent but deep lungful of night air so sharp it tried to cut my lungs. I was almost out of the woods. The glow of the damn LED lantern signaling the clearing where the boathouse sat was *right there*. But elves were ambush predators. Troy, in particular, was patient and took a wicked delight in springing traps at the last moment. He was taller and faster than me, although I was nearly as strong now. And he'd been trained as an assassin and commando since childhood.

Of course, he knew I knew that. Which meant he knew all my little tricks.

All my habits. All my fears.

That's it.

My way out wasn't letting him ambush me in the trees this close to the finish line and trying to fight my way free when I was outnumbered.

It was doing something nobody would expect.

I burst into a run, which he *would* expect.

There.

Movement to my left, on the side away from Jordan Lake. A deeper patch of shadow in the dark. Troy.

He knew me, body, mind, heart, and soul. Which meant he knew the last thing on Earth I'd ever do was jump into Jordan Lake, especially in February. Especially here, at the boathouse where I'd nearly died for the first time.

I had to win this. I owed it to myself, for all the hard work I'd put in. I'd *earned* this win. I was as good as any elf, and I'd prove it.

The shadow that was Troy angled to cut me off.

I planted a foot and, instead of trying to get past him, pivoted and hoofed it for the lake. As I ran, heart pounding, I made sure the flag was secured in the pocket of my Darkwatch-issue pants. There was a bluff—

I almost didn't see it in time to turn my headlong run into a shallow dive rather than a tumble.

"Arden, no!"

Troy's shout was the last thing I heard before hitting the water.

The slap of cold nearly knocked me out, as did the rock I would have smashed into headfirst had I not dropped my shields and thrown up a bubble of Air as I leaped. The rock shifted. I flailed and managed to turn in time to take the rest of the impact on my feet. It jarred through my thighs, numbing my legs almost as much as the icy water did.

Dropping my bubble was the last thing I wanted to do, but I still had to get to shore. Sofia, my undine friend, had guided me into a passive Water ability that would let me hold my breath longer than I could otherwise. Val, her dea sister, had taught me a little self-warming trick with Fire, but that would make steam rise from the freezing lake and give me away. I'd just have to hurry and swim before I froze to death.

Fortunately, the finish line wasn't far.

As I kicked off, two more splashes disturbed the water behind me. One was almost certainly Troy. The other would be one of the Ebon Guard. A rescue rather than a capture probably, but the joke was on them. I was passing this exam, come the ninth circle of hell or the high water of this Goddess-damned lake.

Grimly, I stayed beneath the surface and kept kicking. The lake was deep on this side, with short beaches and steep drop-offs. Some folks who jumped in didn't come back up, even when the weather was nice.

Again, I wrenched my mind away from the memory of almost being one of them. I refused. Kept kicking. Let the imagination of Troy's fury at the fool move I'd made keep me warm.

Almost there.

Almost—

The pillar of the dock was suddenly in front of me so fast I almost swam into it. I hauled myself out, gasping for breath. Sofi's little trick didn't work as well for sylph-born me, for all I was a primordial now.

Digging deep, I pushed myself into a run. If someone tagged me before I reached the lantern—

Air currents shifted, and I dodged, hitting the ground and rolling as an arm passed overhead.

"Here!" Allegra shouted. "She's out. She's over here!"

I found my feet and launched myself at the lantern in a dive, crashing into it to send it flying just as Allegra's grip closed around my ankle.

I would have sworn I'd touched the lantern before she touched me, but I was busy trying not to throw up or choke on big heaves of icy air that sliced my lungs at the same time.

It had been cold enough before without being wet and exhausted. Now I was paying for it. I opened the bond with Troy, knowing he'd be worried, then jumped to find him practically on top of me and, as predicted, furious.

He melted out of the night as he dropped his shadows, dripping lake water. "What in the ever-loving fuck was that?"

Oh boy. I was in big trouble.

Troy's fury was always as icy as his power signature, but the swears—those were the biggest giveaway. I was too tired to move though, so I just laid there shivering as Etain hurried over with two of the silvery emergency blankets I'd gotten way too familiar with in the last few years.

Troy snatched them from her, knelt in front of me, pulled me up into a seated position, and wrapped both around me with rough tugs. "*Never* do that again."

I scowled. "You giving me orders, Troy?"

"You're damn right I am. This is training. You're my subordinate here. That was fucking dangerous. Headfirst into a lake? In February? Into *this* lake? What the hell, Arden?"

Temper flaring, I inhaled to snap back at him—and caught the rotted-herb scent that said he was terrified. The gold flecks in his hazel eyes, the ones that apparently marked an elf who was too close to what the elves had once been for the modern standards that'd kept them from being discovered pre-Reveal, flashed in the low light. His grip stayed locked on the blankets, holding them tight around me rather than taking one to warm himself.

Glancing away, I remembered we had an audience: Troy's sister-cousin Allegra Monteague and Etain Bossence, my half-elven captain of the Ebon Guard. Haroun Carrell, the other of my personal bodyguards, also wet and shaking. Apparently, he'd been the second splash. Lachlan Sequoyah and Felip Luna, who doubled as healers. And maybe worst of all, Omar Monteague, aka *the* Captain, looking on with arms crossed and a heavy scowl on his dark face.

I grimaced, face flaming, and lowered my gaze. I kept forgetting it wasn't just about me now. There were people who would die for me, even if it was my bad call. "You're right," I said stiffly. "That was reckless."

Troy, ready to keep fighting, blinked and sat down. "What?"

I shrugged, annoyed and embarrassed now on top of being cold and wet. My cold hardiness only went so far in temps this low. "I knew you'd wait to strike until I was almost home free. Y'all needed to see if I could do the first part of the test, so while you could have taken me earlier, you wouldn't have known if I could find the flag and disarm the traps. I figured everyone else would hang back and let you flush me out in case I lost it at being ambushed. If they were behind and on the far side of the lake and you were in front, the only way out was the lake itself."

He stared at me in consternation as I recited my thought process, report-style, then started rubbing my arms. The blanket made a crackling noise, and Haroun fished a lighter from his pocket to light the nearby fire kettle. The lighter sputtered a few times before he gave up and let Allegra light it with a dry one.

I could have lit it myself, but Troy was right—I might be High Queen of House Solari and Arbiter for the Carolinas demesne, but he gave the orders in training exercises. One of those had been not leaning on my powers unless my life was in danger. I was cold, but I'd be fine, so I hadn't coaxed Fire to me to light the prepared wood myself.

Behind me, Allegra said, "She's not wrong, T. Batshit crazy, but she anticipated the strategy and found a tactic to counter it."

Troy wasn't having it. Heat scalded me in the bond. "She dove. Into. The lake."

"Which you were counting on her PTSD to stop her from doing. Another point to her for mental toughness."

He glared at her then transferred the look to me. "The flag?"

I shifted and dragged it out of the cargo pocket.

Troy shook his head, scrubbing his hands over his face. "Nobody tagged her before she hit the lantern?"

"Allegra did." I couldn't quite keep the sullen note out of my voice.

"Nope." She moved closer to the fire. "You knocked over the lantern first. You won, sis."

"I did?" My heart lifted. I needed some damn good news.

The Triangle—the country really—was going to hell in a handbasket as conservative politicians elected in the last year overturned early wins we'd secured for Otherside rights and protections, rolling back laws defending us. I'd instigated the two Reveals that'd outed the vampires, werewolves, elves, and witches, so all of Otherside was blaming me for the upheaval. The Darkwatch had suppressed as many records as they could, but I was still reeling from having my privacy largely stripped away in the media frenzy that'd followed the aversion of the Wild Hunt and the quieter backlash from Otherside.

We'd won. But lately it was feeling like we'd lost, and I didn't know what to do about it other than what I had done: step back and mind my business for a little while. All I knew was that I wanted more than anything to feel safe and in control. Hence, taking Troy up on his suggestion to take my training regimen up a notch and into the first level of the full Darkwatch program.

Troy glanced over his shoulder at Omar. The relationship between the two was strained as hell these days, but Omar Monteague was Captain of the Darkwatch, at least here on the East Coast, and still had the final say in who passed its tests.

Omar's lips pressed together in deep disapproval. Then he shook his head, much as Troy had. "It was a near thing, but she did win. If the lantern had been a getaway car, she'd have made it. At least close enough to be covered by backup." He arched an eyebrow. "Alone, she'd be in trouble. But that's why we don't send agents alone." A glance at Troy, one that might have been remorseful from anyone else. "Usually."

My heart pounded as I waited for the judgment.

I'd been training for the last year for this. Busting my ass daily alongside Troy, Allegra, and whichever of the Ebon Guard wanted to try me after Maria and the rest of the parliament had accepted me stepping back from dealing with mundane affairs, as much to calm the rest of Otherside as the mundanes. I'd needed something else to do with my time. Hell, even the wereleopards had helped with my training.

Self-defense had seemed like a good idea. Complaints from the elven conclaves in Richmond and Charleston had gotten louder. I knew from experience and with the Sight that I'd need to defend myself sooner or later. Troy might not always be there to save my ass.

And frankly, I was hoping if the Houses heard I was properly Darkwatch-trained, they'd either think twice about coming for me or have to send a large enough force that Omar or Etain would hear about it.

Omar sighed heavily. "Take one of those blankets, son, before you freeze to death and leave House Solari without an heir."

Annoyance flashed from Troy at the word "son" from his uncle and adoptive father, but for once, he let it rest as the bond echoed with both my frustration and Troy's embarrassment.

The topic of heirs was a touchy one. One I refused to think about just now. Heat faded from my face as I stomped the thought down and pushed it into a box.

I nudged Troy, and he stared at me before shaking himself and taking one of the blankets. Sometimes, we were a little too tightly meshed together and it took a moment to separate whose thoughts were whose.

We all moved closer to the fire, although Troy hung back a little. I might have dived right in, but I had trauma around water—the lake. His was around fire, specifically fire in braziers in the dark and what his grandmother and sister had done to torture him to within an inch of death. I shifted to stand in front of him, both to put a physical barrier between him and the fire and because leaning my back against his front would soothe him. We were both wet and cold. It wasn't like I could make it worse.

The snarl of emotions in the back of my mind loosened, although he didn't embrace me like I knew he wanted to. This was still a training exercise, and Omar was still the father figure who'd raised him and been his military superior.

The Captain studied me. "The conditions are satisfied." As my heart leaped, he held up a hand. "I don't like *how* they were satisfied. What you did was dangerously unconventional and almost criminally reckless. Your king and a member of your Guard followed you in because you could have—*should* have—cracked your head open and drowned. They could have followed you. Losing either you or Troy would throw the entire Eastern Seaboard into chaos because of how much you've destabilized the region by reorganizing the power structure and allowing Maria to hold the seconds of the New York and Miami coteries. I'm not convinced we've seen the last of Sergei or Roman Volkov, but you refuse to have either of them killed."

I flushed again as he shook his head with disappointment, equal parts ashamed for putting people I loved and cared about at risk and angered at being called out like this. But I pressed my mouth shut and took the feedback. Partly so that Troy, who was already pissed off, wouldn't be drawn into an emotional feedback loop in the bond.

Omar nodded approvingly when he saw I could hold my tongue. "As a Darkwatch agent, you've passed the first of the three physical contests. I'll give you that."

I straightened, despite my embarrassment at how much I wanted this approval.

Then he continued. "But part of being High Queen is neutralizing threats. So far, you've done that by burning House Monteague to the ground, killing the queens of Luna and Sequoyah in personal combat, upending the wereclan leadership, empowering your vampire ally to execute a coup a good century or two before she would have earned the place, and using elemental power to put the fear of the Goddess into the mundanes, which I suspect is the only reason you've managed to continue living in your little house in the woods rather than being chased out of town." He stared me down, his dark eyes unimpressed. "What are you going to do when you have to deal with a threat without killing it, burning it, fighting it, or bullying it?"

"I'm not a bully," I snapped. I'd killed bullies. After giving them the opportunity to change, of course. I wasn't an asshole.

Omar's eyes glittered. "Aren't you?"

The clearing was dead silent except for the crackling fire. Everyone around it looked like they wanted to be somewhere else, and at my back, Troy was stiff, the bond conspicuously quiet as he walled himself away.

"I was *defending* myself. And the people who looked to me."

"Okay." Omar crossed his arms. "Now you've defended yourself into becoming the single most powerful Othersider on the East Coast. Possibly on the continent, maybe in the world. So, a word of advice, Arbiter? Learn to step softly instead of always swinging a big stick. Because most of the world is not going to see things like the people around this fire do, and most of them will not love you enough to forgive a heavy hand."

With a last inscrutable look at Troy, Omar turned to leave.

He paused only to call over his shoulder, "I'll enter her success into the records, son, and your qualification as a trainer. Physical only—she's not a full agent. Not without passing the rest of the tests. And never without Aether."

I was too pissed off to thank him for deigning to give me what I'd earned.

Chapter 2

Troy waited until we were at home and alone to let me in on his thoughts. Quite the feat, given that it was easier for us to be in each other's heads than not most days. He almost never argued with me in front of our guards, but in private? I'd earned his trust that I wouldn't maliciously or intentionally punish him for speaking his mind, so he spoke it.

He squared up to me as soon as the front door was shut and locked and the new security system reset. "It meant that much to you to pass?"

I flinched. His soft not-quite-disappointment in my recklessness was harder to face than a shouting argument would have been. I wrestled with the resentment that sparked, until he reached for my hand and towed me toward his body despite the fact that we both stank of stagnant lake water and sweat.

Not mad. Just scared, I reminded myself.

"I guess it did." My words were muffled against his chest. "I'm sorry I scared you." I fought off a smile and failed. "And that I made you go for a swim in February."

He sighed, although the bond echoed more with resignation than annoyance. "Not like it's the first time." Pulling back, he kissed my forehead. "You did well, cariñamí. I'm proud of you—even if I wouldn't mind thrashing you for the scare."

I couldn't help the zing of heat that raced through me. Not just from the pleasure of his being proud of me or the elvish term of endearment he'd let his guard down enough to use. Sometimes our sparring—very fairly called a thrashing on his part—ended in very hot sex.

Okay, more often than not. We'd always had a physical attraction edged with violence. Once we'd worked out our opposing viewpoints, it had become downright hot.

"Don't tempt me," he murmured, picking up both my mood in the bond and the shift in my scent under the reek of lake water.

"Sorry not sorry." When he gave me a stern look from under an errant lock of black hair, I added, "What? You're hot when you get all grouchy and bothered."

He snorted, and the thin thread of tension broke. "You're the only person I've met who thinks my moods are hot rather than scary."

"I'm sure Allegra has opinions—"

"She always does."

"—but *I* happen to have expert insights."

"I'm going to expert insight you into that thrashing if you don't leave off and take a shower with me."

If he wasn't inclined to hold onto my foolishness, far be it from me to encourage him. I was much happier to follow him under the hot spray and let him soap me up, then rinse me off. The tawny brown of his hands slid over the darker sienna brown of my body and skimmed up my flanks. Then he pinned me to the wall by the throat as the other hand dipped back down between my legs.

"Yes," I said before he had to ask.

The hot weight of dominance thundering through the bond told me what he wanted. Having the world's only living elven king twice bonded to me came with plenty of advantages but also a duty of care. He needed physical reassurance to feel balanced and at his best: casual touch, sex, and occasionally a little blood. All of which I was happy to give him, because damn but he made me feel good as he took what he needed.

His mouth fell on mine as though he was going to devour me while his fingers worked between my thighs. No matter how much I moaned and writhed, trying to slide his fingers into me, the hand around my throat kept me in place. Shit. He was going to make me beg. I had it coming for scaring him the way I had, but I didn't beg. Ever.

Until he made me.

My heart raced with anticipation, and he drew back to study me, a predatory gleam in his gaze. "You know what I want."

I nodded, panting. "You're not getting it."

Resistance was part of the fun.

Troy didn't bother responding. He simply pulled back, made sure we were both rinsed clean of soap and conditioner, turned off the water, and followed me out of the shower.

Tension stretched as I sorted out my hair and we went through our bedtime routine. He didn't touch me, but he didn't have to. He had Aether and a direct link to my mind.

I nearly choked on my toothbrush when he leaned on the Aether, sending teasing tendrils of it through my nervous system, and I couldn't quite stop a whimper as I finished brushing my teeth then fled to the kitchen.

Part of resistance was giving him something to chase.

He let the tension draw even tighter as he took his time following me out, stalking me with the smooth grace he'd always had but which had been elevated as he allowed himself to become what he'd always had the potential to be. He was deliciously dangerous in the best way, and my body tightened as he came after me.

There was nowhere to run in my little house, but I tried, vaulting over furniture, gasping as his fingers brushed my arm. I managed to make it to the bedroom and shut the door on him...but not the one that connected to the bathroom.

I tried whipping open the door that led to the kitchen again as he burst through the bathroom door, but he slammed it shut and leaned on it, trapping me against it with his body and stealing another demanding kiss.

Once upon a time, his nearness and the scent of herbs and burnt marshmallow—the scent of a high-blood elf and powerful Aether magic user—had terrified me.

Now, I couldn't help another muffled noise that was definitely all frustrated want.

He quivered at it and the scent of my desire, the reverberations of it through the bond, and then he was tired of toying with me.

Before I could take another breath, I found myself pinned to the bed. Most of the time, Troy used the extensive bedroom training he'd received as a royal to serve me. Much less frequently, he used it to destroy me in the best possible way, unraveling me layer by layer until my soul was as bare and open as my body, dragging the kind of pleading from me I would have said I'd die before voicing until taking him to my bed and my heart.

This was one of the latter times.

Pleasure he usually coaxed from me was commanded. I held out as long as I could, but he kept pulling back just as I reached the edge of my climax.

"Say it," he growled in my ear as I gripped the sheets in frustration. He curled two fingers inside me almost lazily, keeping me at a fever pitch but not giving me enough to push me over.

I moaned, lips pressed tight to stop myself. Not that it did any good, I had the walls down in the bond. He knew what he was doing to me.

"Say. It."

"Please." The word burst from my lips as he applied a little more pressure.

"Please...what?"

I growled. I bucked and fought. When I tried pulling on Air, he sent a pleasure sting through the bond, distracting me from my magic by short-circuiting my nervous system with an overwhelming surge of ecstasy that he muted before it reached my lower regions. I tried again, faster this time, but he knew my tricks as well as I knew his. Again, the overwhelming pleasure left me groaning as he kept working me with his mouth and fingers. If it was possible to die of great sex, odds were good I might one of these days.

If he'd get around to it, that is.

If I surrendered.

"Goddess *damn it*, Troy Solari, fuck me!" I tried to inject command into my voice, but he had me in melty little pieces and all I managed was desperation.

Teeth flashed in the dark as he smiled. "With pleasure."

And then he was in me, moving torturously slowly, controlling my efforts to take more from his body with his weight pressing me down, his grip pinning my wrists overhead.

"Never." He thrust. "Scare me." Another thrust, deeper. "Like that." Deeper and harder still. "Again."

I don't know what I said, what I promised as I babbled my pleas and assurances, but he finally let me tip over the edge, shifting his grip on my wrists while I was distracted so that one still held them and the other bracketed my throat again, under my jaw. There was no escaping him, and rather than being terrified, I wanted more.

"Bite me," I said when I'd finished, more breath than voice.

He slowed his movements. Hunger surged, hot and sharp in the bond, and he didn't bother hiding it from me. "You're sure?"

"Yes. Fuck, Troy, please, claim me, I—"

He picked up the pace again and stole the rest of my words. With my enthusiastic consent, he wouldn't ask twice. He grew rougher as, in the bond, his anticipation reached new heights. A shift of his jaw dropped his shark-like secondary teeth.

"Ready?" he growled.

"Do it."

Troy wasn't a vampire, to transmute pain to pleasure with the glamour in a locked gaze, but the trick he'd adapted to use between us more than worked. He covered my mouth to catch my scream as he ripped another orgasm from me and turned my head in the same movement, exposing a stretch of my neck.

The bite to the meat of my shoulder should have hurt like hell, given all his teeth, but I was lost in an ecstasy that was the opposite of a vampire's—soaring to heights rather than spiraling down to bliss.

His movements lost their grace, and he groaned as he finished.

We stayed as we were, his forehead against my jaw, coming down together. Gradually an ache grew in my neck, and he soothed it with another ripple of Aether. He couldn't heal the bite, like a vampire or a Sequoyah could have, but he could ease the pain of it until my own accelerated healing kicked in.

"Don't go anywhere." He kissed me and slipped out of bed to get a towel. We hadn't used a condom in a while, which would have been incredibly stupid except that apparently, I was like most of the elf-blooded—fertile only when my stress hormones had dropped long enough to menstruate and ovulate. Hadn't happened since the initial announcement of puberty, no surprise. Since I was effectively infertile for the time being and we'd both gotten the requisite health checks, we'd agreed to enjoy each other sans barriers. I hadn't fallen pregnant after the first accident, or the second, or after our intentional discussions. And if I did...well, I'd chosen him, and the House would need an heir eventually, even if I avoided thinking about it for the time being.

He helped me clean up then curled around me, holding me tight. "I love you. And I will be damned if I lose you."

I pushed closer, wanting to be as close to him as possible and trembling in the rippling aftershocks of excruciating pleasure. The icy chill of the lake was long gone, burnt away by the inferno he always kindled in me. "I love you too. And I'm not going anywhere."

With that reassurance, he gently ran his tongue over the bite he'd given me. He didn't have healing magic in his saliva like a vampire. He just liked and was grounded by the taste of me. I shivered as the motion sent more shocks of pleasure through me. This was only the second time he'd claimed me like this. I'd goaded him into it the first time without entirely knowing what it meant for him. This time, it was a penance for my earlier rashness. We'd learned the importance of keeping the scales balanced between us and of healthy, mutually enjoyable outlets for some of our more violent urges. Sparring was more usual. This felt better.

I'd needed it as much as he had. For a moment, I scrambled to rein in spiraling panic at the realization that I didn't recognize my own life anymore. When Troy paused in his aftercare, I pushed that thought away for later. I didn't know what was triggering it, so I didn't want to talk about it.

"Thank you," I whispered before he could ask what was wrong.

He grunted. "For what?"

"Knowing what I need better than I do and finding a way to give it to me."

Shock blanked the bond before love surged in to replace it like a tsunami. He didn't say anything though, just held me so tightly that I thought I was going to burst for a minute. "I will always at least try, cariñamí. Always."

I drifted off, knowing I was guarded if not safe. A mated pair of gytrash patrolled the grounds; the fae black dogs were sworn to me as part of a deal with their king. A couple of the Ebon Guard would be out there as well, and in here, I had Troy. Anyone who got past all that would have to face my wrath as a primordial elemental, and nobody was keen to do that after I'd leveled parts of downtown Durham with Air, Fire, Earth, Water, and primordial Chaos while saving the world from the kickoff of the Wild Hunt.

I'd passed my exam. My king was falling asleep at my back, breath slowing and body relaxing. I followed him down, spiraling into darkness.

A darkness that was a little too dark.

It was a dream. I knew that immediately, just as I knew it wouldn't shift to the windswept seashore as long as Troy was nearby. I didn't know what that was about, but I knew it was related to him. To the Aetheric bond and distance between us. Or lack thereof.

But it also wasn't the impossible white blankness of the unframed Crossroads.

It wasn't a normal dream.

It wasn't anything at all, and nothing at all happened.

All the same, I couldn't step out of the dream like the djinn had taught me as a child, and I felt odd. Almost like I was being watched. But the only people who could possibly be watching me were gods or djinn. The djinn were allies, and the gods were silent.

Nothing was *wrong*, per se. But it wasn't quite right. And while I wasn't actively being threatened, I definitely didn't like it.

My life was already too far out of my control without adding creepy dreams.

Chapter 3

Morning brought Allegra bright and much too fucking early, a whirlwind of far too much energy for the fact that elves were supposed to be nocturnal, she was dating a vampire, and I personally wouldn't be up before ten without a good reason.

Troy rose to get the door while I went to the bathroom and evaluated the bite, poking it gently in the mirror to elicit a dull stab of pained pleasure. I healed faster than human-normal from most things, including vampire bites.

Elf love bites were another story.

I sighed and mentally steeled myself for the ribbing I was in for as I shrugged into a robe. Maybe she wouldn't notice. In the bond, Troy did the same mental fortification as I finished up and stepped out of the bathroom.

Allegra's dark locs were pulled up into a tidy bun, and her amber eyes were alight with either mischief or excitement. Probably both.

"Morning, Allegra," I said. "To what do we owe the exceedingly early pleasure?"

She started to answer, eyes twinkling with the amusement they always held when she'd managed to get us out of bed early. Then she scented me and frowned. "Were you wounded during the trial, Arden?"

"Nope."

Her eyes narrowed, and she scented the room again. Her gaze darted from me to Troy to the bedroom and back to me.

I couldn't help flushing, equal parts embarrassment and anger at her nosiness.

Crossing her arms, she settled back on a cocked hip. "Troy."

He lifted his eyebrows.

"Did you—"

"Do you really want to go there?" His tone had the flat emptiness it took on when he was avoiding something.

"If you're going feral—"

Troy's expression twisted in annoyance, echoing a deeper ire in the bond. He didn't give much away to most people, but his sister and I were another story. "I'm not feral, Alli. I wish you'd stop with that."

"There's a reason you're the only king."

"Trust me, I know."

I stepped closer to Troy, leaning against him as he lifted an arm to cuddle me in. "I asked him for it, Allegra." Begged him, really, but she didn't need to know that. Especially when I was short-tempered and feeling protective. "Let him be."

She pressed her lips together to give me a stern look. "Arden—"

I lifted my chin and let my expression go icy. If Troy was reacting like this, there'd been things said outside my hearing that he hadn't mentioned. Allegra was one of the good ones, one of my original Ebon Guard and the leader of the Ebon Rebellion that'd helped me topple the other Houses in the Triangle, but she still had some funny ideas about tradition, culture, and keeping Troy safe. They were closer in age than most elven cousins or siblings, and with her twin Darius still in exile, Troy was all she had left for family other than her estranged father. She'd been Troy's knight growing up as well, saving his life in the attack that'd left the long, heavy scar over his heart, and old habits died hard.

Didn't mean I had to tolerate it, especially if it was hurting Troy.

Clearing her throat, she resettled her posture to a parade rest and started again. "My queen. There hasn't been a king since Atlantis."

I arched an eyebrow at her, stroking Troy's back to soothe some of the irritation. He rested his chin on my head, the bond still thrumming with agitated frustration toward his sister even as he was apparently content to let me handle her. He didn't let me fight his battles very often. This must have been going on much longer than I'd thought.

I kept my expression and voice firm. "I'm aware of the history of elven kings. Is there a reason you're picking this fight?"

"The other Houses will be watching him. Closely. The Guard regularly scrubs whatever comes up about you both on the internet, but we're working on the assumption that spies have infiltrated the territory among all the supernatural refugees."

I connected the dots. "So you're afraid that if it looks like he's behaving too far outside human norms and elven restrictions, they'll be reminded why they murdered men like him."

Allegra flinched at the word "murder" but that's what it was, and we all knew it. "Yes."

"Concern noted," I said.

She made a frustrated noise. "My queen—"

"I get it, Allegra. I do. Nobody wants him alive and kicking more than I do." I raised my brows when she opened her mouth to protest.

Troy and I had become something akin to Aetheric symbionts over the last two years, as the tracking tag he'd placed on me early in our acquaintance warped, deepened, was torn away, re-established, and then used to resuscitate me after the Wild Hunt with some of his aura. If one of us died, I strongly suspected the other would follow in short order.

Softening my tone, I said, "I'll be careful to keep it covered up."

"It will start scarring eventually," she said. "I noticed the scars from the first one last year but assumed it was something else because Troy couldn't possibly be that—"

"Enough." I rubbed my eyes, way too tired and hungry for this discussion, and Troy squeezed me before slipping away to get tea, coffee, and breakfast going.

Diplomacy. I needed diplomacy. I loved Allegra like the sister I never had, and she loved us both the same way, even if it was expressed in a fierce and sometimes—to me—wrong-headed overprotectiveness. "I appreciate your looking out for us. I won't promise not to do it again"—a surge of hopeful hunger in the bond, quickly muted, made me blink—"but I will remember what you've said and be careful about showing the mark. Okay?"

Allegra didn't look happy, but she pressed her lips together and nodded.

"Thank you. Now. Good morning." I went to her and gave her a hug. I didn't usually hug people, but elves were touchy-feely, especially in family groups, and it was the fastest way to let her know I wasn't going to hold this against her. For now, anyway. If she kept hassling Troy, we were gonna have a much more forceful conversation.

She returned it quickly, sensitive to my disposition, and relaxed back into a wry casualness. "Good morning yourself. I've got news."

"You'd better if you're getting me up before ten," I grumbled.

From the stove, Troy asked, "House Ead?"

Allegra shook her head and grinned, all good cheer once more. "Better. Desmarais."

"What?" Troy turned from the bacon just starting to sizzle. "Lyon Conclave?"

"Yep."

I glanced between them. "Lyon?"

"Our cousin-House in France," Allegra said. "Their Conclave wants to send observers. We've got international attention now."

Frowning, I leaned back and crossed my arms to hold in a spike of territoriality. "Wait wait wait. An observer. From another conclave—another *country*. Here. What does that mean?" A tendril of calming energy curled through the bond. "Exactly as it sounds," Troy said. "A pre-arranged visitor plus two attendants, representing each House, to see how we're doing things here."

I held myself firm against the attempt at soothing me. "Why?"

Allegra got up to snag two of the mugs Troy had set out. "I imagine because of that mess a few years ago with the low-blood, the one they sent people to bring home after disgracing and exiling her."

I hadn't heard this story, but from Troy's slow nod and distant expression, he had. "The one who took off with a vampire vagabond. Goddess but the reports made that out to be a complete mess, especially when Maria got involved."

Allegra narrowed her eyes warningly at the potentially uncharitable mention of her girlfriend, the vampire we'd helped become the Mistress of Raleigh.

I'd get details later. "Okay, but why do they need to come here, to *my territory*?"

Maybe I wasn't as good at hiding my feelings as I'd thought.

Allegra filled one mug with coffee then dropped a Ceylon teabag and hot water in the other and set that one in front of me. "Because there's some things that are best seen to be understood."

Her gentle tone told me she saw and got why I was upset. Sometimes the elven hormones hit me hard now that they were activated by Troy's constant presence, and I'd only been dealing with them for just over a year or so, not a lifetime.

Annoyed, I took hold of Air and sent a zephyr swirling through the air plants hanging from fishing lines tied to little glass bulbs suspended overhead. I didn't want to be comforted. I wanted to be *safe*. I'd done a lot of shit I hadn't wanted to do to put myself in the position of being untouchable. Killed people, even, when I'd tried to say I wasn't a killer. Exposed myself as an elemental to the fucking Raleigh police department and then to all of Durham and the world.

Think. I need to think, not feel.

A puzzle piece clicked into place. "This is why you're so upset about Troy biting me."

She grimaced at my outright acknowledgment but nodded. "We've all got to be on our best behavior."

I smirked, unable to help myself. "I dunno, I thought he was pretty damn good last night."

"Arden!" Allegra pressed her hands over her ears. "Goddess save me from you two. Fucking shameless."

Troy's expression matched mine as he brought plates to the table, and I leaned over to kiss his shoulder when he sat down, pleased that his earlier irritation was soothed by my oversharing. I preferred to be more circumspect, but her attitude had pissed me off.

"Thanks for breakfast," I said.

He nodded then pointed at Allegra with his fork. "I'm not the one you need to be worried about if there are observers, and you know it. Don't use me as a punching bag because you'd do things differently than Etain."

Ah. That explained quite a bit. Allegra had technically been "promoted" to princess because we needed a female heir for House Solari to keep the other East Coast Houses off us, and for the most part, that worked for her. She got to be a diplomatic envoy to the Mistress of Raleigh, which as far as I could tell meant all but becoming Maria's solidaire and spending a lot of time in her bed. A good gig, but Allegra had been trained for more militaristic pursuits.

Her scowl all but confirmed that she was chafing a little. "I wasn't wrong to say what I said."

Troy gave her the flat look that said he was out of patience, and I squeezed his thigh under the table. He speared a jumble of chive-and-cheese eggs and ate them, not looking away from his sister.

"Fuck, okay, fine, I'm sorry," she muttered, dropping her gaze. "And yeah, Etain is good, but I'm better."

"Alli, you're top ranked in everything I haven't beaten you at," Troy said. "That doesn't mean Etain isn't as good at her job as you would be, if in different ways."

I smiled and worked on my own breakfast. Troy used to have a massive chip on his shoulder about anyone who wasn't a high-blood elf. His defense of my half-elven captain of the Ebon Guard was the result of a long and painful journey for both of us.

"Fine," Allegra said after clearing half her plate. "Points taken. I apologize." She sounded sincere, which brought my shoulders down from around my ears until she glanced at me again. "But the fact that observers need to come remains, and you need to sign off on it, Arden."

Because I was High Queen.

I sighed and pushed away my mostly finished plate, never having been big on breakfast. I only ate it now because it staved off power hangovers and kept Troy from going mother hen on me.

He snagged one of my uneaten pieces of bacon. "Remember our talks about diplomacy?"

"Yes." I dragged the word out, childishly, because I didn't negotiate or diplomate or whatever. I investigated. I dug into stuff. I got answers. I could play charming if it got me those answers, but I wanted to get to the point and close the case. Even if I'd had to let go of Hawkeye Investigations, my private investigation agency, I was still a PI at heart.

Troy didn't indulge me. "This is a good first step. House Desmarais are distant cousins of ours with ties occasionally refreshed by marriage. They've already got precedence—"

"Failed precedence," Allegra broke in.

Troy nodded. "But not for lack of trying on their part. Their exile didn't take the offer to return home, assuming our intel is correct."

Allegra scowled but nodded, allowing the point.

"Failed precedence or not, they've already been open to the idea of reviewing crime and punishment," he continued. When I focused on my tea instead of answering, he sighed. "If I vouch for them, does that matter?"

I glanced at him. He wouldn't vouch for anyone if he wasn't certain of my safety.

"Yes," I allowed grudgingly. "But I don't understand what they *want*."

Allegra finished her last bite of eggs and set the silverware down with a light, frustrated clack. "Exactly what we've said. To observe. To talk to elves in House Solari, both high- and low-blood. This is important but not unusual. Anytime there's a shift as big as the one you've led, Arden, there's a period of adjustment and evaluation."

"Look at it like this," Troy said. "You've done something so unique that other elves want to learn from us."

I snorted, unable to help my amusement and disbelief. "Elves want to learn from an elemental and a king they'd rather have killed."

"*Yes*, Arden." Exasperation was leaking into both Troy's voice and the bond. "Is that so hard to believe?"

I just looked at him and pulled on Air long enough to let my eyes flash gold, a reminder of how I'd gotten to this position: by being forced to kill three other queens, destroy their Houses, and claim their incomes when they couldn't accept an elemental as a being deserving of life, let alone as the queen of a House that was mine by birthright, and when his choices had put him on the block next to me.

Sighing, he raised his hands then shook his head sharply at Allegra when she started to say something.

"T—"

"Leave it. Let her think," he said. "This would be big news even if she wasn't who and what she is."

Mollified, I settled back in my chair and drank my tea. I wasn't happy about this. At all. After months of being able to mind my own business, my plate was starting to fill up again. Otherside moved slowly, especially compared to humans, but it looked like my hard-earned breathing space was all used up. I was so anchored in the Triangle that it was easy to forget about the world beyond, but they clearly hadn't forgotten about me.

I couldn't help but feel like the target on my back was getting dusted off, and I didn't know if I was ready to be thrown back into the thick of things.

I could definitely assume it'd mean threats to my safety though.

Chapter 4

As I always did when I needed to think big thoughts, I headed for the boulder I'd overturned into the Eno River at the foot of the slope behind my house, leaving Troy and Allegra to have sibling time. The two gytrash, Bás and Marú, trailed me through the woods, keeping out of sight even if I could still pick up the faint tang of sulfur.

I was never alone anymore, which elicited a confusing blend of feelings when I paused to think about it. I was elf-blooded, so I had social hormones that meant I really did feel better having friends around—and especially having Troy fully moved into my house. At the same time, I'd been raised by the more independent djinn, and I'd been solitary most of my life for my own safety. I missed the freedom of not having to tell half a dozen people where I was going and the anonymity of pretending to be a magical null, even if it was a box I'd outgrown and flat-out destroyed.

Troy, I thought, understood it. He'd been forcibly alone for the months he'd been surveilling me for the Darkwatch to keep the secret of my existence—and his deal with me—from spreading. Probably for longer than that, now that I thought about his struggles with readjusting to being social again last year. So as much as I was allowing him and Allegra private family time, he was also allowing me alone time.

The steady flow of water had carved out a small island around my boulder, and I leaped the mini stream to scramble to the top. This was where I'd come to think after a lot of the shitty stuff that'd happened to me in the last couple of years, and Troy would know to seek me out here. From my perch, I embraced Fire and directed it to the pit in the center of the clearing, already prepared with wood in the center of fire-blackened stones.

Despite the chill of the early February morning, I didn't really need the warmth—one of a sylph's passive abilities was to adjust the air temperature in the immediate area to their comfort, and that power had grown as I did. But as a primordial, having all my elements readily available was soothing. Air had always been there. Fire in the pit or from the sun in a pinch. Water in the river, roaring and running high, muddy with the recent rain. And Earth cradled me through the boulder I sat on, icy with winter's chill at first.

I walled off the bond with Troy, leaving just enough of a gap that he could sense and find me but not so much of one that he'd be knocked out by my merging with nature's flow.

With the massive boost in my magic during the Wild Hunt, I'd had to be more conscious of taking time away. When I'd been a private investigator keeping everything supernatural locked down so tight that even Othersiders couldn't tell if I was a mundane or a null, I'd gotten away with pushing through exhaustion and working myself to the bone.

It'd taken one training incident to teach me that wasn't possible anymore, not without consequences Troy alone was powerful enough to help me manage. Exhaustion and short temper didn't blend well with primordial magic. The downed trees edging my accidentally widened backyard attested to that.

So here I was. Meditating or whatever.

I couldn't really shut my brain off—exercise was the only thing that got me to stop thinking so hard all the time—but at least I was spending time with the elements. I sent tendrils of power into the earth, connecting with it and letting it connect with me. Strengthening the ties that grounded my magic. Looking to see if there was anything amiss throughout the Triangle.

Callista might have had Watchers, and eventually I'd need to look at getting people beyond the Ebon Guard and the Darkwatch to support my rule here, as much as it bothered me to take another step closer to being like my homicidal former guardian. For now, my magical ties to the region told me a fair amount when I paused to listen. Not in words. In vibes.

Raleigh was off, as usual lately. There were ongoing protests there, off and on, depending on whether a vote had come to a head or an asshole politician or celebrity had said something foolish. Chemical weapons—tear gas and the like—had been used on the protestors supporting Otherside on more than one occasion.

Funny how it was never used on anti-Otherside gatherings.

The chemicals had seeped into the land. It was a stretch for me from here, but I'd been doing what I could to rebalance the environment before it could do too much to poison the earth and groundwater. It pissed me off to have to do it, but I called it a penance for not doing better at leading the two Reveals.

People had died. Kept dying. And trying to stop it got me called a bully by the Captain.

"Stop blaming yourself, Arden."

I withdrew from the elements and came out of my trance with a deep inhale at the sound of Troy's voice. "What?"

"Blaming yourself. Stop." He jumped the small rivulet as easily as I had and clambered up to sit beside me.

Grimacing at being caught at it and at the stiffness brought on by sitting unmoving on the cold rock, I sat up and wrapped my arms around my knees, opening the bond enough to get a sense of his emotions but not his thoughts.

Troy wrapped his arm around me and pulled me close but said nothing.

It seemed like we'd been doing this for ages—meeting at this rock to have deep discussions and usually some kind of fight. The first time had been after my toxic werewolf ex had left me. That'd been a fight for Troy and me. But also maybe the first of several turning points.

"Why'd you come here, the first time?" I blurted out. It wasn't what I'd meant to say, and I don't know why I thought of it now, almost two years later.

Troy frowned. "After Volkov left?"

"Yeah."

He winced. "You scared the hell out of me when we fought the lich. I guess I wanted to make a point." He squeezed my arm then stiffened. "I was dreaming about you around then as well."

I frowned. He'd never told me that before. "Dreaming about me?"

Dread curled through the bond. "Subconscious response to Keithia and the Captain beating the hell out of me on a regular basis for letting you keep your head."

"Ah. That explains how you suddenly understood what I meant about the law saying who has power and who's controlled." I leaned into him. "I'm sorry."

"Yeah." Darkness bled into his tone and whispered through the bond. "My nightmares aren't your fault though." A flash of embarrassed heat. "None of the dreams are or were."

That heat implied that some of them might have been sexual? Interesting. But not something to rib him about, not when he needed to trust me enough to keep being vulnerable. I shifted to wrap my arm around his back and rub his side soothingly. We'd killed the people responsible for his nightmares.

After a minute, he shook himself and blew out. "Thanks. Sorry. Sometimes..."

"I get it." After another minute of watching the river roar by, I said, "The observers can come."

Troy frowned. "I was expecting you to be more stubborn about being convinced."

"Yeah, well..." I smiled wryly. "Surprise."

"What changed your mind?"

"I can't keep hiding. It didn't do me any good as a sylph under Callista's thumb. It has done worse than nothing as a primordial, Arbiter, High Queen, and whatever the fuck else people have stuck on me."

Troy grunted his agreement and thought about it for a moment before slanting a suspicious look my way. "What's the catch?"

I snorted a laugh. "You have to take point."

"Me?" He frowned. "They'll be expecting to treat with the High Queen."

"She's delegating to her more than capable king and attending any meetings as the impartial Arbiter of the Carolinas."

He mulled that over, probably as much for the politics of it as the fact that I ruled the Carolinas in name, not fact. I'd been too busy to secure the full territory Callista had claimed, and eventually it would be a problem. One I'd been avoiding.

"Do you want me to play High Queen?" I asked as he kept thinking.

A poke through the bond made me twitch. "You're not *playing* at it, Arden. You *are* High Queen."

"Because you say so."

"Because it's true. You know I don't lie. Not when it comes to you." He studied me. "Is that why you want me to take point? Imposter syndrome?"

I started to answer a quick no and then realized that actually, yeah, that was part of it. I let him read the conflicting emotions in the bond as I looked for the right words. "I want you to do it because you've been working hard on reform. It's important to you. To me too, but it's your mission now."

It was his turn to shut his mouth on a quick denial. We'd had several talks about him needing to claim something for himself rather than living only to serve others. The first of those had involved him admitting—with considerable elemental persuasion on my part—that reforming the elven Houses and stopping some of their brutal practices was something he wanted and could accomplish, given a platform.

A platform he now had, even if the circumstances surrounding the Reveals and the subsequent backlash meant he had to be very careful about how he wielded it.

"Fair," he murmured finally. "And it would make the point to the observers. They'll assume you're holding my leash, but that's not entirely a lie."

His smile took the sting those words might have had. The bond leashed both of us. Letting him bite me was a public, if frowned-upon, proclamation that he was my equal. But if push came to shove, I outranked him now, being both the House's ranking female and stronger magically.

I leaned over to kiss him. "You're the best choice because you know what this is about. If I stand as Arbiter rather than High Queen, any political blunders I make aren't a threat against the Houses—they're about me settling into managing the territory and being a hardass about it. Besides, you know Maria won't stand for both of us playing elf politics."

He grimaced. "There is that. And she'll use it. She has before." At my confused frown, he added, "The Desmarais exile was a half-elf serving as solidaire to a vagabond Maria's age. The report I read said her mother was dying and they wanted her home. Desmarais elves turned up in Raleigh and stayed at The Umstead instead of making proper arrangements with Keithia. Lydia, the solidaire, chose the vamps over her mother's people. This is the first time in five years House Desmarais has been in touch. They were livid."

"Shit, that's a big deal."

"Very. I wasn't here for any of it, so I've just read reports, but reading between the lines..." He considered, then winced. "Maybe it is a good idea for me to take point on this one. Your situation isn't exactly the same, but I don't know how...okay...they're going to be with low-bloods. Might be worth the slight of not being greeted by the High Queen."

"Good. Then it's settled." The blood purity of elf politics irritated me, but I had to pick my battles for now. "Let me know how I can help when you're ready. Carte blanche on negotiations, whatever you think best."

A weighty feeling came through the bond, like he was honored by my trust, and I kissed him again. He caught me, cradling the base of my skull and drawing me into one of the really good kisses that always left me a little shaky.

He grinned when he released me, knowing my brain was a little scrambled and pleased that even after a year and a half together he could still do that to me.

"On that note," he said, "what about your birthday?"

"What about it?" I scowled. Beyond indulging in drinking an entire bottle of very fancy red wine and having a wild dance in the moonlight, I didn't celebrate that. Ever. Certainly not since meeting Troy.

"I let you talk me out of planning a party for you last year. Why not do one this year?"

Looking down, I fidgeted and picked at my thumbnail. "I never had one before. I see no reason to start now."

"It'd make a statement."

"It'd be a spectacle." I voiced my real fear more quietly. "*I'd* be a spectacle."

Troy rubbed my arm soothingly. "If you truly don't want to celebrate, I won't push again. But there's a political angle."

"There always is." I huffed. Being the Triangle's power couple meant nothing was straightforward anymore. "Talk me through it."

"Aside from the observers from Lyon, there's the rest of the territory. Nobody's really seen you in almost a year. It starts to look—"

"Like I'm afraid. Which makes us all prey. Shit." I shifted free of his arm and flopped back on the rock, taking solace in looking up at the sky. "Then why was Omar calling me a bully?"

"Partly because he's an ass who has a twisted way of trying to help people," he said. Neither of us said Allegra's name, but we both were thinking about apples and trees. "Partly because you haven't done anything like this though. You stay in hiding and only come out to kick someone's ass."

I flinched at the blunt but accurate assessment, grateful for the bond telling me he meant the words with as much love as honesty. He'd almost certainly stay with me no matter what, but another thing we'd learned was that our unusual situation would be more livable if we were brutally honest with each other in a way most people probably couldn't be.

I rose to a crouch then tugged his knee. He opened his body so I could settle between his legs, my back to his front. Hugs were okay when they were full-body embraces from Troy. His arms tightened around me, and we watched the river together as I wrestled with the idea that I needed to be at least a little more public.

"I assume you have ideas already?" I finally asked.

He hummed an affirmative.

"Where?"

"The bar."

I slumped against him in relief. "Thank Ishtar. I thought you were going to say The Umstead."

"That was Maria's suggestion."

"Of course it was." Her coterie owned the five-star hotel, and she had a taste for luxury. "Political clusterfuck waiting to happen though."

"That's what I said." He kissed the corner of my jaw. "That and that you'd likely take my head if I tried to push you that far into the spotlight."

"Y'all just go around making plans behind my back," I grumbled.

He nipped my neck. "That's because it was going to be a surprise party."

I froze then twisted to look at him in horror. "Please tell me you're joking."

His eyes shone with wicked glee. "It was going to be a whole ball. With a massive cake and—" I was already shaking my head, eyes wide, when he cut off with a laugh. "Don't worry, cariñamí. I reminded them what happens when you get overwhelmed."

"Good." I faced the river again and tried to relax.

It was just a birthday party. And it'd be good for public relations. A way to step back into my role without having people wondering if someone was about to get their ass kicked. How big a deal could it be?

Chapter 5

A pparently, the answer was a very big deal.

Troy and Maria were in one of the better phases of their odd and sometimes violently antagonistic personal friendship, so they divided and conquered. Troy took the arrangements with the Lyon Conclave delegation. Maria did the needful to turn what I'd kind of thought would be a few friends at the bar I rarely went to anymore into An Event™. Noah, as her second, accompanied me to Southpoint Mall to shop for something to wear, dragging me in and out of every department store the day before my birthday.

I didn't know whether to be terrified or embarrassed.

Both. Both was...not good, but felt appropriate.

"It's a *birthday party*," I snarled at him as he held up yet another dress. "At a *bar*. Ishtar preserve me, Noah, what—"

He pressed the hanger into my chest and kept pushing, backing me into the dressing room I'd just emerged from thinking we were finally done.

"It is *not* just a birthday party," he said. The quiet tone did nothing to hide his malicious pleasure, and his grin was so wide he was almost showing fangs. "And you are the *Ar*—"

"Okay! Fine." I snatched the dress, which had to be the eleventy-millionth I'd tried on.

"Just be happy we're not at the bridal shop," he said. When I whipped around, he batted his eyelashes at me. "They have fancier dresses."

I ducked into the dressing room to escape, heart pounding.

Technically, Troy and I were engaged. I'd asked him to marry me in a spur-of-the-moment burst of joy at the beach last summer. He'd accepted. We just hadn't filed formal paperwork or done the rest of the ceremonial shit because an elemental queen marrying an elven king would drop a bomb into Otherside's already volatile political situation. The djinn in particular would lose their shit, and they were my shakiest connection aside from the elementals, who would also react poorly. Everyone outside the Triangle—Otherside and mundane both—seemed to think Troy was a bodyguard or a tool. Or a phase.

For now, we let it go. We had something deeper than any ceremony or legal formality could confer. But I hadn't worked up the courage yet to ask anyone what an elven wedding looked like or what the next steps were to formalize everything.

Power couple shit.

I tugged the dress on, expecting another itchy, uncomfortable one that didn't sit right on my body. But it hugged me, slinky and cool as I zipped it up the side. It fell to my knees but had a slit halfway up the thigh on one side, where I could hide a small knife in a thigh sheath. The iridescent beads on it shimmered against a black so perfect that it reminded me of the In-Between. The high front and cap sleeves hid most of the Lichtenberg lines and knotty scar tissue under my right collarbone, a gift from one of the gods of the hunt in our first encounter. Only part of Troy's bite was visible, and that could be anything if the lighting was dark and the viewer didn't have the scent of sex to back up their assumptions. The low back showed off part of my tattoo, a kestrel fighting the East Wind. I wasn't exactly model slim to begin with and had bulked up in muscle since starting my Darkwatch training routine, but this made me feel more feminine and, hell, *queenly* than I had in ages.

I imagined Troy next to me in a suit and smiled. He'd outshine me—he always did in formalwear or in anything really, being the ultimate success of his birth House's strict breeding program for both appearance and magical strength. But I might actually keep up with him this time.

When I emerged, Noah was on the phone. His eyebrows shot up. "A moment, Michael, apologies." He tapped to put his call with his boyfriend on hold. "That's the one. You look stunning. Modern yet elegant." He studied me with a critical eye. "And the green-gold sheen in the beads will bring out the color in your king's eyes."

I glanced around the dressing room, but we were mostly alone. Still, I gave Noah a wide-eyed warning look not to say *king*.

He waved me off. "Modern slang."

I rolled my eyes. Noah was just as irreverent as Maria, and there was no scolding him. "Tell Doc Mike I said hello."

The necromancer had been my friend before anyone else's and before any of us knew he was a necromancer. Back before all of this had started, when I was still just a private investigator and Doc Mike had been—still was—the medical examiner overseeing the Raleigh morgue.

Winking, Noah went back to his conversation.

Slipping back into the dressing room, I got out of the dress and idly checked the price tag. My eyes bugged, and I swallowed hard, reminding myself that each of the queens whose incomes I'd taken as compensation for attacking me had been millionaires individually and I could easily afford it now.

Still. Another reminder of how much my life had changed in just a few short years. I tried not to cringe as I swiped my credit card at the checkout counter, as much for the price as for the cashier's frown of near recognition as she kept glancing at me.

Noah gave me air kisses to the cheeks as we parted at the curb. "Glad we finally found you something. Imagine the shame if you'd arrived wearing—"

"Yes, thank you." I'd been on the receiving end of enough barbed evaluations of my fashion sense that I didn't need another. I couldn't help my smile though. Noah was mercurial at the best of times, and the way things were going in Raleigh right now meant these weren't the best times. Maybe he'd needed this outing as much as I had—a chance to play at being normal. I squeezed his arm. "Really, Noah. Thank you. You're a miracle worker."

"Oh, I know." The bashful tilt of his head belied the cocky words. Then he perked up as my two bodyguards for the evening, Etain and Haroun, joined us from wherever they'd been keeping their distance. "Any chance at dinner?"

"No," the two half-elves said simultaneously.

"I had to ask." Noah grinned. With a last, surprisingly respectful incline of his head, the vampire headed for his car.

I turned and offered Etain and Haroun apologetic looks.

"Don't worry about it," Haroun said softly. He was almost as relaxed as Iago Luna, my chancellor, and a good counterbalance to most of the high-energy people who usually surrounded me. "Teasing, as usual."

As usual? "If he steps out of line—"

"He's fine, ma'am," Etain said. "Maria's coterie are all incredibly well-behaved with us half-elves." A small, satisfied grin curled the corner of her lip up. "And they're not stingy on returning favors."

I kept my face carefully blank, having thought her and Haroun were an exclusive item. What my people did on their days off was none of my business, and with Allegra more or less living at the coterie's nest, I trusted she'd keep an eye on our people. "Okay. If that's ever not the case, you know I'll take care of it."

Haroun smiled, and Etain nodded.

"Good." I stepped off the curb, heading for my gunmetal grey Honda Civic hatchback. "Let's get home. There's a storm coming."

△▽△▽

My birthday fell on a Saturday this year. The moon was two days away from new, which meant elven power was nearly at its peak. Troy's power signature leaked through his shields a bit more during the new moon, which I suspected was the other part of the reason why we were having this party at the bar that served as the local Otherside community's gathering place. The Umstead might be vampire-owned, but it was a mundane space. I owned the bar, my kobold friend Zanna managed it, and a witch named Sarah was our head bartender with a mixed team of witches, wereleopards, and werejaguars making up the bulk of the staff. The spells wreathing the building had managed to keep mundanes away so far, so it was the safest place for the kind of high-powered individuals on the guestlist to congregate without having to worry about the inevitable slip-up of a power signature burst or a fang flash or the partial shifts the local weres might fall into if a dominance question came up.

It also meant we could all be real, which was what mattered most to me. Troy wasn't the only one struggling with the accelerated boost in his power level. Mine had jumped beyond reason, and if I wasn't paying attention, my power signature subjected people around me to the auratic feeling of being in a wind tunnel.

The troubling part, though, was that if the wrong people did catch wind of it, all the Triangle's power players and our guests from Lyon might be at risk. That was intolerable, so I played the bully and ordered Omar Monteague to manage security when he'd sneered at Troy's request.

It really was a diplomatic event. Technically.

And fuck it, maybe I was just a little excited about having my first birthday party in my now twenty-eight years of life. Maybe I wanted the people who'd followed me from the start to have a chance to relax and enjoy themselves in a gathering like nobody had seen in decades. Or centuries. Callista had kept everyone at each other's throats. For all my stumbling, I was bringing them together.

The bar was packed when Troy and I arrived. Music was going only a little more quietly than it would in a human bar, in deference to Othersiders' better hearing. The scents of various boozes and bar foods were thick in the air, enough to overlay the mixed scents of were, elf, vampire, elemental, witch, and fae. New lights had been hung, and flowers in tasteful arrangements graced side tables with artful platters of finger food. I only managed not to gape because of Troy's anchoring nudge in the bond. It wouldn't do for the Arbiter to look like a bumpkin over a disco ball and some fairy lights.

I mean, it was more than that, but the effect was even greater. I had to blink back tears as the people packed into the big open space—bigger now that all the tables had been cleared out to make a dance floor—cheered as soon as the door shut behind Troy and me.

Omar might have called me a bully, but at least for now, it was nice to have a reminder that I really did have friends who cared about me.

Fortunately, I was saved by Zanna. The small fae bounded from her stepstool to the top of the bar, a microphone in hand, and the throbbing bass of the electronica music I loved lowered. "Lords and ladies, masters and gentlefolk, I present the Arbiter of the Carolinas, Arden Finch Solari, High Queen of House Solari and the Triangle. Her oathed and bound consort, Troy Solari, acknowledged King of the House." And because she was a kobold, she glared at the crowd and saucily added, "Show some fucking respect, or your beer won't be beer anymore."

I arched an eyebrow at her as everyone in the room bowed, but she only grinned to show sharp teeth. And notably, did not bow herself. She didn't bow to the gods either, so I wasn't surprised or offended in the least.

As the guests and the music rose again, Maria strode over and kissed each of us on both cheeks. "Fashionably late to your own birthday party. You're a natural, poppet."

Her hair was a rich Tyrian purple these days, a shade some might call wine red if they hadn't been raised by the djinn, rather than the emerald it'd been when we'd met. According to Troy, it was the third color she'd adopted since he'd met her about a decade ago—a lot of change for a vampire. The exquisitely cut wool fit-and-flare gown accented with a stole feathered in black plumage was consistently her.

"Maria," Troy said, a warning note in his voice.

She waved him off. "Oh fine. You're a natural, *Arbiter.*"

I just laughed. "Thank you for arranging everything, Maria. And for lending me Noah and taking the time from negotiations."

"What can I say?" She surveyed the room with a predatory gleam in her eyes. "There's so much opportunity here." Her darted glance at Troy caught him giving her a stern look and she laughed. "And here I thought *the Arbiter* had pulled that stick out of your ass."

"Not quite," he said, nearly a growl.

I popped up on my toes to kiss his cheek. "It's okay," I whispered. "Have fun tonight, okay? Let's build bridges or whatever."

Maria smirked at Troy. "You should listen to her."

Fortunately, Allegra swooped in, dressed in a beautifully tailored suit with patterns stitched in shimmering thread, and looped her arm through her girlfriend's. "Leave my brother be, darling." She grinned at me. "Happy birthday, Arden."

"Thanks."

Allegra winked. "Come on, Maria. If you're good, I'll let you do that thing you haven't had the balls to ask me about yet."

From Maria's suddenly rigid stance, there was a hell of an offer on the table. The elegant incline of her head confirmed it. "If you'll excuse me, Arbiter, Your Majesty."

They slipped away, leaving Troy and me a moment to gather our wits and catch our breath.

"That will never not be weird," he muttered as we continued toward a booth at the back, where a cluster of unfamiliar elves watched us.

"Which part?"

"Maria offering formal titles."

I couldn't help my laugh. "Agreed."

I was still smiling as we approached the table with our guests, and if anything, it made them look at us with more suspicion as they rose from their seats, knelt, and bowed their heads.

Internally annoyed at House formalities, I smoothed my features and said to Troy, "Introduce us."

He gave the same small nod Maria had. "My queen, this is Samarre of House Desmarais, cousin-House to Monteague, Jacinthe of House Proulx, and Luc of House Lavigne, all of the Lyon Conclave."

Samarre was a dark-skinned woman with hair pulled back in elaborate braids, much as mine was for the evening. She was heavily muscled, with the look of a trained fighter. Jacinthe was as pale as Samarre was dark, and Luc was closer to the local Monteague mold, with tawny brown skin and straight dark hair. I was surprised Samarre was the Desmarais, although she might have been adopted in. Then again, not all the Houses were as strict with their family lines as the Chapel Hill Conclave, let alone how Keithia had been with the Monteague royal line.

"Majesties," they said.

I inclined my head to the degree I thought Troy had shown me, and he sent a reassuring tap through the bond. "I'm here as the Arbiter tonight, but rise and be welcome."

Samarre did so first, looking like there was something she was fixing to say.

"Speak," I said.

She glanced at Troy, who'd fallen into a parade rest slightly behind my left shoulder. When he gave a slight nod, she said in a heavy French accent, "Forgiveness, Arbiter. It's just that you remind me of someone I used to know."

Probably Lydia Desmarais. Troy's voice whispered through my mind, though he kept his face blank. *The half-elven scion exiled here.*

I was grateful for that little trick. We had a vampire-like telepathic connection now, although we had to be careful about using it, both because I tended to react and because sometimes it meant speaking words the other had thought, which could be embarrassing.

"I'd heard of Ms. Desmarais's trials here under my predecessor." I chose my words carefully, still not quite sure what the hell had happened or what I should say about it. The Sight flickered, saving me. "We do things differently now. You are, of course, welcome to observe and come to your own conclusions."

A nudge from Troy.

"And I'll make myself available should you have any questions that our king can't address." At Troy's affirmative Aetheric caress, I added, "Troy will be your primary contact and host for the duration. I'm sure you can understand the political implications of my direct involvement in your visit, given our local power structure."

Samarre nodded, her dark gaze flicking between Troy and me before she inclined her head again. "Indeed. Thank you for your time, Arbiter. If we might borrow the king, we'd be grateful for the chance to be reacquainted with customs on this side of the Atlantic."

"Of course." I brushed Troy's arm in lieu of giving him a kiss. "I look forward to speaking more later."

As I moved back to the rest of the room, the triad closed on Troy. He sent a little burst of reassurance—I'd handled my first foreign diplomacy encounter as I was supposed to—then walled the bond up a bit so he could focus on them.

Fine with me. I'd spotted a few faces I hadn't seen in a while: Val and Sofia Pérez and Laurel Kerr, the three elementals who were still the only ones willing to associate with me. I couldn't help my smile as Val waved me over.

She grinned. "Look who finally arrived."

"I know. Late to my own damn party. Took forever to figure out how to hide a knife in this dress."

Laurel snorted and said in a Scottish accent, "She's the most powerful being on Earth and she's worried about hiding a knife."

I let the ribbing go. "We might have banned bronze in the territory, but that doesn't mean—"

A presence at my side pulled my focus. Etain. When she had my attention, she leaned in close and spoke low. "We have a situation."

"Fuck's sake," I muttered. "I haven't even greeted everyone yet. What kind of situation?"

"The kind involving dead humans."

Chapter 6

Adrenaline zinged through me, strongly enough that Troy sent a questioning dart.

I sent one back with the sense to hold and grimaced at my friends. "Back in a sec, y'all, sorry."

They made various faces but waved me away. Maybe it should have stung that they were used to this from me, but I was too busy focusing on what the hell had gone wrong.

I led Etain to a quieter corner behind the bar. "What the fuck do you mean dead humans?"

"Exactly that. Maria's man Oscar just called it in. Don't look at her."

"What the hell happened?"

"We don't know yet. But the body was left in public. Very public."

Fuck.

Troy, we have a problem. Don't rush over now, but when you get to a break—

Got it.

I smothered the wave of concern that came from him. "Maria's people are on it?"

"Yes."

"Where's the body going?"

"Dr. Miller."

I blew out a relieved breath. Doc Mike would know what to do. Better still, he was in our corner. "Okay. And is it obviously an Otherside-involved death?"

Etain grimaced at the technical terminology. "It's a drained human body with unhealed fang marks in the throat and the bend of the arm, left in the alley behind Claret."

"So about as stereotypically vampire as it can get in an area known for vampire activity. Shit. We need to get ahead of this."

"Oscar already got in touch with Dr. Miller. But, ma'am..."

My stomach sank as she trailed off. "What?"

Troy joined us. "What's wrong?"

I leaned close. "Vampire attack at Claret. One mundane dead in a very obvious way."

He frowned. "Someone's calling Maria out. Or you."

I was afraid of that. "Looks like it. Etain, what were you going to say?"

"Ma'am, it gets worse. Another body was left at the gates of the governor's mansion."

Cold seeped into my stomach as Troy stiffened beside me.

This was bad. Really bad.

"How the fuck did this happen?" I hissed. "They just— What? Walked a corpse up to a secure building and left?"

"Arden," Troy murmured warningly.

Taking a breath, I gathered myself and slipped an arm around him in an effort to ground myself. "We'll discuss this later, Etain. I assume Oscar has things in hand or Maria would have left. Keep me posted."

"Yes, ma'am," she said. Even under the multicolored fairy lights, I could see she'd paled. With a quick bow, she wove through the crowd.

I caught Maria's eye from across the room.

The Mistress of Raleigh nodded, knowing what our little huddle had been about, and made her way over with Allegra. "I'm heading out now. I'll deal with this, Arden."

I wanted to snap at her, but I'd learned the hard way not to overstep in Maria's business. If I stepped in without an invitation, I was going to have to do the kind of thing that broke friendships, and I really didn't want to do that in public, at my birthday party. But this was a massive fuckup on her part. I stayed out of her business because she assured me she was handling things and because Allegra was there more often than not.

If this was the shit that went down, I needed to have a serious discussion with both of them.

"Fine. But, Maria, I expect a report. Soon."

Her mien chilled. "Of course, Arbiter."

With a curtsy that seemed mocking, she left.

Grimacing, Allegra said, "I'll see if I can get ahead of it on our side."

She gave Troy a quick kiss on the cheek and followed Maria out. Heat crackled under my skin as I pushed down the urge to call Fire.

Sensing it, Troy stiffened. "Toro ben?"

It was one of the few elvish phrases I could keep in my head. "No. Everything is really not good. It's my fucking *birthday*, and this is what I have to deal with? But let's have a drink and go say hi to the weres so we can pretend everything is fine until Maria tells us how much of a clusterfuck we're dealing with."

He grunted his agreement and poured us both small glasses of red wine, handing me mine as we wove through the room to the table where Terrence, Ximena, Vikki, and Ana had clustered in an unusual mixed-clan gathering. Terrence's Acacia Thorn leopards and Ximena's Jade Tooth jaguars had been allied for a decade or more at this point. The Red Dawn wolf clan headed by Vikki and Ana was newer to the area and bound to the cats by a multi-layered agreement that'd allowed Red Dawn to both claim territory locally and take over dominance from the Blood Moon clan her brothers still headed out in the Blue Ridge Mountains.

Terrence smiled his usual sly grin, his tiger-eye gaze glinting but not shifting to the peridot of his leopard. "Trouble so soon, Miss Arden?"

I matched his expression. "You know how it goes. Somebody's always gotta act a fool."

"Always." He shook Troy's hand, and from Troy's amused snarl, the two were testing each other again. "We still need that rematch, Solari."

Troy's expression became the delighted malice he usually reserved for competitive sparring. "Anytime you want to get your ass handed to you, Little."

Vikki rolled her eyes. "Boys. Always gotta swing their dicks," she drawled in a twangy mountain accent. "Happy birthday, Arden."

Ximena grinned and echoed the birthday wishes, nipping Terrence's throat when he grabbed her and drew her against him with a mock-growl. When Terrence fell back dramatically, as though mortally wounded, she offered a rare smile. "We're not quite ready for the spotlight yet, but if you need us behind the scenes, we stand with you."

"Thanks, Ximena." I smiled back.

The werecats had always been solid allies. On their own terms, of course, which involved keeping their existence under wraps even as the werewolves were outed, but they had a tendency to look out for and protect the underdogs in the area. As far as I was concerned, they more than earned their place in the power balance, even if they weren't public participants like the vampires, elves, witches, and wolves.

I made small talk with them and then circulated the room, sipping my wine and contenting myself with a little bopping and swaying to the Top 40 music now blasting from the bar's speakers, trying to get my mind off the evening's shitshow. If I couldn't do anything about this mundane death in Raleigh, then I wanted to dance, but I couldn't completely let loose here. I prided myself on not forcing people to stay loyal to me with fear and torture—as Callista had—but I had to maintain some kind of decorum, especially with our elven guests from out of town. Not only that, but too much booze would unlock the maenad powers I'd discovered when I was sixteen, powers I didn't want to use in a room full of people I either liked or needed to impress.

Troy kept looking over the room as he whispered in my mind. *I'm half tempted to encourage you to test the maenad thing.*

Not on friends and guests. Trust me. It's bad. Especially given my current mood.

He eyed me consideringly. *You still haven't shown me.*

Because I like you breathing.

That bad?

Yes.

"Stay out of trouble for five minutes." He took my empty wine glass and headed for the bar. Probably to get us both some sparkling water. Troy might not go maenad if he got drunk, but he had a firm one-drink rule. Usually, anyway.

A loud group was approaching from the side, and I turned to see part of the local witch coven: Hope, daughter of one of the coven elders, my bartender Sarah's brother Cam, and Cam's boyfriend Will. The two men were leaning on each other and giggling, apparently having gotten here much earlier than I had, and the life magic lapping from them sent prickles over me.

"Hey, Arbiter." Hope rolled her eyes as Cam staggered and he and Will burst into another round of giggles. She extended a small parcel wrapped in brown paper. "Happy birthday from the coven." Before I could ask what it was, she said, "Save it for later. Instructions are in the box. I need to get these two home before they spell the whole damn bar."

I'd discouraged gifts but was excited in spite of myself and my mood. I didn't get gifts often. "Thank you. Be safe getting home, okay?"

Hope must have picked up on my worry because she stilled and studied me for a moment. "Understood. Should I...pass any message to Momma?"

"Just be careful." I didn't dare say more. Janae could always call me if she wanted details.

"After the fire, we always are." On that solemn note, she herded the rowdy young men out, a mother hen with shitfaced chicks.

Troy fell in beside me as I headed for my office to lock up the box. "What is it?"

"Dunno. Not something to leave laying around is my guess."

He waited outside while I locked it in my desk and then handed me one of the two sparkling waters he carried. "You doing okay?"

I started to say of course but paused to check in with myself and answer honestly. "A little overwhelmed. Still pissed. But I can stay a while longer."

Nodding, he got the door for me. "Then let's enjoy the rest of your birthday party."

He didn't need to voice the unspoken reminder: because if there was a dead human in Raleigh, the shit was about to hit the fan.

△▽△▽

Morning brought banging on my door for the second day in a row. I wasn't any better disposed toward it this time.

"Fuck off," I grumbled against Troy's neck.

I'd only just gotten to bed a couple of hours ago after playing the gracious host and trying to focus on the guests celebrating my nativity rather than disappearing to my office to start figuring out what was going on with the human death in Raleigh. I hadn't even opened my birthday present from the witches yet.

Amusement flicked through the bond as Troy kissed the crown of my head and slid from bed to get the door. It'd be someone we knew or the wards on my property, the now semi-sentient plants on the perimeter, the gytrash, and/or the Ebon Guard would have stopped them.

Didn't mean Troy liked me answering my own door.

I'd stopped fighting him over it. I told myself it was picking my battles, but in reality, I just didn't fancy getting out of bed. It was that perfect temperature where the feeling of sheets against skin seemed to disappear, even if cold was seeping in with Troy's absence. I kept the windows cracked year-round for airflow, counting on my passive power to keep the room at a bearable temperature.

Sleep had almost reclaimed me when Troy's call dragged me back to wakefulness. "Arden, you need to hear this."

"What?"

He sent a sharp nudge through the bond, hot with impatience.

With a put-upon sigh, I got out of bed, found pajama bottoms, a T-shirt, and my robe, and shuffled out of the bedroom only to blink in surprise at who stood on the other side of the half wall separating the dining area from the entry.

"Noah? It's been a while since you've been up this way." I didn't like the blank look on Troy's face or the frustration in the bond. "Did something else happen?"

Maria's second usually vacillated between amusement and derision, but today he was just grim. "An update on last night's deaths."

"You brought it in person?" I took a deep breath. This was going to be bad. "Tell me."

"There were more than two deaths last night. We found and hid the rest before the mundanes could discover them, but the attack was intended to overwhelm our resources."

That sharpened my focus. "Attack?"

Troy's expression cracked a moment, showing thunder before he got himself back to neutral again. "The Masters of New York and Miami send their regards, apparently."

I snarled. "Excuse me?"

Noah gestured to the table.

I nodded then snagged Troy's arm when he shifted toward the kitchen.

Breakfast can wait. You're King. I'm Arbiter, I whispered in his mind.

He pivoted smoothly to sit beside me, still looking neutral and feeling wrathful but with a fresh edge of grim pleasure. He might play the role of dutiful househusband exceptionally well, but we both knew that A, his talent for governance was more valuable and B, the vampires needed the reminder that he wasn't just my bodyguard and consort.

When we were all seated, Noah crossed his arms and looked at the table, as though trying to figure out where to start. "We've had a lot of newcomers to the territory," he finally said. "Refugees, mostly. Some applied for coterie membership. Some requested vagabond guest rights. We're one of the few safe zones in this part of the country."

I nodded, biting my tongue to stop from saying we knew all of this or something else that would put his back up.

"Maria and I know what it is to be hunted and abused, maybe better than most. And unlike many moroi, we're not inclined to perpetuate the cycle."

"So, you welcomed all comers," I said, trying to hurry the story along. Troy nudged me with a foot under the table, and I ignored him. "And presumably some of those were spies."

Noah stiffened. "They were."

"No good deed goes unpunished," Troy murmured.

That seemed to settle Noah somewhat, and I wondered when I'd started playing bad cop and Troy good cop. He had the better relationship with the Raleigh coterie though, a history that went back a good seven years now with Maria directly.

"In all, six humans were murdered last night." Noah sighed a breath he didn't really need, hinting at the depth of his exasperation. "We found four before they were discovered by mundane law enforcement. We're not convinced they were all vampire kills. But the one at the governor's mansion definitely was, and it's obvious."

Blood drained from my face. "Fuck."

For a good decade, North Carolina had had a conservative legislature and a liberal governor. The state was purple in presidential years. The Triangle itself was blue, most solidly in Durham. But in the most recent election, the state had flipped solid red with the help of some blatant gerrymandering supported by the state supreme court and some inflammatory lies from the newly elected politicians. The new governor had gleefully reversed all the pro-Otherside gains we'd made between the Reveals and the election. He hadn't quite managed to push entirely in the opposite direction—a few key roles were still held by progressives or Otherside sympathizers, especially here in Durham, and the Darkwatch was managing a few others—so we'd been able to keep a balance. Barely.

This would fuck us. Royally.

Noah grimaced. "If I hadn't received Santiago's message, I would have said this was a human frame job. The Sons of Seth, maybe." He sneered at the name of the new anti-Otherside group. They hadn't been listed an official terrorist organization yet, but they were on the Southern Poverty Law Center's list of hate groups to watch. "We should be so lucky."

"It's war then?" Troy asked in the same quiet tone. If it wasn't for the intensity in the bond, I'd think he was bored.

"It's war," Noah confirmed. "Or it will be if they don't get Giuliano and Luz back."

I sighed and massaged my temples. "Remind me why Maria still has them?"

"Assurances." Noah shrugged. "And it would have worked—if we were still governed by the Détente."

From the look he leveled at me, I knew exactly who he blamed for the grey area Otherside now operated in.

Troy lifted his chin. "That's not fair."

"Are you speaking as the king of House Solari? Or as her lover?" Noah asked snidely.

"As king." Troy's cold tone said exactly what he thought of that swipe. "The Arbiter can't be held responsible for the poor decisions of vampire city masters."

"But she is responsible for the fact that there were Reveals at all and how things went after."

"And she's sitting right fucking here," I snapped. "Noah, I thought we were done with this argument. Your mistress volunteered. If I hadn't led the Reveal, Callista would have forced the Sequoyahs out. It was happening no matter what."

"And vampires were the face of it," Noah said bitterly.

"Yes," I said. "Again, Maria volunteered. And *you* were all too happy to volunteer to be the poster boy in the moment if it secured you political advantage among your people. Which it did. Don't give me this shit."

Then I saw it. The reason why he was acting like this.

"This is about Doc Mike," I said. "And them sending the bodies to him."

Noah nodded once, a sharp jerk of his head that showed the depth of his emotion in its restraint.

"That means there's pressure on him."

Another nod.

I studied the vampire. "What aren't you telling us? Why did you come in person?"

Noah didn't answer at first, looking out the window for long enough that I wanted to smack him. Then he said, "Michael has a choice to make."

I frowned. "That being?"

"The choice he's been making for you since you called Maria in to clean up the mess the sorcerer made of his office." The vampire's glare was hot with an emotion I couldn't quite read. Resentment, maybe. "Whether he protects Otherside or himself."

Chapter 7

I leaned back in my chair and crossed my arms. "How is that a choice? He's a necromancer for fuck's sake."

Troy sighed. "He's not out as a necromancer though, Arden. He's barely out as a sympathizer and has a secret vampire lover. He's Otherside-adjacent at best. Publicly, at least."

Noah's stony expression confirmed it. "And he's been getting threats."

"Oh, Noah." I reached across the table to squeeze his arm. It was solid as stone, and he didn't react, so I pulled my hand back. "You didn't say anything about this when we were shopping."

"He was safe with Rani playing babysitter, and I needed a night not to think about it." Noah closed his eyes and pressed the heels of his palms against them. "I can't fix it for him because I won't leave him. I'm too selfish to break up with him and he feels too guilty to leave me."

"Because he loves you," I said softly. "And wants to give you more than secrets."

Troy and I exchanged a look. We knew this dilemma.

Noah nodded, still avoiding our eyes. "I don't even know why I'm telling you this, except that I..."

Troy caught on before I did. "We wouldn't kill Dr. Miller, Noah."

The vampire looked up, snarling to bare fangs. "It'd be the last thing you did, Solari."

I stiffened, but Troy rested a restraining hand on my thigh. After a moment, Noah backed down. "I just—don't hurt him. Please. Whatever the outcome of this investigation is."

"He's one of my oldest friends," I said stiffly. It was hard not to be offended. When had my reputation gotten this bad?

"So was Roman Volkov," Noah said. "Yet he's—"

"Exiled and banished because he tried to kill Troy and seriously threatened me," I snapped. "He's *not* dead. For Ishtar's sake, Noah. I could have killed him. I would have been within my rights. Some are saying I should finish the job sooner rather than later, Roman and Sergei both. But I am *trying* to be better than Callista."

I couldn't sit there anymore and take this, and my power was buzzing along my skin. I rose to pace the living area, dropping my shields to let some of the tension off. I didn't care what Noah thought of my control.

Silence hung in the room. Both men were wise enough to shut up until I'd gotten some energy out with pacing and a small zephyr sent to sway the hanging air plants and the parlor palm. I let the men sit a little longer, fetching some copal incense and bringing it back to the table to light it before sitting down again.

"What is this choice?" I asked in as measured a tone as I could. "It's not like we can do a cover-up with a dead body discovered at the governor's mansion."

"There's a new sequencing test," Noah said. "From Verve Health."

Troy frowned. "We destroyed all their samples."

"Which gave them the opportunity to pivot their operations, apparently, since they needed to start from scratch anyway." Noah shrugged, looking irritated. "We only just found out. They reached out to Michael first thing this morning. They want to use this murder as a test case."

My stomach roiled. "A test case? Isn't this a little too high-profile?"

"That's exactly why they want to do it," Troy said. "Confidentially, I'm sure."

"Precisely." Noah nodded. "Arden—Arbiter—something big is coming. We don't know what. But I think someone has been watching Michael."

Troy closed his eyes and shook his head, like he should have seen this coming. "He's the perfect target."

I nudged him to explain in the bond.

"For the mundanes, Dr. Miller is a known, or at least suspected, Otherside sympathizer. But he's also an employee of the state. For those who are paying attention or have the resources to spy, he's a deeply devout Christian in a gay relationship with a vampire in a red state."

"Shit." A headache blossomed. "They're trapping him between his beliefs and applying pressure."

"Exactly," Troy said. "We thought he'd fly under the radar because the relationship is circumspect and private. But all it takes is one Freedom of Information Act request."

I connected the dots. "The Umstead."

Troy nodded. "And the public records that have you, me, Noah, Maria, and Dr. Miller present at another obvious vampire murder."

"Along with Estrella Luna and Detective Rice." I grimaced.

Too many connections to Otherside. Estrella was Ebon Guard, in deep cover as a crime scene investigator with the Raleigh police. Detective Clayton Rice was basic human, but he'd grudgingly agreed to help me—help Otherside—if I agreed to help with cases the mundanes couldn't manage. That was another arrangement it'd be easy to twist, and Rice would be happy to have the excuse.

"Why do I have a feeling one of Santiago or Matthias's people put in a FOIA request?" I said.

"Because it's what I would do if I wanted to discredit you," Troy said. His grim tone held hints of the obstruction and outright murder I knew he was thinking about as options for dealing with this. "Find all your connections—all those the Darkwatch and the Ebon Guard weren't able to eliminate or bury, at least—and apply pressure. We just counted on the Détente to rein in excess within Otherside." He shook his head. "Goddess. Betraying their own people though? That's beyond anything I would have thought any Othersider would do."

Noah sighed, looking grouchy. "They've outmaneuvered us by pushing a return to the Dark Ages to punish us for the Reveal. How do we use this information to protect Michael?"

"And you," I said.

"I don't care about me. I want Michael safe."

I put on my Arbiter face. "I need you both safe. Don't fuck around on this, Noah, and don't do something rash. Maria has too much going on to have to pick a new number two, and you're too valuable to the alliance."

"Oh, well if *I'm* valuable—"

"Stop," I said. "Accept it at face value. I need both you and Doc Mike in place and doing your jobs."

Noah narrowed his eyes at me. "You know, Arbiter, there are days I truly dislike you."

I sighed. We'd had such a nice time shopping the other night, but that would be nothing in the face of the physiological responses vampires developed in response to a prime blood source. I didn't know if Noah fed on Doc Mike, let alone had made the medical examiner his solidaire, but vampires were jealous and possessive of the people they thought of as theirs. Doc Mike definitely qualified as having a big neon sign that read *Noah's.*

"Fortunately," I said softly, "I've had twenty-eight years to get used to the idea that a fuck ton of people dislike me enough to want me dead. Are you making that kind of threat?"

The vampire froze, gaze darting between me and a suddenly too-quiet Troy. "No, Arbiter."

"Good. It would be a shame to have to deal with a vampire succession on top of everything else going on. Like I said, we need you where you are. But I will not abide threats." A small voice whispered that I was being a bully, just like Omar Monteague had said. But I had a burgeoning crisis on my hands and no time or patience to coddle anyone. I pushed through the guilt knotting in my stomach. "Let's recap. We have a confirmed threat of war from the masters of New York and Miami. The conditions for avoidance are the release of their people from Maria's custody. I assume that if those conditions go unmet, we'll have more dead mundanes?"

Noah nodded. "Probably higher profile or more violent."

"Fine. I'll speak to Maria."

"She won't let them go."

Troy shook his head. "And there's the other reason you came in person."

Frustration tightened Noah's expression at being caught out, but he nodded. "My mistress is too young and too new to power—"

"Aren't we all?" I interrupted. I wanted to pull my hair out. I'd thoroughly fucked the Triangle's power structure in ways that were still becoming clear to me a year and a bit later as I caught up with written and unwritten rules that Callista had kept me ignorant of.

Arbiters were apparently supposed to have reached a century before stepping into the role, usually after having shadowed the previous one. Elven royals would be at least sixty before ascending without a vizier or older adviser. Troy was barely half that, I was four years younger, and we'd killed or driven off everyone older except the Captain, who was sworn to the Darkwatch. Vikki Volkov was in her twenties and leading a brand-new werewolf clan, the first headed by a mated pair of women in a deeply conservative and traditionalist faction, just to add complication. Terrence and Ximena might be the only ones of the expected age for their faction. The wereleopard and werejaguar clan leaders were both older than they looked, as were their seconds.

Noah just stared at me flatly.

I didn't look away. I loved Maria as a friend and ally, but she wasn't the only one who had a lot to shoulder in a role she'd been all too eager to claim when Torsten was killed. Luck and my strength as a primordial who could face down the gods were what had kept the Triangle safe until now—that and Troy's emergence as a king with a power signature of his own. I'd thought it meant Otherside accepted our right to rule.

Apparently, it just meant they were looking for the right time to strike.

Noah finally looked away, mouth twisting like he'd bitten into a lemon. "This wasn't how any of it was supposed to go. We did the Reveal because it was supposed to make us safer."

"I know," I said. "We are all doing our best."

The empty look he gave me then scared me, a baring of his soul's fears that I never expected to see from him. "What if it's not enough? How do I keep Michael safe then?"

I couldn't help my shudder. There were nights I laid awake with the same question about Troy. He'd been kidnapped and tortured nearly to death once. But I couldn't dwell on that.

"I will talk to Maria," I said again.

"Even if it means pulling rank?"

I nodded, hoping I kept my dread that it'd come to that from my face. I'd become friends with the other faction heads. Maria in particular. But I was an arbiter. That meant negotiating—without killing anyone—first and foremost and finding a way to end this standoff without anyone losing too much face. Or at least gaining enough from it that any losses were tolerable and wouldn't cause resentment.

"And Verve?" Noah asked.

I glanced at Troy. We could try breaking in again. I'd gotten in alone on a penetration test, and then we had broken in together. Third time might be the charm, or it might be what undid us.

He tipped his head side to side in the barest movement. *Risky*, he murmured in my mind. *Maybe too risky.*

I agreed. One environmental failure was a fluke. Two would be suspicious. They knew what I was now. Or at least had an idea what I could do.

Troy's expression hardened as he fell back into the mien of the Darkwatch agent he'd once been, knowing where my mind had gone even if I hadn't answered. That knowledge was a direct threat to me, one he'd kill without question to eliminate.

"Leave it with me," I said to Noah, hoping I'd answered before he could start to wonder if Troy and I had a similar kind of link as Noah had with Maria. We might have an option with the hackers in the Ebon Guard or the Darkwatch but that was a discussion we might need to raise with Omar. "That's a delicate one. Can you have Doc Mike stall in the meantime?"

Noah grimaced. "He won't be happy about it. But I suppose none of us are going to be happy about any of this."

"Bingo," I said. "But, Noah, I do want to protect Doc Mike. I wouldn't have called Maria after the sorcerer dragged him into Otherside business otherwise, and Troy and I wouldn't have gotten him away from the lich's lair if we didn't value him and care about him as a person."

That was stretching it a little. Troy hadn't given a damn about Doc Mike back then and would have murdered him without hesitation if he'd been ordered to do it. But that was then, and we were a long way from it.

Either way, Noah nodded. "Thank you, Arbiter." He blew out a sigh. "I guess you know what it is to be afraid for the one you love."

"I do," I said.

Troy nodded, and a curl of protectiveness swirled through the bond.

"Fine." Noah rose. "I will do what I can to stall Michael and influence my mistress. Do not make me regret it."

With a last firm look, he pulled up his hood and saw himself out into the grey morning.

When the coterie's black BMW i5 had pulled away from the house, I slumped and scrubbed my hands over my face. "When did shit get so complicated?"

"When we became sovereigns."

Troy's equilibrium did nothing to soothe me. He might have been born to power and groomed for leadership, but me? I was still trying to convince myself I deserved this. That I was the right person for the job and hadn't irreparably fucked all of Otherside because I'd had a personal issue with my former guardian.

"What now?" Troy got up and headed for the kitchen. Suppressed hunger gnawed at him in the bond, reminding me I should eat as well.

I thought for a minute, reviewing everything we'd discussed with Noah.

"Detective Rice never called." I rapped my fingers against the table in a rippling cadence. "That means one of two things. Three, maybe. One, he doesn't trust us to deal with him fairly. Two, he thinks he doesn't need us. Or three, he's being prevented from doing so by his superiors."

"Or four, he sees this as his opportunity to follow through on his own beliefs."

I grimaced. Troy was right. The detective had made it clear he didn't see Othersiders as people. That'd been true when we first struck our deal right before the Wild Hunt, and nothing had changed in that time.

"Okay. So...hm." I got up and made tea, partly so Troy wasn't playing servant and partly because I liked bumping against him in the kitchen. "Sounds like we have a case."

He slanted an amused glance at me.

"What?" I couldn't help my grin.

"You've been itching to play PI for months."

"I'm good at investigating shit." I pressed my lips together before I could say that I was much better at it than being Arbiter.

Troy knew I was thinking it though, and he arched an eyebrow at me before turning back to the stove. "When are you going to start believing in yourself?"

I didn't have an answer for that.

I had no reason not to believe in myself, and I knew it. Rationally anyway. Sometimes, when I lay awake thinking about all the shit I'd already done and everything that still needed doing, I reminded myself that I'd removed a celestial and stood up to the gods of the hunt. But for all I'd accomplished, I knew I was tolerated at best in Otherside. Elementals were still the elves' scapegoats in the rest of the world, and the elves held most of the power in Otherside.

"A case then," Troy said after a long enough silence that the tea and coffee were ready.

I relaxed, which I figured was his intention. "Yeah. Noah's right. Maria isn't going to just let Luz and Giuliano walk. Or their entourage. Not after holding them this long."

"Not at first. She's been hunting powerful blood for as long as I've known her, and now she has it on tap."

I frowned and took my tea and his coffee to the table. "You think she's drinking from them?"

"Almost certainly. She's not just holding them for assurances, or she would have released the entourage at the very least. Their masters sent a colonizing force—vampires strong enough to take and hold new territory." He ground pepper into the pot of grits and added cheese then poured it all into a bowl and topped it with the shrimp that had just finished cooking, finishing with a squeeze of lemon over my bowl. "They weren't counting on you to be there, let alone be that strong."

I snagged both bowls and went to the table, delighted with the change of pace from our usual bacon and eggs—high-protein fare we both needed but which I tired of after a while. Shrimp and grits was a treat, and I couldn't hold back my hum of pleasure at the mouthwatering smell. Troy joined me, and after I thanked him, we ate in silence while thinking through the angles.

I sighed. "She'll want something. Never mind that it's what needs doing." I ate a few more bites. "This case isn't just finding the vampires responsible and administering justice. It's also finding who in the territory betrayed us by not reporting their presence. Or worse, who covered for them."

Troy nodded and stole one of my shrimp, unruffled.

I envied the simple acceptance that this was how life was. People wanted what you had and did shitty things to take it from you. I knew it was true—I just didn't accept it.

For better or worse, I had to do something about it now.

Chapter 8

While Troy called Allegra to either get her take or offer a courteous forewarning of our intent to investigate, I went to the bedroom for the birthday present from the witches. I'd stashed it in my closet, behind the wall of Air protecting the lightning arrow Mixcoatl had shot me with, the godblade in its lead-lined box, the prince's pendant I'd taken from Leith Sequoyah's body, and the Monteague prince's pendant Troy refused to wear anymore. I wanted to get him one for Solari for his birthday in a few months, but Nils, the tomtar smith Callista had retained, had vanished after her death. I didn't know if a geas had been lifted or if he simply preferred the relative safety of the Summerlands, but it meant we were without a fae smith or jeweler for the time being.

Replacing the wall took a bare thought, and I turned the box over in my hands. Most witches weren't like djinn with their gift of prophecy or the Sight, but they did get nudges from their guides and Spirit.

I sat on the edge of the bed and pulled the twine free then unwrapped the simple brown paper. A notecard fell out.

Spirit says you may need to see what can't be seen, it read. *You already have enough pendants. Hopefully this is inconspicuous enough to go unnoticed. Activate it with a drop of your blood at Mercury's hour, preferably on Mercury's day, and be mindful you don't lose it.*

A looping J told me Janae had sent this. Intrigued, I opened the small box and found a gold band set with a black stone on one side. The other was etched with a symbol I took to be either planetary or fixed star magic.

"See what can't be seen." I plucked the ring out, admiring it. Whatever magic was in it, it matched my father's gold-and-onyx pendant and would easily pass as a bit of House vanity.

I turned the card over, looking for more clues, and shook my head. This was beyond odd. Talismans weren't handed out lightly, nor, I would have thought, so casually as this one had been. They took a great deal of effort, time, and money to make, not to mention needing to wait for a favorable astrological transit. This was no ordinary or idle birthday gift.

Troy came in while I was considering it. "What is it?"

"A ring." I held it up for his inspection, dropping it into his palm when he held out a hand. "A talisman, one that can be further activated with a drop of blood."

His head came up sharply, and the points of his secondary teeth flickered as he grimaced. "Blood magic."

"I know." It wasn't illegal or even immoral to practice blood magic if one had the proper consent or used their own blood. But it took a powerful witch to do it, and I hadn't thought our local coven had one. For Janae to gift me a ring like this...

Something about it made my stomach sink.

I wasn't a djinni to have full command over the Sight or to use it to look beyond the immediate moment. Doing any kind of divination or metaphysical deep-seeking had always made me anxious.

Troy eyed the ring like it might bite him. "Did they say what it does?"

"Not in so many words." I held out my hand, and he gave it back then wiped his palm on the leg of his pants. "Apparently, it will help me see the unseen."

The bond flattened with a grim sensation. "I don't like that."

"Neither do I. My mom might have been good with prophecy and shit like that, but I've avoided it. I don't love that I'm getting a nudge to explore the unseen right as shit hits the fan."

Troy rubbed one hand over his face. "If there's one thing that's true of you, Arden, it's that nothing ever happens one thing at a time."

"Tell me about it." I couldn't keep the grouchy note out of my voice.

He bent to kiss my forehead to let me know he hadn't meant it as a dig. "What's the shape of things?"

I lay back on the bed, studying the ring as I thought. "Vampire terrorist attack on humans in Raleigh in an effort to get me or Maria to move. Maria likely to be reluctant to give up her hostages. Elven contingent from France in town. And the witches think I'll need to see the unseen."

Troy stared out the window, hands on his hips as he worked through it.

Grimacing, I remembered something else. "Oh. The In-Between."

His attention snapped to me. "Excuse me?"

I sat up and propped myself on my hands. "The other night. I had a dream. I thought it was just a dream, but there was something super weird about it. And the last time everything in my life started converging, the gods were involved."

"So, it might not be just a dream, and we might have more gods to worry about?"

"Eshu-Elegba did say that they weren't done with me just because the hunters had their turn."

Troy swore far more colorfully than I'd heard from him before, and the bond lit up with hot rage, although his tone was ice cold when he spoke. "They can't have you."

"I don't think that's for you to say," I said softly.

He stalked toward me and leaned over, catching my chin and forcing my face to tilt up in a rare show of dominance. "They. Can't. Have you."

I just looked at him. We both knew that the gods would have their games.

"It might be nothing," I said.

"Might." Releasing me, he sank down beside me and pulled me against him as he sighed, methodically bringing his temper back under control. "We'll deal with the gods if and when they come. Vampires first."

"Agreed. What did Allegra say?"

"She'll work on Maria. See if she can get her to invite us before you have to pull rank, given how badly that went when Dari held the governor hostage."

"Fine. Meantime, we go pay Detective Rice a visit. I don't need her permission for that, even if he is in Raleigh." I rapped my fingers across the table. "I know how law enforcement thinks. They're going to try to move fast and pin this on Maria. And by extension, me, at least as far as the rest of Otherside is concerned."

Troy kept his face blank, but from the bond, he wanted to grimace. He had a healthy respect for the detective on a professional level and a deep dislike of the man on a personal level. Besides having a chip on his shoulder about Othersiders, Rice had forced me to out myself in front of the Raleigh SWAT team and police command, something Troy wouldn't forgive for the threat it represented to my safety.

He didn't reiterate that opinion though, just said, "I'll get the Ebon Guard ready."

I tilted my head to breathe in the scent of him where his ear met his jaw, soothing and grounding myself ahead of what I knew was about to turn into a long day, then kissed him there when the whisper of my breath gave him goosebumps.

"I'll call ahead," I said. "Wouldn't want to be shot on sight or anything."

Annoyingly, Detective Rice stalled me. Claimed to be too damn busy to make time to see someone not officially involved with the case and said I'd have to wait until later in the afternoon. I secured an appointment and hung up, discomfited. Something was wrong, something more than Rice having a bug up his ass about Otherside.

With nothing to do about it, I called Doc Mike to offer my support and then started working on a response. As a public figure, I'd have to say something eventually. Sooner would have been better than later, but I wanted to know what angle Raleigh PD was taking first.

When we finally left, Troy got us there in record time. I was pretty sure there was a spell involved, because there was no way a convoy of three black SUVs should have made it through the usual Durham-to-Raleigh traffic that fast without an accident or an arrest. He'd always gotten places ridiculously quickly, and I didn't think it was just his habit of driving at least twenty over the speed limit when he had somewhere to be.

The speed wasn't what scared me. It was the deadly silent focus and complete lack of road rage as he squeezed his Acura MDX through spaces I might not have dared in my smaller Honda Civic hatchback, sport model or not. Our two escort cars tag-teamed, working seamlessly with Troy to create or claim space—somehow without being challenged by any of the other aggressive drivers.

"You need to teach me how y'all do that," I muttered when we were safely parked. "Nobody gets out of *my* way like that when I'm driving."

He smirked for a moment before slipping back into bodyguard mode and checking that the Ebon Guard were in position before escorting me inside.

The Raleigh police department was the same as always, at least on the surface. What wasn't the same was no longer having to wait on the uncomfortable plastic chairs. No, VIPs like Troy and me got whisked straight back to an interrogation room. The illusion of privacy with absolutely none of it.

Troy remained standing at a parade rest behind me and to my right—closer to the door—when I took the seat facing the two-way mirror. The bond was completely open, but all I got from him was laser focus—and then a small curl of reassurance as my emotions bounced all over the map. I sent him gratitude back, knowing the effort it took for him to come out of bodyguard mode even that much while he was working. This was my first time engaging with the mundane police since an unfortunate incident shortly after the Wild Hunt was averted, and I was anxious as hell.

It didn't help that we'd traded the uncomfortable chairs of the main area for the similarly uncomfortable chairs of the interrogation room. I'd been here before and had used a tiny amount of magic, which meant I had an anchor in the physical location already. I could sense the body heat rising on the other side of the reflective glass.

They're watching us. Not just the camera in the corner, I sent to Troy.

I suspected as much. How many?

I concentrated, closing my eyes and leaning back in my chair like I was bored and ready to take a nap. *Hard to tell. The heat signatures are clustered together. Four, maybe?*

Boring. A hint of savagery curled through the bond as he thought on strategy and tactics to hunt whoever was watching us. More an exercise to stave off said boredom than actual intent, although the man did believe in being prepared.

Keeping my face straight was an effort, but I managed.

One more in the observation room.

Troy sent an affirmative pulse just as the door swung open to admit Detective Clayton Rice.

"Detective," I said, not bothering either to rise or offer my hand. "It's been a while."

"Finch. Monteague."

Something ugly curled through the bond at Rice's calling Troy by his former House name. But we hadn't publicized House Solari's existence among the mundanes, and Monteague was still his legal name just like Finch was mine, even if we both went by Solari in Otherside. All Troy did was nod though.

The detective took a seat, as always looking like a typecast character in a TV series in the small chair: big, Black, and bald, but he'd grown a short beard and moustache in the time since I'd seen him last. He was dressed in his usual pressed slacks and starched button-down shirt, although the shoulder harness he wore overtop was a new and aggressive note I didn't appreciate. Troy neither, from the way he went from wary to deadly in the bond.

Rice noted the threat Troy represented, as always, and only got more tense as Estrella Luna slipped into the room, scuffing her feet intentionally to sound more human. Estrella was one of our Ebon Guard, in deep cover as a mundane—for now. We weren't sure how much longer the arrangement could hold.

"What's CSI doing here?" I asked. "Ms. Luna wasn't requested."

"No, but we have a dead human and she's become something of an expert on weird cases. Kind of like yourself, Finch."

I flicked a glance at Estrella, but she maintained her cover and stared back with the same vaguely hostile expression I knew Troy was wearing. Must be a Darkwatch thing.

"Ms. Finch," she said. "We have a number of questions about the body. The medical examiner seems to be having difficulty confirming that this is in fact a vampire murder."

Good. Everyone was playing their role so far. Not so great was the pressure I felt at realizing they were all counting on me to get us out of this.

Focus, Arden, I thought at myself.

You're fine, Troy whispered in my thoughts. Accompanying the thought was a pulse of pure arrogance, one that made me sit up and lean forward even as Troy's reflection showed him crossing his arms and shifting to cock a hip.

"What makes you think I can answer those questions?" I asked.

Rice snorted. "You're here for a reason."

"I am indeed." I smiled, drawing on a memory of Callista to make it sweet and venomous. "While I neither confirm nor deny the possibility that this was a vampire attack, I wanted to remind you"—I glanced at the two-way mirror then the camera in the corner—"and all of our guests and viewers at home, that the vampires are *my* people."

I held up a hand to stop him interrupting me when he opened his mouth, easing my shields down just enough that the hint of my power signature leaked out to make him flinch.

"I am aware," I continued, "they agreed to abide by the laws of the United States of America, the state of North Carolina, Wake County, and the City of Raleigh. However, that agreement was reciprocal. Just as they abide by the law, the law is obliged to deal with them as it would any citizen. That includes probable cause, Miranda, due process, and innocent until proven guilty. All that American as apple pie stuff."

Detective Rice drew himself up like he was offended. "I know my job, Finch."

"I'm so glad to hear it, Detective. It'd be unfortunate if we had to have a more serious discussion." Again, I offered the venomously sweet smile that seemed to put everyone, mundanes and Othersiders both, on edge. "Now that that's out of the way, I wanted to extend my condolences on the deaths and assure you that my team and I are looking into it." I paused a beat. "As agreed."

"I think you'll find this is too big to be left to your little detective agency, Finch." Rice looked like a thunderhead. "A body was left at the governor's mansion. That's a clear threat."

I held back my initial response, studying him. We all knew it was a threat. Me saying otherwise would clearly be a lie, one I couldn't afford to be caught in, even if I didn't particularly care about lying to the mundanes under normal circumstances. At the same time, I needed him to leave this to me and give Doc Mike room to work. I certainly didn't need Noah doing something drastic because his partner was being threatened.

"I can appreciate your concern," I said, choosing my words carefully. "And I want you to know it disturbs us as much as it does you. Possibly more. This is well outside the boundaries of our laws, and the perpetrators will be brought to justice. You have my assurance."

That was the truth, the whole truth, and nothing but the truth. I'd be damned if I let a couple of jackass vampire city masters on opposite ends of the coast ruin everything I'd fought so fucking hard to build here.

This time it was Rice's turn to hold back his initial response. "I appreciate that, Ms. Finch," he said after a beat. "I assume that means you'll accompany us to serve Maria?"

Chapter 9

M y expression hardened so fast Estrella sat up straighter.

"Run that by me again?" I said softly. My shields dropped a crack more, and I left them that way.

Behind me, Troy did the same, allowing just the hint of the feeling of an icy midnight wind to whisper through the room.

Estrella's eyes widened, and she paled as she leaned away, creating space between us as much as she was able without physically getting up and moving.

Rice, looking uncomfortable as hell, crossed his arms and inhaled, the opposite to Estrella as he tried to make himself bigger and prove he wasn't afraid of us. "We'll be serving Maria with a search warrant for Claret."

That'd be disastrous. The coterie's nest was under the wine bar. Aside from her hostages, they'd have human blood pets, junkies, and solidaires.

Maze? Troy sent.

No. This is being recorded.

I can handle that.

Wait. Exposing Troy as more than my personal security detail was not a card I was willing to play just yet. I tilted my head to study Rice and let a question roll through my mind to trigger the Sight.

"You have no grounds," I said.

"The hell we don't." His brows drew down, and his scent...wobbled. It was the best way I could describe it.

He's got nothing, Troy confirmed.

Yet.

I let a slow, understanding smile spread across my face. "Keeping in mind, of course, that I'm neither confirming nor denying vampire involvement, a possible vampire victim does not mean *my* vampires did it. That'd be like saying you found a gunshot victim and picking a human business at random to search. Only maybe not so random because you've probably already done some kind of exceedingly biased profiling rather than processing the evidence."

"Your vampires, any vampires—a vampire did it." Rice glared, as much, I thought, at being pinned by his own laws as for his abiding anti-Otherside statement.

"So you've said." I shook my head. "But I'm sure you're aware we've had newcomers and there is no proof that *Maria's* people specifically were responsible."

He started to respond, and I held up a hand again, speaking over him.

"How about this, Detective? A compromise. I will speak to Maria and investigate this to the fullest extent of both mundane and Otherside law. And report back, of course."

He scoffed, and Estrella's dark eyes darted between us at the contest of wills.

"If I let you investigate, Finch, you'll let the perp go," Rice said.

I frowned. "Is that what you think?"

"Damn straight." Rice's chin tipped up. He really believed that.

On the other side of the two-way mirror, heat rose, and a low buzz told me people were arguing but not what they were saying. I leaned back and smiled up at Troy. "Would you mind seeing about some water?"

"Of course, ma'am." The thrill of the hunt shivering through the bond told me he'd heard the buzz too and understood the assignment.

As he slipped out, Rice snorted. "'Ma'am'? I'd swear you were sleeping with him."

"I believe we were talking about legalities, not speculating on my security team's duties. Unless you wanted me to file a complaint for sexual harassment?"

He scowled. "That won't be necessary. But the point stands. You'll let Maria off the hook."

"Why would I do that? There's no upside for me." I let the bafflement I genuinely felt show on my face. "We have nothing to hide. That was the point of the Raleigh Reveals. And I assure you, Otherside law gives me far more leeway than human law when it comes to handling a situation like this."

Rice rolled his eyes. "You keep hinting that you'd kill your own people. I don't buy it."

Annoyed with his attitude, I let my approximation of Troy's dead-eyed assassin mask slip over my face. "Buy it or not, I don't care. You can leave this with me. Or you can send officers to Maria." I grinned then. "What's that meme? 'To fuck around is human. To find out is divine.' And my dear Detective, I've had my run-ins with the divine. I survived to walk away."

I tilted my head, holding back the *will you?* purely to avoid suggesting that Maria might kill someone.

Arden, they're arguing legality. Some want a tighter case before going to Maria. Some want to send a SWAT team and be done with it.

Thanks, my love. Well done.

Keeping my expression hard at the burst of cat-like pleasure from Troy was a challenge—words of affirmation turned him into a purring kitten—but I managed.

"Put it this way," I said, as much to Rice as to our wider audience. "You have three options. Option one, you go in now with your warrant and see what happens. You might get a hit, you might get a miss, or you might find more than you bargained for in a way that has nothing to do with anything but does more harm than good. Option two, you go in now with SWAT and start a war you can't finish."

Troy re-entered the room with three mini-bottles of water as I smiled again with Callista's venomous sweetness. When I lifted a hand and called Air and Fire to let the smallest crackle of lightning dance over my fingers, Rice and Estrella both paled. I let go of my power before anyone could feel truly threatened.

That was unwise, Troy sent as he set the bottles on the table and resumed his position at my back.

So is letting them barge in on Maria or think they can push us around. I refocused on my point. "Or you let me *do my job* and have faith that, just like I fixed the hostage situation at the governor's mansion and delivered justice then, I will do the same now and not throw away two years of work building bridges."

Rice hesitated.

I sighed, suddenly tired of this. I fucking hated negotiation. I could do interviews. I could do pentests. I could draw information out of a stone and investigate the hell outta anything on three planes. But having to convince people of something they didn't want to believe despite it being the truth was like pulling teeth from a wyvern.

"Just think of me as your personal fixer, okay? I'll handle it." I cracked open my bottle of water and took a sip, just to look like there'd been a reason I sent Troy out of the room. "If you don't trust my motivations, trust that I have too much to lose by letting this spiral out of control."

The detective and Estrella studied me for a long minute.

I held my tongue this time. The Sight nudged when I thought of something else to say, warning me to silence. They'd go with my plan or not.

"Give us a few minutes, Finch," Rice said.

He rose and waved for Estrella to precede him out of the room.

I inclined my head in a bare nod and leaned back in my chair, crossing my arms and trying to look bored. I let my attention wander around the room as I focused on Troy. *What's the situation outside?*

People pretending to work. It's obvious their attention is focused here. Somebody met me with the water, so they're watching the feed live. My bet is all the force's higher-ups are on the other side of the glass. We're not exactly unknown anymore.

Unfortunately.

He sent a coil of reassurance through the bond. *Would you rather the alternative?*

I barely managed not to snort. *What, being in Callista's box? Or dead? Fuck no.*

Troy held back a response as the door opened and Rice re-entered alone. Rather than sitting, he shut the door and loomed next to it. Troy stiffened, not bothering to hide his dislike for the room's one exit being blocked by someone who was physically bigger than him, even if Troy would have no problem taking Rice in a fight even before the fists started flying.

Rice wasn't a complete idiot. He caught Troy's shift in posture and moved, rubbing his arms without realizing it as Troy's power signature spiked before being pulled back down.

"You have a deal, Finch," the detective said. "We'll give you twenty-four hours to produce either the killer or solid evidence proving the innocence of Maria's people."

"Seventy-two," I countered, more to be contrary, although I didn't like being boxed into such a narrow timeframe.

"Thirty-six. No more. Don't push me. This case is too high-profile, and we can't afford the optics of looking like we're favoring you people."

Favoring us people. Even if it was just what we agreed and well within the law.

"Fine." I rose and extended my hand, just to force him to shake it or look like a coward. "You'll hear from me in thirty-six hours or less."

We shook on it, and I met his power-squeeze with one that left him wincing. He didn't used to be like that, and I was inexplicably saddened to find he'd shifted that way with me.

"Don't fuck this up, Finch," he said.

"Don't try to follow us, bug us, tap our lines, any of that. You either trust us, or you don't. And if you don't..." I shrugged. "Your choice on how you seek divinity."

His scent did that sideways twist again, and I had a feeling he was going to leave this meeting and call off a team. "Understood."

"In that case, enjoy the rest of your day, Detective. I'll talk to Dr. Miller and see if there's anything he can share with Ms. Luna as well."

"I appreciate your cooperation." Rice's sharp-bitten words suggested that was the last thing he was thinking.

"I do what I can." With an ironic smile, I let Troy get the door and shadow me out.

We kept our eyes on our surroundings and our thoughts to ourselves until we were in the car.

"Fuck," I muttered. "Why do I have a feeling I missed something?"

"Because you did." Troy offered a half-smile when I snapped around to stare at him then shook his head. "You're always going to miss something. That's not personal to you. It's a fact of both life and leadership. Even the Sight can't tell you everything."

"I need to be better than that."

He shrugged. "You can try. But if I can offer a word of advice..."

I slumped back in my seat as he got us out of the parking lot. "Always."

"Don't put that pressure on yourself." The words were spoken with the softness that said he was revisiting mental demons.

I rested my hand on his thigh and leaned in for a quick kiss. "You're right. And you're a gift. Thanks for keeping my head on straight."

Troy smiled crookedly. "At least it means losing mine for a bit comes to some benefit." He sobered. "Seriously though, Arden, we're doing the best we can with what we've got."

"I know that intellectually."

"You're just used to carrying everything by yourself."

I made an agreeing hum, too frustrated to speak.

"Well." He smiled again. "Good thing you have me now."

That made me grin. "There is that."

Pleased, he dropped a hand to cover mine and squeeze it.

We really were good together, even if we bickered like djinn sometimes or ran headlong into the obstacle course that was our respective traumas.

My mood twisted as I looked out the window. Some of the shops and restaurants were boarded up, either damaged or in anticipation of it. There was more broken glass on the street than used to be normal. Fewer people out, and those moved quickly, scanning for threats. Spray-painted slogans defaced more buildings than before, both for and against Otherside. Things had definitely taken a turn for the worse. This wouldn't improve anything. And I felt helpless.

"What's wrong?" Troy asked, having caught my mood shift in the bond.

"I just hope..." I sighed, knowing I was about to sound silly. But we'd committed to directness and honesty. "I hope I'm worth everything you went through to be with me."

He stayed silent until we were in the parking garage adjacent to the coterie nest's hidden secondary entrance. Only when we were parked with the engine off, and the Ebon Guard parked and finding positions, did he turn to me.

"Never. *Ever.* Suggest that you're not worthy. Not in my hearing. Not outside of it. Never doubt it."

I froze, holding myself very still as his power signature weighed heavy in the car.

He was pissed. The gold flecks in his eyes caught the sunlight and seemed to flare. "You may have a lot to learn about being High Queen and Arbiter. But don't you dare doubt yourself. I managed to avoid falling for anyone, being maneuvered into any relationship or so much as sleeping with anyone after my majority—until I met you." He caught my chin, almost rough with his grip, and perversely it turned me on. That was almost but not quite enough to distract him, but he refocused even if his pupils dilated. "I love you. And the minute I think you've done something unworthy of our oaths or your station, I will tell you. Until then, trust that I know you're doing your best."

I swallowed hard against the lump in my throat and fought back tears, wishing I had that same level of faith in myself. "Okay."

Troy pulled me to him, kissing me with the firm dominance he usually saved for the bedroom. My mouth opened for his tongue of its own accord, letting him anchor me.

I blinked when he pulled away and nodded at whatever expression was on my face.

"Let's go see Maria." His voice was more controlled than mine would be.

I just nodded, ashamed at how little I trusted myself in my new role. I'd fought and killed to be where I was. Why the hell couldn't I just own it?

"It'll come," Troy murmured. As usual, he was scanning the street, the rooftops, the doorways and windows for any threat, but he still had a corner of his mind turned toward me. "Have faith."

"Yeah," I whispered.

Inhaling, I found some of the arrogant confidence I'd put on display for the Raleigh PD and straightened my spine. If I thought the cops were difficult, I wasn't going to make it through this meeting with Maria. I might be the new power broker and fixer in the Triangle, but Maria had helped me get there. I hadn't donated blood to her since the Wild Hunt for various reasons, one of those admittedly being a need to feel like I'd be able to maintain control if I had to. Callista might have cowed Torsten—Maria's sire and predecessor—but Maria and I had a different relationship out of necessity.

"There you go," Troy said at the shift in my attitude.

I sent an appreciative pulse through the bond as we approached the back door. The fae magic that whispered, *nothing to see here, nothing to see, keep walking* hadn't worked on Troy or me in ages, and the vampire lounging at the door straightened as we approached.

"Oscar," Troy said. "The Arbiter is here to see your mistress."

If Oscar had had any blood in him, he might have blanched. As it was, he wavered a little. Troy tended to have that effect on people—and I supposed I did too these days.

"Of course," Oscar said. "Is the mistress expecting you?"

Troy nodded. "I called Allegra this morning."

"Ah. Excellent. This way, honorables." Oscar unlocked the door then swept us in.

We passed another vampire, one I didn't know, whose eyes widened as Troy and I both dropped our shields enough to loose our power signatures as soon as the door shut behind us. It was equal parts courtesy and threat. Courtesy to forewarn Maria that sovereigns were on her territory. Threat for anyone who might try to stop us meeting her. With Torsten the Viking, Keithia Monteague, and Callista all dead, Troy and I were the only locals strong enough to have a signature. Maria would know who was here before her people could call down to announce us.

The only question was what kind of mood she'd be in when we reached the throne room.

Chapter 10

T he ever-present fire was built higher than usual on the far side of the Raleigh coterie's underground throne room, chasing out the February chill. Vampires were pretty damn flammable, but they all seemed to have an abiding love for fire.

In what I took to be a good sign, Maria, wearing a long-sleeved, amethyst-colored dress in what had to be velvet, was sitting near the massive fireplace in the seating arrangement of red jacquard chairs she'd had brought out from her old living quarters. She had nicer stuff now and could afford to replace these, but I suspected she kept these pieces as a reminder of where she'd started.

She watched Oscar escort us through the gauzy curtains with wary eyes from her chair next to Allegra, who was lounging in jeans and a hoodie on the long couch next to Maria's chair with nowhere near her girlfriend's stiff formality.

Allegra sat forward, leaning with her elbows on her knees. "Wondered when you two would get around to coming down here." She waved a hand over the small spread of meat and mead. "Look, we'll make it a double date."

I was too busy trying to get my fear of underground spaces under control and figuring out how to level out my interactions with the vampires to do more than offer a small smile. I was used to Noah being mercurial. Maria had started getting touchy when

Troy or I were here, despite her easy friendship when we were anywhere off coterie territory.

Maria's nostrils flared for a moment. "I have a feeling the situation has developed since your call earlier, sweets. They smell like the precinct." She breathed again, more deeply, as Troy and I stopped short of sitting. "Like Detective Rice."

Frowning, Allegra took our scents as well. "T, I thought you said you were going to investigate the vampire angle."

"We are," he said.

Maria sighed, an indication of nerves, given she didn't really need to breathe that much unless she was speaking or fighting. "Sit. Be welcome in my nest. My table is yours, my hearth is yours, and my roof is yours, while you are here."

Troy and I answered in unison. "We honor our hostess. While your nest is ours, our strength is yours."

"Lovely. Sit." She waited until we'd each taken one of the two armchairs that completed the set, raising her eyebrows to see Troy seat himself rather than stand as a bodyguard behind my chair. "It must be serious if you're here as King and Arbiter then. How bad does Rice want me staked and burned?"

I winced. "He didn't say it quite like that. But if we don't show them either a killer or proof of your innocence in thirty-six hours, they're sending a warrant."

She rolled her eyes. "We can deal with a warrant. We have very fancy lawyers who charge me a lot of money for their services."

Troy shook his head. "SWAT will be right behind them. You try a glamour to stop them from coming down here, someone will notice. And react accordingly. They're looking for any excuse."

Allegra swore viciously, muttering under her breath as her expression hardened into that of a guard captain planning to defend against a siege.

I spoke over her. "You know how this ends, Maria."

"I'm not freeing Luz and Giuliano."

Troy shrugged. "Then you either find the killer in twenty-four hours or produce a scapegoat we can put to death."

Fury sparked in Maria's coffee-dark eyes.

I raised a hand. "It's not a threat."

"Yet," she snarled. "And have I mentioned how fucking annoying it is when you two tag team? Hekate preserve me but you're like Team fucking Rocket."

I blinked, wondering whether that was the reference I thought it was.

Allegra stiffened, looking like she'd just realized that she might find herself having to pick sides between the brother she'd been sworn to protect and the woman she loved.

"Yet," Troy agreed, ignoring the jab. He sighed and filled a small plate with prosciutto and peppered salami. "Speaking as your friend, I don't want it to come to that. But speaking as King of House Solari, we've got observers in town, Maria. From Lyon. You must have seen them last night."

A predatory smile flickered across her face. "I thought a couple of the out-of-towners smelled familiar. I would have thought they learned better after their last visit."

"They did," he said. "They're staying in our territory this time, not yours."

Both Allegra and Maria glanced at me, like they expected me to slap Troy down for claiming equal rights to and responsibilities for the Chapel Hill-Carrboro-Jordan Lake territory held by House Solari for the elves.

I just arched an eyebrow back and made my own plate of nibbles, more because it made Troy happy when I got my protein in than anything else. We'd made it clear he was here as King and I was Arbiter.

Maria leaned back in her chair and steepled her fingers. "I won't turn one of my people over to be killed. That's not how I do things."

"Okay," I said around a mouthful of smoked ham. "That's definitely fair. I didn't like that option either. But it means you either put all your people on finding who did this, or you make Santiago naming the killer or killers a condition of releasing Giuliano and Luz."

Eyes narrowed, Maria looked at me over steepled fingers. "What makes you think releasing them will fix anything?"

"I know Miami and New York are behind this. Time's up on the blood bank."

She sneered. "I already told you, I won't—"

"You will." I held her gaze and softened my voice to the register that said I was serious. "And I'm speaking as Arbiter. I indulged you in holding them up to now because strengthening you secures the area. But this?" I shook my head. "Maria, this is an epic clusterfuck that severely damages not only the whole demesne, but also Otherside in general and myself in particular. You don't want me telling you what to do with your territory, fine. But that means *you* fully own this fuckery and the risk it poses to the rest of the Triangle—hell, the state, given the body was dumped at the governor's mansion. How in the nine circles did *that* happen?"

Maria had drawn herself up to sitting with the poise of a snake about to strike.

Tension stretched until Allegra brushed Maria's hand. "Maria," she said gently. "The Arbiter is within her rights, and you know it."

With a hiss, Maria spun to look at her. "You're on her side?"

"I'm on *your* side, bae. Which is why I'm reminding you that Callista would simply have done what she did to House Sequoyah had this happened under her rule. Don't bite the hand that shelters you"—she turned to glare at me—"even if it's attached to someone who could learn more tact."

I pressed my lips together until Troy nudged me in the bond. Inclining my head, I said, "Of course. I appreciate the feedback." At the same time, I let my power signature spill out fully. "The point stands, however. You had to know part of the investigation would be asking how exactly an out-of-town vampire or vampires managed to walk a bleeding corpse through the streets of downtown Raleigh and not be seen until said corpse was propped against the literal gates of the state governor's residence."

Maria looked down then, grimacing, and I realized all this posturing was because she'd been badly embarrassed.

"You're...not wrong," she said. "But Arden, I need that blood."

"You need to trust the alliance." This time my softer tone was forgiveness for a friend, and she offered a tight smile to acknowledge it. "Part of assigning Allegra as special envoy was so we'd have someone able to coordinate between House Solari and Raleigh with more independence than is possible otherwise." I sighed again, setting down my empty plate and slumping back in my chair in a way I wouldn't if this was a proper parliament meeting. "We can't afford shit like this, not when the state and most of the country is swinging red on anti-Otherside legislation and rolling back what few gains we've made."

My phone buzzed. I pulled it out to make sure it wasn't an emergency then frowned at the caller ID. Etain, who should have had the night off. "I need to take this." I got up and wandered away, more for the illusion of privacy than the actuality of it, given how sharp the hearing of everyone in the room was. "Etain?"

"We've got a problem, ma'am. A big one."

"Another one? Bigger than Raleigh?"

"Yes, ma'am. The team monitoring federal channels finally hacked their way into one of the newer servers. They found files indicating a new federal agency is being established. One intended to deal with Othersiders."

"Excuse me?" I hissed. "'Deal with' how?"

"From what we've recovered, large-scale surveillance to start, with budget and authorization for search-and-destroy missions. The murder fast-tracked it. They're going to announce it tomorrow. And that local healthtech startup is going to be a vendor of record."

Heat flared in me, and I suppressed the urge to let fire dance over my clenched fist. "Goddess damn all of them. Fine. Thank you. I need to wrap up here. Keep Troy and me posted."

"Yes, ma'am."

I ended the call and stalked back to the group. "Our timeline just accelerated."

"What a surprise," Allegra drawled. "It's almost like that happens every time."

Troy cleared his throat and gave her a reproving look before answering me. "I only caught part of that. Mundanes?"

"Feds." I paced, too amped to sit down again. "*New* feds. Apparently, there've been plans in the works to establish a new federal agency tasked with surveillance and what sounds like is realistically extrajudicial processing of Othersiders." I couldn't help looking at Maria. "Those plans got moved up to tomorrow."

She fell into the utter stillness of the undead, even as Allegra bounced to her feet to pace opposite me.

Troy leaned back in his chair, almost as still as Maria except for the rapping of his fingers on the arm of his chair in an echo of my habit. "The delay in allowing us to come down here today and the thirty-six hours was a diversion. Even twenty-four hours was probably going to be too late."

"Agreed," Allegra said. "We need to get ahead of it."

I let a zephyr swirl into the fireplace, and the fire blazed higher. "Whenever an organization tries to get ahead of an announcement with one of their own, all it achieves is making the people on the defensive look guilty as fuck."

Maria's lips twisted in disgust. "Well, it's not like we can reach out to the agency."

"Can't we?" Troy shifted to sit upright. The bond hummed with intensity. "Or if not the agency, the people involved directly."

Allegra was already shaking her head. "That'll expose our intelligence networks."

Crossing my arms, I made myself stand still and not look up at the ceiling weighing down overhead.

"Arden?" Troy said. "Anything from the Sight?"

Nothing came for a minute. I was still growing into the djinn side of my heritage. The Sight was part of that and possibly the most unpredictable part. I closed my eyes and pondered the question, not trying to force it so much as thinking through doing what Troy had suggested.

The negation was a kick in the gut.

I shook my head. "We'd be better served by not showing that hand just yet."

"Okay." Troy didn't bother hiding his frustration. He knew what I sounded like when I'd managed to tap into the Sight. "Alternate plans. We pull an all-nighter and find something. Or we issue the statement you were working on earlier, Arden. Which we should do quickly. Social media is probably castigating the hell out of Otherside for our lack of response up to now."

"Both," Maria and I said simultaneously. We looked at each other, hesitated, then nodded. No offense taken. She was speaking her agreement as Mistress of Raleigh, and I was speaking mine as Arbiter.

An idea hit me. "Speaking of the Sight, I can try calling Duke. Something like this might be big enough to trigger a vision."

Allegra frowned. "Where's he been lately? Haven't seen him or Iaret in a few months."

I shrugged. "Beyond the Veil, I think. He's been more unreachable than usual."

"If we can't reach the djinn, we can try the fae," Troy said. "Alli's right, we can't contact the people behind the new agency without giving ourselves away. If our hackers do anything to sabotage it, the feds will have incident responders and cyber forensics all over it. The Darkwatch is good, but the feds have more manpower. If we can get a fae, a gremlin to mess with their hardware or, hell, even a kobold or a brownie to curse the home of someone important—"

"It's untraceable." I grinned and sent Troy the equivalent of a pleased high-five in the bond. "We just need to make sure they don't blame the witches for a curse or something."

Allegra scoffed. "The Bible-thumpers would love that opening. But I agree T's idea is the best we've got to increase our window while we also keep hunting and work on this statement, until and unless we can get a djinni on it. There've been rumors about the fae, but people are still thinking pots of gold and fairy circles, not the more malicious stuff."

I nodded, trying to think it through from a mundane perspective. "It has to be flawlessly executed though. If they realize they were fucked with, that will only give them justification to spy on and detain us."

Troy shrugged. "It will. But they're going to do that anyway. Better that we get something out of it."

I didn't like it, but he wasn't wrong. If people were going to cast Othersiders as villains no matter how upstanding we were, what was the point in letting them dictate our actions and resources while continuing to cut our legs out from under us? "Okay. Let's do it then. Separately, I got the statement started earlier today, but it'll have more weight as a joint statement from all the major factions. Maria? Thoughts?"

"Agreed." She tilted her head to look up at Allegra. "Darling, do you mind taking point on organizing the moroi while I help with this Hekate-damned statement?"

"Me?" Allegra looked more startled than I could remember seeing her.

Maria smiled sadly. "I know it's unconventional. But Noah's head isn't in the game today, and neither Oscar nor Lucien or Rani have the instinct or the strategic training yet. You'll think of something they'll miss."

"Of course." Allegra's bright grin said more than words how much she missed some of her work as captain of the Ebon Guard. She leaned over and kissed Maria, a quick brush of her lips that left Maria's pupils much wider than they had been. "You can count on me. Always."

A swirl of satisfaction from Troy made me glance at him. If he was any other elf, he'd see this moment as a threat—the technical heir to House Solari should both he and I fall, clearly partial to her vampire girlfriend. But he was just content his sister was happy and fulfilled, even as he kept a blank expression.

I couldn't hide a sappy smile before Troy caught it.

It's good to see you happy, I sent.

I just hope it lasts.

I barely stopped myself from nodding and giving us away.

"Maria, if you want to start on reviewing the statement, I'll call Duke, Zanna, and the witches," I said to cover myself. Somewhere in the mix, I'd need to come back to Maria letting her damn hostages go. I hadn't missed how smoothly the topic had been abandoned, but there were too many fires right now.

Troy stood. "I'll handle the weres, the Ebon Guard, and the Darkwatch. We'll need a contingency plan. And I need someone taking point with the Lyon observers since I won't be around to play host tonight."

Allegra nodded and jogged for the main door, hollering for Lucien and Rani as soon as it was open.

Maria rose to follow her, skirts swishing. "Come along, lovelies. We've converted one of the bedrooms to be an office space with a big screen. We don't have time to get everyone in a room physically, so we'll have to do this video conference nonsense." She eyed me. "Arden, try to keep the lightning to a minimum, hm? It was expensive to install all this."

I sighed. More time underground meant the odds were good I might start crackling at least a little as my nerves tried to get the best of me.

Now more than ever, I had to have solid control. Something I'd never been great at. I'd gotten better, but I had so much raw strength that I defaulted to using it to batter through problems rather than acting with precision.

But if I didn't have perfect control, I'd do something that would remind the mundanes two primordial elementals had destroyed downtown Durham—and then nothing would keep Otherside safe.

Chapter 11

It was dawn by the time we'd wrangled all the tasks and people and pulled something resembling an agreement together. Duke had been terse and short, with the callstone giving the impression of immense irritation, approving the statement on behalf of the djinn and cutting our connection before I could tell him everything else. Zanna had been more helpful, promising to head to the Summerlands with our request at the dawn crossing hour—so right about now. She liked the honor of being an ambassador, fortunately for us. Even better, she was good at it.

Between negotiating the public statement and then chasing down early leads in Raleigh, we'd lost twelve of our thirty-six hours though, and I was tetchy as Troy drove us home. Drawn tight from too much time underground and too much tension wrangling all the factions into a statement we could all stand behind, one that expressed sympathy for the humans, reminded them that rogue actors did not represent all of Otherside, and offered a veiled threat to anyone—mundane or supernatural—who might attempt a copycat killing.

"We'll get it done," Troy murmured as we pulled up to the house.

The car was full of the smell of egg and sausage biscuits, morning food we'd picked up because I thought it was ridiculous for him to have to cook when we were both equally tired—and I sure as shit wasn't cooking myself.

I leaned against his shoulder when he shut the car off. My brain was too scrambled to find words. I just wanted comfort. He kissed the crown of my head and let me stay propped against him, despite our cooling breakfast, until I could summon the energy to go inside.

We ate in a hurried silence. I couldn't help glancing at my laptop.

"You're getting some sleep before jumping back to work," Troy said when I reached for it.

"I should really—"

"Remember what happens when you push too hard." His tone was soft but implacable, all while being carefully modulated to soothe. He knew how to talk to an unreasonable queen, even if the cue that *I* was that unreasonable queen annoyed me.

I pressed my lips together, wanting to argue with him but knowing he was right. I didn't bother hiding the stubbornness from him in the bond though.

"Cariñamí, it will make no difference whether you watch the statement go out in real time or let the Ebon Guard fill you in. You're not a solo private investigator anymore. You're a queen. With extensive resources and good people." He leveled a firm stare at me. "Delegate."

That pushed me to a flat-out scowl, but he wasn't saying anything I didn't already know. I was just being a contrary control freak. Again.

I glanced at the laptop one more time. Surely it wouldn't hurt if I just checked for five minutes. Stayed on top of things. Got ahead of any problems. I needed to have the answers. It was my *job*—and with Hawkeye Investigations shut down, it was my *only* job.

A smile flickered at the corner of Troy's mouth as the bond sparked with amusement.

"What's so fucking funny?" I snapped.

"I went about this wrong."

I frowned, my annoyance swirling into confusion.

He rose with the easy grace I always envied, his gaze sharp on me as he came around to my side of the table. Stiffening, I shifted to keep him fully in my line of sight. Amusement or not, I knew when he was hunting.

That just made the hint of a smile become full-blown, wide enough to show a flicker of his secondary set of teeth. An intentional "slip," letting me know the game.

"What are you doing?" I asked, breathless in spite of myself. A silly question. More to stall.

"Hunting."

"I know that. Why?"

"Because you need to be hunted right now."

"Like hell." I couldn't help scrambling out of my chair though.

He let me dart around him, standing in the loose ready posture that said he could catch me if and when he wanted to.

"Troy. I just need to check—"

"Yourself."

Before you wreck yourself, I finished mentally to myself. Flushing, I tried to figure out how to get past him. "I know our people can handle this. I'm not *that* much of a control freak."

"Then stop acting like one. Come here."

When I hesitated, he lunged. I got two steps away before he caught my wrist and pulled me against him, turning me so my back was to him and holding me in a loose embrace.

"You need rest," he said. "*I* need rest."

"Go sleep then. I'll be there in a minute."

"A minute will turn into ten and then an hour, and then someone will call with an emergency, and you'll be running on fumes." He dragged his hands up my body, settling them on my shoulders and starting a firm massage that drew a groan from me as he worked the knots that always appeared when I had to do sensitive parliament business. "Come to bed. Even for an hour."

I wanted to argue but couldn't. I could take an hour. I'd been up all night chasing down leads while the parliament refined the statement. I knew what it said and what we had. I had a guess as to how Rice would react. The statement was already sent to Troy's media contacts.

"There's nothing else to be done for right now, and you know it. You're going to sit there, refreshing every news page and social media site, working yourself into an exhausted little tornado. Don't," Troy murmured. A curl of soothing Aether snaked through me, and I let it, shivering as it combined with his hands to drop my shoulders the rest of the way. When he used his grip on them to pull me into the bedroom, I let him.

We could both use a shower, but the more I relaxed, the harder I found it to keep my eyes open. That scared me, and adrenaline jolted me back to myself. "Troy."

The Aether disappeared immediately, as did his hands. "Okay. You're okay."

He turned catering to my reflexive fear into taking the opportunity to strip off his shirt, and of course my libido had to get involved.

"Sneaky elf," I muttered.

I couldn't take my eyes off him though. He was perfect, even with the scars I knew secretly shamed him. The thick one over his heart had been joined by a burn scar under his left collarbone where his old House tattoo had been seared away, a bullet scar under the right collarbone, the faint remnants of an elvish word scratched into his belly, and the braided burn of a lead-and-silver cuff that'd been closed so tightly around his wrist he'd nearly lost the hand. Most of it was punishment from his now-dead grandmother and sister for daring to be with me. Sometimes I felt guilty about that, but I couldn't own his choices. Just be worthy of them.

The scars weren't what I focused on as he stretched and lean muscle rippled. I couldn't help reaching out to trace the cut line defining his hip before it disappeared into his pants.

He caught my hand and shook his head. "You don't want to rest. Go get on the computer."

My jaw dropped. "What?"

"No rest. No touch."

I stared at him in consternation as he let go of my hand, backed up a step, and undid his pants to slide them down. When he hooked his thumbs into the waistband of his briefs and hesitated again, I pulled my attention from that area to his face.

"I thought you were working?" he said.

"I— You—"

He smiled and nodded toward the kitchen and my almost-forgotten laptop.

I made a snarl of frustration that would have made a werewolf proud. "For fuck's sake, it should not be this easy for you to distract me like this! I am twenty-fucking-eight years old, not a teenager!"

One step brought him close enough to whisper in my ear. "Age means nothing when you're part of a mated pair, remember?"

My breath caught in my throat. I wanted to be afraid. He'd explained this to me the first time I'd had a reaction to whatever pheromones he'd started producing when he'd bonded to me. I was his almost as much as he was mine now, and the "almost" was a technicality due to being half-elven rather than full and not having all the hormones or scent receptors.

Troy didn't touch me while I processed that. Didn't speak. Just stood close enough that his body heat warmed the air faster than my magic could.

Then I remembered something: part of being a mated elven pair meant he knew what I needed even if I was ignoring it. He wasn't being relentless because he was especially horny or because everything that'd happened in the last twenty-four hours didn't mean anything to him.

He was doing this because I was probably on the verge of doing something very foolish from lack of sleep and too much tension, and as much as he might enjoy verbally sparring with me, he knew that would spike my adrenaline in a way that wouldn't be conducive to sleep unless we physically sparred.

That was what he'd meant when he said he was going about this wrong.

Still, my inborn stubbornness wouldn't let me relent that easily. "I guess I could keep you company. While you rest."

"That'd be welcome."

When he stepped back toward the bed and sat on the edge, I stripped faster than I had in a while. When I was down to panties, I couldn't wait to touch him anymore. I pounced, toppling him backward on the mattress and stealing a kiss.

His pleased groan was accompanied by one of his arms locking me tight against him while the other ran along my spine.

"Rest," he insisted when we broke apart.

I sighed. "Fiiine." Then a wicked idea struck me. "But only if I get to give you a massage first."

The bond snarled with conflict. Hot desire and cold logic—if I was massaging him, I wasn't resting, but he adored having my hands on him like that.

"I need a few minutes to calm my thoughts," I said. "And you need to take a break from taking care of me. I know how much it drains you when I insist on talking to the police."

I'd been kidnapped from a police station once. Chapel Hill, not Raleigh, but a detective I'd thought was...if not a friend, then at least a buddy, had rolled over on me to agents he thought were federal but were in fact elven. The East Coast Darkwatch was mostly on my side now, but Troy had been nearby and unable to prevent it. With vampires strong enough to leave bodies all over

Raleigh and at the governor's mansion unseen, I knew he had to be hiding some anxiety from me.

He winced, maybe remembering that kidnapping, maybe at being caught. "Okay. Thanks, cariñamí."

The uncertainty in him melted under my hands once he'd laid flat with me straddling his hips. I interspersed breaking up the knots under his shoulder blades with kisses, letting him know he was loved and cared for.

When he fell asleep under a cloud of contented relaxation, I wasn't far behind.

The stark blackness of the In-Between greeted me as soon as I settled alongside him and closed my eyes. I would have sworn, but speech wasn't a concept in this space. Intention was, and mine was clear enough in my desire to cuss. The too-close stars spun and twisted.

I wouldn't do that.

I tried to find the source of that...voice? Thought? Intention? Whatever it was. I wasn't alone in this space.

Eshu-Elegba told you we weren't finished with you, didn't he?

The suggestion that the gods were indeed behind this elicited a sharp spike of panic.

Why so scared? You'll want our help. Because we want yours.

That didn't make any sense. The two didn't have to be mutually exclusive or inclusive.

They do when you consider the consequences.

The starry blackness twisted again as I tried to step out of whatever dream this was. It didn't work with the Crossroads, though, and it wouldn't work here. Whoever this was had me until they were done with me.

Good, you understand.

I understood nothing.

You do. More than you think. Amusement sent a ripple that countered my fear among the emptiness. *Cause, effect. Action, consequence. Gift, return.*

What the hell did that mean? What gift?

The greatest gift of all. Don't worry, primordial. You'll see. Soon.

And with that, I was booted out of the In-Between to sit up with a choked scream.

"Arden!"

I clutched Troy's arms as he pulled me close.

"What happened?"

"The gods," I gasped. "I think."

"You think?" He freed himself from my grip and started rubbing his hands along my arms. Only then did I realize I was as cold as I'd been when I climbed out of Jordan Lake. "The gods want you to freeze to death? What the hell is going on?"

"The In-Between." I'd never told him what it was like to be stuck there. I'd barely mentioned its existence at all. I hadn't wanted to give him more nightmare fuel. He had enough of it as it was, and this wasn't something he could protect me from, other than by being something that anchored me to this plane. "How long was I gone?"

"You weren't. You were here, physically and auratically, unlike when you get pulled into the Crossroads in your dreams. I didn't realize something was wrong until your body temp dropped. It was that subtle."

I shifted, pulling us both down again with me as the little spoon as my teeth clattered, and sought solace in his embrace.

Part of his aura was twined through my auratic points, since he'd done that to anchor my soul and bring my spirit back from the Crossroads when I'd effectively died stopping the Wild Hunt. For a god to be that subtle? That was big magic. Dangerous magic. Not just for us but for the world. They wouldn't bother me if they didn't want something on this plane.

And, as always, it was the worst possible time for it. Worse than last time, even—we'd had a few mundane matters to set in motion when the gods of the hunt demanded my attention and efforts before. They complicated things, but ultimately, stopping the Wild Hunt had been the impetus behind forming the alliance that was supposed to keep Othersiders in the Triangle and North Carolina safe.

This? This was an open threat when I was already dealing with two others. The master vampires of New York and Miami were willing to threaten the safety of all of Otherside with their barbarism. The mundanes were willing to punish all of Otherside for their politics.

And now the gods wanted another shot?

Possibly worst of all, I didn't know the nature of these gods. The presence had invoked Eshu-Elegba, the orisha who was Master of the Crossroads. It hadn't sounded like the orisha I remembered and, as I thought back to the essence, hadn't felt like him either. Whoever it was had defied categorization—neither masculine or feminine, neither assertive nor receptive, neither day nor night. They simply existed. As though they could be anything.

My breath caught.

"What?" Troy said.

"The tricksters."

And as I said it, the Sight confirmed it, squeezing my heart with the knowledge.

I tucked tighter against Troy, exhausted despite whatever rest we'd managed to snatch. "We're dealing with the tricksters."

Chapter 12

To Troy's credit, he didn't waste time asking how I knew or was I sure. He got straight to the point. "What do they want?"

"They didn't exactly say. Something about a gift and a return."

"They want something back?"

I scooched backward, trying to fit tighter against Troy's body as much for comfort as for warmth. "I guess? I don't know. And I don't know when. They just said soon."

He fell into the brooding silence that said he was working through angles. "Fine," he said after long enough that I'd warmed up. "We'll deal with them when they get here. You sounded like the Sight confirmed it's the tricksters, so whatever you think they want probably isn't exactly it anyway."

"Good point." I mentally reviewed my to-do list, scowling when a piece fell into place. "The feds. They're priority. How much do you want to bet that they're the ones pressuring Doc Mike? Especially if Verve is their preferred vendor. They'll want to find out what exactly their new test tells them. Maybe fine-tune it so they can identify a range of Otherside factions."

Troy made a disgusted sound. "Makes sense."

Hopefully Zanna could arrange for a gremlin or someone to fuck with the government's new agency launch before the press conference was due to start at noon, another piece of information we'd gleaned during last night's work. The urgency would mean one of the greater fae would need to open a hole in the Veil to get around the crossing hours from the Summerlands, but Rí, the fae king, would like having me owe him a favor.

I hoped.

Maria and Allegra were focusing on the hunt for the rogue vampires. My guess was anyone who didn't smell like the coterie would be hauled in for a hard questioning, which would, eventually, be blamed on me as well. My mood soured. There was a faster way to do this, and if I was already in the shit, I didn't see any reason not to do it.

Troy sighed, his breath sending shivers across my neck. "I guess we're done resting?"

"Sorry." I winced. "But we've only got a few hours until the fed presser."

"And you want to go around Maria and talk to Matthias or Santiago."

"Am I that transparent?"

He poked me in the bond with an affirmative but then added, "It's not a bad idea. Especially with what Noah said about the message from Santiago and Maria saying nothing about it last night. Frankly, Arden, I'm concerned."

"Speaking as king?"

"Yes. It never should have come to this. We gave her enough rope to hang herself—"

"And she hanged the whole Goddess-burning Triangle."

"Exactly."

I rolled to face him, asking with my expression as much with the bond if there was any other way—one that wouldn't piss Maria off.

He propped himself up on an elbow and rested his head on his hand. "Trust me, I don't want to deal with a pissed-off Alli any more than you do Maria. But we need our culprit. You've read the reports on how many new vampires are in the territory. That assumes it really is them and not the Sons of Seth doing a frame job."

"Fuck." I rolled onto my back and pressed the heels of my palms against my eyes, trying to see another way. This was the downside of the role of Arbiter being my only job. Since deposing Callista, I'd learned the situation in the Triangle was far from normal. Arbiters existed in territories throughout Otherside, but they didn't rule. They stood as impartial judges, at most, when called in by whichever faction had primary leadership. My destroying the local elven power structure while building an alliance had given me the power to stand alone—and that meant in more ways than one.

Troy waited, patient as ever, although he did indulge himself in tracing a light finger over my skin in a way that was far more distracting than it should have been, given how tired and frustrated I was.

"Do you know either of them?" I asked when I wasn't able to talk my way out of it.

"Matthias is slightly more reasonable. Both are older than Torsten was, and Matthias has larger hunting grounds with less sun to push him toward madness."

"Matthias it is."

"I'll get the number from the Ebon Guard."

I missed Troy as soon as his warmth and weight left the bed, and I didn't bother hiding how much I enjoyed watching him leave the room. He sent a playful Aether sting when he glanced back and caught my expression, pleased as always to have captured my admiration. For my part, the endless politics of big-time Otherside were more tolerable when I had him as my adviser.

He came back with a piece of paper. "Matthias's number is the top one. The second is the number for the gentleman's club he owns as the coterie's main front."

"Gentleman's club." That could mean anything from whiskey bar to strip joint, but I had a few assumptions. "Anything I need to know?"

Troy frowned as he thought. "From what I recall from briefings a few years ago, Matthias's original time was somewhere around the end of the Carolingian Empire."

I blinked. My history was decent, but I'd never really bothered myself with the various European empires.

"Late 800s?" He shrugged. "In any case, the point is that somewhere along the way, he went from priest to mobster."

"So...he'll do whatever the fuck he wants but still be up on his high horse about it, and worst of all, he's got more than eleven hundred years of attitude behind him."

Troy snorted. "Something like that. See if you can draw out his chivalrous streak." He frowned. "Might be for the best that you're calling him. Maria's good, but Matthias is her weak spot."

"Because she's gay and was nearly burnt at the stake as a witch and is now the youngest vampire city master in centuries?" I guessed, putting former medieval holy man and gentleman's club together to get raging dickhead. I couldn't keep the disgust out of my tone; I wasn't entirely straight myself, and either way, it was nobody's fucking business.

"Exactly. Matthias's delight in sinning only extends to *male* sins. Which means her usual flirtation falls on unsympathetic attention."

"Asshole," I muttered.

"Agreed. But asshole holding all the cards. And he knows it."

"He's probably delighted at kicking Maria."

"I imagine so." Troy bustled around the room, gathering up a fresh set of clothes. As he headed into the bathroom, he said, "I need to give some attention to our guests from Lyon today. Haroun's your main bodyguard for the day. Try not to give him too much trouble."

I stuck my tongue out at Troy's back, composing my features to bland agreement when he turned around at whatever the bond told him. I wasn't that much of a pain to deal with. He narrowed his eyes at me but went into the bathroom and shut the door without comment. A moment later, the shower started.

As keen as I'd been to keep working earlier, I was more tempted to avoid everything now by getting some of that rest Troy'd been pushing. But we were up, and we were on a deadline. Troy would handle things for the House. I'd handle the rest of the territory.

Even if it meant stepping on the toes of a friend and ally.

I forced myself out of bed, taking the paper with me and procrastinating by making a cup of Darjeeling tea. The last time I'd stepped into Maria's business had been at the Wild Hunt, ordering Noah to prep a distraction for the first incident at the governor's mansion. It would be harder to come out of this one as the heroine though. The mundanes didn't know what was going on before—and I hadn't shredded a downtown district with primordial unreality, only to set it right in front of an unwanted crowd while I was just come back from the almost-dead.

Troy's mental whisper interrupted. *Stop stalling, Arden. Get it done.*

I sent an annoyed poke back rather than telling him to mind his business, but he was right. After a brief argument with myself, I dug around in my bag for the voice recorder I hadn't stopped carrying. This was still a case. I'd need proof for Detective Rice. It went against the Détente to record conversations between Othersiders, but Matthias had already set it on fire with his attack.

With a huff, I dialed.

It was full morning now, but if the Master of New York City was going to be rude enough to leave a corpse at the gate of the governor's mansion, he was just gonna have to deal with awkward calling hours.

The call rang long enough I thought it'd go to voicemail, and I was composing my message when a deep male voice with a Manhattan accent answered.

"North Carolina area code. Not Maria. Could it be the famous Arbiter?"

"That's right." I pumped up the drawl in my voice as I switched the phone to speaker mode and pressed record on my voice recorder. A lot of Northerners thought Southerners sounded stupid and therefore were stupid. Maria wasn't the only one who could get people to underestimate her. "This is Arden Finch Solari. I'm looking for the Master of New York."

"You've found him, my dear, and don't you have that sweet Southern charm."

"Well, bless your heart, sugar." My grin was more of a snarl. If he knew anything about the South, he'd know the barb for what it was. "I'd apologize for the hour, Matthias, but you and I have a problem."

"By all means, state your piece. Leaders must be ready to serve whenever duty calls, of course."

I frowned at that. "Service, huh? Is that what you call having your people leave a body at the gate of my territory's mundane seat of governance?"

"My apologies, Arbiter, for any inconvenience that caused you."

He was being too smooth. I didn't like it. I held my tongue, not willing to accept the apology and wondering what he'd add if I didn't.

Matthias's sigh whispered down the line. "The truth is, little Maria is going against all custom. I'd hoped you might see your way to helping put a stop to that."

"You colluded with the Master of Miami to stage a coup in league with our local elven Houses."

"And punishment was rendered, as is proper for failure. No hard feelings there. Now we want our people back. Or Maria gone."

"No hard feelings." I let my disgust and anger color my words. Folks had heard what happened when I let my temper go, and just now, I didn't mind if he was afraid of me. "Yet you didn't have the courtesy to reach out to me before declaring war."

"Now, just a moment—"

"No, your time for 'just a moment' was two nights ago. That was a hell of a birthday present, by the way." I made a snap decision, since all my people were already in the know and making their preparations. "Do you know what this bought us, Matthias? Not me. Us. All of Otherside."

The vampire master's tone was hard enough to chip stone. "Enlighten me, dear."

"Well, *sugar*, the mundane federal government will be making an announcement later. There's to be a new agency. Your *temper tantrum* convinced them to provide emergency funding and get it off the ground today."

"And I should care because...?"

I smiled, hoping he could feel its bite down the phone. "Because their mandate is to surveil and control Otherside. Since we're so obviously a clear and present threat to human citizens, after all. Now, you were real close to Ground Zero in 2001, weren't you? You remember the Patriot Act? What the mundanes were willing to do to control their own citizens? *We're not citizens* to them, Matthias, because we're not human. Their legal system has no place for us. No way to control beings who can bend steel bars or glamour minds. What do you imagine they'll do to us?"

Silence stretched. I let it hang.

Troy came out of the bathroom, dressed like a king rather than a Darkwatch agent, in business casual black slacks and a green shirt with a shimmer of gold threads, hair slicked back and expression hard. He ghosted over to sit beside me without a sound.

"This was Santiago's doing," Matthias said.

"No. Fuck no. You don't get to walk it back now."

"Your manners—"

"Are not for you to comment on. Not with what you pulled and not when you can't act with the good sense that should come with your big age. Santiago's doing or not, you sent people down for the coup and were implicated in the current outrage. You pulled me and mine into a personal disagreement with the Mistress of Raleigh and put all of Otherside at risk in the process, without the courtesy of speaking to me first. And Matthias?" I let my voice drop down into a dangerous purr. "I protect what's mine."

Troy tensed, reading where I was going with this. *Easy, Arden. He's proud.*

I shook my head. I had not busted my ass to secure the Triangle and the state only for this arrogant piece of shit and his buddy in Miami to come smashing in.

That's his problem, I shot back to him. *I'm nipping this in the bud.*

"Now, Miss Solari—"

I almost laughed at the taut courtesy in Matthias's voice. I was Miss Solari now, when I'd started with a vague cordiality that wasn't quite respect. "The Raleigh PD wants the culpable party. I need a name."

"I told you, this was Santiago's plan."

"One you signed off on or you would have alerted Maria or me. No. I think you wanted to see what would happen. I suppose life gets boring after a few hundred years. Torsten was hoping to see Ragnarok. You might well be first in line."

To Matthias's credit, he caught on. "You'd give up my coterie to save yours."

"All I'm asking for is the name of the responsible party. Now, I can be generous. Take an hour to think about it. But if I don't hear from Maria within an hour with the happy news, my next call is my law enforcement friends. Your move, sugar." I hung up and switched off the recorder. Having that conversation on record went against Otherside rules and taking it without permission would get my PI license revoked, but those were the least of my current worries.

Troy rubbed his forehead. "We need to work on your diplomacy."

With a smile that was all teeth, I said, "What's that mundane saying? Walk softly and carry a big stick?"

"That was more of the big stick than walking softly."

"I've stayed out of sight and out of mind for almost a year, Troy. In that time, we've gone *backwards* on practically everything. It's time for the big stick."

"I suppose it is." He looked concerned though. "Arden...you know why I worry."

That softened my attitude. "I know. I overplayed my hand with the Houses, and if it looks like I'm about to do the same outside the state, I'll bring people together against me rather than with me. More people with more resources."

Troy nodded and leaned in to kiss my forehead. "And I can't protect you from everyone. I couldn't even when it was just our local Houses after you."

And now it was potentially much worse.

The pain it caused him to admit that lashed me in the bond, and I flinched. There was Omar's bully comment again as well.

I was just trying to make everything better for everyone. Make a place for everyone, both within Otherside and for Otherside in the mundane world, where we could be safe. Where *I* could be safe. I hadn't asked to be born a Goddess-damned primordial elemental or to fulfill a prophecy or any of the shit I'd been pushed into. I'd wanted to be left alone. But every time I tried to be left alone, I got painted into a corner.

So, offense it was.

"I'll be careful," I promised.

"Are you going back to Raleigh now?"

I winced. "I think I've stepped in Maria's business enough for one day. I'll head to the bar and do some research." I took his hand and kissed the knuckles. "Like you said. I have to delegate, and Raleigh isn't the only part of the Triangle that'll need me if this announcement goes over badly. While you deal with the Lyon observers, I should get to work on a plan for what happens when this federal agency launches. Even if we get a reprieve today, they're not going away. And people need to see that I'm working on this."

"Smart choice." Tension eased from his shoulders.

We left together after I showered and dressed. I pressed myself to him and gave him a lingering kiss before he got into his car, as much because I missed him when we had separate things to do as because I wanted to be sure my scent was on him for the Lyon elves to remember he did have a queen backing him.

He might worry about me, but I worried about him too. The local elven Houses were destroyed or mine because hurting me was bad enough, but then they'd gone after him. I didn't know shit about the European Houses, and as he headed down the driveway in his black Acura MDX, I sent a little prayer that whatever was going on with this visit wouldn't turn into a shitshow. I didn't trust that they were only here to observe. Elves were never that straightforward, not when it came to politics.

Troy had been hurt enough by queens stuck in the past and their politics. And like I'd told Matthias, I protected what was mine.

Chapter 13

I went in the back door at the bar, not in the mood to put on a pleasant face. Everyone would know I was in residence, even if they didn't see me come in. I tended to stop shielding so hard once within the protective spells laid on the building so I could have a sense of what was going on in my territory. But I needed some quiet time with the door shut to strategize and be more than just a figurehead or media target.

Well, that and I needed to reflect on some of my recent actions. I set my laptop on my desk and dropped into the leather chair, rocking it back and forcing myself to take a few minutes to think before opening the computer.

Troy had been right to get me to slow down earlier. I needed more of his patience. That call with Matthias didn't sit right with me, and I thought I knew why.

Being called a bully still grated on me.

Troy's comment about needing to be more diplomatic needled too. It wasn't that I was worried about being "nice." Trying for harmony had gotten me next to nowhere with everyone except the witches and the werecats. Even my own people, the local elementals, still kept me at arm's length with the exception of my three friends.

No, I was far more bothered about turning into another Callista. Being the change mattered to me. A certain level of domination, even violence, was necessary to maintain order in Otherside. Too many of us were either apex predators or magically gifted with the means to get our way, and some had lived too long to remember why kindness and justice mattered. But just because that was the way it'd always been didn't mean that was what we had to be going forward.

It was just my shit luck that it was falling to me to drag everyone kicking and screaming into the future again.

I spun a zephyr through the room, letting it ruffle the papers pinned to the corkboard I'd hung up on one wall to complement the whiteboard opposite. I'd given up my office at the coworking space, although I still held Hawkeye as a front for consulting work with the mundanes. The bar was just safer.

There was also the benefit that it was still standing. The coworking space had taken a beating when I blew down half of CCB Plaza.

Shit. Sometimes it felt like I fucked up everything I touched.

Even if it all worked out in the end—for me, at least—I had to consider so many more people now. I didn't have Troy's or Allegra's training. I wasn't used to doing anything more than making sure *I* survived the next day. I could do that. I'd gotten damn good at it. I'd succeeded so well at it that I'd completely rearranged the local power structure in a way that put all of Otherside on notice.

I just...couldn't convince myself I was the right person for the job. They'd all figure it out eventually. They'd find a weakness. And then Troy and I both would be in danger again.

My stomach twisted at that.

A twinge in the bond as Troy turned a questioning thought my way made me mask it. He didn't need my self-doubt and imposter syndrome while he was trying to be living history for our French guests.

I needed something else to focus on. Given my mood, the response to Otherside's condemnation of the murder on social media probably wasn't it.

Duke's long absence was a concern, one I could focus on. If we couldn't get a gremlin in time—and it was looking like we wouldn't—I needed someone who could spy through the Veil from the ethereal realm.

Then there was the oddness of the ring I'd been given. I'd tucked the witches' gift in my pocket, hoping I could get Duke to stop dodging me long enough to come through the Veil and tell me what the sigil on it was for. *Seeing the unseen*, the card had said, but did that mean ghosts? Invisibility spells? Something to do with the tricksters, or something I hadn't even thought of yet?

I trusted our witches. But my magic did weird shit sometimes—being of mixed heritage meant the two halves of Aether blended in me, manifesting in Chaos. Most of the time, that just meant I could counter Aetheric attacks. On a bad day, though, it meant I could warp reality. That meant being extra careful with blood magic.

I'd learned the hard way that it was better to ask for help on some things.

Even if it made me feel even more like an imposter.

I pulled a small silver knife out of my desk and pricked my finger before grasping my callstone this time. Blood called to blood, and as Duke's cousin, I should be able to reach him like this. At least I hoped I'd be able to, because I really didn't want to have to use his true name to summon him again. That always put him in a shitty mood.

Massaging the enchanted hematite hanging around my neck, I said, "Duke." I sat up at the faintest crackle of connection in a corner of my mind. "*Duke*. Listen to me. You can't keep shutting me out or giving me half-connections. Don't make me summon you here."

His voice echoed in my mind, more like a direct phone connection than the whispered thoughts I got when I was close enough to Troy. "What, Arden?"

"I need to talk to you."

"What do you imagine we're doing now?"

"Come on, Duke. Stop being an ass." When he didn't answer except to project boiling irritation at me, I raised the wall between Troy and me higher and tried something else. "I have something for you to look at. An enchanted ring. Blood magic."

"Blood magic?"

A tug on my aura made my skin tighten as Duke pulled himself through the Veil, materializing in his usual corner of the room in a burst of lemon zest-scented Aether. Carnelian eyes glared at me from a version of his true form, rippling flame shot through with lightning, and he sneered to show a hint of black teeth as dagger sharp as Troy's secondary set.

"What's this about blood magic?" he said by way of greeting. "I thought you were smarter than that."

"Hi, Duke. Good to see you. It's been how many months since you've been here in person?"

The door cracked as Haroun, stationed outside, stuck his head in to see who'd gotten past him and into the room. It shut again just as quickly.

Duke glared at the door then at me. "If you're going to be boring, I'll go back to what I was doing."

"What were you doing?"

He shimmered, about to change planes.

"Duke! Come on, I'm not trying to be a pain. I was worried."

The shimmer stopped. "You were?"

"You're my *cousin*. The one blood relative I have left. Yes, I've been worried. Even if you are an utter ass."

With a flicker, he shifted into his usual form for this plane: a tall, lithe young Black man with dark umber skin and laughing dravite-colored eyes, dressed in a sharp suit. He arched a disbelieving eyebrow at me. "You missed me."

Oddly, I had.

Duke had been my guardian growing up, alongside Callista and another now-dead djinni cousin, Grimm. He'd beaten the shit outta me more than once, but he'd also saved my life a few times. His beloved, Iaret, had been instrumental to winning the Wild Hunt. I thought we all—Duke, Iaret, me, and Troy—were finally making progress on the testy elf-djinn factional relationship that'd suffered from acrimony since Atlantis had been shattered and drowned a few millennia ago.

Then Duke had vanished, Iaret along with him, leaving only a terse note that he had things to take care of.

"I mean, yeah." I shifted in my chair, uncomfortable with being mushy like this.

Duke tilted his head to study me. "That means a great deal, Arden. That you say you missed me and not what I can do for you."

"Well...good." I hesitated. Normally there'd be all kinds of ceremony and shit, but not only were we blood but Duke was also over four thousand years old and utterly unimpressed with ninety-nine point nine percent of what I did, Arbiter or primordial elemental or not. Mindful of his mood, I gestured to the chair in front of the desk. "You wanna sit? Have a drink while we talk?"

"No drink." He sat though.

I let myself relax. Duke was temperamental as fuck. I had enough on my emotional ledger without having to fight him as well.

"Talk to me, little bird. And don't bother with pleasantries. I can smell your agitation." His nose wrinkled. "Even with all the elf on you."

I arched an eyebrow at him for being rude about Troy even as I relaxed the rest of the way. If he was calling me "little bird"—a reference to my origin as a sylph—he'd indulge me.

"We've got a few troubles I was hoping you could help with," I said.

"More than someone giving you a blood magic ring?"

"A lot more." I gave him the rundown of everything that'd happened in the last few days beyond what I'd been able to tell him to get his approval for the joint statement, finishing with a smile I knew he'd read as sly. "The right person might find an opportunity in all this chaos."

He threw his head back and roared with laughter. "You do know how to draw me in." Shaking his head, he fiddled with a new ring on his finger. "Very well. It's been some time since I played mundane politics. Spinning the FDR conspiracy was one thing, but this should be far more interesting."

I blew a breath out, relieved, and dug some business cards out of my drawer to slide across to him. "Thank you. I haven't heard from the fae yet, and gremlins aren't the most subtle solution."

"I should think not." He twisted his fingers, and the cards disappeared to whatever cubby-hole he hid things in beyond the Veil. "Now. This ring."

Not the one he was still spinning. I dug in my pocket for the one the witches had given me and held it in my palm. He passed a hand over it, eyes flickering back to carnelian as the lemon zest scent grew stronger. I tried to follow what he was doing, watching via my third eye, but I was an elemental, not a djinni. I could follow the shape of the magic, sort of. Like hearing a melody but missing the full song. Forget reading the sheet music.

"Your talents lie elsewhere," Duke said distractedly. "Focus on Chaos. Rare enough for an elemental to have even your level of control with it."

"About that actually. Talents. And Chaos."

"Wait."

My hand prickled, then he plucked the ring from my hand to peer at it. "No traps. Tidy piece of work. The local coven gave it to you?"

I nodded. "To see the unseen, whatever that means."

He stilled, then his gaze flicked to me and away so quickly I nearly missed it. "The only reason blood magic would be needed for that is to see the true nature of a thing. The lie in a truth or the soul in a body."

I blinked. "Um. Okay. That's kind of heavy. I was thinking more along the lines of ghosts or one of those don't-see-me spells the elves use."

Mischief smoldered in his gaze. "If it worries you, I could hold onto it for you."

"No, that's fine." I held my hand out.

Duke hesitated before giving it back. Djinn loved their magical items, especially if it was something that involved blood or soul magic. "You're sure I can't hold onto it for you?"

"Yeah. I'll be fine." Reluctantly, I pushed it onto the middle finger of my right hand. It fit snugly but not uncomfortably, and a little zing of magic darted through me. "Anything?"

"If you're referring to your aura, you'd have to ask your elf king. He knows it better than I do by now. I imagine activating it would help as well. Wait till I'm gone though. I do hate a mess."

I snorted and rolled my eyes. He cared, given he was here. He didn't want to though. Fine by me. I didn't want to like him either, but he was true to his nature, and where we were now in our relationship was progress. "Thanks for checking it."

"Mm." He grinned. "Mostly I want to see what trouble it causes you when you activate it. From a safe distance."

"Of course you do."

Amusement faded to near boredom. "What else did you want to talk about?"

I grimaced, suddenly cold again. "I got pulled into the In-Between."

He sat up straight, intensity pinching his expression. "Excuse me?"

"Twice."

"And you're still alive? You found your way out? I had to drag you out the last time."

"I wasn't physically there this time. I was asleep. The second time, someone spoke to me."

Duke hissed. "Dreamwalker. I wondered whether Ninlil's talent would pass to you, half-breed that you are."

Pissed off at the slur, I sat up straight and glared at him. Scolding him would do nothing. He knew better and simply didn't care. Which reminded me why I hadn't been all that overeager to look for him for the first few weeks he was gone.

"Oh fine, I'm sorry," he said.

I blinked, surprised by the apology. "Okay, you must be interested then. What's a Dreamwalker?"

He ignored my question. "Who spoke to you?"

"I don't know." I repeated as much of the conversation that I could remember, adding, "I think it was the tricksters. Did you... Are there any other prophecies?"

Duke stiffened as though I'd poked him with a stick. "There are always more prophecies."

That was an odd reaction.

Before I could press him on it, he said, "Is this the first time you've had strange dreams?"

"No. I dreamt of the forest and the beach from the gods' plane sometimes, before we went." I hesitated, uncomfortable, but not wanting to leave something out if it was important. "Troy was there sometimes."

"Did he dream the same?"

"He might have? He mentioned dreams once."

"Chaos spheres." He shook his head and pinched the bridge of his nose, a gesture I always wondered how he managed in his natural form. "Bloody hell, Arden. You should have said something."

I crossed my arms and hugged myself. "About what? All you and Grimm ever taught me was lucid dreaming and stepping out of a dream so I wasn't casting in my sleep. What the hell is a Chaos sphere?"

"We didn't think a—an *elemental* with one element would have the talent, regardless of your strength, and it was enough bother to teach you how to hide the Air magic with all of the bloody elves in this territory." He flickered back to his true form before resuming his preferred human skin. "This is dangerous. Doubly so if the tricksters are indeed up to something. I need to talk to Iaret."

He gave me A Look, the one a four-millennia-old djinni gave a barely-three-decade-old woman he thought was particularly useless.

"*Try* not to do anything impatient or especially stupid while I'm gone. Between this dream business, the Council breaking my balls, and spying on these mundanes for you, I might be a while." He shrugged. "Or not. Depends on whether I can inspire one of them to talk to you before holding this absurd press conference. Either way, at least it gives me an excuse to leave the Old City for a bit."

Without waiting for another word from me, he shimmered, changed planes, and was gone, leaving me with even more anxiety than I'd had before finally getting ahold of him.

What the fuck was a Dreamwalker, and what did it have to do with the trickster gods?

Chapter 14

I needed a distraction from my distraction. It was time to get to work on my actual job—managing shit in the territory.

First priority: the announcement and any reports on fallout.

Steeling myself, I logged on to my various social media accounts. I checked them once a month or so, mostly for research or to keep them from being deactivated. The prerecorded video showing me, Troy, and Maria in her office and Vikki Volkov at her kitchen table was at the top of YouTube and Twitter's news pages, and I grimaced. I hated seeing myself on camera. I didn't like that Troy was a target as the only elf publicly out, although nobody had quite figured out his faction or his role yet and we weren't in a rush to tell. The rest of the parliament—Terrence, Ximena, Doc Mike, Zanna, Janae, and Val, representing the werecats, human sensitives, fae, witches, and elementals respectively—had dropped off-camera for this. Some of us were out or more public about it because others had fewer numbers or other safety concerns.

It was part of why I'd stepped back in the last few months. Aside from wanting to get my life back to what it had been, I knew there was a lot of discontent around my unilateral decision to Reveal the biggest factions in Otherside.

As expected, public opinion was evolving lightning fast. I shook my head at some of the takes. Others made my heart ache and my stomach clench at the vitriol and hate, the willful twisting of what was supposed to have been a message of solidarity and condolences. Troy had told me to leave shit like this to the Ebon Guard and the Darkwatch to filter through, but I refused to ask them to do something I wouldn't. Perversely, I wanted to know exactly how bad it was. I wanted to know exactly what I was up against.

I wanted to be angry because it was safer than being afraid.

I couldn't hide behind anonymity anymore, so I wanted to armor myself in knowledge. All knowledge was worth having...even when it sent daggers of hurt into my soul.

My phone buzzed once with a text message.

Stop checking the news, Troy had written.

The mental walls were still up between us, so it was probably a lucky guess on his part. Or an indication of how well he knew me. Unless I was upset enough that my emotional state was leaking through despite my efforts.

He was right though. Other shit to do.

I spent the next hour plowing through the reports I'd fallen behind on in favor of a birthday party and a murder, growing more concerned by everything I read. We'd had some instances of hate crimes against known Othersiders or their businesses in the last year, but they'd died down somewhat as the news cycle moved on and Otherside didn't retaliate the way the provocateurs wanted us to. There'd been a few deaths, but the community had always been good at covering them up and dealing out justice to the perpetrators where it wasn't self-defense.

Now there were two very public murders. A leak from one of the first responders had the rumor mill cranking and threats flying against vampires. Hope's shop Midday Moon had gotten hit again in the last day, as had Claret—just bricks through windows for now.

I closed my eyes, feeling sick.

Just bricks. They'd tried burning Hope's shop down after the second Reveal.

It could get worse. It *had* gotten worse for a while before coming down to a vicious simmer, like a pot with something burnt on the bottom. With right-wing demagogues in office and an actual non-human demographic to stir their base against, all the crap would get scraped up and boil back up to the top. And this time it'd be even worse because our protections in the mundane legal system had been stripped away.

All sympathy we'd garnered would be gone. The few mundane allies we'd had after the Reveals had gotten tired of protesting and gone home, for the most part. We were back to being targets.

Unless I could stop it.

I hadn't heard from Zanna or Maria, which meant the fae were having trouble finding a gremlin—or simply didn't want to play—and Matthias was playing another game. Maria would either be furious or pleased as punch when she found out what I'd done, and either way, she'd be calling about it. The thirty-six hours I'd negotiated with Detective Rice were counting down, and I was sitting here with nothing but a stomachache to show for it.

"Make a plan, Arden," I whispered. "What's the plan?"

I couldn't sit here. The windowless room offered security but no fresh air, and whatever I was now, I'd always be a sylph first. I hurried out of the office, nodding at Haroun and making a gesture that I was getting a drink as I passed through the door to the main bar.

Sarah, the redheaded witch we'd hired after she'd been fired from her last place for being the one to Reveal the witches, took one look at me and said, "Rum or sparkling?"

I couldn't help my bitter laugh. "I wish the answer was rum. Sparkling. Thanks."

"Coming right up, boss." She filled a highball and slid it over after dropping a slice of lemon in for me.

"What are you hearing?"

Her green eyes flicked over the bar. It wasn't unusual for it to be busy when we opened at late morning—it was one of the few places in the territory where various factions could meet safely—but it was busier than usual. "Lots of fear."

"I can imagine."

"Lots of people wondering what you're going to do about it."

"What do they think 'it' is?"

She eyed me. "Between the leak from the first responders and your parliament's statement, some are certain it was one of us. A vampire. But who?" She shrugged as she got a rag to wipe up the bar. "Some rumors about that as well."

I frowned. "Does someone in the community know something?"

"Someone always knows something." Her tone was darker than usual. Sarah was our sunshine gal, or she had been. The last few years had been hard for her. She wasn't quite as much of a celebrity as Troy and me, but she'd had her share of trouble. "But Arbiter, the thing that worries me most is the number of people saying it's a frame job."

"Sons of Seth?"

She nodded tightly.

I put that together and barely managed to keep my expression blank. "Sarah, we cannot afford to have Othersiders playing vigilante."

Her gaze was hard when she pulled it off the room and onto me. "Then I hope you find the real culprits soon, Arbiter."

"Working on it." I toasted her and headed back toward my office, walking past it and the door down to the basement sparring studio to stand outside the back door.

Haroun followed me out, leaning against the wall on the other side of the door. The half-elf was one of my favorite bodyguards because he didn't say much unless asked and his calm demeanor helped me stay calm.

I sipped my water and closed my eyes, reaching into the earth underfoot to ground myself. "How are things with the Guard?"

"The usual. Some complaints about a half-elf being in charge, but Etain's handling it."

"Do I need to step in again?"

Haroun's snort made me open my eyes. Amusement had his lips in the smallest curl, although he didn't stop scanning the area as actively as Troy would have. "As funny as it is to see you put high-bloods in their place, you have bigger worries right now. I'll tell Etain you offered though." He sobered. "And hopefully this mess with the vampires will remind everyone that we have to stop fighting each other if we're going to have a chance against the mundanes."

The callstone at my chest warmed before I could answer.

I held up a hand to warn Haroun and then grasped it. "Yeah?"

Duke's voice in my head: "Would you take a meeting with this federal agency?"

"Are they offering?"

"I might be wearing a face I think could convince them."

I grinned, glad to have a djinni in my arsenal again. Their shapeshifting abilities went down to the genetic level, although the match was imperfect or incomplete and their magic remained djinn Aether no matter what their shape.

With a silent prayer that he and Iaret could convince more of their people to actively work with me, I told Duke, "I mean, yes, but what happens if the owner of that face doesn't remember giving that instruction? Or when their security system tells them that they were in two places at once today?"

Delighted malice slithered through the callstone.

"No, Duke. We're not there yet." I was not going to let him kill a mundane when that was what had started my current problem in the first place.

"Then your other option is to let me curse the very expensive equipment being set up for this conference. Tick tock, little bird."

I almost told him no. But I was still pissed with how all of this was playing out. Some of those tweets had been disgusting and vicious. Hate crimes just waiting to happen in real life. "You know what? Curse it with truth. Then change your face and give them my card when they realize shit's not going to plan."

Duke's rich chuckle sent goosebumps rippling over me as his mind pulled away from the callstone.

Haroun shook his head and pulled out his phone, texting Etain, no doubt. "Today just got a hell of a lot more interesting."

Interesting turned out to be an understatement.

Under any other circumstances, it would have been hilarious to watch the den of lying jackals on Capitol Hill squirm as they tried to announce their plans only to find words they hadn't intended spilling from their lips. If they'd chosen noon for its symbolism—the light of truth and righteousness and all that—then I was happy to grace them with it.

Troy loomed behind my chair, arms crossed and everything locked down. He'd made his excuses to the Lyon elves when I'd texted him an update about what I'd done and hightailed it back here. He wasn't exactly happy, but he agreed this was the best we could do with the situation.

As for the politicians...clusterfuck didn't begin to cover it.

"We're here to announce a new federal agency," the All-American white man on camera was saying. "A turning point in our relationship with the residents of this country."

"So far, so good," I muttered.

"Wait for it," Troy said.

The suit on camera said, "This agency has one mandate: to hunt down these supernatural sons of—"

The crowd gasped. The speaker clapped a hand over his mouth, wide-eyed.

I twisted to look up at Troy. "Boom."

Savage amusement shone in his gaze. That man was marked. "In more ways than one."

More suits were hustling down to the podium. One, an older, greyer white man, smiled smoothly at the camera. "Well! You never quite know a person, do ya?"

I smirked. "True enough. Let's see what you have to say, asshole."

"I'm Senator John Wright. What Mr. Rankin meant to say was, we don't know what exactly these vampires and werewolves and such want. We need to be sure everyone is safe."

Troy snorted. "All that means is that he believes what he's saying."

"We need a better understanding of these other people among us. These, 'other siders' as they call themselves." The air quotes he raised made Otherside into a joke rather than a people, and I scowled even as he continued. "To that end, the Bureau for Supernatural Investigation has a mandate to seek, investigate, and if necessary, detain, any person or group suspected of being a supernatural terrorist."

Furious as that made me, I couldn't help a laugh. "Wait, Supernatural Investigation? Sin? Are they seriously calling themselves Sinners? First the Sons of Seth, now we have to deal with honest-to-Goddess Sinners? Or would they prefer BuSI-bodies?" Because there would be bodies on the floor before this was all over if I knew anything about how mundanes worked.

Troy shushed me. "They said terrorist. That means they're going to use the Patriot Act against us."

All my dark amusement fled. "Fuck that."

Troy didn't bother answering. We both knew it was true. Hell, I'd pointed it out to Matthias. The government wouldn't go after half the listed white supremacist hate groups, or any of the human-supremacist groups, but after watching the hard crackdowns on pro-Otherside mundane protests over the last year, we both knew they'd be coming down like the hammer of their god on any collective group of Othersiders before we could do more than squint at a human.

The senator was still talking. "We have a number of plans in place and ready to execute—"

He froze, frowning. That wasn't what he'd meant to say.

"Got ya," I snarled.

Troy was already swiping out a text.

The asshole on camera tried again. "That is, we aim to do whatever we have to do to keep humans safe."

Again, he frowned.

I sneered at the laptop screen. So that was his ploy. He was going to try walking the fine line of liberty and justice for all, when "all" really meant only those he considered people—humans like himself. Maybe even only a certain subset of humans who physically looked like himself, but that might matter less now that they had the monsters under the bed to hunt.

Might. More than likely, it just added another tier to the grotesque layers of privilege in this country.

We were deeply fucked.

With a grating professional smile, the senator cut his losses and wrapped up. "We'll be announcing more in the coming days. Until then, God bless these United States of America. Stay safe. Stay aware. And go with God."

Implying somehow that those of us who weren't human were therefore ungodly. I snarled. I knew more about the gods than any of these assholes. I'd fucking met some of them.

The camera panned past the confused-looking crowd before cutting to some mainstream political commentator, and I muted it, spinning the chair to look up at Troy.

Everything about him—expression, posture, the feeling leaking through the walls in the bond—had dropped into cold, murderous fury. "They're going to come for you."

"I know."

"Then tell me now what I'm allowed to do to get you back. Because I will burn the world to the ground if it means protecting you."

I stared up at the love of my life. Asked myself what the world was worth compared to me. And chose myself so I could choose him. Because Allegra had hinted too many times that if I died, so would he. The Aetheric link between us had bound us too tightly, to the point of being symbionts. We could draw on each other's strength, aura, or magic if necessary. Troy could resist for a short time—we'd learned that the hard way after the Wild Hunt—but if I didn't come back, I didn't have much faith that he could break the link in time to prevent himself from being dragged down with me.

I couldn't allow that. I refused. He'd been through too much.

"Then burn it," I said.

His gaze hardened, the moss-on-sandstone color shifting to shadowed labradorite. "You mean that?"

"I want you to live, Troy. That's my only order to you, High Queen to King. Live. If that means burning the world to save me, then that's what you're worth to me. Every. Fucking. Thing."

His eyes widened, and he rocked on his feet as a drop in the bond said he was shook to his core.

I lifted my chin, daring him to tell me he wasn't worth it. Daring him to defy me as High Queen when I never pulled rank on him.

"Arden—"

I sprang to my feet, caught his jaw in both my hands, and kissed him fiercely.

"You are *mine*, Troy," I said when I pulled away. "I know the greater good matters. I know it does. But *you* are the greater good for me. You are the *only* person who has ever made a choice to help me to their detriment." I closed my eyes, rested my forehead against his, and forced myself to breathe. "Maybe I'm too selfish to make the call. I have chosen myself and my survival at every turn. If what I'm doing—if my survival contributes to what *you* see as the greater good, then burn the world down. We'll start fresh." I swallowed hard. "But if I've stepped wrong? If I'm another Callista? Let me go. Or kill me yourself."

"Arden!" Troy's grip tightened on my arms to the point of pain.

"I mean it. Just do what you can to break free of me first. I don't want you dragged down with me." My throat thickened, and tears stung even to think about it.

He didn't have an answer. The bond was too full of conflicting emotions.

My phone rang. A blocked number showed on the caller ID coming through on the new Google Voice account I'd set up for dealing with mundanes and had printed on the cards I'd given Duke.

Troy moved to my laptop and pulled up some complicated Darkwatch application, tapping a few keys to start a program that would block my location from being traced. He pulled a second device from my drawer and flicked it on. I had no idea what that did, other than add another layer of obfuscation, but he insisted on using it on the occasions when I didn't know who was calling. The magic on the bar wouldn't do any good to turn away a drone strike or a tactical team with GPS coordinates. If police were willing to bomb an entire city block in Philadelphia in 1985 to get at a handful of people, they wouldn't hesitate to take out my bar on its separate parcel of land now.

At Troy's thumbs-up, I cleared my throat, took a breath to compose myself, and answered it. "Finch."

A man's voice, clipped and tense with a Virginia accent, said, "Ms. Finch. I have Senator Wright for you."

I almost—almost—said that I didn't know any Senator Wright, but I'd played my trick. This must be who Duke had given my number to. "I can make time for the senator."

As I waited for the phone to be passed, I looked up into Troy's eyes and watched him become the Darkwatch agent he'd been when he met me. The one who'd thrown me into Jordan Lake with a concrete block tied to my ankles because he had orders and a mission to complete.

"As my queen orders, so shall I obey," he whispered.

And I shivered, knowing that one way or another, our fates, and that of the world, were sealed.

Chapter 15

"**M**s. Finch," the polished, vaguely Southern voice from the press conference said. "The strangest...individual...handed me a card with your name and this number on it."

"My associate grows on you." I leaned against the desk and played with a whiteboard marker. Troy could hear the phone call just fine without me putting it on speaker.

"I'll take your word for it."

A silence fell, one I bit my tongue to stop myself from breaking.

"What are you, Finch?" the senator blurted.

Troy shook his head, and I squeezed his arm to reassure him. "I am what I need to be."

"I see. But you're not human. I've seen the footage from Durham. Quite the mess you made. Fire and lightning and such."

"Not human," I agreed. "Although I should think that's obvious. Nothing human could have stopped the gods."

The Ebon Guard and later the Darkwatch had done their best to scrub my fight with Orion and the gods of the hunt from public record, but there were bound to be videos in places not even motivated elves could find—and that assumed there weren't elves motivated the other way working to provide the same information to my enemies. We still hadn't figured out which way House Ead was going to swing. Obviously, one of those videos had made it into Wright's hands.

"Which means your associate isn't human."

"I imagine you have lots to do, Senator, and so do I. Let's get to it."

"A straight talker. All right, Ms. Finch. You're not human. More than that, you're powerfully non-human."

"I believe we've covered that."

"Look, I don't know what the hell you did to my press conference, but I can't afford that kind of nonsense going into the next election cycle." After a brief hesitation, the senator lowered his voice. "I want to make a deal."

Troy stiffened. *Careful, my love. More cautious than with Matthias, please.*

I sent an affirmative nudge back. "I dunno if that's in the best interest of me and mine. Your good ol' boy seemed pretty dead set against Othersiders. As in, he'd rather see us dead than deal with us fairly. That doesn't seem conducive to making a deal."

The line hung silent for a few heartbeats. Then the senator said, "I'm sure you can understand that an agency like this attracts a certain type."

"Much like your police seem to, I'm sure."

"Now, Ms. Finch, that's not quite fair."

"Isn't it? How many of them were found to be active Klansmen again? Besides, you just admitted there's a 'certain type' interested in joining this new agency."

The senator sighed. "I can see we're not going to find common ground on this."

I punched up the Southern in my accent. "Bless your heart, Senator, but I'm still waiting to hear what 'this' is to begin with. I simply wanted to be sure y'all had my number in case you were tempted to try something foolish."

"And what would be foolish, Ms. Finch?"

I hated when people kept using my name. It was unnatural, a contrived way to create false intimacy or indicate that they were paying attention or that you were important. A thing that smarmy businesspeople and too-clever politicians did and idiots fell for. In short, it was the sign of a liar who wanted you to believe they were telling you the truth.

Diplomacy, Arden. Troy sent a near-smothering wave of pressure to counter my urge to snap at the man.

I took a deep breath in. Held it. Let it go. Chose my words carefully. "Foolish would be me saying anything that could be construed as a threat. I have no interest in harming mundanes or in allowing those people I represent to do so. But since we were talking about you and your shiny new agency, foolish would be pre-emptively assuming Othersiders mean harm."

Wright spluttered a laugh. "You can't seriously expect me to believe that *vampires* don't mean humans harm?"

I squeezed my eyes shut at the near-identical question Detective Rice had originally asked me and answered much the same as I had then. "Vampires have had to join the twenty-first century to blend in. Most are big on consent. We have rules, Senator, rules we follow in addition to those of the society we live in. Killing mundanes draws attention we don't want."

The senator pounced, like he'd been waiting for that opening. "Do tell? Then what's this about a dead man with fang marks outside the gate of the Raleigh governor's mansion?"

It was my turn to hesitate as I debated how truthful to be and how to speak what truth I was willing to give him. "Much like the humans, we have certain parties who are struggling with our new reality and acting out."

"Acting out? A man is dead, and you call it acting out?"

"Six Othersiders and twice that many mundanes have been killed by human anti-Otherside movements in the last year, mostly by the Sons of Seth," I snapped. "If you're happy to give those actions and the resulting deaths a name that makes you feel better, I'll use the same."

Troy gave me a hard look. *Reel it in, Arden.*

I pressed my lips together and fisted my free hand to wrestle down a spark of lightning, wanting to punch Troy for prodding me on this but glad he was here. I'd learned to come out swinging to defend myself if I was discovered for what I was. He'd learned to keep his head down and look harmless to do the same. We—Otherside—were going to have to do something in the middle to make it through this.

A heavy sigh on the other end. "There's a long road ahead if we're to have order, Ms. Finch."

"And peace," I said.

"Peace. An interesting word. Are we at war?"

"Honestly, Senator? Some days it feels like it. Every day, I receive reports of homes and businesses run by Othersiders, even suspected Othersiders, being attacked. Vandalized, windows broken, burned. And like I said, I'm trying to tell my people that we will get through this, even as we and our supporters are being killed. Their murderers walk after sham trials with openly sympathetic juries."

"I don't control the justice system, Ms. Finch."

"And I don't control all of Otherside. Just my little corner down here in North Carolina. All I can say is, we've been watching over the years. We've seen how the government deals with school shootings and domestic terrorists and extrajudicial police murder. Frankly, my people don't have much hope of seeing justice, and we know it. We've watched support plummet in the last year, even among our so-called allies as they get tired or bored and move on to something else. That, more than anything, is where we are both going to have trouble."

"How's that?"

"You've got an election year coming up. I've got a slim margin of control over an influential area and a number of people with voices others are currently inclined to listen to. If we don't keep both our peoples happy and reinvigorate our supporters..." I trailed off and let him fill in the blanks, even though the whole conversation felt icky.

"I can see we have a similar understanding of the shape of things, Ms. Finch. How about this? I'll take what we've discussed here today back to my committee. You take my willingness to have a conversation back to your people. We can talk again in a few days."

"What committee would that be?"

"A confidential one."

"No deal then."

Troy poked me in the bond, and I poked him back with a finger. I had a feeling. The Sight.

"Be reasonable, Ms. Finch."

"I can be reasonable. What I'm not finna be is naive. I spent too long trusting that people would tell me the truth eventually and nearly died for it on more than one occasion."

The line hung silent, and I let it. He wouldn't have reached out to me if he didn't need something. Not want, *need*. For better or worse, I was the most powerful public Othersider. He knew that, while parts of his base might well want to see every Othersider lined up and shot, the public would probably be turned off it. Eventually. Vietnam but on home soil. Maybe even international observers.

Or worse for all of us, Otherside would go to war. We'd kept to the shadows up to now because the mundanes outnumbered us as a whole and because my little alliance was unusual in our willingness to back factions not our own. We were too insular and too jealous of our territories and claims. If the mundanes turned on the vampires, the elves or the weres would sit back and wait for the territory to be cleared out and vice versa, a pattern that would repeat until it was too late, given how reluctant the rest of Otherside was to get on board with my new program.

That said, while there weren't many of us, Sherman and his march had nothing on what a pissed-off primordial elemental could do all on her own. If the gods thought I was enough to remake the world, I'd be damned if I let the humans think they could walk all over me and mine.

Another hefty sigh, this one sounding irritated as fuck. "I will see about getting you security clearance. Cards on the table, Ms. Finch. I need an ally in Otherside. I'd like that person to be you."

I stiffened, even as Troy did the same. We frowned at each other.

"Is that so?" I asked cautiously. "Given that video you've seen, that seems to be a risk."

"It is," Wright said bluntly. "Some of those around me would say that we don't negotiate with terrorists and that you are one."

I flashed cold and then hot. We'd been right about the Patriot Act.

"At the same time," the senator continued, "you are the only clear leader we've managed to identify among the supernaturals other than the vampire Maria, and you seem to outrank her. Furthermore, I don't know what on God's green earth that giant snake you killed was or where those monsters came from the October before last, but I can sell you and your people as our very own superheroes." He paused. "If you work with me."

Troy rolled his eyes in open disbelief and flipped his hand in a "wrap it up" gesture.

"Well, you know how to reach me if you get that clearance. Good talk, Senator Wright."

I hung up, setting the phone down to scrub my hands over my face, then went up on my toes to wrap my arms around Troy's shoulders and kiss him. "Thanks. For being here and for keeping me grounded."

One of his hands slid around me. The other switched off the little scrambling device then stopped the tracker-jamming app before joining the embrace. "This isn't exactly what I had in mind when you made me king. But..."

"What?" I said when he trailed off.

Flustered anxiety rippled through the bond. "It's what I'm supposed to be doing. What I'm good at."

I grinned against his chest then tilted my head up to kiss the corner of his jaw. "Why are you anxious about that?"

He hesitated before answering. "Once we had a guest at Keithia's mansion. They watched me lead the training cohort. Told Keithia I was a born leader." The bond soured. "She had me beaten for showing off. Other days, it'd be because I wasn't pushing hard enough. Everything I did was wrong. Even when it was right."

I froze.

In the eighteen months or so since we'd gotten together, I'd slowly learned pieces of Troy's story. He'd had the hell beaten out of him on a regular basis as part of his "training," starting around the time his father had been tortured and exiled for the so-called crime of bonding to his mother and continuing up through our initial acquaintance.

I'd unknowingly killed some of the people responsible before learning all this, so there was that, but it didn't magically erase the nightmares that plagued him or the coping mechanisms he'd developed. Or the intensification of the inborn desire to please a queen I'd found most elven males exhibited. Not only was he predisposed to take care of me—his queen and mate—but it'd become ingrained behavior as a matter of survival, even when it was to his detriment.

We were working on it. Not always in the healthiest ways—I was a private investigator, not a therapist—but the Aetheric bond between us helped. He knew where my head was at most of the time. Knew I loved him beyond reason and had long since forgiven him for following orders and drowning me not long after we'd met thanks to what he'd done to make amends. He was still moody as fuck on top of being as stubborn as I was, but he let his considerable yet well-controlled temper show more. I took that as the badge of honor that it was. He wasn't allowed it before, so he'd buried it except for passive-aggression and stubbornness. He wasn't allowed much of anything beyond his duty and his oaths. Emotions, relationships, love, grace, dreams, all stripped or withheld from him. It'd made him a particularly effective commando and sometime assassin in the Darkwatch, and he was still terrifyingly skilled in those roles. But he was, under the violence and the murders and behind the walls, self-sacrificing to a fault, deeply committed to doing the right thing, and undyingly devoted to me.

It'd taken me a while to see it. He'd nearly died before I had.

"It's okay, Arden. I'm okay." Troy squeezed me. "I'm just glad..." He broke off.

I waited, letting him order his thoughts.

"I would never wish for some of what's happened, to either of us or the Triangle. But if it hadn't happened, I'd still be counting down the years until forty."

"Why forty?" I frowned. Troy was thirty-one years old, thirty-two in May. Forty was maybe a quarter of his full lifespan, maybe less given he was closer to what pureblood elves used to be before they'd started interbreeding with humans to reduce their power and better stay beneath the notice of mundanes.

"I always assumed Keithia would have me killed by then, since I'd made it clear I wouldn't be studded out to breed like a dog. Better that than her turning me into my father."

Shock hit me hard enough that I completely dropped my shields, and my power signature flooded the room.

The door creaked as Haroun stuck his head in. "Everything okay, majesties?"

"Fine," I said faintly, not taking my eyes off Troy.

The door shut again. Troy just looked at me, letting me see some of the deeply buried pain still hiding in him before he boxed it up and put it away.

"We have more important things to think about," he said. "I only told you because..." He sighed. "I don't know why I told you. The anniversary of his exile is coming up. It's been on my mind. I needed to say it out loud. So I can stop thinking about it."

Short sentences. He wasn't okay, for all he was holding himself together and saying he was. He'd had a phase like this late last winter and into early summer, keeping everything in order publicly and then sitting on the deck alone for hours at a stretch, brooding. He hadn't explained it, and I hadn't pushed, too focused on pulling him out of the pit I could sense him falling into however he'd let me, terrified that I was going to lose him to the demons his family had planted in his past. Looked like I had my answer as to which particular ones came for him at this time of year. That he was telling me now rather than bottling it in and brooding alone said how far we'd come, but that didn't mean he was all good. Not by a long shot.

I closed my eyes and squeezed him, pouring as much love as I could into the bond. "Troy, I will *never* punish you for being what you're meant to be. I'm a pain in the ass sometimes when you're right and I don't want you to be, but I'm so, so grateful that you are who you are. That you've had the training you've had and that you're my opposite. My balance. I love you. I love you so much. I hope you always know that."

"I know, cariñamí. I know. It's why I love you. Part of it. And why I even considered entertaining your request earlier. It's why I'll do as you've asked if it comes to it."

"I don't want it to come to it." I ran my hand up and down his back, offering what comfort I could. "I'll try to be better about defensive reactions."

He just kissed the top of my head.

We'd both try to be our best for the other. It was part of why we worked as counterbalances and were so effective as a team. But we were in uncharted territory, not just for ourselves but for Otherside.

Me as the first primordial elemental since ancient times.

Troy as the first elven king since Atlantis.

Vampires breaking the Détente and killing publicly for the first time in centuries.

Mundanes preparing to hunt us all down with the backing of the federal government.

Elected officials wanting to use Othersiders as their personal team of superheroes to win re-election.

And the trickster gods waiting somewhere at the margins, looking for some kind of return on a gift I had no knowledge of them giving.

Chapter 16

A crowd was waiting for us when Troy, Haroun, and I made our way to the main bar.

I pulled up and barely managed not to do my usual startled blink. Zanna and a lanky fae I took to be a gremlin were on opposite sides of the bar, chatting over beers. The Lyon observers were in the big corner booth, waiting for Troy and me from the way their attention sharpened as we emerged. Noah was in another corner, Ximena scowled from the far end of the bar, and Laurel was trying to keep a low profile as far away from the Lyon elves as she could. To cap it all off, Sarah and Hope were in what looked like an intense conversation out front. The usual regulars and dealers were gone. Everyone here was somebody, on some level.

All conversation stopped as everyone noted our arrival. Hope glanced through the window, spotted us, and pointed. She and Sarah came back inside.

The fuck? I sent Troy.

I don't know. The observers were going to stay at the old Sequoyah mansion at Jordan Lake.

I shivered at the reminder that the place not only still existed but was actively being used. Leith Sequoyah's Redcap conspiracy was what had started the path to where I was now, and I didn't like that house. I'd killed him there. Become a killer there. Become the Arbiter there. Or at least taken the first step.

"I have a feeling y'all are here to see me, him, or both of us together," I said as blandly as I could. "Who's here because of the mundane press conference?"

Everyone raised their hands.

"Right. Anyone here for private business?"

Everyone raised their hands again.

I decided to handle it like I would interviewing witnesses as a private investigator. Divide and conquer based on urgency, vulnerability, and utility to the case. The case, right now, being the vampire murders that were still the top of my to-do list with fucking Matthias not answering me.

"Mundane update first then, since you're all here and nobody else is. Right?" I counted again to make sure we had a rep from every faction as Zanna nodded. Elves, weres, witches, fae, elementals, vampires. Noah would update Doc Mike, so that would cover human sensitives. We just needed one of the djinn.

I gripped my callstone and thought hard, keeping my voice in my head so that only I—and Troy—could hear it. "Duke? There's been a development. Do you or Iaret want to come for an informal parliament meeting?"

"Shame to miss the fuckery going on here, but I suppose it helps to be informed."

With an auratic tug, Duke used his blood tie to me to orient himself and shimmered into the room. He bowed his head, and a moment later, Iaret phased in beside him.

She grinned to see everyone assembled, and although she took her preferred mundane shape—a small, slim woman with blue-black skin, tight curls hugging her scalp, and an elegant bearing—her eyes stayed the sparking fire opals that were natural to her. "Arden, dear! Lovely to see you. Staying in trouble, I hope?"

The Lyon elves tensed and reached for weapons.

Troy held up a hand. "Hold."

When our guests kept their hands on whatever they were hiding at hip, waist, and ankle, he stepped between them and the djinn and let his power signature blow through the bar in an icy wave that dragged frozen fingernails down the spine of everyone in the room. His voice was almost as cold. "I said hold. You're here because we do things differently in this demesne. One of those differences is our alliance, which includes the djinn. If you want to attack them, you go through me."

Duke and Iaret smirked behind Troy. Iaret blew a kiss, one everyone in the room could feel the sharp edges of. Neither djinni liked high-blood elves, with Troy a minor exception, mostly because he'd helped free Iaret and worked with all of us to stop the Wild Hunt.

For their part, elves did what they could to kill djinn almost as enthusiastically as they usually did elementals—Troy included.

He'd been the one to kill Grimm, more because she'd been trying to kill me.

I got distracted for half a second, wondering if even then, Troy had started falling for me, then pushed the thought aside and moved forward to stand shoulder to shoulder with him. "Not just through my king. Through me as well."

"I love when they're pissed," Iaret said behind us. "It's Chaos incarnate. You can *feel* the universe shifting off its axis. Delicious."

The Lyon elves tensed. Then the oldest, the one who looked like she could be one of Iaret's cousins—Samarre—eased her hand away from whatever was under her jacket.

"Apologies, majesties," she said in her French accent. Then to my surprise, she inclined her head. "My queen—my former queen—taught us better, and we are guests here. Of course we'll oblige."

The others followed her lead when she gave them a hard look, their movements slow and their gestures tight.

Iaret danced forward, testing them. "Well, that's no fun."

"Iaret," Duke said soothingly, "remember our little king here has star iron and he's used it before. Maybe don't piss him off, hm? Besides, we like him."

Iaret turned, tilting her head to consider Troy. "I suppose we do. He did help us with the Wild Hunt." She grinned to show black teeth as sharp as any mako shark's, one of the small similarities the djinn shared with elves, minus the color. "*That was fun.* Arden, dear, I hope if you're calling us all together again there will be something equally as fun on the table."

I did my best to hold in a sigh. Iaret had been trapped in a smoky quartz enhydro crystal formed of her own soul for a good thirty years. She'd come out of it alive but not entirely sane when I, backed by Troy and Duke, had freed her from it. Some days were better than others.

This was maybe not one of the better ones.

I met the eyes of everyone else in the bar. When nobody else seemed inclined to make trouble, I said, "Round on the house, Zanna, if you please."

Troy gave the elves and the djinn a last warning look before stepping away to help Zanna and me serve the group. Sarah hustled to the back, re-emerging with snack platters of meats, cheeses, and pickles.

Salt, booze, and oaths, the foundation of peace in Otherside.

Ximena's approving nod when I placed her usual in front of her reassured me. I'd found the werecats bigger on service leadership than the rest of Otherside, so it wasn't a surprise but it was satisfying. They had high standards, standards based on what one did for the community in whatever capacity they were able, rather than who one was or how powerful they were. The wereleopards and werejaguars might be the smallest factions, both locally and in the United States Otherside community, but their focus on character and action made me work a little harder for their respect since it could and had to be earned rather than commanded.

When everyone had a drink, I said, "As we all come here in allyship, let us leave thus."

Everyone in the room echoed me, and we drank deeply.

"Welcome to our guests, representatives of Houses Desmarais, Proulx, and Lavigne from Lyon, France, and..." I turned to lift my eyebrows at our gremlin friend.

"Call me Ruprecht. Gremlin. He/him." He smiled slyly, blue eyes peering from behind a fall of dark blond hair like he was scoping out possible targets for mischief.

"Ruprecht the gremlin. Welcome. Thank you all for coming." Not that I'd invited them, but courtesy never hurt. The bond shared Troy's approval, and I relaxed a little more, despite the difficulty of the subject. "You've all seen the press conference by now?"

Nods and affirmations.

"Fine. You have Duke to thank for the unusually honest nature of that event." I nodded to Duke, who smiled almost as mischievously as Ruprecht had. "And for the fact that after the presser, I received a call from someone involved. This stays confidential to faction heads and parliament reps." I fixed everyone with a hard look and let lightning crackle over me to make the point.

The Lyon elves reached for weapons again before Troy's glare quelled them and Samarre reluctantly waved them down. Much like my first meeting with Allegra, even nominally friendly elves got spooked by seeing their ancestral boogeyman in the flesh. Doubly so when powers were on display.

When everyone was as settled as they were going to get, I shared as much as I was comfortable sharing, conscious of the fact that the Lyon elves would take the intel back to Europe and Ruprecht would take his back to the fae king after helping us. "The feds are looking here for leaders in Otherside. Thanks to the Wild Hunt, Troy and I are on their radar."

We exchanged a look and I held myself back from adding, *for better or worse.*

Ximena's lip curled. "Leaders for what?"

"I'm not sure yet. If the djinn are free, maybe we can find out."

Iaret grinned. "Oh! A mission!"

I turned to her. "No deaths please, but feel free to make deals if you want."

Her eyes narrowed. "I don't need your permission for that."

"What you do reflects on me and impacts my ability to keep all of us informed and safe." I let those words hang for a moment. Everyone needed to understand that. "It happens that I think having a few US government officials in Othersiders' pockets might help us with leverage later. Besides"—I grinned, trying to get her to go along with something more than threats—"think of how much chaos and opportunity it would bring to have the US government in your pocket rather than dead. I'm surprised you haven't gotten more involved there."

Iaret's fire-opal gaze sparked. "We've been busy with Council business. But yes, that does sound fun. Very well. Deals only. No deaths. Unless we have to protect ourselves."

Or get bored, Troy said grimly in my head, ever the realist. *I'll let the Captain know, just in case we need to do a cover-up.*

I answered him and Iaret both. "Thank you. Anything else?"

Noah rose. "What about Detective Rice? Did he know about this?"

"I don't know what the detective did or did not know, but I have a strong suspicion that he was aware and that it influenced the short deadline we have as much as the need to keep the city from descending into riots again does."

He shook his head and scowled. "We're being outmaneuvered. This is unacceptable."

Troy said, "We're a handful of people going against multiple government and law enforcement agencies as well as our own people. Don't let your personal stake in this influence your judgment, Noah."

"Personal stake." The vampire sneered as the visiting elves watched with raised brows. "Shall we talk about your personal stake? And the Arbiter's?"

Troy and I just looked at him. Noah brought up our relationship like a dagger every time he was unhappy, never mind that his mistress was dating Allegra and he had a necromancer boyfriend. Noah loved to stand in his glass house and chuck stones.

I was bored of it but tried to keep my tone light. "Which is, as always, why I'm acting as Arbiter and not High Queen in non-House matters. Believe me when I say Troy and I have no problem keeping each other honest, when it comes to it."

Behind us, Haroun coughed. When I glanced at him, he flushed a deep red. The poor man had probably accidentally seen the sexual aftermath of one of those disagreements on at least one occasion.

"Sorry," he said.

By this time, the Lyon elves weren't even bothering to try keeping their expressions neutral and were openly watching all of this like I'd grown horns and Troy had a tail.

I clapped twice to cover my own embarrassment. "Okay. That's all I've got on the situation with the human feds. Noah, let's step back to my office so you can get home and get to bed. Laurel next. Everyone else, I'll see you in the order you arrived, unless you have information about the murder in Raleigh."

Nobody protested so I headed back to my office, leaving Troy to decide what he'd do. He stayed, probably trying to counterbalance Noah's implications of undue influence.

When the door closed behind us, I sat and gestured for Noah to as well.

He took the chair opposite and leaned on the desk, intensity crackling in his gaze. "We haven't found the killer yet."

"How close are you?"

"How in the nine hells should I know? We need you to stall for more time."

"You drove up here in daylight to tell me that?"

Noah reached in a pocket and slammed something on my desk. "I drove up in daylight to give you this."

An odd little implement rested on the desk, a piece of metal with two thick, pointed prongs and a handle.

It was obvious what it was—something to mimic a vampire bite, although it would be imperfect, given vampire teeth were more like conical wedges, not the mostly round thing in front of me.

"Where did you find that?" I asked.

"In a gutter near where one of the other four bodies was found."

I frowned. "Are you saying not all of the bodies were vampire kills?"

"That is exactly what I'm saying."

"Were they all drained?"

"No."

"How many were?"

"The one at the governor's mansion and three others."

"Leaving two that weren't us."

"'Us.'" Noah narrowed his eyes at me, as though he didn't trust that I was considering myself alongside the vampires. "Yes. And Michael can prove it. But to do so will force him to say that four *were* us."

"Fuck." I leaned back in my chair. "So, are Matthias and Santiago working with another group, mundane or Otherside? Or is this just some real bad luck?"

"Whatever it is, we need more time. Take that to Rice."

I bit my tongue to stop from asking why he didn't do it, since the drive down the road to a Raleigh PD station was much shorter than the one up to me in North Durham. None of us could trust that an Othersider, especially a vampire, who put themselves in the hands of law enforcement would walk back out again, at least not without glamour, which would blow the tentative truce like a powder keg.

"I'll take it," I said. "Assuming I'll be able to move in Raleigh without pissing off Maria all over again."

"Thank you." He gave me a steady look. "I know you and Michael are old friends. But Arden...please stay away from him until this is over. He's under a lot of pressure as it is, and you don't have a low profile anymore."

The implication that I was a danger to Doc Mike hurt. But I couldn't deny it was true. Mouth tight, I nodded.

As Noah rose to leave, his phone rang. "Mistress."

My hearing had gotten better as my power grew, so I caught Maria's terse question about his location.

"In Durham. With the Arbiter, delivering the evidence I found this morning."

He put me on speaker when she insisted. "We're listening."

Maria sounded furious. "Arden, did you speak to Matthias after you left here?"

"Yes. Did he finally get around to supplying the name and whereabouts of our bad actor?"

"Hekate *damn* you. I just got a call from Santiago. He's pissed off about something Matthias said, that *you* said, and declaring open war on the Carolinas demesne in general and the Raleigh coterie in particular."

I gritted my teeth. "He did that when he and Matthias killed mundanes and left them for the public to find."

"I was handling this, Arden!"

"No, Maria. You weren't." Tired of Noah and Maria both, no matter how much I liked them as friends, I let my voice chill and fixed Noah with a stare so he'd know I blamed him equally as her second. "There was one simple fucking solution. You refused to take it at any point in the last year and a half, up to and including this morning. You were being selfish and insisting on holding onto not only Luz and Giuliano but their entire entourage."

"As is my right."

"As would be your right if you weren't part of an alliance. How many times do we have to go round this carousel?"

"So it's all my fault."

The bite in her words felt like it should have drawn blood, but it only made me angrier. "Oh no, it's definitely mine as well. I should have insisted on sending at least some of the entourage back months ago. But I took a fucking vacation after dying to stop the Wild fucking Hunt instead of handling my responsibilities and was too much of a coward to stand up to a friend."

A questioning nudge curled through the bond from Troy, and I dropped my walls enough that he could tell I was physically fine but furious.

Do I need to come back there?

No. I'll explain in a minute.

Maria hadn't filled the silence I'd left explaining things to Troy.

Noah, at least, finally had the grace to look ashamed. As her second, he should have been pushing for the same. The power boost they got from drinking from Othersiders—including other vampires—had come with too high a price to pay.

Now all of us would have to pay it for them.

Chapter 17

Diplomacy. I had to salvage this diplomatically, or the alliance was fucked. "Maria."

"What, Arden? What?"

"Noah can fill you in on the details, but the mundane feds reached out. They want to talk. But I'm on shaky ground right now. I need one less front to fight on. Help me end this. Give Matthias and Santiago *something*."

"I can't. It's not just their blood I need. If I can't root out their saboteurs and secure the territory, they'll see me as weak. There will be more attacks, Arden. More coup attempts. If not by them, then by other city masters. Maybe even the Modernists among my own people."

Setting aside the idea that she saw the interlopers as saboteurs rather than murderers, I said, "We will help you with that. I know Troy will. *You* know he will. You two have been working together for what, nearly a decade now? His sister loves you. He and I both care about you and Noah and Doc Mike. Trust us."

"It's a big ask."

"I know. But you trusted me to help you beat them in the first place, right?"

Maria snorted, and there was a rustling sound like she'd sat down. "Once upon a time, I trusted Torsten to save me. And I lived. Well. I didn't burn at the stake for delivering babies and creating herbal medicinals. I just spent the next hundred years as a plaything to be drunk from at his or Aron's whim. Even when I proved myself clever and useful, they took advantage of me. So yes, in a pinch, I trust you. But I have lived too long to be comfortable letting things get to that pinch."

Noah's expression was grim. This was the first I'd heard about any of Maria's past beyond her nearly being burned as a witch during the Inquisition, so I assumed her telling me was an indication that she wasn't in a good headspace.

I took a breath then another. Tried to push my frustration down. This could all be so. Fucking. Simple. But Othersiders had long lives, and all the trauma that went along with it stayed nearly as fresh as the day it'd occurred unless we found solace in madness, which led swiftly to death.

I couldn't blame her. But my frustration was also valid.

"Think about it," I said. "We have a few hours left until sunset and the end of the thirty-six-hour window Rice gave us. I can't get on a plane and burn down Miami or New York without starting World War Three, but if there's something else I can do, tell me. Please just remember you're part of something bigger than your coterie now, and a federal agency with a mandate to control Otherside is breathing down my neck. I cannot fight on two fronts."

"I'll think on it," she said after a few heartbeats. "Noah, be a dear and see if you can get the good doctor to stall a little longer."

"Yes, Mistress."

The call ended, and I met Noah's gaze. "Talk her around, Noah. Please. I know you're frustrated with me. But you and I both know she's held them long enough."

"I know." His mood had flipped from anger to tired sympathy, not unusual for the mercurial vampire even if it made my head spin some days. Then he was back to wary. "More importantly, I know that if she doesn't let them go and harm comes to your House, you won't hold Troy back from retaliating. Even though you could."

"That's right. I won't. You can call that unfair or playing sides all you want, but it'd be his right as King, even if I wasn't High Queen. My job as Arbiter is to keep the balance. If Maria allows it to be broken, I won't hobble Troy from doing what he thinks best to reset it."

"Fine. I'll talk to her, *if* you promise me that you'll shield Michael from any fallout."

"Of course I will. I already promised you that. He's still my friend, Noah, and he's just trying to do his job trapped in the middle of a shitty situation. I've been there. I don't like him being in the same place."

After a long stare, he gave me a last nod, pulled up his hood, and slipped out.

Not quite ready to face Laurel, I examined the thought that'd started bugging me when Noah brought up Doc Mike. The test case. For Verve Health's new test, whatever it was, the one Noah had mentioned when he'd swung by my house. All of this was too shittily convenient: six dead mundanes, all public after almost two years of zero confirmed vampire deaths. But not all of them done by vampires.

An uncomfortable idea formed in my mind, and I sat bolt upright.

Troy.

After a moment, he sent back a distracted, *Yes?*

What if the feds are behind some of the deaths?

Surprise rippled through. A minute later, he stalked into my office, shutting the door firmly behind him. "What do you mean the feds?"

"I mean, Noah says not all of the deaths were vampires." I pointed at the little implement still resting on my desk. As Troy picked it up and sniffed it, I added, "There is no fucking way that in the same week, a federal agency is ready to go on the drop of a hat, a new test that can hypothetically identify Othersiders is ready, and we have multiple high-profile murders."

He scowled. "Too many people handled this for me to get a clean scent. But you think an Othersider is working with the mundanes? And that this was all orchestrated?"

I nodded. "I know it sounds like a conspiracy theory—"

"But it makes sense. And you seem to be one of Fate's focal points."

Making a mental note to dig into what that meant later, I summoned a zephyr to get the air in the room moving and let off some energy. "So that leaves us with the question of, assuming an Othersider is helping the feds, are they local? Or is it someone in New York or Miami trying to force Maria's hand and benefiting twice over by making government contacts?"

"Matthias sounded surprised earlier."

"Surprised about the agency? Or surprised that our information network is good enough that I knew before the trap was sprung?"

"Fair question." His gaze unfocused as he thought through it. "I can have Etain divert some of the Ebon Guard's resources to investigating it, but that leaves us with fewer resources to monitor the Richmond Conclave. I can't figure out what House Ead is up to. Also, continuing to push on this will piss off Maria."

I winced. "She's already pissed. Matthias refused to play ball. He called Santiago. Santiago called Maria and declared war."

He stared at me. "You could have led with that."

"Sorry. Had an idea. But I pushed Maria—diplomatically—to just end this and give them back their people. Noah will work on her."

"What was your stick?"

"Noah knows that if we have all-out war and it impacts House Solari, you're within your rights as king to take whatever action you deem necessary."

Troy hesitated, studying me. "And you'd allow it?"

"Like I told him, my job as Arbiter is to keep the balance. If that means getting out of your way..." I shrugged. "You're the royal. I care about building the House back up, but I can't sit back on my responsibilities as Arbiter any longer. I took the power. I have to use it. And that means letting you do you."

Joy flashed in the bond, warming me as he grinned and stole a kiss. "If someone had told me I'd find a queen who gave me what you have, I wouldn't have believed them. Have I mentioned I love you?"

"Never hurts to hear it again."

He leaned closer to whisper in my ear. "I love you." The gold in his eyes sparked as he walled off a thought, but he just smiled when I narrowed my eyes at him. "Let's get Laurel in here, before the Lyon elves give her a heart attack."

I spent the next hour and a half listening to everyone's factional concerns about the events of the last few days, trying to suppress my anxiety to get back to the case. The elementals and werecats had the usual concerns about being outed with the increased scrutiny we were all now under. Laurel wanted additional assurances about the intentions of the Lyon elves, which I gave with the usual caveat: the territory was open to anyone peaceable, and they'd be bound by the same rules as the rest of us.

The witches wanted to negotiate using the Ebon Guard for defensive surveillance again. I sent them back out to talk to Troy. Etain technically answered to me, but I had to be consistent in how I was handling elven matters. Treading such a fine line with Raleigh meant staying hands off and leaving it to Troy to coordinate the use of elven resources with Etain and Omar, especially given what he said about the Richmond Conclave.

With the djinn handling the feds, Ruprecht was freed up to be backup for any local situations in the event we couldn't work things out in Raleigh. I offered him lodging and all the beer he could drink in exchange for staying on retainer, an offer he was delighted to take—especially when I told him the vehicles and technical devices of the Sons of Seth were his to fuck with as he pleased, if he could ferret them out. It was about time I had an effective non-lethal option for dealing with them that wouldn't pull resources from the Ebon Guard or the Darkwatch, and a motivated gremlin was the personification of Mercury retrograde. Maybe it would keep them too busy to bother us while I sorted out the rest of this mess.

Duke and Iaret had gone back to their mischief disguised as surveillance, which left our guests for last. Troy came back in for that part, having left me to deal with the rest solo for the same reason I'd sent the witches to him.

My office was a little small for the four elves now crowding it, or maybe that was just my general discomfort and wariness with unfamiliar elves.

Samarre and the other elfess took the chairs on the other side of my desk. The remaining elf leaned against the wall next to the door, probably mirroring Haroun on the other side, while Troy settled into a parade rest at my side. As always, our guests took careful note of how Troy and I interacted—or didn't. I don't know what they were expecting, but it never quite seemed to be what we gave them.

"Majesties," Samarre said. "Thank you for seeing us."

"Thank you for your patience." I offered a small professional smile. "You've come at an interesting time."

"So it seems. High Queen, may we be frank?"

"Of course. I appreciate honesty and directness."

Despite her question, Samarre glanced again between Troy and me then exchanged another look with her triad. "The situation here isn't what we'd expected at all."

Troy shifted slightly, cueing me to let him answer. "How so, Samarre?"

Again, the looks, like once more we'd thrown them off.

"That, for one," she said. "A High Queen who not only permits a king to live but sets him as an equal in uncertain territory? Allows him to speak as counsel?"

However that was intended, it irritated me. I took a breath and smoothed it down before Troy could poke me though.

"I'm not in the habit of limiting people," I said, "let alone killing them for being what they were born as. Aside from being a shitty thing to do, it's a terrible waste of talent. I need the best to get us through the current upheaval. It costs me nothing to say Troy is it."

The other elfess, Jacinthe, tilted her head and studied Troy. "We've heard reports that she nearly died after the Wild Hunt. You could have been rid of her and ruled solo. You're certainly strong enough, my king."

This time it was Troy who had to rein himself in, keeping his expression blank and his voice flat while the bond roiled. "I would rather die myself."

"Because you're bonded to her," Samarre said.

"Does the reason matter?" Troy replied.

Samarre and Jacinthe looked at Luc, their third.

He shrugged. "I never gave into the temptation. There was no reason that mattered enough for me to risk the punishment. That there was for him, that he took the punishment and she came for him..." Another shrug. "They have my vote."

I frowned. "What are we voting on, exactly?"

I refrained from asking how the fuck they knew so much about our personal history. We hadn't told anyone to keep it a secret, partly because rumors might help accomplish Troy's goals to reform elven society. That might well be what'd happened here, but it was still weird to me after living so privately for the vast majority of my life.

Samarre leaned back in her chair and steepled her fingers. "How much do you know about the situation with Lydia Desmarais?"

Troy crossed his arms. "Half-human daughter of the House's heir-apparent. Exiled here, under my grandmother's auspices, about six years ago. Took up with a vampire vagabond and caused some trouble with the local Houses before falling off the map with him."

"Those are the basics, yes." Samarre sighed heavily, looking much older as she gathered her thoughts. "Lydia's mother was disowned for staying with her human lover. The girl's father. All the same, there was no one else to be heir when Princess Delphine was fatally poisoned. I was among those dispatched here to bring Lydia back to reclaim her place as heir."

Surprise flickered through the bond. Troy asked, "A half-elf as heir to a high House?"

That answered one of the questions I'd had when this originally came up—why a delegation had been needed to recall an exiled half-elf. I smirked. "So I'm not the only one?"

Troy shot me a look. "You're you, Arden. Half-human low-bloods are far more common. And there should have been someone else—a sibling or a sister-cousin—to step in as heir."

"Yes," Samarre said, eyes glittering with something dangerous. "There should have been. And would have been, had our queen not started murdering them all in paranoid fear that they were a threat."

It wasn't hard to make the jump of logic. "You think your queen had her own daughter poisoned?"

"I'm her knight. *Was* her knight. I was very good at my job, and there were very few people who would have been able to achieve it. Queen Blaise is one of them."

Troy frowned. "That's quite the accusation against the High Queen whose auspices you're supposedly here under."

Jacinthe smiled grimly as she shrugged. "And yet we are here. Admittedly with an ulterior motive."

Stiffening, I tilted my chin up. "What's that?" I asked coldly.

"Not just observation. Also a request. Sanctuary."

"Sanctuary," Troy repeated when I stared at them in consternation. "What does that mean to you? For how many and on what terms?"

"For now, just us three but with plans to bring six more. In exchange for permission to settle and find employment in the territory, we offer our services. All of us are fully Darkwatch-trained, even if we took other paths to service."

I held up a hand. "Hang on. You want me to consider allowing settlement of a triple triad of Darkwatch-trained elves who have only now admitted an ulterior motive, after guesting in my territory for two days? While we're in the middle of handling a serious mundane situation?"

Samarre nodded, and her gaze flicked to Troy before coming back to me. "We understand it's highly unusual and that you in particular have an understandably bad history with our kind."

"That's a damn understatement," I snapped.

She nodded. "That's why we're also prepared to offer information to sweeten the deal."

"What kind of information?" Troy asked.

All three of our guests sank into a deadly stillness as they focused on Troy, and Samarre said, "We know where your father is."

Chapter 18

I had to shield hard to block the backwash of Troy's emotions into me before their intensity could spark my magic.

Despite his inner turmoil, Troy made no outward reaction beyond the chill in his voice. "You're going to want to be very careful of what you say next."

They said nothing at all as Samarre reached slowly into her jacket, pulled out her phone, and tapped it before sliding it across the desk. "Proof of life."

The dark, grainy photo could, if I squinted, look like an older version of Troy, gone almost fully grey.

He wasn't convinced. Or didn't want to be. "That's not proof of anything." When Samarre tried to speak, he held up a hand. "And even if it was, I won't be bought. Not at the cost of the demesne's security. Certainly not at risk of my queen. We welcomed you here in good faith. As observers. This is something else entirely."

I didn't need the bond to know he was furious. His temper was a slow and carefully controlled one, but when it went completely, a bull in a porcelain shop had nothing on him. I'd only seen it fully expressed once in the two years I'd known him.

We might be on the verge of the second if I didn't step in, and I didn't know what he'd do if there was nothing to throw or fight.

Reminding myself about diplomacy, I rose to signal the end of the audience. "I'm sure you can understand our need to consider what you've brought forward today. Was there anything else you wanted to observe during your stay?"

Luc and Jacinthe shook their heads, looking like they knew they were on thin ice. Samarre slowly replaced her phone and studied us before doing the same.

"Very well. If you'll excuse us, we'll be in touch when we've given your request due consideration." The words sounded stilted and formal to me. Fake. Everything about being "diplomatic" felt fake to me. Maybe that was why I was so shitty at it. It was different from hiding. When I had to hide, I was still me, just quieter. This felt like...not me. "Oh—and please stay at the residence. This isn't a good time to go wandering."

The Lyon elves rose, bowed, and saw themselves out, leaving Troy and me to deal with the bomb they'd dropped on us.

I started to reach for him and halted when he tensed ever so slightly. Most people wouldn't have noticed it. He was good at locking himself down. But he was my mate. I knew his reactions, his body language, better than my own. He might crave the comfort of touch physically, but he didn't want it, or want to want it, if that made sense.

I turned the reach into a gesture toward the door, keeping my own expression locked down. Our guests weren't the only ones on thin ice when it came to Troy and his blood father. That was not a topic anyone raised lightly, even me. Maybe especially me, because I knew how much it hurt him.

Haroun took in the mood as we left the office and wisely held his tongue. We let Troy lead us out, and both of us sat in the back seat without a word, knowing Troy's protective tendencies went into overdrive when he was troubled. It wasn't fear of him, just respect. It helped that Haroun was one of the few neutral parties we had; as a half-elf he was weak enough magically that he didn't register as an overt threat for Troy, and as a male, Haroun didn't register as an overt threat to my increasingly active elven instincts. He'd also been one of our first recruits, so we trusted him the most outside of Allegra, Iago, and Etain.

I wanted to thrash the hell out of Samarre and her blurry photo. This was the last thing we needed right now, and they were trying to play the game of Houses. Fine, maybe they legitimately did want to settle in the Triangle. I didn't blame them. Loads of Othersiders had moved here. But no elves. I wouldn't allow it even if they'd asked.

But I would if it meant Troy had a shot at reconnecting with his father.

That was a wound that needed lancing and healing. The timing sucked, but the necessity was there. I wrestled with that, distracted from the vampire problem, until we got home.

As we parked, Haroun said, "Will you two be good with the gytrash if I head over to HQ for a breather?"

"Yes," I said before Troy could answer. "Give us an hour or two before you send someone else over."

Haroun grimaced. "Etain—"

"Doesn't have final say."

"As you command, my queen."

I squeezed his arm to take the sting out of my words, and he nodded before sliding out of the car and into his own, adjacent to where we were parked.

As Troy and I got out, he blocked me from going inside. "I don't need you to run interference for me."

"I know."

"So, what was that?"

"That was running interference for myself."

He frowned down at me, the gold flecks in his eyes sparking as he looked for the lie.

"They offered terms for settlement in the Triangle. I need space to deal with that without feeling like there are elves underfoot everywhere as it is." It was a thin argument and a shitty one in more ways than one, and we both knew it. But there was a note of truth in it, and we both knew that as well.

"Fine," Troy said. "Let me know what you decide."

I grabbed his sleeve as he turned to go inside. "Talk to me."

"I can't. Not right now."

Worse than I thought then.

As I was debating whether I needed to push him or leave him be, and whether the reaction was because of his father or my continued wariness around elves in general or both, he sighed. "He's my father, Arden."

Even with the bond, I didn't know what he meant with that, so I bit my tongue.

He paced then stooped to snatch a rock and hurl it into the trees hard enough that a crack rang out from whatever tree it'd hit. "How the fuck could they know about him? Why use him as leverage?"

Throwing things. We were on the edge then. At least it was rocks outside this time, and he was still talking.

Still, I couldn't help my wince and sent a tendril of blended Earth and Water to see if there was any major damage to the tree. Just bark. "I don't know how they know. But the first thing Omar asked when I called him the first time was if you'd made your father's mistake. My guess is if they knew about an exiled Monteague—"

"Veisi," Troy said miserably. "He was a Veisi before he was given to my mother."

"Okay. If they knew about an exile and they knew or assumed you'd bonded to me and they have any kind of psych profile on you like the Darkwatch had on me...Troy, your light in the dark has always been to do the right thing. It used to be orders. Now it's the greater good. They probably took a shot on your seeing righting the wrong done to him as a step toward the greater good."

He started to answer then shut his mouth. Another start. Then, "I need to run."

I held back a sigh. I needed him focused, but more than that, I needed him to be okay. Running was better than the alternative. "Go. I'll stay in, unless you want a hunt."

"No. I need to think. Not distract myself." He offered a tight-lipped smile. "But thank you. And for staying in."

Where the wards were strongest and the gytrash and whichever of the Ebon Guard would be coming on duty could keep an eye on me in his absence, giving him one less thing to worry about. I was familiar by now with his penchant for using exercise, but especially flat-out runs through my woods, to deal with his demons.

"Go on and change. I'll have something ready to eat when you get back." The one time I could remember to cook without being flat-out starving myself was when he was like this. When he was hurting too much to keep the iron fist of control clenched and needed care. He'd never ask for it, of course. Or at least not yet.

I might forget to take care of myself a lot of the time, but I was determined to be better to him than everyone who'd used him before I'd claimed him. Yeah, I reaped the benefits of claiming an elven king in the bedroom, and in security, and in having nice things because he thought of them when I rarely did. But neglecting the flip side, the way he'd been abused and denied anything that'd help him feel grounded and secure and loved, would make me almost as bad as Keithia. I'd show Troy it was safe to be himself and safe to need rather than always to be the one on top of things, always seeking the right way to be perfect.

Eventually. Somehow.

Rather than get defensive about taking care of himself, or argue that he was fine, he brushed a distracted kiss on my temple as he passed me to go inside.

Definitely, definitely bad.

I did a quick boundary walk at the edges of my property, restrengthening the wards before going in. Troy was already gone, somewhere closer to the river and moving fast even on the rough, semi-mountainous terrain. I'd start the food when I sensed him on his way back.

In the meantime, I had a call to make. Detective Rice's deadline was hours away, and I had nothing.

"Damn Maria," I muttered as I made a cup of chamomile tea. I hated the idea of calling Rice with a failure. It was my Goddess-damned *job* on the line. My reputation. That was all any of us had in Otherside. It was how Callista had kept control of the territory for at least four hundred years.

And here I was faltering a year in.

No. Fuck that sideways.

Diplomacy. What was the diplomatic action? Even if I hated the idea, I felt obliged to give it a try. Even if I could get away with handling Otherside my way, the mundanes played by a different set of rules.

I sat with my tea in my favorite armchair. It was old and stained, but even Troy with his upscale royal tastes didn't dare suggest replacing it. It was the one thing—other than him and strange elves in the demesne—that I got territorial about.

How did I bring everyone together in the absence of a threat like the Wild Hunt?

That'd made everything easy before. Everyone knew what the Wild Hunt was, and nobody wanted the world to end, themselves and their dreams included with it.

Guiltily, I thought about the trickster gods and what they might want. But the tricksters weren't the organized force the hunters were. It wasn't their nature. They were a group in name only, united more by their effects than their goals. And both effects and goals were never quite what you thought they were. Not only that, but I had no idea what they wanted. Or what even one of them wanted.

Only that they were looking to me to deliver it.

I'd have to find another way forward. That meant playing nice. And nice, for Maria, meant catering to her paranoia. She'd been chasing strength and power for as long as I'd known her, and as long as Troy had known her. Hunting elves had gotten her in trouble with her sire and former master, Torsten, more than once. She'd kept doing it, until both Aron—Torsten's original second—and Torsten himself were dead.

That was it. I needed to find a way to give Maria power to replace what I was demanding she give away.

Steeling myself, I called her. Her heavy sigh greeted me, and I wondered when our easy, once-flirtatious friendship had become so burdened.

"Hey," I said. "I have a proposal for you."

"Do tell, poppet."

Pet names. Maybe she wasn't pissed at me, but something going on there. It couldn't all be about me, lone primordial and Arbiter or not. Hell, maybe it was simply because it was the middle of the afternoon and I'd woken her up. "What if I played bait?"

"Excuse me?"

"Our deadline is almost here. I get that you're not comfortable releasing a whole pool of blood donors when we have war on our hands. You need someone to help you shoulder the risk. Right?"

She didn't answer immediately. "What's the catch, Arden?"

"No catch. I need this resolved. I'm not willing to stoop to Callista's level." I snorted. "You know I care about you, Maria."

"And here I thought your stopping the blood donations was to put distance between us."

"You had your hostages and your throne. You didn't need me."

"You think?"

I checked the bond. Troy was still running hard, walls mostly up. Almost at the farthest point of his typical run. He'd be on his way back soon, so I needed to get food going. "Maria. What's the point of all this?"

"I suppose I'm wondering where I sit now that you have a king."

I let that rest, giving it due consideration. Maria had offered a partnership—sex, blood, politics, and whatever else I might want. She'd more than hinted at taking me as a solidaire before it'd become apparent I was a primordial elemental and destined for more. And despite our butting heads now, she'd been one of my most consistent supporters. Most other people I'd have let hang themselves, but there'd been a spark between Maria and me since she sidled up to me at Claret and figured out I wasn't what I was presenting myself to be.

"You will always matter," I said. "And hell, I'm sure I'll always find you cute as hell. But I'm bound to Troy, and him to me, and we're both happy with it. And for the record, he didn't make me stop the blood donations." A moment in the car with him flashed through my mind, the jolt of remembered pleasure as Troy confidently told me he knew his place. "That was my choice. So, I offer myself now. Either we draw out Matthias and Santiago's people and have our scapegoats, or time runs out and you give Matthias back some of the entourage to buy time before they launch an attack. Tell them I ordered it so you don't look weak."

"Blunt as fuck, aren't you?"

I didn't reply. We didn't have time to play games.

"Fine." Her voice lightened, sounding forced, but at least she was trying. "I suppose it's not every day a city mistress has a primordial elemental as collateral. Speaking of—what's your lover boy think of this plan?"

"He's occupied."

She barked a laugh. "You didn't tell him."

"I'm calling as Arbiter. And your friend. I told you, Maria, Troy and I do keep things separated as much as we can, even if I'm going to pay for it later."

Amusement threaded her voice. "Oh please. You love it when he gets wound up, or you wouldn't be with him. That damned elf has been the bull to Fate's picador his entire life. Just pray you're not the matador, hm?"

I shivered. "I certainly try my damnedest not to be."

That was the second time today someone had mentioned Fate. It sparked a thought. If I was a focal point for Fate, and this moment in time really was one...why hadn't Duke had a vision like he had before I was captured by the Recaps? Or had he? If not him, then maybe another djinni. I refused to believe nobody had seen anything. Maybe that was the "Council bullshit" Duke had mentioned.

Another thing to dig into.

I bit back a sigh and refocused on Maria. "Sorry, what?"

"I said don't worry. You're good for him. Or rather, you both are good for each other." She paused. "Keithia was going to kill him."

That choked me up, given what Troy had said earlier. "I know. *He* knows."

"Good. Then hopefully he'll stop hating himself. Or fearing himself. Whatever it is."

Troy's mental health was not a topic I was going to discuss further. "Do we have a deal, Maria? I need to take something back to Rice when our time is up. I'll give you our culprits for the most recent attacks, but you've got to let some of the New York and Miami coterie go."

"Back to swinging your proverbial dick."

"Tiresome, I know, but it's this or I can try Callista's methods."

"You wouldn't."

"Correction, I'd rather not." Even as I said the words, I realized they were true. "I will not fail after one year when she managed four hundred. You can call that petty if you like, but I have a chance to do things better." I bit my tongue before I could say that Maria was kind of a shitty friend for not helping me—and all the rest of us—by just. Giving back. Her hostages.

She picked it up anyway. "You're that tired of me?"

"I'm that tired of you making this difficult when it doesn't have to be, and I'm tired of being the friend who bends over backwards to make shit work. This is it. No more offers. We get it done in the next six hours, or I follow Troy's playbook—the greater good above all and regardless of cost."

"Be here in two hours then." She hung up, sounding pissed.

Let her be pissed. I was too, and wondering if I could afford the luxury of friends anymore. So far, all it seemed to be getting me with the Wild Hunt over was dead bodies.

Chapter 19

I was still brooding over the call when the back door slid open and Troy came in, smelling of the woods, the muddy chill of winter, and the frighteningly delicious scent that was all him. He was still breathing hard, which stirred the air molecules in the room, adding to my general agitation.

I looked up from the steak I'd just put on the grill pan as he drew nearer, reflexively drawing myself up. Troy had always been intimidating—not just because he was tall, all lean muscle, and a vicious fighter. Not just because I was an elemental facing an elf who was even stronger with Aether than any others I'd met, especially now that the new moon was further amplifying that power. He had presence, even when he wasn't trying to avoid notice by suppressing it.

He wasn't trying now.

This was almost as close as he got to his full self. A good sign, given where he'd been earlier. His secondary teeth weren't out, but he crackled with an unchecked power signature and shone with sweat-slicked skin.

Fat from the steak popped as I turned to face him fully, heart pounding and breath short as much from trepidation as arousal. Every liquid step bringing him closer sent prickles over me. Gold sparked in a gaze of shadowed labradorite, and a hint of burnt marshmallow teased under the scent of crushed rosemary and sage.

Most of the time, Troy worked very hard not to look or act like the apex predator he was. It'd been a matter of survival for him, much like me hiding my true self as an elemental under an elven death threat had been. The people controlling us would have hurt us. The mundanes would fear us, and they attacked what they feared. One way or another, something bad would happen if younger versions of ourselves had come out of our boxes.

It was part of why we understood each other, in the end. Why we were together—because we recognized that in each other. And he'd never intentionally hurt me. But that didn't stop some part of my brain from screaming that I needed to pay attention to the stalking elf approaching on footsteps quieter than death with the chill of a power signature ripping through the room.

From the slow upward curl of his lips, he liked my reaction.

I didn't know if I let him catch my chin or if he was just that good.

"You looking at me like this is dangerous," he said. Violent delight danced in the gold flecks in his gaze as he pinned me against the sink. "And you know it."

It took me a few heartbeats, but I pulled myself together even if my voice was raspy. "Go take a shower before the food's ready. We need to leave for Raleigh in forty."

He stared down at me. Tension stretched tight. A tremor shook me. Just when I thought I'd break, he stole a kiss and was gone almost as quickly as his lips brushed mine.

Freed from his touch, I closed my eyes and shivered before pulling myself together and turning the steaks. I might be the most powerful being locally or anywhere, but Troy? He held my heart and soul. And that made him more dangerous, no matter what I told Maria about us keeping our business separate.

Because if I was honest, I'd been trapped in Troy's influence for a long time, even before I knew who and what he was.

And with all this talk of Fate, I was starting to wonder if there wasn't something more to all of it.

△▽△▽

"I don't like this, Arden."

I wrapped my arm around Troy's waist and drew him closer as we walked down Blount Street, two blocks away from the governor's mansion. We'd eaten quickly and gotten down to Raleigh in record time. He'd washed away the intensity he hadn't managed to run off and was back to his normal. For now. The topic of his father wasn't closed yet, but I couldn't afford to do anything more about it just now.

"I know," I said. "And I'm sorry. But it seemed like the fastest way to hit our deadline without losing Maria as an ally."

He wrapped an arm around me absentmindedly, keeping me within the sphere of influence for his don't-see-me spell and playing to our cover of being just another couple out for a stroll. Not at all the power couple of the East Coast. "I know. And it's fair. But—"

"Yeah. At some point, no more breaks."

The feeling in the bond said as clearly as words, *You said it, not me*, but Troy held his tongue and focused on his nose.

"Nothing," he muttered. "Raleigh is even smaller than Seattle, but there've still been too many people here for me to parse out a crime scene."

That was new. "You were in Seattle?"

"Omar sent me there for my initiation."

Before I could answer, my phone rang. Blocked number. "Shit."

"Answer it." Troy drew me against him as he settled back against a building. To an outsider we'd look like just another amorous couple enjoying an outing, temporarily distracted by a phone call.

Sighing, I did so. "Finch."

"Ms. Finch. A pleasure to speak with you again."

I ground my teeth at the familiar voice and forced a smile when Troy squeezed my hips. "Senator Wright. I hope this call is to tell me you've gotten the security clearance I asked for."

"As a matter of fact, it is."

Keep it quick, Troy sent. *I don't have any tech to block the tracking on your number.*

"I'm a little busy at the moment," I said. "Tracking down murderers isn't the easiest work, as I'm sure you're aware. Can I call you back in a few hours for next steps?"

Hesitation. Then, "I'm afraid we need to speak now, Ms. Finch."

He's got someone tracing you. Troy's grip on my hips tightened again, even as he kissed me. *Is this a battle we want to fight here?*

Better here than in Durham. I hesitated then added, *Maria made the bed.*

So, she'll sleep in it. Grim satisfaction tinged with regret came through Troy's thoughts at that. *Fine.* He nudged me away and took a few steps farther down the street to make a call.

I refocused on my caller. "Okay, Senator. What do you need from me?"

"Not much, Ms. Finch. Not much. I just need to understand a few things about how the power structure works for you locally."

In other words, he needed us to bullshit long enough for a trace to come through on my location. But I wasn't in Durham. I was in Raleigh—Maria's territory. It was with her blessing, and technically within my demesne, but far enough from my woods and my home that I was able to wrestle down some of my protectiveness.

"That's quite a nebulous ask. Care to be more specific?"

"I was hoping you might come to DC to discuss in person."

"No."

That set him aback. "No? No what?"

"It's a full sentence on its own, and I'm not in the habit of repeating myself. Even for senators."

"Now, Ms. Finch, we wanted to speak to you because you seemed reasonable."

"Funny how being reasonable involves considerable inconvenience for me. There's a brave new world of video calls if you'd like to see my cute face when I tell you no to meeting in person. Now was there anything else? Or are you just making small talk until your tracking program locks on?"

"I don't know what you're talking about."

"See, I'm not in the habit of allowing people to lie to me either. The stated purpose of your agency is to surveil Otherside. Presumably, that puts me at the top of the list. I'm allowing this conversation to continue purely because I don't care if you know where I am right now, given I'm doing the job I'm supposed to be doing and it's not a secret that I'm investigating the recent tragedy."

"It is supernatural-related then?"

"I didn't say that."

"Then in what capacity are you assisting in the investigation?"

"Surely whatever file you have on me includes a notation that I'm a trained and licensed private investigator," I said drily. "Which reminds me—your agency wouldn't have anything to do with the odd coincidences of sudden deaths and a local healthtech startup pressuring our local medical examiner to try out a new test right before said agency was announced, would it?"

"I'm sure I don't know what you're talking about, Ms. Finch."

Which in my mind was a yes. This was a waste of time. "Then if you'll excuse me, I have actual work to do, and it seems like you're more interested in dicking me around. We'll chat later, when I'm not on a deadline and you actually have something for me."

I hung up as Troy returned.

He gave me a look of consternation. "If you were just going to hang up on him anyway, why not do it before they could get a lock on your location?"

"Like I told him, I don't care if they know that I'm doing my job. It plays to my advantage to be seen to be urgently investigating the situation. Trying to keep the peace and all that. You good?"

Troy nodded. "Etain will send a few more half-elves down. Just in case. Thana will come as well, in case we need another high-blood."

That would be treading a fine line. Aside from Allegra and Troy, high-bloods were technically banned from vampire territory after the mess with Leith Sequoyah scuttled their trial of open borders, and all of the Darkwatch-trained half-elves in the area were now sworn to me. But the human-blooded were allowed passage through any Otherside territory—with, of course, the trade-off that they could be hunted as a human would be. Another thing about Otherside I didn't love, but I didn't have the answer for that particular tangle just yet.

"Thank you," I said. Better to have them and not need them. I was starting to get a funny feeling, like a pot was simmering. Not surprising, given the city would be under a curfew in an hour. Preventative measure after the property damage last night. But there was something more, something sharper, and it itched like it was pointed at me.

"Arden?"

I looked up at Troy.

"Where'd you go?"

"The Sight. Something's bugging me, and I think it's to do with all this. It's gotten worse the longer we've stood here."

He frowned, keeping his attention on the street and buildings as he muttered a refresh of the don't-see-me spell in elvish under his breath. The scent of burnt marshmallow spiked and was gone, too subtle for a mundane to catch. A vampire would though.

"This bait idea isn't working," Troy said in a low voice. "And I can't pick up an old scent under everything else. Let's head back to Raleigh PD and see if we can talk some sense into Rice."

I nodded, still distracted with trying to figure out what was bugging me.

Troy slowed.

"What?" I asked.

He held up a hand to wait then spoke softly into the mic strapped to that wrist. "How many?"

Shit. That meant there was trouble ahead.

"Got it. Do not engage. We're waiting on a few more friendlies and can't afford the headlines. If they try Arden and me, we'll handle it." He lowered his wrist, and when he met my gaze, he'd slipped back into the headspace he went into for Darkwatch work. "There's an armed group converging ahead. Likely coming to protest at the governor's mansion."

I let the spike of adrenaline slash through me and rode it to focus. "Can we find another route?"

"No. They're coming from all directions. For once the idiots didn't announce themselves on social media."

"Only way out is through then."

"Yes." His gaze flicked past my head, never still. "We should be able to make it if we tamp down our power signatures. If we can't, your training should be enough to take them down without magic. I strongly recommend we stick to the physical if we can't get past them."

My pulse jumped, thudding at the understanding that the Darkwatch training Troy had given me actually be put to use for the first time. "You're lead."

He studied me, approving of what he saw if his quick nod was any indication. "Let's go."

I fell in slightly behind him to his left. We rounded the corner—and came face-to-face with a group of mostly white men, all with the orange bandanas the Sons of Seth tended to wear.

I ducked my head and stuck close to the wall of the building to stay out of their way as we approached, trying the first line of defense I'd learned well before meeting Troy: not looking worth hassling. Between that and Troy's don't-see-me spell, we managed to slip past them.

Someone started up on a bullhorn behind us, shouting anti-Otherside slogans and riling the crowd.

This is going to get ugly, Troy said.

Fast. And I bet you the police will find a way to be too busy with Maria to stop them.

No takers.

We made our way down the street. I forced myself to stick to Troy's measured pace, not rushing but not hanging around either. As we neared the same police station we'd been at the other day, a SWAT truck rumbled past us, flashing lights as the siren whooped. There was far less traffic than usual, and what remained got out of the way fast.

"They're going toward Claret," I blurted. We'd both seen this coming, and yet it still kicked me in the gut to see it. "We still have time on the clock, and they're already moving."

Troy grimaced. We both wanted the SWAT team to be going to the Sons of Seth protest, but neither of us was that naive. As one, we changed direction and headed for Claret. This might be Maria's mess, but I was the Arbiter and we were still her friends—for now. We couldn't let anyone get the idea that Othersiders in the Triangle were ripe for the picking.

The street outside Claret was blocked off when we got there, and a crowd was gathering outside barricades set up in front of the wine bar. A handful of police—including Detective Rice—were assembled within the barricades in a setup that said they'd started well before the deadline we'd been given. The metal shutters were down on Claret's windows, and Maria stood out front in her black bodystocking and combat armor, hair pulled up into a no-nonsense bun. No katanas this time, but she was deadly fast in hand-to-hand. Her tiny stature and purple hair made people underestimate her, which was how she liked it.

She spotted me first, and her eyes went black as she pulled a glamour. The crowd gave a collective wobble, making it easier for Troy and me to push through.

With a pointed look at the police, we hopped the barricade to stand beside Maria.

"Glad you two could make it." She smiled to show fang, antagonizing the humans. "Any joy?"

I shook my head. "No."

She sighed. "Fine. I will hold to our deal, even if there's going to be hell to pay."

"There always is, one way or another," Troy said.

Maria gave him an annoyed look.

Rice cleared his throat. "If it's all right with y'all, we were in the middle of something. Finch. Monteague. What are you doing here?"

I turned and glared at him. "My job. Which I still had twenty minutes to complete before all *this*."

"You weren't going to, and you and I both know it."

"What I know is that you're making a mistake," I said. "Maria and her people aren't responsible."

"And how would you know that?"

"If you'd been at the station, I could have told you all about it." I fingered the little tool Noah had found, now tucked in my pocket, and decided to keep it there. Too many people might learn such a thing existed if I showed it here. "But now we're in public, with fucking news cameras setting up across the way, because y'all decided this spectacle was more interesting than actual terrorists marching on the governor's mansion."

Rice frowned. "What terrorists?"

"The Sons of Seth," Troy said. "My team is tracking the ringleaders. We'd be happy to offer assistance in the form of information sharing." He looked at the collection of police and SWAT team officers. "Assuming, of course, you redirected these resources to deal with them."

A police officer behind Rice spat. "They're not terrorists. They're damn heroes."

Chills of dread swept over me. "Ugly" didn't even begin to cover how this night might go if the cops were so focused on making Maria the bad guy that their inaction emboldened a group with a history of attacking Othersiders.

And it wouldn't be just this night. There'd be more.

I couldn't let it happen.

"Rice, I know you think we're all demon spawn or whatever, but I have proof it's not Maria's people who are responsible."

"What we discussed was you finding the perpetrators."

"We discussed that, yes, and we are actively working on it. But we also discussed finding evidence that it was someone else. I broke precedence and custom to get you that evidence."

"I'm afraid my superiors no longer accept that deal." He smirked, pleased as hell to be getting the upper hand on me.

Troy looked like he was planning strategy as his eyes darted. "Detective, this is a mistake. Maria isn't the enemy. None of us here is."

The same officer as before spoke, louder this time. "Y'all are about to be under arrest."

I gave him a share of the look I was giving Rice. "I can't be under arrest because I haven't broken any laws and you have no probable cause for anything else."

"Your existence breaks the laws of nature and God. That's enough probable cause for my favorite judge. But obstruction will do. We're trying to serve a warrant."

I loosened my grip on my power signature, just a little. "I don't think Senator Wright will be very happy if I'm in a cell in Raleigh when he'd like me to be in Washington, DC shortly."

That wasn't what I'd wanted to say, but it was smarter than asking if he really thought a cell could hold me or Troy, or Maria for that matter. Breaking free would expose more elven and vampire secrets and too much of my strength, but I wouldn't be held captive. Not again.

Fortunately, it shut everyone up and bought us a moment of pause.

But in that moment, the Sight flared to life.

Chapter 20

"Something is wrong," I whispered. The Sight was screaming, clenching my heart in a fist and twisting hard.

"There is a clusterfuck of police trying to get inside my nest. I know something is wrong!" Maria smelled of pissed-off vampire, hot iron and wet ash.

I kept my attention internal, trusting Troy to keep watch.

Detective Rice edged forward. "Get out of the way, Finch, or I let Officer Smith here arrest you. US Senators don't have jurisdiction in Raleigh so he's just gonna have to get in line and file the paperwork."

"Just hang on a fucking minute!" I snapped. "Something is *wrong!*"

"You're obstructing the lawful—"

And then I spotted them. Or sensed them, rather. Dead zones in the crowd.

People who felt like Maria, who didn't breathe and whose heart only beat more than once a minute in a fight or when they drank.

"Maria," I said urgently, "Are all your people inside?"

"The coterie is on lockdown," she murmured, too quiet for a mundane to hear. "They're off the streets. Allegra's holding our exit. What—"

Rice moved, trying to grab me.

Troy intercepted him with a snarl, dropping his shields to let his power signature slash through the space and spook every mundane present. "Back off, Rice."

Every *mundane* spooked. But not every presence.

I couldn't read life signatures like the witches could, who drew on life for their magic. But I could read things like air molecules moving around bodies and in and out of lungs. The waters of the body rushing through it. The faint electric spark of a nervous system.

And I could tell, even if belatedly, when they were reduced or absent. Especially in a packed crowd that crackled with energy.

With Troy holding off Rice, I turned to Maria. "If all of your people are on lockdown, why are there vampires in the crowd?"

Maria's eyes widened.

"Troy! It's a trap!" It was all the warning I could spare before drawing Air to me and using it to corral most of the police.

Our bait hadn't worked because it wasn't me they were after. Whether that was because Matthias and Santiago were that focused on Maria or because they were hoping I'd change my mind and stay out of it didn't matter. Either way, we were about to have a shitshow of violence on our hands—one that would set not only the Triangle but all of Otherside back to a point that might be unrecoverable.

Troy spoke into his wrist mic, rapid elvish. Something about move in and snipers. Maria was snarling an update to Allegra on her own headset.

And the first rogue vampire attacked.

I snatched him with another coil of Air as he leaped from the crowd, trying for one of the cops I hadn't managed to kettle. He bared his fangs, snarling soundlessly as he fought magic he couldn't see or smell.

Maria hissed when I dragged him closer. "That's not one of mine."

"Then let's assume the other five aren't either!" Splitting my attention and managing fine control had never been my strength, but I had to now. I snatched another vampire trying for one of the SWAT team on the edge of the crowd.

How many do we need alive? Troy whispered in my mind.

You're the strategist.

He spoke into his wrist mic again, more elvish, staccato enough that I could follow it. "Keep two. Arden has them. Subdue the rest."

Most of the mundanes had fled as soon as they realized magic was happening. Those who stayed were looking for something to use as a weapon or pulling them from their coats, so the SWAT team and the Ebon Guard found themselves on the same side if with different targets.

One by one, the Guard found the vampires and took them down with stakes and silver. The stakes would paralyze them. The silver would poison them. We could finish the killing later, when we'd gotten the information we needed and the mundanes couldn't see how it was really done. Let them think their favorite movie tactics were enough. We couldn't put Maria's coterie at risk.

The cops had realized they were trapped within an invisible barrier and were losing their damn minds hammering on it though, their shouts muffled.

I used a loop of Air to lift Rice over the top and drop him on the other side of Troy and me from the barrier.

The detective stared at the sky and then me with wild eyes. "What in the name of God is going on? What was that? What did you do to my people?!"

"I held up my side of the bargain and saved their lives," I snapped. "There are six rogue vampires in the crowd. Four are down, two are captured. This was a setup. Someone wants violence here. Public violence. Is that what you want, Rice? Blood in the streets of Raleigh?"

He snarled. "You are all so goddamn unnatural."

"Rice." I kept my voice low and even, needing him to hear me and not see me as a larger-than-life threat, even with my eyes glowing in the early evening darkness. "Listen to me. Someone wanted this confrontation. Who does it serve?"

"Release my people."

"No. Not until we're done talking." I pointed to one of the vampires I still held trapped and suspended with Air as two pairs of the Ebon Guard passed, dragging all four of the downed vampires to Claret's door. "There's at least one of your possible culprits for the murder. That means you call off your dogs and leave Maria, Claret, and the rest of the vampires and their properties the flying fuck alone."

"I'm supposed to take your word for it? Leave vampires in her hands?"

I wanted to scream. To shake him and Maria both. Did he really think he was going to hold four vampires in the damn *jail*? Or the morgue, for that matter? Everyone was being so Goddess-damned unreasonable, and I was tired of being the big girl.

"Yes," was all I said, although my tone was clipped.

I could help him along, Troy said.

Don't. Not yet. Maybe it would be the wiser choice, but I was determined to protect the knowledge of elven powers—protect Troy—as long as I could.

"Come on, Rice," I said. "The situation is out of control. Even if Maria let you in, you've got a media circus, rogue vampires, and—"

Before I could add the Sons of Seth, angry shouts drawing closer by the second announced that they were adding themselves.

I grimaced. "Shit."

Troy shifted, positioning himself between me and the end of the street where the shouting was coming from while still keeping an eye on the increasingly panicked police. "Fighting on two fronts wouldn't be my first choice, Arden."

"It's not mine either. Rice?"

The detective scowled. "They haven't done anything. You're holding my officers captive with magic."

"Fine," I snapped. I dropped the wall of Air. The ones who'd been pushing against it cried out as they stumbled. "They're free. I suggest you get the fuck out of here. Or regroup. Whatever you want to call it."

"And where are you going?"

Troy glanced our way. "We're leaving," he said firmly. "Your people are too riled for Arden's safety to be guaranteed. Maria needs space to get your confessions."

Rice frowned. "I thought you had proof?"

"I have their leader on an audio recording," I said. "But if you don't want an ironclad close to this case—"

"We need to go, Arden. Now." Troy kept his voice low and quiet, but the bond carried an increasing edge of tension. I got the feeling he was resisting the urge to grab me and hustle me out of here.

I dragged the last two vampires closer and dashed them against the wall to stun them then glanced at Maria. "You good?"

She nodded, thin-lipped. "Thanks for having my back. I'll handle the confessions and the executions."

Rice stiffened. "Hang on, executions?"

Shaking my head, I said, "I told you once before, Rice. Otherside justice is hard and fast. When we have a guilty party, we can't afford for it not to be. Not if we're going to maintain peace with you humans, for all you don't seem to give a shit for doing the same."

Troy jabbed me in the bond. "*Now*, Arden, or we fight them."

"See you later, y'all. It's been super un-fun." I spun on my heel and hustled in the opposite direction of the shouts, sensing Troy following behind me.

"Stop right there, Finch!"

I would have kept walking, but the scrape of metal on leather and the sudden lethal focus to Troy's side of the bond told me we'd crossed a line we couldn't uncross. I turned, hands up, to find Rice aiming his service pistol at Troy, who'd moved to stay between me and the line of fire. Behind Rice, half a dozen officers drew their weapons as well.

My blood froze. Mundane bullets wouldn't hurt me unless they were jacketed in bronze. Special order. But the lead alloy in a standard bullet would poison and likely kill Troy. Painfully.

Go, Arden, he said. The bond carried grim lethality. He might die, but he'd do it taking every single one of them with him.

No fucking way, I sent back. *You do not get to martyr yourself for me. Not today. Not over this.*

"Get on the ground!" The same officer who thought the Sons of Seth were heroes edged closer. "On your knees! Hands behind your head!"

Arden—

I said no. My mind raced for an idea. After the battle against the gods in Durham, my powers were generally known, even if nobody had connected them to my being an elemental yet. I guess when you didn't have magic, all magic just looked like power. To save Troy—and Maria, Allegra, and my Ebon Guard—it was worth the exposure. *Play along.*

Frustration snarled the bond as Troy followed my lead and knelt in front me.

Maria's face was a blank mask as she did the same, and the Ebon Guard followed.

And as I reached the ground, I drew on Earth.

I love you. Brace yourself, I sent.

What—

I sent a pulse of magic into the ground. Nowhere near as flashy as lightning or balls of fire. Less impressive than blowing everyone down with a wall of Air. Earth wasn't my strongest power, but I was more than good enough to manage this.

The earth under the street heaved. The cops lost their footing. I threw a wall of Air between us and the police, just in case a gun went off. Sent another call into the earth, willing it to shift and buck. Added a thread of Fire. Willed the metal in the underground pipes to corrode and burst, poured heat into it until every grate and sewer was billowing steam.

Troy shot to his feet as soon as we had cover, pulling me to mine and backing me away while I kept working, trying to focus on disrupting the mundanes, not hurting them. I pushed aside a flashback to when Troy and I had infiltrated Verve and the distracting warm-and-fuzzies that butterflied through my stomach.

We made a good team.

"Go!" I shouted, waving at the Ebon Guard. "Get the cars!"

They didn't wait for Troy's confirmation, just took off.

A gunshot rang out. The bullet hit my barrier and ricocheted into the ground.

I sent another pulse of Earth in a rolling heave. I couldn't see through the steam, but I sensed bodies dropping as asphalt cracked.

Noah burst from Claret's front door, more vampires behind him. In a flurry of motion, all six rogues were dragged inside. Maria followed. A final shutter clanged down over the door.

Everyone was safe.

For now.

I let Troy pull me into a run. Neither of us held back or tried to hide our speed.

A squeal of tires ahead was the Ebon Guard with our rides.

"Split up!" I said. "Better they not have us both if we're stopped."

Because if they did get one of us, they'd have a hell of a time keeping that one until the other arrived as the proverbial cavalry.

Troy snarled but obeyed, jumping into the passenger seat of his MDX while I slid into the back seat of my Civic when someone threw it open from the inside.

Haroun caught me and stopped my slide. "Good?"

"Go!" I said.

Thana Luna, one of the ex-Darkwatch full-bloods, hit the gas. We shot ahead. Troy's car followed.

As the adrenaline drained from me, it was more than the comedown that left me shaking. It was rage too. Troy had included the psychological training in his Darkwatch regimen for me, so I could handle it better now. But I was at the end of my tolerance for jumping through hoops.

"Where to, ma'am?" Thana asked.

"The bar please. There's some hell to pay, and I intend to collect."

My voice came out as cold as Troy's would have. That made me proud.

I didn't even mind the heavy silence it created in the car on the drive back.

Chapter 21

The chatter in the bar cut off as Troy and I stormed in, not bothering to tamp down our power signatures.

"Raleigh is off-limits," I announced to the room at large. "There's been a situation, and I need to ensure it doesn't get worse."

Nobody answered as I kept walking, although Zanna hopped down from her stepstool and followed Troy and I through to the back.

"What situation?" she asked when the three of us were in my office.

Troy leaned against the wall near the door and glowered. He'd have words for me later, I was sure, but for now we were in an emergency situation and he'd defer to me.

"The mundane police are aligned with the Sons of Seth. Openly." I swiped that same message to the other faction heads and parliament members: Terrence, Ximena, Vikki, Janae, Laurel, Val, Doc Mike, and Maria, just in case she'd missed that part amidst everything going on. I'd fill Duke and Iaret in later.

I had a missed call from a blocked number, which I cleared. The senator could wait. We'd rushed everything trying to beat a deadline nobody had any intention of keeping. I hadn't trusted the feds to begin with, but it still pissed me off to act in good faith and have that spat on.

Zanna sneered. "Did you expect otherwise?"

I sighed. "No. Not with how they treat their own marginalized populations. But I would rather not have found out while trying to hold them and the Sons off from Claret under gunfire. What's Ruprecht up to?"

She grinned mischievously. "Still looking for work."

"Fantastic. Duke's got the new agency covered, so if Ruprecht is able to sneak into Raleigh and wreak some havoc in every police station down there, I'd count it a valuable service. Whatever he can do without exposing himself or coming to harm." I doubted he would. The fae could spin all kinds of illusions and were even better at being unnoticed than elves using spells or vampires using glamour.

My request got a dark smile from Troy. Normally the Darkwatch alone would be tasked with this sort of thing—sneaking in and destroying records or hacking them from the outside. But the elves were overstretched, and the fae could damn well help with something.

Zanna's grin widened to show pointy teeth. "Anything in particular?"

"Tell him to have a field day with any and all servers or other hardware. I want zero records available of any warrants, arrests, convictions, nothing so much as a damned parking ticket. It's time to reset the playing field. For everyone." They might have cloud backups. But not of everything. Police budgets went more to weapons better suited to a warzone than investing in tech upgrades since the Reveals. If the mundane police weren't going to consider our rights, I'd free myself of the burden of worrying about ordering the commission of crimes to protect Othersiders. More chaos would give Maria room to move. Or room to do a cover-up if she needed to kill to protect the coterie. "If Raleigh PD have so much damn time on their hands, let them busy themselves rectifying their records."

"I'll let him know." Whistling an annoyingly cheerful tune, Zanna left.

For once, Troy didn't say anything about overplaying our hand. A thought that was more of a feeling reverberated between us, that maybe we'd all been playing it too carefully up to now and a change in strategy was needed. The lesson I'd learned personally two years ago—that no matter how much you kept yourself in a box and made yourself small and non-threatening for other people, they would still project their own fears onto you. Troy had learned it too, especially as it became more widely known that he was a true king, power signature and all, in contravention of elven law and tradition.

Fine. Diplomacy didn't work for me anyway.

We'd be the things that went bump in the night instead.

We wouldn't go out of our way to harm or kill mundanes or the rest of Otherside, but after today, I wasn't going to tell my people they couldn't do everything in their power to defend themselves. We'd tried playing by the rules. We'd tried being accommodating.

They were afraid of us either way.

It was time to establish Otherside as a sovereign power. I wasn't sure how yet, but I'd come to my own power breaking all the rules and I'd be damned if I stopped now. If power was all that anyone respected, then I'd quit restricting mine. It'd make me a target, but I had faith in the people around me.

Troy straightened from his lean against the wall and eased into the chair opposite me. "They're definitely going to come for you now."

"Or you, now that it's clearer you're more than a bodyguard. But I know. We'll be ready."

He studied me. "You're handling this well. Better than I expected for your first real engagement."

Heat rushed through me at his approval. I wasn't too proud to say I admired him and his skills. "You trained me well."

That earned me the flicker of a smile. "I don't love that you used your powers like that. But I know why you did it."

I shrugged, flushing hotter as love curled through the bond, and tried to brush it off. "They know what I'm capable of. I need you as my ace in the hole."

"You're protecting me."

I just stared at him, daring him to tell me not to.

Another almost-smile. "Just promise me you'll be careful, Arden. If Raleigh PD will go this far in front of news cameras and the general public, the feds will go further." His expression melted into a frown. "I'm surprised we haven't had air surveillance yet actually. The Darkwatch is keeping an eye on drone and helicopter traffic, but there hasn't been anything yet."

"They'll track down the cars eventually, even with you swapping the plates."

Which he knew. We'd parked at one of the nearby garages and walked over to the bar, rather than parking out front for that reason. The wards on the building only stretched so far. We'd almost certainly been on the news, but Troy's don't-see-me spell had been enough to get us to the bar without notice.

We looked at each other, both knowing but not wanting to say that we might have to get out of town for a while. I was able to—we'd tested it—but I'd start to feel peculiar and get outright bitchy if I didn't work enough magic to make a connection with the land, water, and sky at my new location.

"There's always a royal progression," he said lightly.

I wrinkled my nose.

"I'm trying to get rid of the queenly responsibilities I already have, and you want me to go on progression?" I sent a teasing dart through the bond along with the words so he'd know I didn't resent the elven responsibilities, just didn't know what to do about them.

He snorted. "I wouldn't push it yet anyway. Not with Matthias and Santiago declaring war. We need to re-solidify control of the demesne, or we'll have more and worse threats and border probes. The House is too new to open us up to that kind of trouble."

"I was hoping you'd say that. You know how much I hate sleeping in a bed that's not mine."

My phone buzzed before he could answer. I checked the caller ID then tapped to put it on speaker. "Hi, Maria. Troy's here too."

"Of course he is." She sounded tired, or more tired than usual. "Just as well. Wouldn't want my oldest non-vampire ally to feel left out."

Troy's expression hardened. "It's not about feeling left out. It's about—"

"Securing your new House. I know, sugar puff. So, in the interest of doing so and reducing the likelihood of another clusterfuck like today, I'll meet you halfway."

Tired all over again, I scrubbed a hand over my face. "We need all of them, Maria."

"And I still need to not risk my coterie. The moroi who attacked the police today all smell like Santiago, so I will release all of Matthias's people except Giuliano."

I glanced at Troy. He grimaced but nodded.

"It's a start," I said. "What's the plan for the rest?"

"Get Santiago to stand down, and he can have everyone except Luz."

"Do you really think they're going to just let you keep their seconds and not do anything about it?"

"Come on, Arden. I need some kind of assurance. They've moved against me three times now."

"The first time was at Evangeline's invitation," Troy said, voice flat at the mention of the now-dead sister who'd tortured him. "Matthias might be reasonable enough to make a deal. Especially once we find out what the federal government wants with Arden."

"Other than a pet elemental," I muttered.

Maria huffed a sigh.

"What's Alli saying?" Troy asked.

"No. Oh no. You do not get to use her against me."

I rolled my eyes at the drama. "Nobody's using her against you, Maria. She's a solid strategist, and you know it. It's part of why we made her a special envoy. So we could all work together on making smart decisions."

The silence told me Allegra had probably sided with us.

Maria confirmed it after another few seconds of sulking. "She told me to send the coup plotters back."

Probably six months ago or more, Troy thought at me. *Alli wouldn't have let it get this bad.*

I didn't know what Allegra would or wouldn't have done, given she was head-over-heels for Maria, but that sounded about right.

"So, you're ignoring the advice of your brilliant girlfriend, the request of your oldest non-vampire ally, and the order of the Arbiter of the territory." I kept the words bland to lessen the sting, but this had to end. Right now. For real this time.

"I take your point," she said stiffly. "Fine. Matthias can have everyone if he agrees to a cessation of hostilities, starting immediately and lasting for the next decade. I would *request* that Giuliano stay as an honored guest rather than a prisoner. To...maintain good relations. And *you* are negotiating it, little miss Arbiter."

I let the snark pass since I was getting what I wanted and firmly believed in picking my battles. "Agreed."

"Agreed for House Solari," Troy echoed.

"Good. As for Santiago, that pissant doesn't get a flying rat fuck of anything until he withdraws entirely. I get the deaths of the moroi who tried to attack today, and I keep Luz regardless. She's their battle leader, and she hates me."

Fear wasn't a good look on Maria, but we were finally getting somewhere.

"I will see what I can do," I said. "Thank you for being reasonable."

"Call me when it's confirmed." She ended the call.

Troy blew out a breath and slouched, eyes closed. "Progress."

"Something like that."

The gold flecks in his eyes glittered as he opened them. "Don't tempt fate, cariñamí. The Fates and the gods all seem far too interested in you as it is."

I winced then gave in to the part of me that wanted comfort, rose, went around to his side of the desk, and dropped into his lap. His arms curved around me, and we sat for a minute, just existing as he tucked his face against the curve of my neck and breathed in my scent.

"I need to call Matthias," I said when I'd settled somewhat.

He tightened the arm around my waist, steadying me as I leaned forward for my phone. "And then home. And bed."

I didn't argue. It'd been a long, violent day on only a few hours of sleep. He made a satisfied grunt as I settled back against him and dialed, holding me close and getting more comfortable. The chair creaked alarmingly, but I'd spent extra on sturdy chairs after an orc stopped in and nearly broke one of the old ones.

Matthias's voice was cold and hard when he answered. "Miss Solari. I'd ask to what I owe the pleasure, but I'm not sure it's a pleasure."

"Would getting your people back be more to your liking?"

The line hung silent. "Is this bait?"

"It's a peace offering. Maria recognizes that Santiago is the driving force behind this mess and is willing to be reasonable if you are."

"Is she now?"

"Mm-hmm."

"Terms?" Matthias asked.

I repeated what Maria had said.

"A full decade of peace? In these times?"

"You're lucky she's so accommodating," I said drily. "I'd have pushed for a century."

Troy pinched my hip, a warning to be nice, even as his lips shifted in a smile against my neck.

"I see." Matthias said. "I need more. If I pull out now, Santiago will be furious."

"Santiago's demesne is thirteen-hundred miles from yours, and he has to pass through mine to get at you. If he does, you'll have all your people to defend your territory. I fail to see the danger, unless the vampires have expanded into hacking or other digital sabotage."

"Hmm."

Which could mean they had and Matthias didn't want to tell us or they hadn't and I was making sense. I let him think.

"You said there was a new mundane agency," the Master of New York finally said.

"There is. And a US Senator who's being a pain in the ass about getting me on board."

"How about this, Miss Solari. I will accept Maria's terms. I will leave Giuliano there as her honored guest, as she calls it, with the expectation that he truly be a guest and be free to move about the territory in the same way any of her people are, as well as being free to contact me whenever and however he likes. But I also want a direct alliance with you."

Troy went still at my back, cluing me in to the idea that something about this was unusual or off.

I squeezed his arm so he'd know I understood. "What does that mean, exactly?"

"What are the terms with your people there?"

"We come to each other's aid as and when needed, in line with the gifts and needs of each group," I said. "The witches don't fight, so they provide medical support and safe haven. The elves and vampires commit to using their resources for the whole territory, as and when called for. The weres, djinn, fae, elementals, and the few human sensitives working with us provide other services to support the whole, whether that's construction work, vehicle repair, surveillance, information gathering, security, or anything else suited to their resources, talents, and occupations."

"That's everyone but the gods and the other celestials. You have that many factions?"

"I do."

Something almost like admiration came through for the first time in our telephonic acquaintance. "I had wondered how a child like you ousted Callista."

Ignoring the insult, I said, "That was just me and my king passing through the Crossroads."

Silence met me, and Troy stiffened. He hated the Crossroads. Elves shouldn't be able to go there, and he'd suffered for it badly on the two occasions I'd dragged him through.

"You wield threats so elegantly," Matthias said. "I think I underestimated you."

"It happens. What terms were you expecting?"

"Something far less egalitarian. I'm almost tempted to make another push. These multifactional territories don't last long. Callista was the only one who managed to hold one together for as long as she did, and that by pure force of will."

"I leveled a good chunk of downtown Durham without really trying." I let him hear all the menace seeping through me to Troy and back again in a feedback loop. This was as much his territory as mine, and he'd happily kill outside vampires to defend it. "I don't think you want to test my will, my power, or my allies. Especially given how cranky I get when I have to leave home. And how much my king hates it when I'm cranky."

Matthias sighed. "No, I expect I don't want to test you at all. This whole business with Santiago was a folly from the start, but I need to expand my holdings or kill off some of the more ambitious of my flock."

"I hear Miami is lovely in February," I said blandly. An impulsive statement, but if Matthias went along with it, it'd potentially solve a problem. "Jacksonville's even bigger, but everyone's too afraid of Santiago to settle in north Florida even if it's unclaimed."

A surprised bark of laughter came down the phone. Then a long silence. "You want me to move against Santiago?"

"It's not my style to tell other faction heads what they should do unless they're trying to step into my business. If you wanted to take advantage of Santiago being distracted, with a number of people where they shouldn't be, to make a move on a large and growing yet bewilderingly unclaimed city...well. That would free me up to think about things like who I might be able to protect should the feds finally pull their heads out of their asses and get to dealing."

Savage pride and deep approval shot through me from the bond. Maybe I was getting the hang of actually being Arbiter and not just holding the title.

"You have a unique perspective, Miss Solari. I almost find it refreshing."

"Just almost?"

"I have eleven centuries. Unique and new aren't all that comfortable anymore. And yet this would solve my problems neatly."

"Some things really can be that easy. If we let them."

Matthias thought that through. "Very well. Cessation of hostilities against the Carolinas demesne for a decade. Giuliano stays there as an honored guest, *if* he may join your parliament and keep me apprised of goings-on. You keep me personally updated on this federal agency. And I take north Florida. Charity—Mistress in Atlanta—will need to be placated, but she's been dealing with Santiago's madness for centuries. I'm sure I can convince her of the benefits of joining forces."

"Agreed. I'll take it back to Maria and have her contact you for whatever y'all need to settle things."

"In that case, I'm pleased to end on a high note. Good night, Miss Solari. And to your king."

The call ended.

"Well done, cariñamí." Troy's pleased purr sent chills over me. "Very well done."

I slumped against him and blew out a breath. "I would really rather just sit in the woods."

"Which is why people will keep testing you and why you'll keep outthinking them."

"Huh?"

"That's your strength. You don't actually want any of this. So, you look for the easiest way to do things that still protects our people. Not the way that saves face or gains you more power. And you're a newcomer to power plays, so you do things even I wouldn't think about."

"Oh." I shifted and half-twisted to kiss the corner of his jaw. "Thanks. I just... Shit doesn't have to be as hard as everyone makes it. They just refuse to see a different way."

"I know. It'll be a long road. But we'll get there. And I'll be with you for all of it."

There were other long roads we'd have to travel. I hadn't forgotten the Lyon elves' offer to give us information about Troy's father in exchange for settlement rights, or the trickster gods, as I dealt with the situations with the feds and in Raleigh. But I could only get there one step at a time, especially if everyone else was determined to rain on my parade and throw rocks while they were at it.

Chapter 22

We were almost to the parking garage where we'd left the cars when the bond sang with tension.

Someone's following. Troy didn't change anything about his gait, didn't look around, even.

I trusted him to know though. *Where?*

Thirty feet back. Mundane. He kept walking past the street that'd take us to the parking garage we'd parked in. "Still want ramen for dinner?"

"Sure." Now that he mentioned it, my stomach was rumbling, and the ramen place on East Chapel Hill Street was damn good.

Troy murmured a light obfuscation spell, something that would lessen the likelihood of our being recognized or easily remembered, and we got a table near the front window. After we ordered, he swiped out a quick text under the table and told me the reply. *Etain's sending Thana to take a look and do something about it.*

Even though I knew how well he suppressed his emotions, I'd forgotten what a good actor he was. They were two different skills, and he managed to pretend nothing was wrong as he actually made me feel like this was a planned dinner, not a last-minute diversion so he could figure out who was following us. I slipped into the charade as our meal was served and had to keep reminding myself not to act like we were together.

He finished his shio and pushed the bowl away, checking his phone again under the table. *Looks like it's feds. Two of them.*

I scraped the bowl of my tonkotsu before pushing it aside to snag some of the pickled vegetables we'd gotten as a side. *Orders?*

That got me a genuine smile. No acting or falseness in it. "You're going to take orders?"

"You're the one who knows what he's doing." I was tempted to lean across the table and kiss him, but we weren't certain if the mundanes knew he was more than a live-in bodyguard. That'd change as soon as they figured out where I lived and realized my one-bed house was too small for him to be sleeping anywhere but with me, but I still wanted to protect him as long as I could.

You can't protect me forever, Troy sent, answering the sense he was getting in the bond rather than what I'd said.

Let me try.

His phone buzzed. "We're good. Let's go."

He'd paid as soon as all our food had come out, so I snagged a last piece of pickled melon and then pulled my coat on. The bond sharpened to wariness as he preceded me out the front door and stayed on the side nearer the street.

We made it to my car without incident.

I got in the passenger side, slouched in my seat, and rubbed my temples. "What did Thana do?"

"Influence spell. Not a mindmaze, but enough of an aura sting to strongly encourage he get lost. Plus a tracking tag." Troy got the car started and got us on our way.

"Okay." I grimaced. "Shit. They're going to figure out they don't know all of us."

"They already know there's more than vamps, weres, and witches. They haven't figured me out. There's speculation about the fae." He lifted a shoulder in a shrug. "Like I said. You can't protect me forever."

"I know. So be it." I needed to change the subject. "What are you thinking about the Lyon elves' offer with your father?"

Despite my light tone, the wall slammed down in the bond. "I don't want to talk about it."

I let that sit between us, again wrestling with whether it was better to push him or leave him. He was as stubborn as I was, and he'd carried this wound for a long time. He had several like that, deep and festering. For all that being with me—being my king and living to his fullest potential, rather than as a beaten dog—was helping him heal, that wasn't all he needed. And I couldn't be the only source of healing for him.

This, he had to own for himself.

Besides, the Lyon elves were still here, waiting for a response. He'd been the one who wanted them here, so I'd allowed it. If I wouldn't let Maria off the hook on something that affected the House, I couldn't let him off either.

I tried to keep my sigh as quiet as I could, not wanting him to think I was upset. "I understand this is hard for you."

He grimaced, keeping his eyes on traffic as we left downtown Durham and turned toward Eno.

"Troy...if you don't decide, I will." I braced myself, as much against my own fears as his reaction. "And I will tell them yes."

He almost ran a stop sign, a signal of how upset he was. He was usually the better driver under pressure out of the two of us. "What?"

I swallowed and strove to keep my voice even. "I wouldn't dare to tell you what you need. But you have wrapped yourself in brambles over this. Nobody gets in, and nothing comes out. And, cariñomí, it's killing you. Little bits at a time. You hold Omar at arm's length even when he's not being an ass. You don't talk to Allegra or me about it. You just...hold it. While it poisons you."

He kept driving, not looking at me, and I held my peace until we got home.

We needed to rest. I needed a shower and some sleep. We both did. But we stayed in the entryway, me leaning against the end of the half wall separating it from the dining area, him pacing the living room in an unusual display of agitation.

I thought he was going to shut me out again and was already resigning myself to it, because I wouldn't willingly cause him more hurt.

When he did speak, his voice was stripped of its usual melodic intonation. Flat. Dead. The Darkwatch agent and killer. "So you'll make decisions for me now."

My heart skipped. "Troy—"

"What if I said I didn't want to take their deal?"

I was glad he'd shut the bond down from his end. He wouldn't catch the burst of frustration coming off me. First Maria, then Matthias, now him. "Then I would happily respect that because you made a choice."

"But you said—"

"I said if you *don't* decide, and then I explained why I would take that action. Yes, I have personal fucking issues with allowing more elves in the territory, for good Goddess-damned reason. But *you are more important*. I would allow any number of elves into the territory *for you*. Because they're our people and more importantly this is *your father*."

He stopped short and gave me a flat look. "*Our* people? You can barely stand to be around more than a triad of full-bloods you don't know."

That hurt, but it was fair. I forced my temper down and answered as honestly as I could. "I lived almost my entire life under a death sentence that most elves outside this territory would still be happy to carry out, especially now. It is hard for me to find trust when I'm still an active bounty and the other elementals don't feel safe coming out because of elves, not humans."

"You think I don't know that?"

"I know you know that, which is why I'm trying to figure out why this is upsetting you when I just told you I would be willing to find a way to move the fuck forward."

"So you think I can't protect you."

I gave in to my frustration and scrubbed my face over my hands then drew on Air to send a zephyr swirling through the air plants hanging in their little bulbs.

Troy watched me warily but waited for my answer, his expression daring me to lie.

"Your ability to protect me has nothing to do with any of this. My fear might be irrational." I gave him a steady look. "But so is whatever this is."

He glared at me. "And what is this?"

"Deflection. When we promised to be brutally honest. I was honest."

That sparked on his temper and his pride. His word was his bond. Always had been, even before he swore he'd never lie to me. His chin went up, and his mood chilled to subzero.

I went to him but didn't touch him.

"I didn't say you lied," I said in the softest tone I could. Not out of fear of him. He'd never hurt me, at least not without my explicit and enthusiastic consent as some kind of sex game. But because he was going to break over this if he didn't bend, and we were in the middle of too many clusterfucks for that to happen. "I know you would never lie to me. I know you would protect me or die trying. I know you love me more than anything that has existed, or exists now, or could ever exist. I know. And I love you the same."

Troy blinked rapidly. His breathing picked up, and the muscle in his cheek jumped hard as he tried to lock himself back down.

I reached for his hand. He stiffened but let me take it, and I drew it to my chest and splayed it so he could feel my racing heart. "This scares me, Troy. The hold it has on you. *It scares me.* Because I'm afraid I will lose you over it somehow."

All of a sudden he drew me in tight. I grunted as I hit his chest and the wall in the bond dropped at the same time, flooding me with his fear and pain and anger to make me shake with it.

His voice rumbled in his chest against my ear. "You will *never* lose me. I would have to die for that to happen."

"That's what I'm afraid of," I whispered. "That someone figures out how to use this against you and they lure you in and kill you. I can't let that happen. So, if that means letting the Lyon elves settle here, letting them think they have shit figured out with your father so we can at least face the threat this information might become, so be it."

Troy stiffened, and I grunted again as his arms tightened around me then shivered as his mind raced through mine, picking up thoughts and feelings like fingers sliding through hair. We could do it to each other but almost never did because it was invasive and uncomfortable. But I restrained my reflex to push him out and made myself relax into it, offering up everything. I needed him to understand I was on his side.

"You really think this is something that could be used against me?" he asked.

"Not think. Fear." I snorted as I squeezed him back. "I guess neither of us is rational here. But I felt your reaction. If these three know where your father is, who else does? Who else has put together the pieces of your past and thinks you'll put yourself in their pocket?"

"They'd be idiots to think that."

"Some people are more than willing to fuck around and find out. And Troy, please know that I'm speaking as your love, not your queen. But I cannot afford the cost of that. Not after what Keithia did. Not again."

He shuddered at the reference to his torture. "That's fair."

We stood there, holding each other. Apologizing in silent ways for the hurt caused, with the bond and our softening touch.

When I thought he'd bear it, I went on my toes to breathe in the scent where his ear met his jaw and kiss that spot, letting his pheromones ease through me and soothe me. Letting that feeling swirl back to him. Peace. Comfort. More than a little arousal. But most of all, acceptance.

Whatever he needed, we would make it work. Because we loved each other. That love had already toppled tyrants and an entire political system. It could bear this.

It had to, because after everything I'd gone through to claim him, I refused to let him go over this. Unless he wanted to go, and then I'd just try to live with my broken heart.

Frightened by that idea, I offered him another tentative kiss.

He leaned back enough to catch my chin and made it a proper one.

Relief shuddered through me. I hadn't fucked this up. Yet.

"You're right," he said when he released me, holding me steady as I swayed a little. His voice was still rough, but it was a more vulnerable emotion than anger this time. "This is— It hurts. A lot." His thumb swept over my lower lip. "And I'm sorry I'm taking it out on you."

I offered a wry but loving smile. "I'm the only one you can do that with."

He started to answer then frowned. "That's not fair."

"To who?"

"To you."

I shrugged. "You don't do it often. And I know I've done it to you. Part of being a power couple, right? We can only show this side of things to each other." I lifted my eyebrows. "At least until there's a therapist strong enough in Aether to take us on."

His expression blanked then cracked. A laugh slipped out. "Us. In therapy."

"Yeah. Somewhere between saving the world, dealing with the gods, and fighting prejudice against elementals and elven kings."

"Mental health *is* important," he said solemnly.

"Exactly. So, talk to me. Or Allegra. Or Maria. Or Haroun. *Somebody*, Troy. Please. I'm not alone anymore, and neither are you. Never again."

He kissed me again, deeply and passionately enough that the earlier frustration and upset all channeled into arousal. I enjoyed that dynamic with us, and he knew it. All of our fights ended in hot sex, or had so far, and I wanted it now.

Or maybe after a shower and a nap. And a decision.

"So?" I asked. "What're you thinking?"

He sighed. Looked away. Then the bond and his expression firmed. "I've been thinking about seeing him again every day for the last twenty-one years. Wondering if he was alive. What he'd think of me. Of what I've become." Troy studied my expression. "I was afraid you'd be upset if I admitted I wanted this. That you'd leave me. I know you have reason to be wary of us. Of elves. It's hard sometimes."

I rubbed my hands along his back. "For me too. I'm sorry. I'm trying."

"You are. I'm reminding myself that you have reason. And that if you can forgive me—love me—after everything I did to you, we can figure something out with the rest of elvendom." His gaze searched my face again. "You'd really accept the deal?"

"Yes. I need to move forward. And so do you. Two birds with one handful of seed."

"Okay." The bond jittered with agitation, and his muscles locked up as he came to terms with his choice. "Then...I want this. I want the deal. We could use more Darkwatch-trained full-bloods on our side if out-of-territory factions are going to move against us. And I'm not convinced House Ead or the Richmond Conclave won't. But mostly because I need to know. About him."

"Then we'll accept the deal. And Troy, whatever you need to feel good or safe or okay with any of this, we'll do. Okay?"

"Yes, my love."

We were decided. Troy's father would be returned. And the Lyon elves would have sanctuary.

With the alliance with Matthias, that was two problems solved in a few hours.

Now I just had to figure out Santiago and the US government.

Chapter 23

The morning sun was slanting at the angle that said it was later rather than earlier, and the air was warming when the feeling of being watched pulled me to full consciousness.

Even as I gasped awake, a firm hand gripped my waist and pulled me closer to the middle of the bed. I drew on Air and barely had time to realize the perceived threat was Troy in one of his more intense moods before his body was pinning mine, my wrists trapped to either side of my head and my hips weighed down by his.

"Good morning," he said.

Even if I'd had the breath to answer, the purr of his voice made my body tighten. I froze, looking up into eyes the color of moss on sandstone, flecked with a brighter gold than when I'd met him. The ghosts of his past weren't there this morning. Just him. And a fuck ton of lust.

A small sound of want escaped me before I could stop it, and Air fled with it.

He chuckled, a dark, predatory amusement threading through the bond as he leaned closer to my ear. "I'll never get tired of this."

"Of what?" I managed to ask after a few panting breaths. The bond was open, and I didn't know where his desire ended and mine began. There was only *want*.

"I knew two years ago that I had the most powerful sylph in generations asleep in my bed." He trailed kisses down my neck. "But I never dreamed I'd have her as my fiancée. Or that she'd be this much fun to seduce. Over and over again." The kisses made their way to my breast, and I arched under him as he rolled a nipple in his mouth before moving on. "There's always a hunt with you, even if it's not the one I'd expected to find. I like this one better. It never ends."

My heart rate picked up, and my pulse thudded against his grip on my wrists. He was in a very good mood if he was bringing up the time he'd held me prisoner without guilt. We'd both been too exhausted to fuck last night, but a good sleep and a weight off his mind had Troy in fine form.

And I was about to reap the benefits.

It made me wild. I wanted it. Wanted him. I lifted my wrists. Or tried to.

"No you don't." Troy shifted back up and pressed harder against them, gripping tight.

I fought harder. He liked it. I liked what he did in response. Loved the affirmation of trust as I gave myself over to him, the surety that settled into him as I accepted all of who and what he was.

A faint snick said the sharp secondary teeth had come out a moment before they pinched on either side of my throat.

Elves were predators. Elementals were not. A fact he enjoyed reminding me of sometimes.

I squirmed in his grip, and a whimper escaped me before I could control myself. The Darkwatch regimen he'd put me through had been combat. Not bedroom play, even if most of our sparring sessions had ended in sex. And with the bond open like this, I could. Not. Think.

"Troy," I whispered.

His teeth pinched harder, drawing a groan from me as my hips bucked upward.

With all that Allegra had been going on about him "going feral," I should have been terrified. But I trusted him. I knew what he wanted. And as always, I resisted giving it to him. Not to be cruel. But so that he could find pleasure in taking it.

He withdrew, shocking me as my throat and wrists were both freed, and I gasped as he slid down between my thighs and kissed the inside of one.

"Alli was right about biting your neck. But they won't see everywhere." His tongue pressed against my femoral artery. "Trust me?"

"Yes!" I needed *something* before I burned alive from the inside out.

He bit down lightly, just enough to break the skin. Not on the artery but above it, in the meat where I wouldn't bleed out if one of us slipped. A dart of Aether flooded me with pleasure as he did, and only his firm grip stopped me from tearing up my own damn leg on his teeth as I came.

"Fuck," he muttered when he'd taken enough blood to satisfy him.

Then he eased off the Aether sting, hid his secondary teeth, and set about eating me out with a purpose, holding my hips down with a forearm when I tried to arch against his tongue. His fingers joined the party, slipping into me easily and curling against just the spot he knew would draw another orgasm from me. No magic. Just passion.

I came hard and was too lost to remember to muffle my shout lest the gytrash or whichever of the Ebon Guard was on duty heard me.

Troy didn't bother quieting me. He just kept going, drawing me to the edge again before drawing himself back up my body and sheathing himself in me in a smooth motion.

This time, he swallowed my cries in a kiss, not stopping the driven movement against and in me.

The words "I love you" fell from me like a prayer when he shifted to kiss my neck. He nipped me again with the blunt teeth. I'd have a bruise rather than a bite, but I didn't care either way. I arched up against him—or tried to. I might be almost as strong now, but he'd always be bigger.

He trapped my wrists again, watching pleasure build in my face.

"Troy, please."

"Please what?"

"You know what!"

"Tell me, my love."

"Aether. Please. I—"

For once, he didn't make me finish begging.

Troy had an affinity for minds, like all of his birth House. But he'd taken what he'd learned, and what he'd been subjected to, and twisted it from unbearable pain to overwhelming pleasure. His special trick.

He was an incredible fuck without it.

With it? I was ruined for anyone else. And he knew it. And delighted in it.

It was the reassurance he needed after last night's fight.

Pleasure flooded me as his hand covered my mouth.

Every nerve danced on the edge of pleasure and pain, never crossing into what hurt, even as what felt good shorted my brain. A burst of Air flew from me and something on the nightstand clattered to the floor.

Troy came when I did. Tight, hard thrusts that drew another layer of pleasure.

The next time I was fully aware of what was going on, I was on my side and in his arms.

Light kisses brushed the back of my neck.

"I think we both lost ourselves on that one," he said.

I groaned something I hoped he'd know was agreement and shifted closer to him. A sharp pain jolted through me from my thigh, immediately soothed by Troy numbing the nerve endings with Aether. It'd finish healing in a few minutes, or at least enough not to hurt. Until then, I'd stay where I was. In his arms, safe and loved.

"It will never not surprise me that you think that," he said.

"Think what?"

"That you're safe with me."

"Not think. Know. No question."

Love flooded me as he kissed my neck again, trailing his fingers along my flank. "I know that mentally, but..."

"Yeah. Same."

"What?"

I tucked myself even tighter against him. "Everyone else is afraid of me. Deep down. They posture and snap and snarl, but they do what I say because they're afraid of the primordial elemental. You know what I am better than anyone. And you still risk me destroying the Goddess-burning Triangle making me come like *that*."

Troy's low chuckle sent goosebumps over me. "I think that's a compliment."

"It is."

He leaned closer to whisper in my ear. "Then it'll never end."

I shivered. "It had better not. You're *mine*."

"And you're *mine*. As well as the only one I'd submit to belonging to."

I didn't need to say, *likewise*. He could read it curling through the bond.

We laid there, recovering, as the sun crept higher. There was work to do. What'd happened in Raleigh had probably sparked riots, and there'd be hell to pay for fleeing the police, even if we'd done nothing wrong. We both knew it. We were both, uncharacteristically, avoiding it all to stay in bed, wrapped up in each other.

Words jumped from me before I could think them through. "I want us to have a life just for us."

Troy's fingers stopped tracing patterns across my skin. "In what way?"

"I don't know. But I want this. More this. More..." I thought hard, trying to articulate the feeling. "Happy. Just existing."

His smile made me shiver as his lips curled against the back of my neck. "We'd get bored."

"That's true." I thought some more. "But we haven't had time to be us. And I haven't—"

The thought hit me like an earthquake. I hadn't menstruated yet. Which meant that for all this was the most peaceful time in my life, I was still effectively sterile. I hadn't felt safe enough for my body to agree to even think about—

I pushed the thought away.

We needed an heir for the House. Not just naming Allegra a princess. A blood heir. Mine and Troy's together. But it wasn't the need of the House I was thinking of. It was something deeper that I was too afraid just now to work through. Something that jangled against the ragged edges of my fucked-up childhood and made me doubt myself even more than being Arbiter. I couldn't take a step like that because of external need or obligation. That was selfish. I had to do it because of want. And while part of me did want, the other was terrified.

All I'd known growing up was abandonment and fear and pain. There was no way I could—

"What's wrong?" Troy asked.

I held onto the thread of gentleness in his tone. Reminded myself that brutal honesty was our policy. "I feel safe with you. But not with the world. Or myself."

He was quiet and still as he turned that over. There was a pulse of wary hope in the bond that he buried almost as quickly as it sparked, followed by sadness.

"We came to power a good twenty to forty years early," he said cautiously. The fingers tracing my flank slipped to draw slow circles around my lower belly, confirming that he did indeed know where my thoughts had gone. "We have time."

"We do. For now."

Troy read the truth in that as well and said nothing as he pulled me closer. The way shit was going, one of us might die sooner rather than later. Both of us.

Which only snarled my thoughts further.

"You gonna talk to the observers today?" I asked, risking setting him off again to think of anything else.

He grunted a yes, still thinking on what we'd just been talking about.

"You need me there?"

"Not if you have plans. They'll be dealing with me when they get here. Might as well start now."

"Good. I need to head to the bar and check in with Ruprecht then follow up with Maria about what happened yesterday. Divide and conquer?"

"Works for me. Just be careful. And tell me if you get followed again. Raleigh PD might have their hands full for now, but the feds won't give up easily."

"I'll be sure to tell you." I rolled in his arms to give him a solid kiss. "You want first shower?"

"I was hoping you'd join me." His gaze darted to my thigh and back up. "Unless you need a little longer."

I pulled away, lifting my knee to check. The bite wouldn't heal completely, not this fast, but was healed enough that it wouldn't hurt to get it wet. "I definitely love the accelerated healing part of being a primordial."

The grin he gave me didn't show the sharp teeth but was predatory all the same. "As do I."

He pushed me to my back, nibbling my neck to make me squirm and giggle before continuing his roll and getting out of bed.

We took a little longer in the shower than strictly necessary, but I wanted to make sure he was definitely okay before we went our separate ways for the day. Last night had been one of the harder ones we'd had together. Disagreements on strategy or the management of the territory were relatively easy even if we both had a stake in our arguments. The personal stuff could get nasty. Especially given our families' shared history, our individual traumas, and our snarled and violent interpersonal history.

I also wasn't the best at opening up in relationships or doing all the little things that cemented two people together. But I was trying. I wanted him to enjoy being with me, not just be tied to me metaphysically. He might say I deserved his loyalty and sacrifices, but that didn't stop me from wanting to earn and reward them.

It must have been enough because the bond hummed with focus and purpose rather than dread or anger as he left, leaving whichever of the Ebon Guard had been posted up on night duty to watch over me.

That whole situation bugged me—that we were still keeping one of the Guard at my house. I'd been fine with just the wards for a long time. Troy had only powered through them to help me with the rabisu because he'd focused on the idea of protecting me and then had acted to do so, for all he'd scared the bejeezus outta me when he did. But in the year and a half since the Reveal, nobody other than the gods had made their way through without an invitation. Or Duke, with his blood tie to me.

Even if someone else did make it through the wards, they'd have to get past the gytrash, the fae black dogs who were more than happy with their situation haunting my woods. Then this hypothetical intruder would have to hit me with bronze to stop my magic, and I wasn't new to my powers anymore. If they managed that, I had my Darkwatch training now.

Yeah. Maybe it was time to talk to Troy about freeing up the Guard to focus on things other than standing around outside. Like tracking down whoever had been following us yesterday evening rather than waiting for them to push past the magic and the tech keeping my life private.

Meantime, I had other concerns.

I washed up the breakfast dishes and then headed downtown with Thana, parking in a different deck than yesterday.

"Anything big on the docket today, ma'am?" she asked.

Like Troy, she kept her attention more on the surroundings than on me as we exited the garage. Also like Troy, she carried the burnt marshmallow scent of a heavy Aether practitioner rolling over her herby thyme and oregano scent. But otherwise, she had the same brisk efficiency all of the full-blooded ex-Darkwatch elves exuded. I didn't know how she felt about me, but she was one of the guards I liked best. Didn't fight with the half-elves—and more importantly, didn't consider us less-than. We'd had a few problems with high-bloods thinking their heritage or House mattered more than their skill and ability to play well with others. Those either came around real quick or were released from service.

I kept my own eyes moving, taking an active part in my own defense as we waited for the light to change to cross Morgan. We had a bit more of a walk to get to the bar today, but it was better than being predictable. Especially now that we might be tracked.

"Couple of things," I said. "Need to follow up on Raleigh first and foremost. Probably a boring day for you."

"Boring is good," she said. Our paces matched as we crossed the street. "I'm not in a hurry to reveal what we can do, if I'm honest, ma'am."

"Good. I don't want you to."

"Ma'am?" She pulled her eyes off the surroundings long enough to frown at me.

I lowered my voice, knowing her hearing was sharp enough to hear me. "All Troy showed in the second Reveal was shadows and teeth. The letter of the agreement with the alliance is that y'all are Revealed. Not how much. I want the rest kept quiet."

"What if there's an attack? The tag I put on the guy yesterday says he's still in the Durham area. They're not done yet."

Sighing, I thought it over before giving my reflexive response. Hobbling my bodyguards wouldn't help anything, even if I wasn't convinced I needed bodyguards at this point. I was known, but so were lots of people. Unlike lots of people, I could handle myself.

"I won't tell you not to use the training at your disposal," I finally said. "But I would ask that anything not publicly known be a last resort. Especially if they're not going for a kill."

"That's a very fine line, ma'am," Thana said grimly. "And realistically, one that's hard to discern in the moment."

"I know. But if an elf overreacts or rushes in and gets killed? With this new blood test or whatever it is that Verve has? You know they'd experiment on a body if they got to it before we do. At the very least they might start testing people in positions of power or influence."

"Ah. And that would lose us some key placements."

I nodded, glad she got it. We were speaking quietly, but I still tried not to say anything too obvious while in public. I'd worked as a private investigator long enough to know that you never knew who was listening or where. Especially with the government taking the steps it was.

And with that thought, the Sight flared to life again.

Chapter 24

I missed a step and nearly tripped.

"What is it?" Thana hissed as she caught my elbow and steadied me. She'd been around me often enough and long enough to know I didn't just stumble on thin air.

"The Sight. Something's wrong."

"Do you know what?"

"Government. I think. I was thinking about listening devices and the government."

"Now?"

"I don't know." I couldn't keep the frustration out of my tone. Some djinn could give a what but not a when with their Sight-driven prophecies, like Duke. Some could give a when or a where but not a what. Others didn't have the talent at all. Mine, via my djinni mother, was a shadow of what a full djinni would have, even if it apparently made me a Dreamwalker. Which I still had to figure out what that even was. "All it tells me is when I'm on the right track."

"It's definitely not the same guy as yesterday. Tell the king and the captains. I'll keep watch."

As I took out my phone to alert Troy, Etain, and Omar that we might have a problem, a faint *ka-thunk* off to the side distracted me. Out of Darkwatch-trained reflex, I pulled on Air and threw a wall up.

A beanbag thudded into it and fell to the ground before it could hit me in the ribs.

I didn't have time to swear before a burly man came out of the shop we'd just passed and lunged for me.

Thana slid between us, smoothly grasping his arm and breaking it at the elbow. "Run! Get out of the ambush zone!"

Pride stung me, but she was the bodyguard.

I ran.

We were nearing the edge of downtown, but there were still too many people in the area for me to risk using my magic at its full strength. I snarled. That had to have been their plan. Trust that I wouldn't risk civilian casualties or have an optics coup if I did.

And while I was faster than a human, it meant nothing if I was stuck in a crowd.

Fuck. Downtown Durham was the perfect trap. Not only was it my seat of power, but I was also personally committed to it and to the relationship with the mundanes living in it, whether they knew it or not. I wasn't in a hurry to destroy the city again after shattering pieces of it trying to save it. I wasn't going to risk throwing Otherside in a bad light by lashing out with magic. And the buildings and people meant I couldn't move at full speed.

Jordan Lake flashed through my mind. My Darkwatch trial, not the other events that'd happened there. I'd been cornered then too. But I'd found my way free.

I can do this.

Rather than continuing to the bar, I cut west down Hunt Street. The zoning was a mix of residential and commercial here, and there was a skate park down this way I was hoping would give me room to work.

No joy.

A black SUV, bigger and louder than the hybrid ones favored by the Darkwatch, pulled across the middle of the street to block my path, lights and sirens going.

I threw up a wall of Air as a gun was leveled. The pop it made was off—and rather than a bullet, a dart hit my wall and fell to the ground.

The fuck?

A scuff warned me there was someone behind me, and I threw up a wall all the way around myself, blocking two more darts. Okay, so whatever this was, they wanted me alive. That gave me options. Troy would be pissed. But if I was taken, I could potentially learn more about who was behind this.

A small comfort because I didn't have much faith in what would happen when we got to wherever these fuckers were going. But if they were using darts, it was because they didn't know about what bronze could do to me.

"We've got her cornered, sir," the first shooter said into one of those classic clear earpieces with the spiraling wire. "Some kind of magic in play though. We can't get to her."

I snarled, trying to keep my mind clear of the spike of adrenaline and the concern crowding my mind from Troy as my phone buzzed, still clenched in my hand.

"What do you want?" I asked. "Who are you working for?"

He didn't answer. Typical.

We were in a standoff, just like when Troy and I had fought Callista. Only this time, I was alone, stuck in broad daylight, downtown, with people's houses and livelihoods surrounding me in addition to enemies and Goddess knew how many civilian cell phones. These assholes could last a lot longer than I could as well. It didn't take much power or effort to maintain a wall of Air, but the longer I dragged this out, the more of a media circus it would become and the more information they could gather about how long I could hold if pushed.

Shit.

I had to end this.

Now.

I pushed the wall ahead and behind and lunged forward with all the speed I had.

All thought stopped.

There was only action. I reached for the dart gun as my Air punch hit the guy in front and staggered him. I twisted the wrist inward like Troy had shown me. Took the gun. Shot first the guy in the car then the driver as he scrambled for his own gun then the two in the back seat.

The dart gun clicked.

Hands closed on my arm from behind.

I fought them off.

I'd never put Troy's training to the test in a real combat situation, but I mopped the floor with the bastards.

It was almost too easy. In hapkido I'd always held myself back. Tried to hide my speed and strength out of necessity. When I'd nearly hurt a human, I'd quit the class and reluctantly called Troy for help. Training with him—an Othersider, an *equal*, even if I hadn't quite known what I wanted from him yet at the time—had given me new confidence.

Confidence I used now to stand alone. As had been my goal for years.

I downed all my assailants, barely sweating in the February chill as I swept the area for more.

I found one. And metal. Up high, on a roof. Away from the immediate combat.

I spun, already throwing a whirlwind and preparing myself for the punch of a bullet, but I was too late and I'd miscalculated the angle for the wind.

Pinch.

Frowning, I tugged the silly little dart out of my neck the moment before another pinched me. What the fuck was it with these darts?

Before I could summon Air to block the third, my muscles suddenly gave up. I dropped. Dizzy. Limbs slack.

Ketamine? What was it the werewolves had been drugged with at the Wild Hunt?

It didn't matter. I was down.

I didn't go out. Not completely. But the world was muffled, and I barely felt the bite of asphalt against my cheek, gritty yet distant. My emotions were muzzy.

Troy's, pouring through the bond, were more so.

I couldn't summon the wits to do anything about it.

Footsteps crunched on grit.

"She's down. Yessir, we got the demon. She took out three teams though. No sir. By herself. Hand-to-hand. There was another female, but we lost her. Disappeared when she couldn't make it to Finch. She was there, and then she wasn't. Another demon, maybe."

Good for Thana, even if she'd disobeyed orders using some magic. Maybe they were going to kill her. I wouldn't have wanted that. I liked her. And we couldn't afford to give the feds a body.

A rough grip pulled my hands behind me and fastened my wrists together at the small of my back with the annoying ratcheting-plastic sound of zip ties.

Ridiculous. I started giggling. Zip ties couldn't hold me. Whatever this drug was might make me senseless but—

Another pinch, and I was gone.

△▽△▽

I woke up in a dark, shaking box.

My head pounded. My mouth was sticky with dried saliva. My muscles ached from being twisted and tied, my body crumpled on the rumbling floor.

I couldn't see anything. I blinked. Then again, squeezing them tight before trying to see again. My eyes were open, but the world was dark. I froze, remembering the weight of collapsed earth overhead, of too little air and no light. I'd been trapped, buried alive, underground, and nothing but the scent of dirt and death and rosemary and sage and burnt marshmallow and—

Troy. And Troy.

When I got my claustrophobic panic under control, I realized all those scents were a panicked memory, not real. It wasn't the underground lich's lair or anywhere underground at all. It was the back of a mundane van, and said mundanes were so busy bitching about Othersiders that they hadn't noticed their drugs had worn off and I was awake.

Hooded. Bound at wrist and ankle. But awake...and able to reach my magic.

I could also reach Troy. He was still nestled in the back of my head, despite however much distance was between us now. Too many emotions blended for me to separate them out, but topmost was rage.

I reached for him. Stretched through the bond and anchored myself in him. We couldn't speak mind-to-mind at this distance, but I tried. Soothed what I could of the fury that threatened to overwhelm his reason.

I'm okay, I sent, even if he couldn't hear it. He'd sense the gist of it.

Immediately the rage flattened. Narrowed. Focused to a point. He had a destination for his mission now. A purpose.

Troy was always at his best when he was set to a purpose.

As for me, I wasn't truly okay. When I reached for my land, the places I'd tied myself to with magic, they were all well to the south. We were probably somewhere in Virginia and heading north.

North-ish. North and east.

Ah.

So...the feds. Or someone wanting me to think they were the feds, if they had any idea I could recover this quickly from three—four?—darts of whatever sedative they'd hit me with. I vaguely remembered being called a demon. Fools. They wouldn't know what to do with a real demon. But given what'd been exposed by Duke's spell at the press conference, this could be the new agency as easily as the Sons of Seth. Two sides of the same coin, working toward the same aims.

Despite the grim situation, calm settled over me. I stayed as still as I could and kept my breathing even.

The last time I'd been kidnapped, I'd panicked. Or the last two times, really. So, this wasn't my first rodeo—and more to the point, I wasn't who I'd been. Troy had seen to that, first by setting himself against me and then by aligning himself with me.

I was stronger now. Faster. Better trained. And didn't need to hide who or what I was any longer.

That made me smile, an ugly, dangerous curling of my lips that scraped against the rough fabric of the hood. I might be fucked. But this time, I could unfuck myself. And from the sense of the bond, Troy wasn't far behind us and gaining fast.

As I calmed, my sense of Troy did too. We both fell into the deadly focus that was his default for a mission.

I had options.

Recalling my training, I centered myself in my senses. Moving vehicle. Human scents only, all masculine. I sent blended Water and Fire into the space in a questing tendril, counting circulatory and nervous systems. Four in the back, aligned as though on side benches, with me in between. Two in the front, one driver, one passenger. Gun oil. Snacks, some kind of protein bar. We were moving at speed, so a freeway. Likely 85 North.

I closed my eyes and fed those sensations back to Troy then dropped my shields further, reaching for my surroundings.

"Fuck but this bitch creeps me out," one of the men said as my power signature spilled into the space.

The other men agreed, and someone kicked my thigh.

I didn't react, having had plenty of practice trying to lure Troy into thinking I was down. They had no idea how creepy I could be.

Reaching for the nature at the edges of the freeway was hard while moving, but at Troy's urging, I'd learned. Trees were generally somnolent in winter as the cold forced the deciduous varieties to shed their leaves and the conifers to drop their cones. Grasses died back. But there was still a day-night ebb and flow of energy, if I listened for it.

Still day. They must have put me in their vehicle and fled north as quickly as they could. I'd come round faster than I'd thought.

Some metal moved ahead of us. A truck. Some more metal far off to the left—traffic in the other lane. Not many witnesses.

Good.

I reached toward Troy again, trying to gauge how far behind he was. Not too far. Thana must have gotten away quickly and gotten a message off when she couldn't get to me.

Support was coming, which meant I could afford to be a little reckless. Because while there might be some strategic value in finding out who had me, there was more than one way to do that.

Causing a car accident and seeing who came for the wreckage was more appealing to me than allowing them to get me all the way to whatever secure facility they had prepared. Troy and whoever was with him would be able to break me out, but why make them do all that when I could save my own damn self?

I didn't want to hit more vehicles than this one. These other drivers hadn't asked to be caught up in what was becoming a war between the mundanes and me.

But I'd been taken too many times as it was. And I was not about to let Senator Wright, or whoever had orchestrated this, take me again.

Once or twice, early in our acquaintance, I'd threatened to blow Troy's car off the road and wrap it around a tree. A freak accident of nature. An unexplained tornado that, if he survived it, would be hell to explain to his insurance company.

It would have been a strain then. It'd be easy as breathing now.

I reached for Troy. Sent him as strong a sense as I could that everything would be okay. Then I pushed through the throbbing headache and reached for as much Air as I could hold. Fashioned a small cocoon around myself. Shaped the rest into my best approximation of the front end of a Mack truck as apprehension skyrocketed from Troy.

And then I slammed my truck of Air into the side of the vehicle.

Impact.

The crunch of metal and plastic.

Weightlessness. Confused shouts. Fear scent that made my mouth water in a way that hadn't happened before.

Second impact.

I grunted and hissed in pain as I hit the edge of my cocoon. All it did was soften the blow of landing, not eliminate it. Even I couldn't get around physics without warping reality.

Roll.

Roll.

Roll.

Between the disorientation and the pain in my head, I lost control of Air and my cocoon shattered.

Third impact.

I hit a hard surface.

Piercing pain.

No more movement.

Hiss and ping of the engine. Pained groans. Some of them mine. Some from my kidnappers. Earthy-metallic scent of human blood. Cloying scent of gasoline.

It took me a few heartbeats to realize that A, I'd survived my admittedly ill-advised plan and B, Troy was equal parts horrified and furious. I'd been too focused on control and ignoring my pain to wall him out, and he'd felt every terrifying heartbeat of the crash.

I reached, trying to reassure him, but a stabbing pain in my side twisted it.

He knew where I was. I had to concentrate on myself. I had to get out.

The only sound was creaking metal and wind moving through shattered window glass. I couldn't manipulate plastic, but I could melt it. Gritting my teeth against the pain, I twisted my hands, coaxed Fire to me, and let the heat of a small ball of flame melt the zip ties enough that I could jerk my hands apart. The plastic gave reluctantly, dragging out in long, searing strings that stank and burned against my wrists, but I was free.

When I yanked the hood off with a flinch for the pain in my right flank, I found myself in the back of a transit van laying on its side. My pain was from a twisted piece of metal that'd sheared off somehow in the crash and caught me in the side.

Fuck. Not good. The bright ozone scent of me was stronger as blood dribbled with every throb of my pulse.

Shuddering, I centered myself again and finished my evaluation.

Four human men lay in the space with me. Two dead. One on his way. The fourth unconscious. Two more in the front, both alive but unconscious, the driver dangling by his seatbelt.

It could only have been moments since the crash, but there would be bystanders. Soon. If I was really unlucky, this wasn't the only van for this group. I needed to move.

Quick eval of my flank. The metal shard had missed my liver—I thought. Hoped? And it wasn't too deep. I could move. If I had to. And I did have to, even if I was reluctant to pull the metal out.

I fought agony as I got to my feet then fished in pockets and gathered wallets and tech. Anything that'd help the Ebon Guard or the Darkwatch figure out who the fuck these assholes were.

Then I made my way to the back doors of the van, melted the hinges with Fire, and blew them open with a burst of Air.

The leather backpack I used as a purse was wedged in the corner that met the ceiling on the side nearest the ground, and I scooped it up. Unzipped it as my vision swam. Wallet. Keys. Phone.

Good. At least I wouldn't have to have the Darkwatch hack my phone and erase everything.

I dropped what I'd stolen in my bag, zipped it up, and slung it on my back. Stumbled out and onto the grass. Fell to my hands and knees, gasping, dizzy with pain, as the metal piercing my side dug deeper with the fall.

Troy was still getting closer. A few cars were pulled off to the side of the road. Mundanes were shouting.

I had a choice.

Let them come down and save the three humans who still clung to life.

Or spark the leaking gasoline and cover evidence of myself.

By the tenets of Otherside in general and the Darkwatch in particular, there was no choice at all.

I let exhaustion pull me all the way to the ground and reached for Fire.

Chapter 25

T roy was definitely close because as the gasoline ignited and sent a searing hot ball of fire skyward, pure horror washed through the bond.

I'm okay! I sent.

I wasn't really except that okay meant alive. All my moving hadn't helped with the bit of metal in my side, and the heat of the burning car would have killed or severely burned anyone not gifted with Fire and Air.

But the sense of it—of me being alive and still in control of myself—returned Troy to the state of laser focus.

I wanted to stay put. Help was coming. I'd done enough, both to free myself and destroy the evidence of an Othersider in custody. The fire was too much for humans to dare getting close, and there were no sirens yet. Troy would reach me first.

Still. I was too close to the road.

I drew a breeze to me to diffuse the heavy black smoke for cover and dragged myself deeper into the trees, drawing on the strength from the cold earth and the sleeping plants. Not like a witch would draw their energy and kill them, but more of a borrowing. A kinship. I was them. They were me.

Thunder rolled overhead.

With a curse that was more thought than spoken, I let go of the elements. I couldn't afford to draw a storm to me, certainly not a thunderstorm in February. They weren't unheard of in the mid-Atlantic but combined with a car randomly flying off the road and a sudden explosion would spell Otherside.

Pain jabbed deeper in my right flank. I dropped, pressing my hand around the metal. It had to come out before I healed around it, and it staying in while I moved meant it was continually cutting me up anew. But I didn't know if it'd cut anything vital, and if it did come out now, I might bleed out too fast for even my accelerated healing to save me.

"Arden!"

I blinked my eyes open. I must have blacked out, from pain or concussion or the aftereffects of whatever I'd been drugged with.

Troy was weaving through the trees at top speed, a dizzying blur to my pounding head.

Closer to the road, the kidnappers' van still burned. Smoke still fled skyward, forcing a helicopter to stay back. Sirens screamed in the distance; presumably the freeway was backed up by now.

We had to go.

I pushed myself to a seated position, grimacing at the fresh burst of pain.

"Stop moving," Troy snapped as he reached me. "What—"

I lifted my arm to show him, and blood drained from his face. Then fury tightened it as I forced myself to rise.

He glared down at me. The bond throbbed with equal parts fear, anguish, rage, guilt, and horror.

I didn't get it. Until I remembered this morning.

Fuck.

Just this morning I'd hinted that I wanted a family. And now I did this—put myself in an extreme amount of danger when help was already on its way.

"Sorry," I whispered.

Anguish won out, and he scooped me up before I could fall, careful of my wound.

Two more elves melted out of the forest. Samarre and Thana.

Great. Just what I needed. Politics while wounded.

Samarre, Jacinthe, and Luc insisted, and they were already at Ebon Guard HQ, Troy said when I stiffened. *I didn't have time to argue.*

Any healers?

Not yet. We couldn't risk them since we didn't know what we were going into. I called in for one when the vehicle blew.

Fair. I focused my efforts on staying conscious as the elves cast overlapping don't-see-me spells.

We emerged from the woods, moving slowly both to avoid jarring me too much and to prevent breaking the effect of the magic. All mundane attention was on the car fire that was now half a mile up the road. I reached past the pain and summoned a burst of Fire and a buffeting wind to send the flames from the van fire higher and keep the helicopter busy. Some of the trees at the edge of the road were burning, and while I felt a pang for their destruction, at least it'd destroy the evidence of my blood trail. None of the mundanes in their vehicles noticed as the elves slipped back into three vehicles caught in the traffic.

Haroun was in the back seat of Troy's SUV, and he caught my feet to guide me in then laid them across his lap, grimacing at my whimper of pain.

Etain twisted to look at me from the front seat. "Goddess damn it, what—" Her nostrils flared as the door slammed and the scent of my blood filled the tight space. "Shit."

Troy ignored her, focusing on making sure I was comfortable with my head in his lap and that the blanket Haroun had pulled out was covering my injury.

"Crack the windows," Troy said distantly, his full attention on checking me over.

Etain frowned at him. "But she's—"

"She's going to settle from the drugs and the endorphins blocking the pain of being moved in a minute. And then she's going to be a wounded sylph in a small dark box surrounded by elves with no moving air," Troy snapped. "Crack. The

Goddess-burning. Windows. Unless you want us to end up like the motherfuckers she flipped off the road and incinerated."

With an elvish swear, Etain did as he said.

I shuddered, finding a measure of calm as light slanted in through the crack in the heavily tinted windows and fresh air flowed through the car. Then the shudder turned into shaking. Heat became cold. My skin felt clammy and too tight on my bones, and I couldn't quite catch my breath no matter how quickly I panted.

"She's going to crash," Troy said. "When she goes, I might go with her, depending on how bad this puncture wound in her flank is. I think she's blocking me from some of it, but she's worse now than twenty minutes ago. If I go, you're in charge, Etain. Phone in anything you can't handle to Allegra."

"Yes, sir," Etain said.

I tried to find my voice, either to reassure or to protest or...something. But the world was spinning. Too fast. My stomach cramped.

"Gonna be sick," I whispered.

"Breathe," Troy said. His hand settled over my forehead, fingers pressing into my temples.

A groan escaped me as the pain was numbed from my nervous system, and the dizziness eased.

"Better?" he asked.

The cessation of pain dragged me into unconsciousness before I could answer him.

△▽△▽

Waking was more comfortable the next time, even if consciousness was spun out of another dream of the In-Between and chiming laughter.

I jerked, and the dream released me. I woke choking on a gasping breath as I reached for Air.

"Whoa! It's okay, my queen."

I turned toward the feminine voice and found a blond elfess at my side. Fi Sequoyah. Darkwatch-turned-Ebon Guard, undercover as a surgeon in Chapel Hill.

"Ophelia."

"Good, you know who I am. What's your name?"

I humored her as I fingered the tender but healed skin where I'd been wounded, since I'd probably concussed myself at some point. "Arden Finch Solari, High Queen of what's left of the Chapel Hill Conclave, Arbiter of the Triangle territory and the Carolinas demesne."

"Very good. What's the date?"

"Far too close to my fucking birthday for me to have to put up with this shit."

She smiled and let that slide. "And who's he?"

I turned my head to follow her pointing finger and tried to sit up. "Troy!"

"Shh, lay back. He's fine. Or at least not physically harmed. We can't wake him though."

Troy lay on a cot next to the one I was on, completely unconscious. The bond was still there, just quiet.

I winced. "I must have been hurt badly enough to draw on his vitality to heal faster."

"We thought it might be that, since you were healed around the metal when you got here. Good to have it confirmed. Probably a fascinating case for a Luna, but Iago stayed in the Triangle and Thana's on duty."

"Stayed? Where are we?"

Fi looked around the darkened area, a large cubicle in a high-ceilinged space lit only by camp lanterns. "This is a Darkwatch facility on the Virginia side of the border. Originally intended to support the Richmond Conclave if they came under attack from the Farkas wolf pack or the Philadelphia coterie. The Captain gave us the access codes."

"Glad Omar is playing well with others," I said.

A gasp at my side had me twisting back to Troy.

"Arden!"

"I'm here, cariñomí."

His gaze swept over me as he tensed, visibly holding himself in check as he realized we weren't alone. "You're okay?"

"I'm fine. Thanks to you." I looked over my shoulder and nodded at Fi. "Thanks to all of you."

"Remind me not to try taking you somewhere you don't want to go," she said lightly. "I'll be getting a nap in. Shout if you need me." She tugged a curtain hanging across the entry to the cubicle mostly closed and slipped through it.

There were other elves nearby, but we were as alone as we could get in a converted warehouse.

"How are you feeling?" I asked Troy.

He frowned. "I should be asking you that."

"You didn't just auratically drain me because you flipped a car off the road and lit it on fire." I kept my tone dry but figured we should get this part of the reconnection over as quickly as possible. He'd been pissed before, in the heartbeat before he'd picked me up and carried me out.

Troy surprised me though. Pride shone through the bond. "You did well. I couldn't follow your thoughts, but you controlled your emotions and found calm. Assessed the situation. Made the best choice available to you to keep a key asset out of enemy hands." He glanced away, and I followed his gaze to my bag, sitting in the corner. "You even managed to secure intel. And most unusual for you, you didn't try to do it all yourself. You got clear and waited for support rather than injuring yourself further."

"Oh." I squirmed, dropping down to the cot and cuddling closer. "Um. Thanks."

He snorted. "I'm still not happy about all of it. But this is good. It's progress. Even if it makes me want to shake you."

I traced my fingers along his jaw and over his lips. "I can't guarantee it won't happen again. I have to keep trying to do this my way."

Troy captured my fingers and kissed them. "I know. And I can't guarantee that I won't go a little crazy over it."

"Damn hormones."

He grunted an affirmative. "It was a lot easier to stay cold before you. But it's worth the trade."

Relief flooded me, and I kissed him. "Glad you think so."

A ripple swept through the bond, kind of like what a sonar scan would feel like if it was physical. "You're all healed up? That shard made its way to your liver on the drive over. Internal bleeding."

"That's why you went down?"

He nodded. His eyes darkened to shadowed labradorite as fear raced through him and was suppressed. "I thought we were going to lose you. Stopped walling you out."

"We're seriously going to have to figure something out about that. That's too big a cost—losing one of us means losing both. The House needs you, and the Triangle needs us both."

"I know. I'll check back in with Iago when we get back. Maybe he's made progress on his study." He frowned and another ripple ran over me. "Did you activate the ring?"

"No?" I tugged it off and peered at it. Now that Troy mentioned it, there was something different about it. A spark of magic that hadn't been there before. "I must've bled on it holding the wound."

His expression tightened. "Let's hope for the best then."

I gave Troy a last kiss rather than answer and eased myself to my feet. Iago had been working on the "auratic entanglement," as he called it, for a year now. It wasn't easy, since the best way to study it was for either Troy or me to be so badly wounded that we drew on the other's aura and vitality for support, but at least he was trying. I didn't want to be severed from Troy again, but I did want to find a way to manage this.

The cot creaked as Troy rose as well, and I didn't bother hiding my admiration as he stretched and limbered. He'd always had an alluringly cat-like grace, but as he grew into his full elven powers and stopped trying to hide himself, it'd only gotten more fluid. He smirked at me and shook his head but was, as always, pleased by my attention.

We held hands loosely as we slipped past the curtain to enter the rest of the space. Like many Darkwatch outposts—or at least the ones I'd been told about—this was a converted warehouse. Concrete floor, support pillars scattered at even intervals, some of which had partitions set up between them to create rooms for bunks or work. Windows higher up where light could come in but not the eyes of snoopers. It'd have bathrooms and a shower somewhere and a cooking area with hot plates or maybe a microwave. Power probably came from solar to avoid drawing from the grid and reduce the odds of gaining someone's attention, since this place didn't have the ozone scent that spoke of a high-tech listening post. Just a place to stay and keep watch.

This particular outpost reminded me of the old furniture factory where we'd recovered Iaret. It didn't have the sawdust or anything else indicating what the space had been used for before, but there was a hollow emptiness that spoke of old ghosts and older days. And blessedly, fans spun overhead, giving me at least the illusion of air flow.

I lifted my eyebrows at the number of people in the room.

"You brought this many?" I murmured. There had to be three triple triads, totaling twenty-seven elves.

"All Thana knew was they were well-trained and numerous. Terrence and Ximena agreed to keep an eye on Chapel Hill while we were gone. Ximena said, and I quote, 'Y'all better rip some throats out for this.'"

Ah. That being the point of the alliance to begin with. Still, I thanked my stars the Triangle was the territory it was. Anywhere else would have other factions moving in to take it or even ambitious parties within the same faction. It was how Maria had come to power—filling a sudden power vacuum.

"I suppose burning alive will have to do." A pang hit me at realizing that's indeed what I'd done. I hardened myself against it. They'd picked the battle. I'd finished it. And I'd finish the next ones, if they didn't learn their lesson this time.

Troy shuddered, and fear spiked in the bond.

I rubbed his back, annoyed with myself for triggering one of his worst memories—being seared with hot iron then having the skin peeled from him in strips. "Sorry."

He just walled me out a little then leaned over and kissed my head, steering me toward the far corner.

It held a briefing space, with a whiteboard affixed to the wall and a table and chair in front of it. More chairs in neat rows facing the whiteboard sat beyond that. Etain sat at the table next to Haroun, scowling at a tablet.

She looked up and shot to her feet. "My queen. My king."

I nodded to her. "Hey, Etain, Haroun. How's things?"

She flushed. "I'm sorry. About the—the injury."

"Why? You didn't do it."

Troy said, "The metal pierced your liver when she took a corner too fast and all of us slid." He fixed her with a steady stare. "Necessary, given we needed to keep the convoy together through a light."

"Yes, sir." Etain still looked sheepish and was ignoring the *I told you so* look Haroun was giving her.

I squeezed her arm, knowing elves preferred physical reassurance. "Hey, I'm alive. Troy's alive. Everyone except the bad guys came out in one piece. It's a win."

"Thank you, ma'am."

Troy sent an approving tap in the bond. "Report."

Etain's expression shifted to savage amusement so fast I blinked. "Whoever it was thinks the queen is dead, sir. And it seems like that somebody is none other than Senator Wright, legislative sponsor for the Bureau for Supernatural Investigation."

"Son of a bitch." I clenched my fists as the Sight flared. "I fucking knew it. I *knew* there was no way this was on the level."

"Sight?" Troy asked.

"Yeah. I just wish it would tell me *before* shit like this happened. Wait—Etain, how do we know this?"

"Because he called Maria to express his condolences and extend her an invitation to come to Washington."

"What'd she say?"

"Put him in a polite holding pattern. When Noah couldn't reach you, he tried King Troy." She glanced at him and winced. "I took the call."

"Good," he said. "I told you, you're in charge if I'm out. Own that. This is only going to be the first attack. We need our systems and processes strong for the next one."

Etain stood straighter. "I will, sir. Own it, I mean. And make sure everything is as strong as I can make it."

From the fire in her gaze, she would. Haroun too. I wasn't the only one with something to prove. Troy had just handed her an opportunity I'd wager no half-elf had ever been given, and she was going to make the most of it. Not just for herself but to prove—whether for herself or for all half-elves—that they were just as good as full-bloods.

I knew the feeling.

Troy nodded. "Okay. Next steps?"

She hesitated, obviously having expected Troy to give the orders, but recovered quickly. "I was thinking, majesties. If the werecats are happy to cover the territory a little longer, we have a solid opportunity to do some recon while the human powers that be think the queen is out of the picture. We're too close to the Richmond Conclave for comfort here, but at the same time, we haven't been able to figure out what they're doing."

I crossed my arms and rapped my fingers along my bicep. "It would be good to have more intel. Seems odd to have a vampire ally in New York but no idea what a conclave on our own borders is doing."

"Agreed," Troy said. "I would have said we retreat back to the Triangle and shore up defenses against Santiago, but with Matthias agreeing to move south and Maria stalling the Bureau, we have options. Briefly. But I would sign off."

There was another missing piece though. "We haven't heard from the djinn in a while. Let's see if Duke or Iaret or both can come here for an update. Then we'll move forward with Etain's idea if we don't have anything from them."

Etain kept her face straight, but the lift of her chin spoke to her pride. Haroun's too—he was smothering a smile.

Troy clapped her on the shoulder. "Make the plans."

We made a round of the space, checking in on our people, reassuring them all was well while munching on some beef jerky Troy had snagged and given me with a no-nonsense look.

Seeing me on my feet helped.

My smile at the idea of taking action helped more.

One way or another, my days of hiding were over. And for once, I shivered with the anticipation of running a hunt as the hunter, rather than the prey.

Chapter 26

To my surprise, Duke sent Iaret alone to speak with me and Troy. There was the usual tug on my aura as he made the connection, and then she was beside us in the curtained-off cubicle Troy and I had woken up in. She took her favorite human shape, the elegant woman with tight-cropped curls and dark, dark skin, dressed in close-fitting black today, which made the sparking of her opaline gaze even more obvious than usual.

We huddled close to speak quietly enough not to be overheard by the sharp senses of a roomful of elves.

"Good, you're alive," Iaret said. "The fools we're observing are all a-tizzy over some explosion or other. Did you blow up a car?"

"Someone kidnapped me," I said. "And did a really shitty job of it, fortunately. I got hit with a ton of ketamine or something—"

I turned to Troy.

"Blood test is being run," he said, anticipating what I was about to ask. "I told Etain to have Ophelia do it before going down."

"Good. Thanks." I didn't want to be caught off-guard again. "Whatever it was, it knocked me on my ass. But not for as long as they apparently thought it should have, and they didn't have any bronze. I woke up, blew the car off the road, stole some shit, and set everything on fire. Including all the agents who'd taken me."

"How delightful!" Iaret beamed, clasping her hands in front of her. "We'll make a djinni out of you yet, my dear. I knew you had it in you."

I didn't know what to say to that.

"What's the status inside the Bureau?" Troy asked, saving me.

"Chaos." Her eyes closed and her lips curled up in pleasure. "Pure chaos."

"You couldn't have warned us this was going to happen?" I said. "That's part of why we sent you."

"We didn't know. We were busy derailing the other plan."

I exchanged a frustrated look with Troy. "What other plan?"

"The one where they're backing Santiago in another coup attempt."

"Oh, for fuck's sake," I snarled. My hunch had been right. "Do they have Matthias as well?"

"No. They don't have info on him other than that there is a master vampire in New York City."

Troy frowned. "But Santiago has become known since the Reveal for his extravagant lifestyle. And ambitions."

Iaret nodded. "So ambitious that he hasn't told dear Matthias of these plans." Her grin widened. "It'll be a double-cross."

"It certainly will," I said. "Because I've swayed Matthias to my side. Admittedly, with the promise that if I saw an opening to drop a favorable word about him with someone influential, I'd do so. But if they don't even know who he is and they're using who they have identified to run ops against us, then taking this to him should settle things in lieu of my good word."

"We need to get ahead of this," Troy said. "Solidify the Carolinas demesne. Then expand. Etain's plan is a good start."

The idea of taking more territory—even if some of it was technically mine, since Callista had claimed both the Carolinas as hers—made my head spin. But the Triangle was filling up fast, too fast, and not only was it exacerbating existing resourcing issues but even the pro-Otherside mundanes whose support hadn't waned were getting anxious.

The anti-Othersiders were getting bolder, louder, and more violent, even as they insisted they were a silent majority. Same old playbook with a new target.

We needed more space. And I needed to insist that the rest of the territory take in more Othersiders. They couldn't all keep coming to Durham, progressive as it was. Beyond the space issue, there was also a simple strategic concern: having a huge chunk of Otherside in one place would make it easy to eliminate all of us if the feds decided one human city was expendable.

Shit.

Troy and Iaret were watching me, waiting for my response. Even Iaret looked unusually serious as I considered my plays.

The vampire Master of Charlotte had loosely allied with Maria, though not with me. I hadn't heard shit out of Roman or Sergei Volkov in Asheville; the Blood Moon werewolf clan had gone quiet as their sister's Red Dawn clan ascended. I'd read an old Darkwatch report about a sea fae who had her own information network in the Outer Banks, one who must have been powerful if Callista hadn't moved against her. That covered mountains to sea in North Carolina alone.

An enormous territory, when I'd just wanted to protect my little corner of it. And now we were eyeing not only Charleston to the south but Richmond to the north as well. We'd have to, if we wanted a buffer between the heart of my demesne and the human federal government.

I sighed. "I guess it's time to step up."

Troy nodded. "I know you'd hoped we'd have better relations with the mundanes before making this move."

"Yeah. But I should have been faster to move when everything went sideways in last year's midterm elections. Nobody else is stepping up. If there's someone stronger than me on this plane, they're either playing smart or coward by keeping their head down."

Iaret's eyes sparkled. "Of course there are beings stronger than you, silly. Otherside goes bump in the night, but the Nightmares eat your soul."

I blinked and Troy tensed.

"The what?" we asked.

"Nightmares. The Grand Court."

Grim calculation slithered through Troy to me as he said, "Why is this the first time we're hearing of them?"

"Is it?" Iaret grinned. "I suppose Keithia wouldn't have told everything to a child she'd have killed if her captain hadn't stepped in. Assuming she knew herself. It has been an age since they stirred themselves. And *I* have been dreadfully busy."

"Iaret, when we have Santiago sorted and ten minutes to breathe, I'm gonna need you to fill us in," I said. "Please."

"Of course. Now, I really should get back to play." Without waiting for a response, she shimmered and changed planes in a burst of lemon zest.

Troy crossed his arms and scowled. "Grand Court."

I wrestled with my intense curiosity. Was I wrong about my dreams being from the tricksters? Was it something from this Nightmare Court? But no, I couldn't afford to dive into that when I had bigger, realer threats right in front of me.

I shook my head. "Later. We know nothing and have nothing to go on. Have Iago search the archives. While we're at it, have him draw up resourcing plans. I need to know how stretched we are here in terms of prey and space before I reach out to the Master of Charlotte, Roman, and this fae Mami Wata out in Ocracoke."

"Yes, my queen."

I bit back a reminder not to call me that as he snagged his longknife from where it rested next to my bag and smoothly slid it home in the sheath he wore down his spine. He was in a headspace. Best to leave him to it rather than pick at him.

We passed a restless night planning. The knowledge that I'd have to face Renaud, the vampire Master of Charlotte, and whoever Mami Wata was weighed heavily on my mind. Sergei and Roman too eventually. But what weighed heaviest was what Iaret had said about this Grand Court. I laid awake, afraid to dream, long after Troy had given in and fallen asleep.

The next morning, I sat blearily in a too-hard chair with a cup of black tea that tasted faintly like coffee, the way hotel room tea did after being run through a shitty combo coffee-tea machine. It was just after dawn, which was far too early to be respectable, for all that elementals were supposed beings of the golden hour. The cots weren't as comfortable as my own bed, the coffee-tainted tea felt like a personal offense, I itched from the separation from my land, and I was beyond tired of playing dead after less than a day.

Ease up, Troy sent as he squeezed the back of my neck in a massaging grip. *Before you have everyone thinking they're doing something wrong.*

I forgot myself enough to glare at him, which would look unprovoked to anyone watching us. Fortunately, everyone had caught my mood and was busying themselves with other things.

Troy just smirked and sipped his own nasty coffee. *He* looked ridiculously well-rested. Even the bond felt fresh on his side.

"I thought you were supposed to be nocturnal," I grumbled.

"I am. I'm also disciplined."

With an effort, I suppressed the urge to use one of my passive powers to mimic his words back to him in his voice or stick my tongue out at him. He caught the feeling in the bond though, and his grin widened, which only pissed me off more.

I closed my eyes and took a breath rather than snap at him further. It wasn't his fault I was a homebody. "Has Maria called yet?"

"No. I imagine she and Matthias were laying out plans last night. They have to sleep sometime, cariñamí."

The sweetname broke through my irritation. I put down my disgusting tea and rose, folded into him, buried my face in his chest, and hugged him. "I think I need to make a tie to the land," I said. "This is fucking unbearable."

"I'd wondered if that was what was going on."

I tried to be soothed by his scent and the rumble of his voice, but it wasn't enough. Apparently, I was too deeply tied to my land to be this far away from it for this long and not suffer. A good thing to learn now, while I had space and time to learn it. The longest I'd been away before was a day trip to the beach. This was pushing twenty hours or so, on top of the stress of fighting the damn government and accidentally faking my death. If I didn't do something to manage it, I might find my magic trying to do something for me.

It...pulsed. Reached for home in a way that felt disconcertingly alive. Like it might sink into the ground or twist the winds of its own accord. That was a risk I couldn't take. Not with how finely balanced everything was and how tight our schedules were. We didn't have time for me to wrestle with control or for Troy to bring me back. Then there were the Lyon elves to consider.

Yeah. An uncontrolled elemental queen would be real impressive. Not.

Reluctantly, I pulled away. "I'll be outside. You can come with if you want."

He hesitated then glanced at Etain. Our captain was running a meeting with brisk, bright-eyed efficiency. *There* was a being of the golden hour, for all that the half-human were supposed to be more effective at dusk.

Or maybe she was just very aware that some of those reporting to her were elves and she had to be twice as good. Especially for an op being run against elves' natural circadian rhythms.

"I'm going," I said. "You decide. But I need the land."

"I'll be out in a few minutes."

Suited me just fine.

I had no idea where in Virginia we were on a map, but as I emerged from the warehouse and turned my face to the rising sun, the air held the faintest brackish tang. That combined with the flatness of the terrain said we were nearer the coast. Pines dominated, for the most part, along with some mixed hardwoods. Similar to home, but the land here was swampier. It tasted like peat to my senses—rotting things turned to richness. It was also colder here, if only by a pinch. Probably should have grabbed my jacket, but I'd been born a sylph. The air would warm up to suit me after a few minutes. It drove Troy nuts when I let the house get too cold for him, but it'd never bothered me as much as the humans' excessive use of air conditioning or heating did.

I didn't want Troy to worry about finding me or to be foolish enough to wander off in potentially hostile territory, so I dropped to the dirt outside the door and set my back against the wall. It was still too...people-y. But it was better than being surrounded on all sides by concrete with minimal air movement.

I reached out with my senses for a check of what was nearby.

A jammer of some kind, humming to my senses. Probably to block cell phone tracking. Cars, hidden under trees and camouflage nets. Birds. Some deer. Something bigger, a bear maybe.

That was interesting. I pulled back before I could draw its attention.

To the north and mostly east was a wide, slow river. A bit farther east was the Atlantic, and my heart leaped to find it. I'd found I liked oceans much better than lakes. Far to the west were the echoes of mountains. Nearer were foothills that remembered being bigger, ancient things nearly worn all the way down.

My magic settled with the stretch. This would do.

I dropped my shields and sank into the land and sky. The walls slammed up in the bond as I did so, Troy trying to avoid being pulled into nature's flow. I would have winced for not warning him, but I was pulled into it myself.

As the sun rose, I slowly stretched elemental tendrils of Air and Fire, Earth and Water, through sky and ground back to the Triangle, reaching, straining, trying to connect myself with my magic there. When I managed it, the relief was so sudden I sat up and gasped.

"Arden?"

I shook myself and blinked a few times, finding Troy sat next to me, fully alert. My coat had been draped over me, and when I flexed my fingers, I found a cloth-wrapped handwarming packet had been placed in my cupped hands. I'd missed all of it. That should have worried me, but I was surrounded by my people. I chose to trust that I'd be safe right next to the wall of the building holding us all.

"Are you okay?" His eyes searched me as much as his attention did in the bond.

I smiled, loving him for taking care of me even if he'd probably been grouchy about me not taking care of myself again. "I'm fine. Much better now, thanks. Connected with home is all. Fed the tie there. Claimed this place."

"Good." He eyed me. "You seem steadier. You ready to go in?"

I'd rather stay out here and just commune with nature, but that wasn't my job. "Yeah. Let's get the party started."

He rose and pulled me to my feet, wrapping my coat around my shoulders and tucking the handwarmer in his pocket without commenting on how out of it I'd been. Maybe he was getting used to it. Or maybe he just knew better than to make an issue out of it by now. It was in my nature to make ties to the land, like it was in his to hunt. We accepted each other.

The Ebon Guard and Lyon elves were all assembled when we walked in.

I cleared my throat and injected a cheerful note into my voice, or as much as I could, given the lingering frustration of not being at home. "All set?"

"Yes, my queen," Etain said.

"Talk me through it."

I did my best to pay attention to the strategy and tactics. I had to learn this shit. I couldn't rely on Troy and Allegra to break it down for me behind the scenes every time. The whole time, I was conscious of the Lyon elves...well, observing. Separate from the rest of the group, for all they'd insisted on coming along. I still wasn't happy with them for the shit they were trying to pull with Troy, but I tried to bury the feeling.

When Etain wrapped up her plan to infiltrate the Richmond Conclave's territory, I asked what I hoped was a smart strategic question. "What if someone is captured?"

Her expression went grim. "Richmond hasn't responded to Omar's attempts to make contact, so we have to assume they're hostile. Standard protocol for capture in enemy territory."

I went cold as my mind scrambled.

"Suicide?" I thought that was what Troy had told me.

Etain nodded sharply.

That made me sick and tired all over again. I crossed my arms, closed my eyes, and bowed my head. I was allowing—asking—these people to go on a dangerous mission. To serve me. They were doing this in my name. That would mean I was effectively signing their death warrant should anything go wrong, when we were only here to begin with because I'd been cocky and gotten caught, something Troy might have words about when we were home, alone, and less stressed.

I'd been almost completely hands off in the running of House Solari, for all it was my father's bloodline and royal title that'd given me the legitimacy—in elven eyes—to re-establish it and claim Troy as mine in weregild. Blood for blood, a prince for a prince. But this went beyond shit like how the Darkwatch and the Ebon Guard worked together or dealing with the fallout from my complete destruction of the Chapel Hill Conclave.

"No." I shook my head as I looked up. Met the eye of every elf in the room. "Not this time. Not for this."

Chapter 27

Cautious hope lit the bond and was smothered as Troy put his walls back up. He wanted me to make this call but didn't want to influence me. I didn't know why he couldn't make it himself, but he'd been hoping I'd go here. He stayed silent though, vocally and mentally.

"My queen?" Etain frowned. "That's— We all signed up for this."

I shook my head again as I saw my reluctance to allow new elves into the territory in a frightening new light. "No. We do not have so many people that I can afford for you to throw your lives away on a fast call made in the heat of the moment. Yes, they might try a Thread of Thorns and extract intel despite your best efforts. I've been through that, so I leave it to you to decide if you can bear it. But anyone taken might also find an opportunity to escape and come home."

I looked around the room again.

There was uncertainty in some eyes. Careful relief in some. Wary interest from the Lyon elves.

I thought of the werecats. Service leadership. Humility. Courage, even when you were small but especially in the name of justice.

Then I committed. "Should I have killed myself when I was taken?"

Nobody answered me. There were a few awkward shifts.

I turned to Troy. "Should I have?"

He kept his expression almost excessively neutral. "There's no recorded precedent for a queen being taken outside of a declared battle or hostile parlay. Mireia's choice last July was technically suicide, even if you wielded the knife. Otherwise, they don't put themselves at that much risk. They have the Darkwatch. Knights. House Guard. Assassins and spies."

"Layers of defense I've either refused or haven't built up yet. Thus, necessitating all of y'all to come after me because I won't stay at home in my lair."

Troy hesitated then nodded, a slow up and down with his gaze anchored on me as he tried to work out where I was going with effectively forcing him to publicly admit that I'd made an error. Hell, admitting it from my own mouth.

"Killing myself never crossed my mind. Escape did. Getting back to y'all did. Gathering intel, covering my tracks." I shook my head again as my gut churned. "For a species that is the slowest in Otherside to reproduce, elves seem ready to kill and die awful quick. Killing each other as weregild or for having too much power or too little or for bonding to someone you love. For what amounts to differences of opinion or upbringing or in the name of purity. That has to end. It *has* to. Or it won't matter what the mundanes do. You'll wipe yourselves out trying to uphold the supremacy of the queens. No. No more mission suicides."

Troy's expression and posture didn't change, but the bond suddenly sang with pure joy, like I'd handed him a gift. Maybe I had.

All he said, in the same carefully neutral tones as before, was, "As my queen says, so shall we obey."

"So shall we obey," the room echoed—including the Lyon elves.

That caught my interest. I frowned at them. "What's your observation here?"

Samarre, ever the leader of the group, took a half step forward. "That you are choosing a long road and a hard one. But one that would have saved the lives of people I loved, had my own queen taken it."

"Same for me." Thana stood. The muscles in her jaw clenched and bunched, and unshed tears sparkled in her eyes. "My queen...this may be the word of a coward. But *I want to live.* I want a family with someone I love. Someone I've held back from admitting I care about because my oaths to the Darkwatch came first. My oaths to die for conclave, House, and queen." Defiance tightened her expression as she looked around the room. "And I know it's my Goddess-damned duty to bear a child, but I couldn't bring myself to do it knowing that I might have to make a choice to die even if there was a chance I could live. If it's not expected? If I'm trusted to find another way?" She saluted, fist to heart. "My queen, I was already ready to follow you because it gave me a better shot at living, even with everyone coming after you. For this? I'm yours beyond death because you give me hope for a future."

That hit me like a kick in the chest.

Suddenly I had a feeling Troy had hand-selected these elves, not just for their skill but for some facet of loyalty to me. It made sense—if they were expected to die, he'd want to make sure they actually would if it came to it—but it meant I was in an interesting position to make this decision. The elves gathered here would be my evangelists, intentional or not. Or they'd decide they preferred the box the old queens had put them in, and they'd leave. Dozens had, rather than serve an elemental High Queen and the king she should have put down upon the manifestation of his power signature.

But given the reaction of our guests from Lyon, I had a feeling we'd find replacements...if I allowed them. And after today, I had to. I'd been letting fear drive me, and the people around me, the people who looked to me, were suffering from the attrition.

Their options were narrowing, their burdens were growing, and I'd been so busy hanging onto my own pain that I hadn't seen theirs.

I had to do better.

Ending the death cult was part of it, but I had to give them options for life. For thriving. And not just them, but the elementals as well. Hurt people went on to hurt others. Maybe if the elves stopped hurting and focused on healing, the elementals could catch a break.

I pulled myself together and nodded to Thana and Samarre. "Thank you for your candidness and vulnerability." Closing my eyes, I gathered myself the rest of the way. Debated a response. Let it fly anyway. "Y'all know I haven't had the best track record with high-bloods."

Troy continued to stay outwardly impassive, but the bond spiked with alarm he quickly walled off from me.

I offered him and everyone else an apologetic smile. "That never meant I wanted y'all to die. Yeah, we're in fucked-up times. We're going to lose people. But if we do, I want it to be because you have something of your own to fight for. To *live* for. The death cult has to stop. So, I'm stopping it. High crimes like treason, murder, and rape will still be sent to trial with death as a possible consequence."

I couldn't change elven society or Otherside society that quickly, even as High Queen, and I had to give Troy room to work as the one who'd be implementing everything for the House.

"But we're going to review all those laws to make sure they're fair. And exile or death sentences for shit like marrying humans or non-elves or establishing a consenting bond between partners, or being captured doing your very dangerous jobs?" I shook my head again and made a cutting gesture. "No. Nuh-uh. People need hope in dark times. We're in dark times. You're no less brave for wanting to live. So, let's build a place together where you can."

Half the Ebon Guard erupted into cheers. The rest sat in shocked silence, like they were imagining new possibilities. Samarre, Jacinthe, and Luc watched me with what I thought was approval, tinged with a new respect.

Imagine that. I hadn't even wanted them here. But between letting my people feel safe to have lives and families and opening an appealing reason for outsiders to choose me, I might be able to rebuild the local conclave *my* way, adding another layer of power and security to my base that might end up saving lives because other factions—like Santiago—wouldn't see the Triangle as easy meat.

Of course, that'd add to my territory population concerns eventually, but I had to offer an alternative to the elves. Not just for my House. But again, for me and the other elementals who were still in hiding. Decency wasn't enough of a reason for many of the elves to do the right thing. Maybe this would be. It'd be dangerous, both because it'd open me to attack and because I'd learned the hard way that when the matriarchy was threatened, they came down swift and deadly on the perceived threat.

So be it. If people were going to die, let it be for something they believed in. Not just what they'd been told they should do.

I was the fucking Eternal Huntress. I'd create an eternity I wanted to live in, or I'd go on a hunt of my own.

With that decided, I turned the meeting back over to Etain. Troy and I jointly approved the plans, and the Ebon Guard got ready to move out. Troy would stay with me, playing bodyguard again. I couldn't tell if he was glad to keep me out of trouble or disappointed not to be going back into the field. He'd been a Darkwatch agent for a long time and groomed by Omar to take over the Darkwatch as captain one day even before that, despite Keithia's plans for Troy. Kings—and queens—didn't see as much direct action, although we were both seeing more than most. We had our own mission though, even if it would be executed remotely rather than in person.

The Lyon elves were staying behind as well. Apparently, observers weren't supposed to engage in espionage missions against other parties.

Fair enough.

How much of all that did you set up with who you picked for this mission? I sent to Troy as the last elves finished gearing up and did final weapons checks before filing out the door in silence.

Etain and I did pick the most loyal to you. But I didn't plan for all that. He shifted a step closer, so our arms were brushing—as touchy-feely as we'd allow ourselves to get as people were staging for a mission.

I think I'm impressed you found three triple triads of elves that loyal to me.

You shouldn't be. Not everything is going well. But people see you're trying. For them.

Sorry for stepping on your toes.

Don't be. It's what I want too. I just couldn't figure out how to raise it.

Probably partly because I'd been all too ready to kill elves before, for all I insisted I didn't want to kill anybody. I sighed, annoyed at how defending myself to the point of murder had been reasonable and justified but also made life harder, and leaned against Troy's arm. Maybe this would help me feel safer too. So we could—

I wrenched my mind away from that direction, still not ready to fully imagine that particular future.

Troy sent a questioning nudge in the bond.

Nothing.

Arden.

The future.

Ah.

Maybe he did get it because he left me in my feels.

Finally, the Ebon Guard were in their cars and on their way, leaving me, Troy, and the Lyon elves alone.

Heedless of our guests, I gave in and slipped my arm around Troy's waist. He curled his around my shoulder, and we made our way toward the door the Guard had left from to find some privacy, move out of range of the jammer, and get to work on our part of the plan: ending this fucking vampire war.

"You really care for each other."

Troy and I turned to see Luc eyeing us with a mixture of confusion and longing.

We answered as one. "Yes."

"I thought it was practicality." Luc looked from Troy to me before focusing on Troy. "She lets you live. You defend her against the rest of our people. Together, you're more powerful. But the connection between you is palpable. A true king of the ages. And a queen of vision, if not of pure blood."

"We're partners in the vision," I said drily, annoyed at my blood coming into question again. Aside from the death cult and systemic abuse, the obsession with blood purity was the most tiresome part of elven culture. "And in everything else."

Luc nodded. "The king tells me you've accepted our offer to settle here. I do not think I recognized until now what a gift and an honor that acceptance is." He made a short bow. "By your leave."

Troy nodded, and Luc headed back to the cubicle the Lyon elves had claimed. Naptime, probably.

As we headed outside, I checked that the door was firmly shut and waited until we'd made it a few steps before letting myself slump against Troy.

He kissed the crown of my head. "We starting with Rice?"

"I guess." I dragged myself upright. "Hopefully having some space and some culprits makes him more cooperative because I'm too tired to deal with him nicely right now."

"You won't be. You're dead."

I blinked. "Shit."

"Don't worry. I haven't lost the knack of playing bad cop." A predatory gleam lit his eyes in the morning light.

I couldn't help my shiver. The curl of his lip at my movement wasn't quite a smile. Some part of him enjoyed reminding me that he was dangerous. We'd fought over it once. I think we both tried to avoid going head-to-head on it again.

"Wait. Check in with Maria first, please," I said. "We were in the right to go around her before, but this time I don't think she'll forgive us."

He nodded and dialed.

I leaned close so I could hear the conversation. A faint click came through as the call connected, and Troy and I exchanged a glance, both nodding. We had an audience.

"Troy! There you are. What the fuck is going on? Where are you? What happened to Arden? Etain wouldn't fucking tell Noah anything!"

He glanced at me.

I shook my head. *We need her trust, or she'll go rogue again. But aside from that click, the Sight flared when I thought about 'listening' before. It's gotta be the feds.*

"I'm in Virginia." His voice was hard and blank, the unreadable Darkwatch agent.

"Virginia." Maria sounded hesitant, like she was afraid to ask about me. "What, in Hekate's name, is in Virginia?"

"Someone took Arden. There was an accident."

Shocked silence held the line, then horror filled Maria's voice. "That fireball on 85? That was her?"

Troy didn't answer, playing the grieving lover the best way he could: by falling back on the safety he found in silence and pretending he felt nothing.

"Oh, Troy. Oh, no."

I was glad we hadn't told anyone outside a trusted few about the risk with the bond because otherwise she would know that if I died, Troy would either be dead or comatose. A silver lining in all this. Nobody would think of it now.

Maria's voice went as soft as I'd ever heard it. "Are you..."

"Etain said you received a call from someone. I need to confirm who."

If she was offended by Troy's brusque tone, Maria didn't give any indication of it. She cleared her throat and went on, back to business. "The personal aide to a Senator Wright, political sponsor of the Supernatural Investigation Bureau or whatever fool name they're calling it. He wants a meeting."

"That's what he wanted from Arden."

Maria hissed. "I see. Well, for better or worse, I can't afford to deal with him right now. M—"

"Don't. Lines are tapped."

She swore in old Spanish. "Let me guess. It's what you'd do."

Troy didn't answer that. He and I had both heard the click and knew it for what it was, even if she didn't. Tapping a cell phone was hard but not impossible.

Not when the US government wanted to invoke the Patriot Act.

"Fine," she said. "I have reason to believe there's going to be another push."

"As do I," Troy said. "Can you handle it?"

She blew out a breath. "Do I get to use all of my resources, or is that crossing factional lines?"

I frowned, until I realized she meant Allegra, who was, after all, still an adopted member of House Solari and technically supposed to be playing the role of envoy and political observer, much like our Lyon guests. There might be other elves or half-elves in Raleigh, but Allegra was the true asset.

Again, Troy glanced at me.

I shrugged. *Would Allegra listen if we told Maria no?*

Troy's lips thinned as he considered that and didn't seem to like the probable answer. "I'm going to make a few more calls to clear you some space. Any resources in Raleigh are yours. On the condition you stay out of Chapel Hill and Durham except at need." His voice hardened further. "Arden was patient with friends. I'm not. Now less than ever. I don't want to be the monster again, Maria. Don't test me."

That made sense. We could send people down to fulfill Troy's offer, or Maria could commandeer them, while at the same time maintaining enough separation that nobody would be making a move for a coup—or if they did, it'd be very clear who we needed to take out. And who was tapping the line. The comment about being the monster worried me though.

Apparently, Maria was thinking the same. "Understood." Again, her voice softened. "We've been...maybe not always friends. But acquainted, for a while." A hesitation. "Don't follow her, Troy. If she's gone, we need you."

"End this, Maria. And ensure your *resources* are well cared for. Or you won't like what happens when I get home. Last chance."

The call ended as Maria hung up.

Troy bowed his head. "I don't even like pretending that you're dead."

I hugged him.

"I keep telling you not to scare me like that again." He crushed me in an embrace so tight I grunted.

"And I keep getting in more trouble."

He sighed, knowing it was pointless to fight over it. "Rice next?"

"Yeah."

"Fine. Then I want to go on a little side mission of my own." The earlier hint of hunter's savagery came out in full force.

I leaned back and looked at him, startled. He never went off-script, off-piste, or off-anything. Troy was by the book. Excellent at it. But there was a way to do things, and that was how he did them.

Wait. No.

The *old* Troy was like that. The one who, like me, had been beaten down and forced small, even if he'd loomed over me in every way back then.

The *new* Troy, the king to my queen, had gone from soldier to revolutionary. He still had all the training and knew what all the books said...which meant he knew better than anyone how to exploit them now that he was slowly freeing himself of what they'd forced him to be.

"What?" he asked as I stared up at him. "Why are you looking at me like that?"

"I guess I just realized how much we've both changed."

Worry pinched his brow.

"It's okay. It's not bad." I went up on my toes to brush a reassuring kiss on his lips. "I'm just— Well, shit. Growth is good. I'm excited to see what it means for you. For us."

This time his embrace was even tighter. We didn't need words to revel in the anticipation we both felt for the future. It was still new for me, to look forward with hope rather than fear or dread, even in the face of current danger. To look forward at all really, rather than being stuck in the loop of day-to-day survival.

For both of us, I guess.

And both our hearts sang at having someone to share the journey with.

Troy cleared his throat and released me. "I'll call Rice. Make sure he stays out of Maria's way."

"Okay. And then we're planning this mission we're going on."

"We?" He looked at me sharply enough that I had to steel myself against backing up.

I gave him a flat look. "Tell me this 'little side mission' isn't to go scare the bejeezus out of a certain senator."

The gold flecks in his gaze sparked. "If it is?"

"Then you'll need backup." I crossed my arms and let the stubbornness cresting in me crash through him in the bond. "You can't tell me a Darkwatch-trained elemental wouldn't come in handy for something. And you're not fighting my battles for me. I didn't go through the training just for self-defense."

"This battle is mine as much as yours."

I arched an eyebrow at him. "Great. We go together in a proper triad."

He fisted his hands on his hips and glared down at me.

"What? It's a compromise."

For a minute, I thought he was going to flash his secondary teeth in a threat display. Then he took in my posture and my rock-solid resolve in the bond and backed down. "Fine. But you stay in cover."

"You're the boss."

Troy's narrowed eyes said he didn't quite believe me.

"I mean it. I might have passed basic Darkwatch training, but you're still the expert. As long as I'm there, what you say goes." Because I wasn't foolish enough to push him much further than this.

With a sharp nod, he accepted my terms. "Rice first. Then we plan. I want this as airtight as we can make it."

I bit back a joke about sylphs and air and just nodded back.

Rolling his eyes at what he caught in the bond anyway, Troy called Detective Rice as I pressed close to listen in again.

Chapter 28

"Monteague." Rice's drawl was a little too forced this time. "Didn't think I'd hear from you again, given you fled law enforcement." When Troy didn't take the bait, he added, "We're a little busy right now."

I rubbed my hand along Troy's back when he stiffened, as he always did, at being called by his birth House. At the same time, I couldn't help my smirk. If Rice was busy, I was willing to bet it was dealing with the fallout of Ruprecht's prank.

"Rice. I'm following up on the situation at Claret."

"Why you? I usually deal with Finch."

"You're dealing with me now."

"Uh huh." Rice's voice went a little too innocent. "Anything to do with this headline news outta Virginia?"

"Detective, you really do not want to test me today. Did you get what you needed from Maria?"

After a long pause, Rice said, "I received a video. A set of videos. Someone left a USB drive on my desk. That you?"

Troy held his silence. He and I both knew what that pause meant, but we let the detective tell us.

Rice made a disgusted scoff.

"I can't use confessions gained under torture in court." The tough-guy act sounded like it was wearing a little thin. Maria must have used what she'd seen during the Inquisition and gone all-out.

"It doesn't need to go to court. Arden's recordings plus a confession equal case closed."

"Now hang on—"

"Have there been any more murders that fit the MO?"

"We'd have a better chance of knowing if *someone* hadn't trashed our IT system. Was that y'all as well?"

I had to press my lips together to stop from laughing.

Fortunately, Troy was more level. "I've had larger concerns than your IT system, Detective. Have there, to your knowledge, been any more murders?"

Rice's silence said no.

"Okay. That's because they got your attention. As they wanted. And then the people responsible were caught. I'm calling you now with a warning: stay out of Maria's way."

"Excuse me?"

"We have house cleaning to do. You remember the Wild Hunt? We advised you to put people under curfew or get them out of the city."

"I don't like where this is going, Monteague."

And I was going to hit Rice if he kept setting Troy off with that House name. His legal name in the mundane system was still Monteague, just like mine was still Finch, but it might be time to change that. Maybe we needed to both legally become Solari, even if doing so might open a whole new batch of trouble if someone poked around in the past and found records of two dead parents on the bank of the Cape Fear River and the infant they'd barely managed to save from drowning after their car was driven off a bridge.

I set that aside and refocused on the conversation at hand.

"—a curfew in place," Troy was saying. "You once told Arden you became an officer of the law to protect your community. Trust me when I say that's the best you can do to protect them now."

"That'll set y'all supernaturals up to be terrorists," Rice replied. "That's the only way I push this through."

Troy and I gave each other a long look. We were already on the back foot. There were no good options.

I closed my eyes and tried to find another way. *So be it. At least if we're fighting the threat, we have a chance to spin it.*

"So be it," Troy echoed. "But, Rice, Othersiders will be putting their lives on the line to protect Raleigh and push out invaders that threaten all of us. If I don't see a damn fine press conference acknowledging that, you and I are going to have an encounter of the sort you most assuredly will regret."

"That sounds like a threat."

Troy's sharp secondary teeth dropped with a snick, and his voice fell to a deadly whisper. "That's because it is. Arden was the pleasant one. Remember that."

He stabbed his thumb on the end call button before we could hear Rice's reaction.

"I'm not sorry." He kept his gaze on the trees.

Rubbing my hands up and down his arms, I said, "I'm not asking you to be. For all anyone knows, I'm missing or dead. Whether they know you're more than a bodyguard or not, they had to see your dedication to me. You said what I'd expect you to say."

"Good." That gaze snapped down to meet mine, hard as the meteoric steel of his longknife. "Because Goddess help me, but I will pay a personal visit to every single one of those human-supremacist bastards with badges if I have to."

"And I'd be at your back while you showed them what goes bump in the night. We're in this together, Troy. Now more than ever."

△▽△▽

Full dark had fallen by the time the Ebon Guard returned. Our three guests were outside sparring, leaving Troy and me to plan our trip to the senator's private residence in Alexandria in privacy. We were hashing out the final details when Troy looked up at the sound of engines pulling into the clearing around the warehouse.

Jacinthe stuck her head inside. "Your people are back. All of them safe."

"Thank you," I called.

With a nod, she went back out.

"This is it," Troy said. "You're sure you're okay with going this route?"

"Boundaries."

He grimaced and nodded. That'd been a lesson he'd learned the hard way with me.

Seemed he wasn't the only one destined to do so. I refused to waste time wondering what it was about myself that made people think they could trespass against me. I knew. I was a woman in a world where, outside of the elven Houses, men dominated. I presented as Black in a society where Black people were systemically and historically excluded and harmed while society debated semantics and tried to excuse or ignore the crimes of the past. And I was an Othersider—outright non-human when the human species excelled at dehumanizing and othering their own kind.

Yeah. I wasn't gonna have it. I had the power to draw a line and allies who'd proven time and again that they would not only hand me the stick to drag through the sand but also be at my back when push came to shove.

I was blessed in a way too many weren't. So, if the Federal Government of the United fucking States of America needed an object lesson in "what we not gon' do"? Fine. I'd play teacher and school them. And when they came for the Triangle—because they would; nothing infuriated the powers that be more than someone standing up for their rights and dignity—I'd meet them with all I had.

Like Sarah had said once: nobody got what they were owed without fighting for it. Not in this society. Not when violence and death were glorified as the ultimate expressions of power.

I supposed the mundanes weren't so different from Otherside after all. Except that we'd spent centuries forced to rein in our excesses, lest we be hunted.

A memory of the hunger I felt in the van at the spike in fear scent curled through me.

Hunter.

Hunted.

Time to change what those words meant to me. Time to stop being prey.

Troy was watching me when I refocused on him, his pupils dilated and his gaze darkened to shadowed labradorite. "Sometimes I'm afraid I'm rubbing off on you."

"If you are, I'm fine with it. It'll keep me alive now that I can't hide anymore."

Etain's voice rang out before Troy could answer me. "My queen?"

"Here." I emerged from our little room.

"We found something. Several somethings." She was grinning ear-to-ear. If half-elves had the teeth their full-blooded cousins had, I was almost certain they'd be out.

I glanced at Troy then led the way to the corner of the room with the briefing area. "Let's hear it."

Etain took her place in front of the whiteboard. "Team One went to the territory of House Hilith. Following last known Darkwatch intel, they found indications that the House Guard was being mobilized—the family mansion was packed, and there were constant deliveries to the house. Food, unmarked boxes. They're getting ready for something."

"Could just be defensive," Troy said.

She nodded. "Agreed. Team Two found similar preparations being made at House Bedoe. But House Ead is where it got interesting."

"Also prepping?" I asked.

"Yes," Etain said. "But not only that. While we were observing, they went to meet a visitor at some private hunting grounds north of Richmond. The car that met them was a nondescript black sedan with DC plates that screamed government even before the cookie-cutter ops guys got out and escorted none other than the aide to Senator Wright to meet Queen Onora's House Guard captain."

Thunder had nothing on Troy's reaction in the bond, and ice had nothing on his expression as he glanced at me.

"They're already working together," I said. We had our answer on Troy's question about what the hell Ead was up to. Then I frowned. "But probably only as of today or late yesterday, or the guys who came for me would have known to use bronze, not drugs."

Etain nodded sharply. "That was our estimation, ma'am."

"Then they're moving fast," I said. "Bronze would have been the first secret they gave up, even as a bit of taster information just to get me out of the way without them having to do anything. So, first contact in the last eighteen hours or so? With the senator's aide clearing his schedule to make a face-to-face meeting late today. Shit."

"We cannot have this," Troy said. "I trust Arden to represent Otherside fairly to the mundanes. House Ead? Not a chance. Not with the reports Omar passed along after the Wild Hunt."

This was news to me. "What reports? I only heard they were complaining about the Darkwatch being subverted. And then that we weren't sure what they were up to."

"They were also making quiet overtures to Houses up and down the East Coast. Looking for an alliance. They quit when Omar told them he wouldn't set the Darkwatch against the gods' chosen, which is why none of us mentioned it. But this is the perfect opportunity for them."

"Dammit, Troy." I rubbed my temples and almost told him I needed to know things like that. But I knew why he hadn't said anything. That threat had probably looked minor compared to what we'd had going on immediately after the Hunt and had dissipated on its own. Still, that couldn't be the process going forward. "Morning briefings are going to be a thing."

"That'll require you to get up in the morning," Troy quipped, deadpan.

I tried to glare at him, but stopping my mouth from twitching into a smile diluted the effect somewhat. "I'm serious."

"Of course. We'll make arrangements."

"Thank you. Etain, please tell me we have some idea what the senator discussed with House Ead."

"As a matter of fact, ma'am, we do." She grinned and pulled a device out of her pocket, something small and black that looked like a fancier version of my audio recorder. "They were warded against djinn and full-blood elves using magic. Not against half-elves with directional mics. They didn't even bother with a jammer."

Troy barked a laugh, looking incredulous. "Seriously?"

Etain nodded, sparkling with enthusiastic pride. "And I've already communicated that to both the rest of the Ebon Guard and Omar, to make sure we don't fall prey to the same overconfidence."

"Well done," he said.

As quickly as Etain had brightened, she sobered, suddenly looking nervous. "Um. You're not going to like it though. Either of you. It's bad."

Troy looked at me, his grim expression echoing mine. "Fine. Let's hear it."

When Etain pressed play, the voice I recognized from the very first call I'd received from Wright's office spooled out, sounding shakier this time. Fear, maybe. "Thank you for agreeing to meet. When your people reached out to the senator's office, we weren't sure what to think. It helps to put a face to a name."

"And a scent," Troy murmured.

I glared at the device. Othersiders actively reaching out to an agency that'd come out with bald-faced bigotry on public television?

"We have common objectives," a second person said. Sounded like a man, deep-voiced, with the faintest hint of an accent I couldn't place. "Objectives it seems you've already taken a step toward achieving."

"That's Sixtus," Etain murmured. "Captain."

I nodded.

"What objectives are those?" the aide asked.

"Primarily, the elimination of Arden Finch Solari as a threat."

"Solari?"

"That's not the most important part. What's important is that you cannot leave Troy Solari alive either."

I went cold. "Motherfuckers."

Troy just slipped into the dangerously taut mien of a Darkwatch agent on the hunt. An air of anticipation hung over him, like he knew where this was going and was just waiting for it to be confirmed.

The aide said, "We were given to believe his name was Monteague and that he was her pet bodyguard or head of security, not some kind of husband or family. What is their relation?"

The elf stayed silent. I couldn't figure out why since they were giving up this much, unless explaining that Troy and I were king and queen edged too close to giving a hint about elven power structure they'd rather keep quiet.

An exasperated huff from the aide. "Fine. What is this Solari business?"

"Terrorists, Mr. Jackson. Suffice to say it's a group that should have stayed dead. We'd like to make sure it does this time." A pause, giving me the feeling that a smile or something had been shared. "And do our civic duty as Americans, of course. Assuming we could be acknowledged as such."

"They use the name of a terrorist group as part of their own name?" Disbelief echoed in the aide's voice.

"We believe in calling things what they are in Otherside."

I snarled at the non-answer serving as confirmation of my earlier thought. They'd collaborate with the feds to remove me and Troy, but they wouldn't talk about queens or Houses. "Bastard."

After a brief pause, the aide said, "This is quite the accusation. How about this, Mr. Ead? I take what you've said back to the senator and see if this is something for the Bureau to investigate further. We'll be in touch."

"Of course. Here's my card. That's my personal mobile phone. I'd advise not waiting too long. Troy Solari—or Monteague, if you wish—is a formidable foe. He might be reeling now, if the headlines from yesterday are what we think they are, but he was never one to let emotion get in the way of what he thought needed dealing with." A significant pause. "If you came for his woman, you're someone who will need dealing with."

"His woman?"

Again, Sixtus stayed silent.

"Fine. I'll take that under advisement. Enjoy your day, Mr. Ead. God bless."

The recording ended.

"What the fuck!" I exploded into motion, too agitated to stand still. "Why would I lead two Reveals and bend over backward to help the mundanes if I was an actual fucking terrorist?"

"Arden," Troy said.

With an effort, I got myself under control and returned to stand next to him, arms crossed and stiff. "Don't tell me you anticipated that."

"I had a feeling it was a card in their hand." That meant it was something he might have done.

Etain's gaze darted between us as I stared at him.

The look he returned was just as flat. "This is war. On three fronts now."

That never worked out well. I didn't need Troy's strategic training to know that. "You're saying we need to move."

"The sooner the better."

"Same plan?"

He nodded.

"Even though they know you'll be coming now?"

Another nod.

Looking like she'd rather not interrupt, Etain softly cleared her throat. "Plan?"

I raised my brows at Troy. It was his mission.

He shifted into a posture that was a little too aggressive to be a parade rest. "I need to pay the senator a visit."

Etain's eyebrows drew down in a hard scowl. "Is that so? Sir."

Troy gave her a flat, dead-eyed look that she held for an admirably long time before dropping her eyes.

She didn't give up though. "My queen said 'we.' You're both going? After what just happened?"

"We'll take a third to round out a triad," Troy said. "But this is even more of a stealth mission than the one you just returned from."

From behind us, Thana's voice. "Take me. As your third."

We all turned to look at her.

Falling into a parade rest, she lifted her chin. "I'm one of the best shadowmancers in the East Coast Darkwatch. Ma'am, you can't draw shadows."

I winced. That was fair, and if this was a super-stealth mission, we had to go in with the best for the job.

Troy studied her. "Show me."

The scent of burnt marshmallow spiked as Thana first drew shadows like any full-blood elf was capable of then, with an Aetheric flex, expanded them to envelop all four of us. It was even stranger than when Troy covered the two of us, darker and colder somehow.

Troy backed up a few steps then frowned and took a few more. "That's good. Arden?"

I guessed what he wanted and, heedless of looking silly, jumped up and down a few times waving my arms.

"Very good."

Thana dropped the shadows. "Am I in?"

"Why do you want to come?" Troy tipped his head to study her. "This is going to be dangerous, and you've got a reason to go home now."

She drew herself up. "Not until these fuckers back off. I won't feel safe until the territory is secure."

And that meant she, like me, was effectively infertile until her body had been free of the deeper stress hormones long enough to ovulate.

"She's in," I said to Troy.

He just nodded. "Gear up. Both of you. Thana, we'll fill you in on the drive." Turning to Etain, he added, "Have half the group fall back to the Triangle. If the Bureau is going to investigate, I don't want to leave our territory with only the werecats as guardians. Secure everything."

Etain saluted, fist to chest. "And Allegra?"

"On loan to Maria to deal with the vampires. You're in charge, Etain. You know the line of succession."

"Yes, sir."

"Good. I'll call Omar on our way up."

Relief flickered across Etain's face. "Thank you, sir. All of you, be safe. I'm grateful for the opportunity, but I'd rather have all of you back in one piece."

I smiled at her, trying to make it as encouraging as I could even though my heart was racing at the idea that we were really going to do this. "You stay safe too, Etain. Don't let the feds fuck up my house—the building or the entity. Got it?"

"Yes, ma'am. You can count on me."

On impulse, I gave her a quick hug.

"You got this," I whispered.

She didn't respond but nodded sharply before moving deeper into the warehouse.

With that, we went to gear up and get on the road.

We had a senator to terrorize, since they were so intent on pinning that label on me. And if they were going to twist my freedom-fighting and call it terrorism, then I had nothing to lose by giving them a reason. Not with my back and Troy's against the wall like this. Appeasement hadn't worked over the course of the last year. Now we had to try deterrence.

Chapter 29

Senator Wright had a house about two hours' drive north, in Alexandria. Or it should have been two hours and some. With Troy driving, it was closer to an hour and a half, despite his being on a terse call with Omar and even with the increased police presence after yesterday's event.

I sat in the back with Thana, where the windows had more tinting and where I could quietly fill her in while Troy handled Omar and kept cops out of our way.

When Thana was updated, I called Zanna. Kobolds weren't known for taking tricks well unless they were the ones executing them, and I didn't need to be cursed coming back to my own house or the bar. Once she finished yelling at me, she agreed it was a good trick and that she'd keep quiet until we'd scared the senator into leaving us alone for at least a little while longer. Then I had to talk her out of sending Ruprecht on another mission unless he was able to get to the Sons of Seth.

It was well into the night when we arrived. The moon was still close to new, and the darkness was deep enough for both elves to be at their best. The senator must have been loaded because it was a damn big house on a massive lot, edged in forest near some state park or other.

Corrupt bastard.

We crept close, a furtive, shadow-cloaked hustle from the woods edging the property, before I hissed and raised a fist in the gesture to stop.

"Invisible fence of some kind," I whispered. The electricity jolted the edges of my awareness. "Hang on." I settled on my haunches and stretched out my senses, feeling for the currents. "Camera trap, maybe," I muttered. "Too many animals around for it to do more."

I pulled back my magic and considered my options. We hadn't had time to do much research for this plan, which meant we didn't know what we'd be up against in terms of security until just now.

"If I short the posts I can find, that'll just tell them something is wrong with the perimeter defenses. Someone will come out to check, likely a guard or a security company." I'd gotten into a building like that on a case, pretending to be the security engineer sent to fix a system I'd tripped by more mundane means, but we didn't need to play those games. Not when we had elemental magic. "The alternative is that I short out the whole damn house." Remembering what I'd promised Troy before we left, I added, "Orders?"

His expression of amused pleasure made me flush. "Since you're asking, a question back to you: Did you decide if you want them to know you're alive?"

"Not really," I admitted after a moment's thought. "I like that I could be anonymous again. But I'm not fixing to be a martyr, and I'm not much of a deterrent if I'm dead."

"Agreed. We don't have the people to hold them off for long without that deterrent. Short the house." He studied me, the muscle in his cheek twitching. He didn't like what he was going to say next. "Change of plan. You're coming in to handle any further security. Thana and I take any guards. We get in and out under shadow. Five minutes inside, tops."

"Understood," Thana and I said together.

Now the trick was funneling my power to a fine enough point to knock out all the electricity but not blow the house to pieces like I did Keithia Monteague's mansion.

"Oh duh," I muttered. I didn't need to target the house. Just the nearest power line, transformer, or power hub.

I dropped my shields all the way and reached farther, finding not just power lines but an underground line and a backup generator. Gas-powered, which was annoying. That'd be easier to explode than to take offline. I'd do that after I cut power from the rest.

"Brace yourselves."

Troy grabbed Thana's hand and put it on my shoulder, keeping one of his on the other.

I inhaled, twisted Air and Fire together to create lighting, and took out every aboveground power source in a five-mile radius. Then I drew on Earth and dug my fingers into the frozen ground, reaching for the metal threads that made up the cable and melting those with a twined burst of Earth and Fire.

Silence crashed down on us as everything electric in the area abruptly shut off, followed by distant shouts from the house.

"Wait for it," I murmured when the elves started to lift their hands.

With a hum, the generator switched on.

"Got ya." I reached for it, trying to visualize it as best I could. It was far easier to work with the elements when I could see what the hell I was doing, but I hadn't needed Troy to tell me that was a weakness. I'd practiced distance manipulation on my own.

It paid off now.

I created a small sphere of Air to contain the generator then kissed the gas in it with Fire. The explosion was contained within the sphere, and I thinned what Air remained within until the fire went out.

"We're clear. On electronics anyway, unless there's something running on its own battery." Eyes still closed, I swept the area to confirm. "Power's out for at least five miles in every direction, and their generator is slagged."

I could have done more, but I didn't see the need for every mundane in the state to lose power on account of one asshole. The people in this area would be badly affected as it was, given it was February and it got cold here without heating. I hated the idea that innocents might get hurt in this, but I needed the humans busy enough with the power failure that they wouldn't respond to an emergency call from the senator's house.

Like Troy had said, this was war. I had to be strong enough to lead it.

When I opened my eyes, Troy was looking at me with proud satisfaction and Thana with shock. I smiled, biting back a comment about how useful it was having an elemental on a triad, and nodded toward the house. "Shall we?"

We ran, full speed. Despite the danger, I couldn't help my exhilarated grin.

I was hunting. Like Troy. *With* Troy, not as prey.

My shields were wide open, and my power signature throbbed like the heartbeat of the night itself. Running like this, as one with a hunting triad at full dark with the cold kiss of the wind on my cheeks—this was living.

You understand us better now, Troy sent. *Good.*

I couldn't even be cross at the implication that I hadn't before. I'd been raised by djinn, and he was right. And this was good. Better than good.

We reached the house.

While Troy covered us with a don't see/don't hear spell and Thana blanketed us in shadows, I felt for the network of nervous systems and blood vessels that'd signal a body.

"One on the other side of this door, another at the back, a third moving along the outside of the far side of the house," I whispered. "Six more in an inner room. My guess is four total hired security, the senator, and four civilians. Or three civilians and the senator's aide."

"Tallies with the profile the Darkwatch ran on the senator," Thana whispered back. "Wife and two kids. Aide is his right hand. And maybe a little more, not that they let on, given he's a centrist politician from a conservative-leaning state."

"Good." Troy dipped into a pocket and came out with a lockpicking kit then knelt to eye the lock. "You'd think they'd upgrade the physical hardware on a sitting senator's residence." He shook his head, disgusted. One of the first things he'd done after moving in with me was upgrade my locks and install a security system in case someone made it through the magical wards.

I just smiled at the personal offense he took at lax security, like it was an insult to his skills and training. He had the lock open in seconds.

The guard on the other side of the door went down as the scent of burnt marshmallow flared and Troy muttered, "Be still."

I stepped over the downed guard, spread a hand over the security system, and zapped it, since it was running on battery. Another small push with Air and Fire slagged the wiring in the entire system. They'd have to rip it out and replace it.

Petty? Maybe. I didn't see a reason not to err on the side of "fuck you" though.

The spells Troy had cast earlier, to be unseen and unheard, were still in effect, but we let our power signatures spill out fully. Mundanes wouldn't know what they were, but they'd experience anything from a mild case of the heebie-jeebies—like Detective Rice did—to a full-on case of the dreads if they were more sensitive.

From the rising voices as we approached the study where I sensed the bodies, it was something closer to the latter.

Good. It'd have that much more impact when we pulled back without harming anyone.

No guards outside the door. Everyone inside. I concentrated then pointed to where each person was. Three in one corner, two of them small. I indicated somewhere around knee-height so the elves would know they were the children. Two more in the center of the room, probably at a desk, likely the senator and his aide. One just the other side of the door. And the guard at the back door.

Thana crept to the back of the house to take out the other guard.

I held out my hand for the lockpick kit, pleased when Troy handed it over without a fuss. A memory flashed through me of picking the lock at Sybil Sequoyah's place. I'd been Troy's backup then too, but I'd been out of my depth and shit-scared. My heart pounded now from the thrill, not fear, and I had the lock open almost as fast as Troy.

When Thana returned with the guard she'd downed slung over her shoulder, Troy cracked the door enough to snatch the third guard and drag him out as multiple people in the room screamed, then incapacitated him with the same "be still" spell used on the other two guards. The security guy slumped. He'd be out for at least half an hour, maybe more.

"Matthews? Matthews, report!" Senator Wright shouted.

The scrape of metal against leather said someone had a gun.

That scared me more than the mission itself. I drew on Air and prepped a wall, not wanting Troy or Thana to take a lead bullet. When I was ready, I switched on my body camera and nodded.

Troy and I entered the room side by side in dead silence, amidst a clinging swirl of shadow.

My eyes had to be glowing a gold almost as bright as the washed-out little camp lantern sitting on the senator's desk, which showed him and his aide behind it, both with guns leveled at us.

The magic Troy was holding combined with the lamplight to make the gold flecks in his eyes shimmer for a moment, and he was menace incarnate as he said, "You're going to want to make a smarter choice with those guns, Senator."

That fool. Pointing a gun with his wife and children in the room? I put a wall in front of them with a thought, leaving a crack at the top so they could breathe. The woman was having hysterics and the little boy wasn't far behind, but the slightly older girl stood in front of them both, hands fisted and pale face twisted like she was trying not to cry.

"It's okay," I whispered to her.

Her little face screwed up tighter as she tried to reconcile my words and the situation.

"Leave my daughter alone!" Senator Wright shouted. "We've been warned about you, Monteague." Even in the dark, I could see the blood drain from his face as he realized he was looking at me. "You're supposed to be dead!"

"*You* were supposed to be reasonable in a general sense and at least somewhat willing to listen to me," I said as neutrally as I could, as though I came back from the dead all the time. In a way, maybe I did. I spread my hands wide in a showy gesture. "You wanted to see me, Senator. I'm here."

"Get out of my house!"

The aide, Jackson, snatched a walkie-talkie from the desk.

With a focused burst of Air and Fire, I fried it.

Jackson dropped it with a curse.

"That's just rude. Bringing in other parties when we're having a conversation." I took another lazy step forward. Troy mirrored me then positioned himself behind me as I sank into a cushy leather chair opposite the senator as though I did this every day and my heart wasn't fit to fly outta my chest. "We are having a conversation, right, Troy?"

"We are." If possible, Troy's tone got even harder. "Unless the senator wants to try some other nonsense. Then I might have to be offended. I believe you were told by some new Otherside friends what might happen if I feel like I need to deal with something."

The aide's eyes flew wide as a full moon as he dropped to his knees and started praying. Apparently, the Ead House Captain had scared the ninth hell outta this guy. Or Troy was.

I snorted. "You know, the gods are listening. But for the moment, that particular one has plenty of followers and no real need of sustenance. Your little wishes probably whizz right on by."

"And what do you know about it?" Jackson screamed.

I just smiled.

"You're speaking to Arden Finch Solari, High Queen of the Chapel Hill Conclave, Arbiter of the Carolinas, and the Eternal Huntress," Troy said. More screams from the corner as the hiss of leather against steel said he'd drawn his longknife from its sheath. "Show some respect."

I held up my hand. "Easy. Ignorance can be excused." I narrowed my eyes, wondering if they could even see my expression in the semi-dark. "Once. Now, Senator, Mr. Jackson, put the guns down."

Maybe they could see. Wright gulped, and his grip tightened on his gun.

"Or don't," I said in a hard tone. "We can play fuck around and find out. But your men outside won't hear the shot, and if that car accident didn't kill me, I won't die this time either."

I made a mental prayer of my own and almost thought I heard ethereal laughter.

"Shoot her! Shoot that unhuman bitch!" the senator's wife screamed from the corner.

I rolled my eyes and slouched in my chair, saying *I dare you* with body language.

With shaking hands, Jackson dropped his weapon. The senator held out a second longer before lowering his gun as his wife cussed him out and called him a coward, threatening divorce or dismemberment or both.

And they called Othersiders violent. She was really making me question my decision to shield her with that wall, but I had a feeling any deaths tonight would be pinned on us, body cams or no.

"Thank you." I sat up, smiled, and assumed a more professional posture. "Now. We have a few things to work out and not much time in which to do it, so I'm gonna talk and you're gonna listen. First: attempting to kidnap me was a very foolish idea and not just because I took it personally. If I go down, there's a lot of very tenuous situations that are gonna go off-kilter, and none of y'all will enjoy that. So don't try it again. Second: you spoke to someone today who said Solari was a terrorist organization. That's outright false." I held up a quelling hand. "And *of course* I'd say that. I'm its leader. But, Senator, believe me when I say all I have ever f—" I remembered the kids and moderated my language with an effort, even if their mother wasn't. "Friggin' wanted is to be left alone. The harder you make that, the harder I'm gonna push back. As a certain man in black once said, don't start nothin', won't be nothin'.'"

I rose. A thrill shot through me as they flinched. Something predatory and hungry.

Shaking it off, I gestured to Troy and myself. "Lastly, we're only here like this because you're apparently one of those men who mistakes courtesy for weakness and thinks everyone is at your personal beck and call. You saw what I did in Durham to protect this plane and the people on it, both Othersider and human." I shifted my wall of Air forward just enough that I could lean on his desk and let him get a good look at my glowing eyes. "So, take this show of strength for what it is: an example and a warning, not a threat. I found you here. Which means I could have opened a sinkhole under this house and dropped it straight into hell. I am choosing not to because I would rather find a peaceful path forward where, ideally, we all leave each other alone. Remember that."

"And let *me* be clear, Senator," Troy said in an icy soft voice. "She's the one giving the orders that keep the rest of us...civil." The faint snick and the senator's gasp told me Troy had dropped his secondary set of teeth. His power signature, already heavy, flared and set everyone in the room freaking out all over again as the chill of an icy wind and the fear of knowing a predator watched you from the deep forest at midnight ripped through the room. "I'm not very nice off-leash. So maybe you don't want there to be occasion for her to drop it."

I forced a grin, worried again about Troy implying that he was truly a monster without me when I knew he didn't want to be, and straightened. With a thought, I drew on Fire one last time to slag all the bullets in every gun I could locate in the room, pulling a little Water from all the sweat pouring off people to dampen the gunpowder and prevent a misfire in the process.

"Good talk, Senator." I threw him a sloppy human-style salute. "Next time, just work with me. Play it straight. I'll do the same. Assuming you really got me that security clearance anyway. Oh, and don't try surveilling me or mine."

To his credit, Wright found some courage somewhere. "If you're no terrorist, why is Raleigh under a curfew due to a supernatural threat?"

The words were spat at me as though I'd been lying, and I let my tone cool accordingly. "You know what Troy said about me being the one keeping Otherside civil? Someone saw I was distracted with y'all's games and is testing that arrangement." I tilted my head as though thinking, but I was more than ready to give up Santiago. "Bit of free info for you. Good faith and that. Santiago, the vampire Master of Miami, is an ambitious bastard who has already attacked Raleigh once before. I stopped him then, so he broke the main agreement governing Otherside and orchestrated the murders a few days ago then tried to escalate it further. We stopped him again. For now. My people are handling it, and it's easier to avoid human casualties if the humans are off the streets."

"Are you telling me there's a—some kind of a supernatural turf war?"

We need to go Arden. Now.

I heeded Troy and turned my back on them, speaking over my shoulder as I headed for the door. "There's always a turf war. Only difference is you know we exist now and some foolish people think that means they don't have to hide anymore. You've been protected from it until recently. Maybe don't try finding out what happens if I'm no longer around."

I offered the brave little girl one last smile and a nod of respect as I left and caught Troy doing the same out of the corner of my eye. She looked confused now, glancing between her now-sobbing mother and me like there was a lesson there.

Maybe there was. I just didn't know if we'd created a little ally or an enemy to worry about in another decade or so. Shame her mother, at least, would certainly twist this event into its worst light. Hence, the body cameras Troy and I wore. We'd need proof of what happened when this was inevitably twisted for political theatre and votes.

As Troy and I swept out in the same swirl of shadow we'd entered in, I dragged my walls of Air after us and used them to slam the doors shut dramatically.

The guards were still passed out in a heap, the last one from outside now among them. I switched off my body cam and stepped over them, resisting the urge to step *on* them. They hadn't done anything to me personally, and I didn't know the circumstances of their working for the senator. Maybe they hated the guy.

Thana fell in beside us. "Think they'll buy it?"

"No," Troy and I said together.

I sighed then broke into a run the elves easily matched as we left the house. "This will just piss them off. Rich, powerful, old, white men hate being reminded that they're no bigger or better than anybody else and that they've only got what they have because the world handed it to them. Especially when it's a Brown man and Black woman doing the reminding."

"They'll try again," Troy agreed. "But it'll either be tomorrow by air strike, or it'll be in a few months when they've spied on us a little bit. It's still early to wipe out a city. They'll try spying first."

"I hope you're right," Thana said.

I grimaced. "Yeah. Me too."

But hopes and dreams were like thoughts and prayers. Well-meaning at best. Empty at worst.

Unless there was action behind them.

Chapter 30

We spent the day sleeping at the outpost before heading home with the remaining Ebon Guard at sunset. Everyone was beat from the stress and long hours. When it was time to leave, folks started filtering out in triads, spacing departures every few minutes. Far enough apart that a bunch of North Carolina plates wouldn't draw attention driving in convoy, close enough together that there'd be aid if we found trouble.

One triad was staying behind. We couldn't afford to leave ourselves open to attack from Richmond or Washington, DC.

The first step in staking bigger claims for my territory.

I sat with that on the drive home. Everyone who'd stayed behind had volunteered. But this still felt too big for me. A step I wasn't ready for. Might never be ready for. Etain and Haroun were riding with us, so Troy didn't scold me for allowing my imposter syndrome to run roughshod over me again. Or maybe he just figured the drive would be a fair amount of time for me to wrestle with it before telling me to get over it and set it aside.

There was no running from feelings. Only facing them.

My thoughts weren't the only thing keeping me on edge. I was buzzing from all the additional land I'd claimed in the last couple of days. The network that was my claim now had hubs in Durham, Chapel Hill, Raleigh, Jordan Lake, Wrightsville Beach over on the North Carolina coast, and now Alexandria, Virginia and somewhere south of Richmond. Wondering how much I could realistically claim and what would happen distracted me from my other worries, and Troy relaxed in the driver's seat.

A little. Anybody driving an average of twenty over the speed limit couldn't relax all that much. I was a speed demon, but Troy took it to the level of art. I wished it was summer. I loved feeling the wind when he drove.

We all breathed a sigh of relief on crossing the border into North Carolina and then again when we passed Creedmoor and into territory held by Vikki's Red Dawn clan.

Troy dropped the other two at Ebon Guard HQ and then continued home.

My land seemed to dance as we pulled into the driveway.

"I'll walk up," I said when I jumped out to open and close the gate behind us.

Troy smothered a flare of concern, looking like he wanted to argue, but the newish gate was halfway up the long gravel drive to slow anyone who wasn't deterred by the wards. The trees and undergrowth were thick enough that, even in winter, it'd be hard to see me from the road in my black leather jacket, especially in the dark.

"Love you," he said.

"Love you too. I'll be up soon. I just need—"

"Yeah, I feel it."

With a grateful smile, I shut the door and got the gate, locking it behind us before closing my eyes to walk up the driveway, spreading my senses through my land and being embraced by it in return. It was quiet with winter's rest and had fallen deeper into slumber in my absence but stirred now like a satisfied dog getting a friendly pat. An owl hooted from a perch among the pines, and everything smelled of cold and damp. Not in an unpleasant way, just in a way that spoke of things happening in their proper time.

This was what I fought for. I had to anchor myself with this—and with Troy—when I was painted as a terrorist or some kind of extremist. The reminder that I was just trying to find space for these moments of connection, to live in peace with people I cared about.

People were going to believe what they wanted to believe. What fit *their* worldview. I could waste time trying to convince them why they were wrong, or I could focus on doing my best for the people who shared my vision. Not stepping on toes when I could help it but not allowing people to up and step on mine just because they could.

Do no harm. Take no shit. The ethos I'd always tried to live by. When they let me.

I walked with that idea bouncing around in my head. That idea of *let*. That was a power word—not in the magical sense but in the sense of who held might and resources. I'd been governed by what other people would allow me to do my whole life. Now I had the strength, allies, and resources to be the one calling the shots, but I was still sunk into this idea that other people were dictating what I could do and how. I was planning actions based on what I needed to do to defend against them, once again on the back foot.

That didn't sit right with me. That didn't sit right at all.

As I climbed the steps to the porch, I turned the concept over in my head, looking for what I *wanted* to do, rather than what corners I was allowing other people to paint me into. I had big dreams at the end of the Wild Hunt, dreams of a new golden age of cooperation among Othersiders and, if not acceptance, then at least tolerance from the mundanes.

Those illusions had been harshly tempered, and I needed to re-evaluate.

When I let myself in, Troy was sprawled on the couch, feet hanging over the edge, eyes closed. "I called Terrence and

Ximena and told them they can stand down. What's got you all tangled up?"

"I'm doing this wrong." I needed to talk it through, but I also needed to stay moving. "You want a fire?" Sometimes he was good with fire, sometimes not. Depended on how bothered he was by other events or his memories and what the fire was in. The fireplace was usually okay, but I didn't want to assume.

He grunted a yes, eyes still closed. I was staying out of his head while I worked through my own, so I didn't know if he was giving me space or just dead tired. Probably both.

As I cleaned out the fireplace, opened the flue, and stacked new logs, I tried to order my thoughts so they'd make sense spoken aloud. With a quick embrace of Fire, the logs caught, and flame danced merrily on them.

"That's better. Thanks, Sparky. Cold in here." He cracked an eyelid. "Now come here."

Shaking my head at his rarely used nickname for me, I went to the couch and clambered on top of him, stretching out with my legs on either side of his and my cheek resting on his chest. "We need a bigger couch. I refuse to believe this is comfortable for you and your long-ass legs."

His arms wrapped me. "I wouldn't say no. But you weren't thinking about the couch on your walk up here."

"No, I wasn't." I sighed and squirmed. I still wasn't used to rationalizing my thoughts, and I cared about his opinion. A lot.

"Do you want to talk or do something else?" Troy asked in a tone that made it as clear as the curling lift of his hips what the something else would be if I didn't stop wiggling.

"Talk. Sorry."

He threaded the fingers of one hand through my curls and started massaging, sending shivers of pleasure over me.

"I don't know what I want," I said quietly after a few more minutes of thought.

"In terms of..."

"Being Arbiter. Being High Queen. I took the titles because they looked like a way forward when what I wanted was first to be free of Callista then to have the space to just live my life. Only the titles came with responsibilities, and I started feeling like I was wearing shoes that weren't mine."

"Because they're too big? Or not the right style? Or they pinch?"

I smiled against his chest, appreciating how he extended my metaphor. "If I said all of those, does it make sense?"

Troy mulled it over, his fingers not stopping against my scalp. "What I'm hearing is you had an idea of what you were signing up for but it's turned out to be more or different."

"Both."

"And as a result, you feel like an imposter, the expectations have wildly changed what your life looks like, and you feel like you're not getting anything you wanted. And that's upsetting."

"Yes." I kissed his chin. "That's it exactly."

"Can I tell you what I've observed?"

"Please."

Another long silence as the fire crackled, gradually heating the room. Troy didn't let me up though, just shifted from massaging my head to my neck. A quick flash of hesitation in the bond accompanied him drawing a deep breath. "You're used to being a victim, Arden."

I flinched. Ouch.

"And I'm not saying you haven't been victimized. Callista messed you up for what? Fifteen years? Twenty? Grimm and Duke helped. The elves did their best to kill you, repeatedly, after Leith tried to use you in his conspiracy. That human cop betrayed you to the Darkwatch. The gods tried to make you their pet. So, you were continually on the defensive. Even when you were looking for a way out, you were defending."

He paused, and I pushed down the urge to get up and pace.

"Fair," I whispered. "Even if I deeply dislike it."

"Fair." He loosened his embrace in case I did want to get up and continued when I stayed where I was. "Cariñamí, if you wanted to abdicate and give all of this up, I'd back you."

I stiffened. "I thought you wanted to be king."

"I said I'd back your choice for yourself. Not that I'd give up what I want."

My stomach clenched, and despite the fire's warmth, I went cold.

"I know what I was born to be. I accept the burdens that come with it. I suffered too much to walk away from it. And I'm comfortable wielding the power. But if you're not, you need to decide now. Before we commit to actions for territory expansion that will cost lives, no matter how careful we are."

This time I did get up to pace.

He let me go, crossing his arms as he opened his eyes to watch me but staying out of my head.

I pulled all the elements to me, creating a small ball of primordial energy I bounced from hand to hand. The corners of Troy's eyes pinched in wariness. If I lost control of even this little ball, I'd level the house and warp reality for a good quarter-mile. But there was too much pulsing energy in me. My land claims and mental agitation wouldn't allow me to just play with a zephyr this time or even with a ball of fire.

What did I want? That's what this boiled down to. That and the question of, if I wasn't the person for the job, who did I think would do a better job?

Troy could certainly handle it. But in my heart of hearts, I knew I wouldn't be happy playing second fiddle to him. I needed my own thing, and I'd long outgrown the mundane work with Hawkeye Investigations.

So, if I set aside the pressure and the expectations, the demands and the coming battles, what was I willing to step up for?

And why did I keep feeling like I wasn't good enough when I'd literally bested every queen in the area and then the gods of the hunt?

Who was I under all the titles?

That. That was what I had lost. My sense of self.

I couldn't figure out what I wanted because I didn't know who I was anymore. Both Otherside and the mundanes had been projecting onto me for the last year and half.

And I'd let them.

Let.

That word again.

But it was true. I'd retreated. I'd stepped back from negotiations with the humans after we got some local bills passed in Durham, Wake, and Orange Counties, telling myself it was my turn to take a break. To rest and recharge and train and just generally catch up with shit I'd neglected while I was saving the damn world.

Really though, I'd tried to go back to living my little life in the woods but with everything around me changed.

And in so doing, I'd allowed everyone else to determine who I would be and what I would do because I hadn't filled the void myself.

Otherside abhorred a vacuum. Me claiming titles didn't fill it on its own. Only action could do that. And for most of the last year, I hadn't taken any.

"Fuck," I whispered. I dispelled the ball of magic, took a deep breath, and exhaled hard. Then did it again as tears threatened.

When I looked at Troy, sympathy filled his expression as he sat up. "Now you see it."

"Yeah."

"It's a hard lesson, my love. I had it beaten into me. A royal who doesn't know who and what they are—even if that who and what is only what they've been told to be by the queen—is fodder for another House's plans. But you needed space to see it on your own."

I went to him and straddled his lap, burying my face against his neck like I could hide from the misery this realization was causing me. I'd had no idea he was being that patient and giving me that much space and time, all while he dealt with smoothing over the disruption to local elven society.

If I'd figured it out sooner, could I have avoided war with the vampires? The situation with Senator Wright?

Troy gently peeled me away from him and squeezed my shoulders. "No. Don't do that. There is no point in dwelling on what might have happened." Something that was almost amusement flickered across his features. "Unless you've learned how to time travel and didn't tell me."

I tried to swallow my answering snort of laughter and hold on to my wallowing mood, but I couldn't. He was right. All I could do now was own it and move forward.

I thought back to some of my musings of the last few weeks. My desire to take a stand for what mattered to me—which was, and always had been, space for me and the people I cared about to live our fullest, best lives. My acknowledgment that I had the most power available among those in my sphere of connection to do that. And now, the realization that I did know who and what I was.

Not just a private investigator. I was lost now because I'd clung to that identity. That *title*. What was coming to me now was something deeper than that.

I was a protector.

Sometimes it came out in investigating things, pulling the pieces together to right wrongs and find the guilty. Sometimes it was a hunt or setting boundaries like in Virginia. Sometimes it was as simple as loving Troy and protecting him from the demons that haunted him—different from mine but still there.

He smiled at whatever he saw in my face or felt in the bond as that idea—protector—settled in my mind. "You found it."

"Yeah."

"And what do you want to do with it?"

I steeled myself. "I want to make sure the people I care about don't have to worry about being hunted or excluded or unsafe. I want *my people*, all of them, to have space to thrive."

He watched me, the gold flecks in his eyes bright in the firelight, waiting for me to finish.

"And that means I need to fight. Not just physically. I need to be smarter. Bolder. I was thinking earlier that there's no point in trying to convince people who don't want to be convinced that Othersiders, or elementals or whoever, are people. But I can present a better vision so that people want to join me. Join *us*. And I can create space for that vision to flourish."

Troy's smile thawed all the cold spots in me. "Good. And it is *us*. I might be focused on the elven aspect, but we want the same thing. A better life for all of us."

Overcome with relief and gratitude, I kissed him.

My big dreams might not have panned out the way I'd planned. I might have lost ground working through my issues.

But now the real work could begin.

Chapter 31

For the immediate time being, that work had to start with Troy concluding the visit with the Lyon elves, with promises to open further negotiations for settlement. Then for us both to go and wrap things up in Raleigh.

The confessions Maria had gained told her where the remainder of Santiago's cells were. Fortunately, they were all cleared out by the time Troy and I made it down to her nest the next day. I thought Maria was going to hit me when I stepped out from behind Troy and pulled my hood down.

She was in my face faster than I could blink, and Allegra catching Troy's arm probably saved her life.

"You little wretch! You awful bitch! You let me think you were dead!"

"Surprise." I grinned, pleased that she cared. Maybe our friendship was still intact, in spite of everything.

Her pale skin flushed deeply enough that I glanced at Allegra and wasn't surprised to find two scabbed dimples in her neck.

At my raised brows, Allegra had the grace to drop her eyes. "Okay *fine*. I will stop commenting on Troy biting you."

That distracted Maria. "You let him bite you? With elf teeth? Hekate burn me, but if I'd known you had that much of a biting kink—"

"Maria," everyone in the room said.

She gathered herself like an empress and flounced to the cluster of chairs in front of the roaring fire. "Be welcome in my nest. My table is yours, my hearth is yours, and my roof is yours, while you are here."

Troy and I answered together as we followed her. "We honor our hostess. While your nest is ours, our strength is yours."

I seated myself in the same armchair I'd been in when we first discussed what to do about this mess. "That was all dealt with fast."

Maria's smile was broad enough to show fangs. "I won't have incursions on my territory."

"Is Detective Rice giving you any more trouble?" Troy asked.

"Not yet." She glanced at Noah. "And our resolution of the situation means the good Dr. Miller wasn't forced to make a choice."

"Fortunately for all of you," Noah muttered, ignoring Maria's sharp look of rebuke.

"And Matthias?" I asked.

"Cooperating." Her expression soured. "I gave him all his people back. Giuli is staying here. A guest, as agreed. He'll likely accompany Noah to the next parliament meeting."

I reached out and squeezed her hand. "Thank you. What about Santiago's people?"

"Those sent to murder humans are all dead. Those sent for the coup are prisoners of war." She smiled thinly. "But I turned all of them except Luz over to Matthias's people when they drove through last night. Leverage. In both cases. Matthias gets a gift of blood to feed his people in his territory push or give to Charity as incentive to keep Atlanta out of it. Santiago can be mad at Matthias instead of me."

That would resolve our local territory issues nicely, as far as the vampires were concerned. If only it had been done before now.

If only I'd owned up to my responsibilities before now.

Still, relief fluttered through my stomach. I really hadn't wanted to keep fighting her on this. "Excellent."

Maria narrowed her eyes at me, her eyes sweeping me like she was looking for an injury. "Are we going to get to the part where you were both pretending you were dead, poppet?"

I gave myself a minute to gather my thoughts, staring at the fire. "What I'm going to tell you doesn't leave this room. Faction heads and seconds only. I've already spoken to Terrence, Ximena, and Vikki, as well as Zanna."

Allegra frowned. "Why isn't this being done in parliament then?"

Troy leaned forward to rest his elbows on his knees. "Because this new Bureau for Supernatural Investigation and, more precisely, Senator Wright, was the one behind Arden's kidnapping. They fucked it up. This time. But House Ead in Richmond got in contact with them. We can't trust that next time they won't have bronze."

I did my best to sit still and not fidget at the mention of bronze. I hated the shit. "That also means they may try for others of our alliance. They already reached out to you, Maria, which means you're likely in the most danger after Troy and me."

"But they think you're dead," she said flatly.

Troy and I gave them all grim smiles.

"T, what did you do?" Allegra asked. "I know that look. That's not a good look."

Pride flickered in Troy's gaze when he glanced at me. "Arden joined Thana and me on a mission."

Allegra's eyes bugged. "*Arden* went on a mission? Where? To do what?"

I grinned. "We put a little fear of the dark into the senator. In multiple ways." I held up my hand to forestall further questions. "Look, the important thing is that we have to assume first that the Sinners—the Supernatural Investigators—are going to start surveilling us."

"Nice nickname," Allegra muttered.

"Second," I continued, "I'm expanding the territory."

That got me stares of disbelief from Allegra, Maria, and Noah.

"I know," I said. "But we need a buffer between us and DC, and us and Miami."

Maria sat back in her chair and looked at me over steepled fingers. "That means you need me to solidify the alliance with Charlotte. Maybe with Atlanta as well. And that we need Richmond and Charleston." She looked at Troy. "You going to war too, sugar puff?"

"House Ead as good as declared it when they told the feds that House Solari is a terrorist organization," he said.

After a shocked silence, Allegra whistled. "Y'all were busy while Arden was dead."

With a last smile, I rose to go. "We were. And there's more to do. I only came in person this time so you could see and smell for yourselves that I'm fine, but we'll likely use the Ebon Guard for communications in the near future. Assume the phone lines are tapped and that we're being evaluated as a threat against humanity." I gave Maria a hard look. "Keep your people in line. No more bullshit, Maria. I cannot afford another situation like this. If we draw attention, it cannot be because humans are dead in the streets."

I don't know what expression I was wearing, but she sobered and inclined her head. "As you say, Arbiter."

"Thank you. See you when I see you. As we met in peace, so may we leave."

△▽△▽

We stopped at the grocery store on the way home. I waited in the car, since we only needed a few things and I wanted to let my current notoriety die down some before being "alive" again.

My phone chirped with an update from Etain. The Food and Drug Administration was fast-tracking Verve's new test under an emergency authorization. A second text followed it: information the Ebon Guard had dug up on the filing for a new super PAC...funded by Verve and a few wealthy right-wing donors.

Great. Healthtech, big money, and lobbying, just in time for the early primary campaigning of next year's presidential election.

Guiltily, I wondered how much my and Troy's little stunt had impacted those decisions. We'd been within our rights, as far as I was concerned. But as far as people like Senator Wright were concerned, we weren't people, and we didn't have rights.

We were animals and terrorists they hadn't figured out how to overpower yet.

I reread the text a few more times, not really seeing the words as my mind tumbled. Would I have done anything differently?

No. No, I wouldn't. Because trying to be nice, trying to show that I was just as "human" as they were, had gotten me kidnapped. It kept getting me kidnapped or shot or putting me or the people I cared about in shitty situations.

The car chirped as Troy unlocked the trunk, and bags rustled as he dropped them in, startling me from my thoughts. When he slid into the driver's seat, his nostrils flared at whatever my scent had done to the interior of the car, and he frowned. "What's wrong?"

I filled him in.

His frown deepened. "How much of a problem do we think this is going to be?"

"I don't know yet. Let's just get home. I want to put aside my glorious and godly purpose for one damn night and do something more satisfying."

The frown morphed into a smoldering sideways glance. "You have other plans for tonight?"

"Yes."

He started the car. "And those are?"

"Showing my king the depths of my gratitude for also being my knight in shining armor."

His voice dropped an octave as he said, "Is that so?"

The scent of singed herbs and burnt marshmallow filled the car the moment before an Aetheric thrum of pleasure ripped through me, leaving me shaking and gasping.

"I like the sound of that," Troy said.

He had me panting on the edge of orgasm by the time we got home. I had never moved so fast to get groceries unloaded or put away.

When the last item was in the fridge, I spun to head for the bedroom, where Troy had been changing the sheets on the bed—and made an embarrassing squeak to find him right behind me. I'd been so focused on getting shit done quickly that I hadn't heard him and hadn't been paying attention to where he was in the bond.

I thumped his chest. "Don't *do* that to me, you—"

He kissed me, shutting me up as he pinned me against the fridge. "I'll do whatever I want tonight, thank you."

And I'd happily and enthusiastically let him. Not the bad kind of let that I'd been worried about earlier but the good kind that was part of a negotiated agreement for the mutual enjoyment of both parties.

"Stop thinking," Troy growled.

Before he could jolt me with an Aether sting, I slid free of his grip and dropped to my knees. "Then give me something else to think about...my king."

That set him on fire, like I knew it would, especially when I opened his pants, dragged his briefs down, and took him in my mouth. He threaded his fingers through my hair, directing my motion.

I wasn't down there long before he hauled me away and to my feet then pushed me to the bedroom.

I stripped before he could order me to and undressed him in turn, lavishing every inch of him—and especially the scars—with tender attention.

He quivered, equally for the abundance of touch as for having everything he was self-conscious about lovingly acknowledged. The ritual slowed the pace, centered us both in the moment. Reminded me of everything he'd gone through, and would again, to be with me. Reminded him I didn't see his scars as failures or mars, but as testaments and proofs of his dedication and ability to survive.

When I was in front of him again, he kissed me with all his skill, lips and tongue dancing against mine as his hand dipped between my thighs.

I moaned, arching into him, pressing against the length of him between us.

Much like he had on the first night we had sex, he nudged me backward, toppling me to the mattress and following me down, smoothly pressing into me as he laced his fingers through mine and held my hands down on the bed.

Rather than moving though, he stayed as he was, pinning me. No. I needed more than this. I needed *him*. When I'd been taken, he'd been in my head. Not just the bond. His voice. His training. His steady presence. I'd anchored myself with him.

And now he was anchored in me.

I wrapped my legs around his hips and pulled him tighter against me then moved against him, taking pleasure as much as giving it. Pleasure sparked in the bond, the delight of being wanted and needed and loved. I moved harder. Faster. Fought his hands to no avail as he lowered his head to my neck and breathed deeply.

"Do it," I whispered. He had to be wanting a bite after nearly losing me. After the first time I'd said it wasn't an everyday thing for me, but these last few days weren't the norm.

"People will notice."

"I. Don't. Fucking. Care."

He hesitated as I kept moving.

"I'm yours," I whispered. "I'm yours and you're mine and—"

Snick.

Inhale.

The scent of burnt marshmallow and herbs then a dart of pleasure. Different this time, lower, deeper, dragging me to the edges of awareness but not drowning me.

Like he was experimenting with how to keep me with him even as he carried me into ecstasy.

I still came when his teeth sank into the curve of my neck and shoulder then again when he shifted his grip from my hands to my hips and took over driving into me with everything he'd been holding back.

When I bit him back, hard enough to draw a few drops of rosemary-and-sage blood to my own tongue, he grunted and then groaned as he climaxed. I kept my teeth in the meat of his shoulder until he was done.

Because I'd figured something out. It wasn't just me being his that he needed.

It was the affirmation of being mine as well.

And to feel grounded in the real, that meant a visible claim.

I hadn't intended to, but I swallowed. The herby metallic taste slithered through me with a jolt of the magic of blood and sex, feeling almost like maenad magic had on the handful of occasions I'd gotten shitface drunk enough to unlock it.

Elementals might not be predators. But this? This man? This love?

This was mine. Troy was mine. I'd claim him every way I could because regardless of who I was, or who stood against me, he was on my side. At my back. And on really good occasions like this one, joined with me as one being, the bond singing with our commitment to each other through anything and everything.

Together, my king and I could take over the world.

And if the world wasn't careful, we damn well would.

Acknowledgments

It has been an absolute whirlwind getting this next Shadows of Otherside cycle off the ground. As always, I'd be lost without the good people surrounding me.

My family gets the first shout-out. From listening to me talk about writing and publishing to flying to NYC to celebrate my first on-stage talk, they're constantly showing their support and cheering me on. I'm always grateful for the gift of a supportive family, and supportive friends as well.

Jeni Chappelle continues to be the best editor and writing consultant ever. There are a few points in the last few months where I felt frustrated and lost for various reasons, but having someone with a clear head and a fresh perspective kept me grounded. We all need someone on our side who believes in our vision and helps us see the way forward.

My beta readers, Callan and Stephanie, are always asking the pointed questions that make me go back and improve a section. That the comments are funny and supportive only helps the process!

The lovely readers on Patreon have done so much to push me to keep developing this universe. I'm pretty sure Troy made the jump from a third-person character to a first-person character in my head because they kept voting to see bonus content for him (or him and Arden). Thank you all for being the impetus behind so much more enrichment of what happens outside of Arden's perspective.

To all of the readers, reviewers, book bloggers, and writing community who support indie authors in general and my work in particular, thank you.

Last (but not least!), since I'm writing this right after returning from speaking at the 2022 Writer's Digest Annual Conference, a thank you to the amazing WD staff. *Elemental* got where it did first because of what I learned about writing from WD resources, and then because the team judging the Self-Published E-Book Awards believed in that story. And now here we are, entering a whole new cycle for Arden.

I hope all of y'all enjoy where we go next.

Also by Whitney Hill

The Shadows of Otherside series
Elemental
Eldritch Sparks
Ethereal Secrets
Ebon Rebellion
Eternal Huntress
Tempered Illusions

The Otherside Heat series
Secrets and Truths
Curses and Faith
Menace and Memory

The Flesh and Blood series (as Remy Harmon)
Bluebloods

About the Author

Whitney Hill is an author and speaker. The bestselling first book in her Shadows of Otherside series, Elemental, was the grand prize winner of the 8th Annual Writer's Digest Self-Published E-Book Awards and a Finalist in the Next Generation Indie Book Awards. Her second book, Eldritch Sparks, was named one of the Top 100 Indie Books of 2021 by Kirkus Reviews.

When she's not writing, Whitney enjoys hiking in North Carolina's beautiful state parks and playing video games.

- Learn more or get in touch: whitneyhillwrites.com

- Get email updates: whwrites.com/newsletter

- Read bonus content on Patreon: whwrites.com/patreon

- Twitter: twitter.com/write_wherever

- Instagram: instagram.com/write_wherever

www.ingramcontent.com/pod-product-compliance
Lightning Source LLC
Chambersburg PA
CBHW060518220726
48290CB00015B/1691